Four lives caught in a net of greed and desire . . .

SIMON . . Nobleman-adventurer, a man without fear, without morals, without love . . .

VIVIAN . Restless, passionate, she was eager to barter her innocence—for the right price . . .

RONALD Handsome, dashing officer of the Queen, he wanted one unreachable thing beyond all others . . .

LATAH . . Primitive child of the mountains, she knew all the twisted paths of love . . .

Four lives, swept into a whirlwind of love and hate, war, and sudden death . . .

"A beautifully written story of loyalty, adventure and heroism."
—*Chicago Tribune*

EDISON MARSHALL has written many historical novels, including *The Viking, Yankee Pasha, Caravan to Xanadu, West With the Vikings** and *Earth Giant.**

An anthropologist as well as an author, Mr. Marshall thoroughly researches the material he uses in his books, with the result that they are both powerful and authentic.

ROGUE GENTLEMAN

Original title:
THE BENGAL TIGER

By
EDISON MARSHALL

WILDSIDE PRESS

Chapter One

In the late fall of 1849, a duke of the blood royal and his duchess visited Devon, my native shire, for the woodcock shooting. Although the royalty of his blood was thin as cream in workhouse milk, his stay among us caused great stir in our nobility and gentry. My twice-widowed father, Sir Oliver Peeltower, Bart., attended some of the functions in honor of the ducal pair, although sitting well down the table. My half brother Howard, twenty-eight, and heir apparent of the baronetcy, was permitted to watch the duke's prowess from a distance of thirty paces. I, Simon Peeltower, six years younger, would have never laid eyes on him except for the odd behavior of the birds.

As by a deliberate affront to a kinsman of the Queen, they made themselves scarce at the great shooting box where he lodged, and settled in enormous numbers in some dank woods of Peeltower lands. My father made bold to tell the Duke so, and the upshot of it was that the semi-royal couple became his guests not only for a day's shooting but for supper at Peeltower Hall, followed by a ball transcending gala affairs of its ninety-year history. Besides the gentry, no less than twelve peers with their peeresses made their appearance, including an earl from Somerset.

Providence, whose smiles had brought the woodcock, frowned when our pantry-maid, Betty Cobbler, brought in a bowl of eggnog for the footman to serve. Tripping on my father's extended foot, she spilled nearly a quart of the rich dish on the head and shoulders of the personage sitting next to him. When she saw it was the very duke, she gave a heart-broken wail and dropped the bowl.

"It seems I'm in the line of fy-ah," his grace remarked.

That sporting gesture did not relieve what seemed to my father, my brother, and the nearby guests a shocking disaster. All of these gathered to his help with napkins and handkerchiefs and condolent cries, and no titter of laughter broke anywhere in the hall. I, an anomaly in a baronet's family, somehow a scapegrace, might have guffawed in my sleeve if I could have watched the performance instead of its malefactress. Betty was standing there twisting her pale hands, a look of abject terror on her usually pleasant, pretty, and healthy face.

When the duke had been thoroughly swabbed, my father, Sir Oliver Peeltower, Bart., spoke in his office as host.

"Your grace, you've been very sportin' about this outrage, which we might have expected from such a sportsman, and a royal duke."

"Thank you, and let's get on with the ball."

"We thank *you* from the bottom of our hearts. It wouldn't have happened if that slattern hadn't been tippling, which I should have expected, knowing what sort she came from, and for giving her a chance, I'm to blame." He turned to Betty. "Get you and your belongings out of my house, and don't let me see your riffraff face again." Flushed, he turned and waved imperiously to the musicians.

They should have played a noisy polka. Instead they began a soft, sweet waltz. Goose flesh all over me, I strode in front of Betty as she faltered toward the door, and spoke to her in a voice more steady than I had hoped, perfectly audible above the low strains.

"It appears, Betty, you're discharged."

She started as though she did not recognize me as a good friend in the kitchen.

"Let me pass, Master Simon," she gasped.

"You're no longer under his orders."

"That I'm not——"

"You heard what he said about the stock you came from. He was referring to your father, George Cobbler, who flogged a squire who'd flogged him in his boyhood, and was sent to jail for it."

She stood straighter, and color rushed into her face.

"I was proud of him, sir, for doing it."

"As the son of the baronet, I'm one of the hosts of this

6

ball. Will you waltz with me?"

I had never seen anything as thrilling as the way she cocked her head as though listening to a distant voice, then lifted it high.

"Master Simon, I'd be pleased for a turn with ye."

"Come here, Simon, this instant," my father called hoarsely.

"Oh, damn it," the duke burst out.

"I'll be with you, sir, as soon as I'm free from my engagement."

Only two couples were dancing as Betty and I moved out, and these immediately retired. All alone on the big, glimmering floor, under the crystal chandeliers, in a silence that rose above the music, we challenged the lightning of the gold-plate gods. Betty held her black alpaca skirt off the floor, and though very white, her face had a serene expression and she kept the measures well. The musicians did not appear to notice anything unusual. Their place in society was hardly higher than hers, and people no worse than they had lately died like flies in the Irish famine. Not one glanced at the end of the room where the master waved his arm.

We made one complete circle of the ballroom, then Betty's hand dropped from my shoulder.

"I thank ye, Master Simon, for the pleasure of the dance," she told me, choking.

I bowed to her as to a viscountess, and waited as she hurried out the door. Then I approached my father, who had risen from his chair. The color of his face almost exactly matched that of his buff waistcoat.

Before I could gain the short distance, Howard spoke to him in a low tone. His lips seemed to shape, "Don't make a scene."

"We'll postpone our interview, Simon," my father said in a rasping voice. "And since I think you've made too free with the nog, I'll ask you to retire."

"I'm as sober as Miss Cobbler was, but I'll be glad to go."

I bowed to the duke and his duchess; and my retreat, as a military dispatch would put it, was orderly. I slept very little the rest of the night, and what sleeping I did was because of the sedative power of one fact: my American mother had provide me with an income of three thousand pounds a year. Of course, except for that, I might have danced attendance upon our guests tonight instead of waltzing with

7

a housemaid. Even so, I had known I must pay the piper.

I breakfasted alone in the kitchen under the cook's kindly but wary eye, then read a Dickens novel in the library. My summons to my father's chambers came just before noon, delivered by a frightened footman. I went there, stolidly as possible, to find him ensconced in a big chair, a brandy bottle in reach, more pained than angry if I judged aright, and determined to keep his self-control.

"Yes, sir."

"Of course you know you've disgraced me before a royal duke and duchess and the best of two counties."

This was much milder than I had expected. "I trust they'll blame it on a ne'er-do-well who inherited bad blood from America."

"By God, I hope so too. I wouldn't want the duke to think you were traitor to your class. I dare say he expected some of this thing they call democracy to crop out in a half-Yankee—one man as good as another, and all that tosh. He showed a deal of forbearance, I must say, when he didn't call for his carriage. Of course he was in good humor over the woodcock—forty-eight brace for him and nineteen for the duchess—and it was true—he said so himself—that I'd spoke too harshly to that tipsy maid."

"She wasn't tipsy, sir."

"Then she was careless, which was just as bad. To put it in a nutshell, the whole affair was a damnable bad show, and 'twill take years to live down. It amounted to thumbing your nose at Queen Victoria—yes, it did, in spirit—my own son in my own hall! Well, Simon, I'll now hear why you did it."

If he had not made that imperious declaration, and instead had asked a civil question, I might have made a soft answer. I was too young with too much indignation stored in my heart to resist the goad.

"Part of it—a fairly large part—was standing up for the girl. I could have done it in a lot of better ways. I think you know the other part, although we've never spoken of it."

"I dare say I do know. I've felt it a long time. Resentment against me on your mother's account."

"That too could have been handled in better ways. While she was still alive and it would have done some good."

"You speak mighty bitterly, Simon. I reckon she taught you to hate me."

"She did not. She didn't hate you either. She wanted me

8

to be a good son to you, and in that way save all she could from the bad bargain she'd made—or her father made for her."

"I'll keep my temper——"

"I don't care whether you keep it or not."

"No, the time's come to talk this over. By her bad bargain, as you call it, she became Lady Peeltower."

I had pictured him saying that in many wakings in the night. But my answer took a different form than I had planned.

"King James used to sell baronetcies that could be passed down for a few thousand pounds. She paid a hundred thousand pounds—rather her father did—for a secondhand ladyship that was no good to her children. An heir was already on the scene. Simon Moore must have been a shrewd trader to accumulate two million dollars, but he'd certainly lost his grip when he made that deal with you."

"Your mother—Lady Peeltower——"

"Let's call her Mattie. I think she'd rather we'd speak of her that way. Pardon my interrupting you. I've wanted to say this for a long time and this is my last chance. You cut quite a figure at the balls in Baltimore, and she was pretty and popular enough that she needn't suspect what you were after. But old Simon Moore was mighty ignorant of the market. Why, he could have bought her a 'The Lady Somebody' for that many quid! She could have been a baroness—maybe a viscountess—the first turn at it too for a titled son—instead of a wretched little baronetess, hardly better than the wife of a knight."

"You're getting the income off half of what she brought me. She might have been happier married to an American —she was homesick and poorly—but where would you be? You grew from my seed. You'd have never been born."

My father had scored a point. And I had inherited from him more than I liked to confess.

"You're quite right. Maybe my realizing that—looking out for Number One—kept me from doing anything to help her. I was old enough. I could have persuaded her to leave you and both of us go to America. Instead I was busy pushing myself with the boys at Eton. She might have got well back home. Well, that's all in the past. What about the future? I've disgraced you, not for the first time, and it would be better for all concerned if I get out of England. I don't want to go to America. I think I'll go to India."

My father sat breathing hard a long time. "There, or to the devil," he said at last.

Chapter Two

In the upshot, we parted amicably. Partly this was from a sense of my own guilt, partly his tremendous relief at getting shed of me.

The rupture had not taken either of us by surprise. It had been developing for several years, and my choice of India for a future home was the result of a good deal of inquiry and forethought. Some of the latter was of a cynical nature. The snobbery I had attacked could be turned to my own use out there. All but immersed in the dark floods it presumed to rule, Anglo-Indian society was probably the most stuffy in the world.

Made up largely of middle-class people suddenly living like lords, its worship of coronets was so fervent that a coolie could easily mistake it for a state religion. In England almost everybody played the game of butter-up and trample-down. One eye was cast reverently on our betters, the other scornfully on our worsers. In India my perch would be relatively higher than at home, and I would take a malicious pleasure in the eminence.

There I could live like a mogul on three thousand pounds —thirty thousand rupees—a year. If I found some full-time interest—ethnology, for instance, to which I was attracted— I could pursue it without thought of material gain. If I wanted to work, the mare would go that much faster. Fond of shooting and indeed shining at the sport, I could find there the best on earth, with no great cost of keepers and beaters and preserves. There was also a possibility of adventures of a much more thrilling sort than I ever had in London.

The fine steamer Alexandria-bound from Lisbon carried a number of bigwigs of the East India Company, as well as some good swords. One of the latter was Colonel Oswald Morrow of the Bengal Army, a florid, truculent-looking man, who had married a beauty from our neighboring Cornwall. His daughter of about fourteen was playing hooky from school until the warm weather, and went about shiny-eyed from the thrill of it.

I took no special interest in the high-colored pullet until I had often encountered her speculative gaze. It occurred to me then that the oddness of her countenance, forfending any thought that she was pretty, might well be the promise of startling beauty. She wore her bay hair as a young girl should, braided and ribboned; but it gave glimpses of lambent flames; and her skin, a pale, pure olive no doubt inherited from her Cornish mother, had a fine richness and gloss. The bones of her face were too prominent as yet, but were delicate. Her figure was too skinny, but I thought it would ripen quickly under the Indian sun.

I thought she might be of an age to investigate a young man of twenty-two, especially since there were no boys of her own age available. When she stood demurely by the rail, eying the great rock guarding the Gates of Hercules, I stopped my walk to ask if she saw any apes.

"There are some on the ship," she answered with rather surprising *élan*. "I don't see any on the rock."

"Gibraltar is infested with Barbary apes."

"I'm not interested in apes, but I was mighty surprised to find you on the ship."

"How did that happen?"

"Your name is Simon Peeltower and you're the son of Sir Oliver Peeltower of Devonshire. A girl friend of mine—well, she's a little older—was at the ball your father gave to the duke."

"What's your name, if you'll kindly tell me?"

"It's Miss Vivian Morrow, and although you're trying to change the subject, I think you should face it fully and candidly. That's what I always tried to do when I got in trouble at school. Dorothy was *horrified* at what you did. She's the great-niece of a peer, and *very* haughty. Of course you've had to leave England."

"Yes—to eat the bread of exile."

"Were you having a clandestine love affair with the maid? I know that kind of thing happens more frequently than the world knows. Dorothy said she was quite pretty in a common way."

I shook my head gravely.

"Well, I haven't made up my mind about it yet."

"Have you discussed it with any of our shipmates?" I asked.

"Certainly not. I haven't even told Papa that you are the one who did it. Papa says he doesn't approve of snobbery

11

but he believes in people staying in their place, and his favorite word is 'discipline.' He's quite influential in India—and I didn't want you to start out there with a mark against you."

"You know, Vivian, that's very sporting," I told her, suddenly in earnest.

"I know a lot of things I don't tell," she informed me with a mysterious look.

Leaving that to sink in, she stalked away. I had not the slightest doubt of her troth, and when after sundown Colonel Morrow invited me to a glass of brandy—a staunch Anglo-Indian, he believed that to drink before then was ruinous to the liver—I found no mark against me. If he had ever heard of the disgrace at Peeltower Hall, he did not connect me with it. I fancied him a rather typical soldier in the Colonial tradition—positive in his opinions, forthright if not blunt, with no time for fol-de-rol and no patience with laxity and sloth; nor could I doubt his competence in his profession and intense loyalty to all that he deemed his own.

With him was a junior subaltern of my own age, Philip Maybank. He was greatly impressed with the Colonel and could hardly conceal his palpitations over being in his company. It was perfectly apparent that Philip—I was calling him that after the second glass—hoped for an appointment to Morrow's regiment, and I amused myself wondering why he desired it and whether he could get it. What I could not do was picture him twenty years from now behaving or looking or in any way like his commander. He had nervous eyes; outside of that he was as mild and sedate, perhaps as dull and commonplace, as any officer I had met.

Raising these questions in a casual way with Vivian, I was given earnest answers on the authority of her sharp eyes.

"Oh, yes, a blind man could see that Lieutenant Maybank is mad to serve under Papa," she told me. "And Papa isn't nearly as averse to that kind of flattery as he appears."

"I would be mad to serve under him too," I said, watching her face.

It looked puzzled only for an instant. "I know what you mean. I ought to be angry with you for the aspersion, but there's so much truth in it, I'll forgive you. You see, I make it a rule to face the facts even about my own family. Papa is what's called a martinet. Do you know what that means?"

"I have a vague idea."

"You and he could never get along. You are fairly clever, and he can't stand to have clever people around him, let alone young gentlemen who dance with housemaids in front of royal dukes!"

"You're not exactly stupid. How does he put up with you?"

"I let him think I'm a fool."

"If he chooses dull subordinates, how can he succeed as a regimental commander?"

"He chooses men who will obey his orders without blinking an eye, and although I say it that should not, his regiment is as well-regarded as any in India. The troops are sepoys—natives—the word comes from *sipahi,* the Hindustani word for soldier—but all his officers are English. It stood like iron at Chillianwalla—I was hardly more than a child at the time——"

"About ten years old," I said wickedly.

"I was going on twelve or thirteen, as I recall it," she went on without turning a hair, "and old enough to be very proud of Papa's regiment. At Gujrat, every man was a hero. The citation from Sir Charles Napier said so. I wished I could have been in India to share in the glory. As luck would have it, I had been sent home to school."

"You've been out to India before?" I asked, unable to conceal my astonishment.

Vivian laughed in a superior fashion. "You might call it that. I was born there."

"Do you speak Hindustani?"

She rattled off some odd-sounding words.

"What does that mean in English?"

"It's an idiomatic expression from the Hindi, but freely translated it would be 'Can your grandmother suck eggs?' "

"Vivian, I can't tell you how much I enjoy your company."

"Wait until you meet Lieutenant Maybank's wife, and you won't look at me again."

"Great guns! He said his wife was aboard! But I haven't seen any lady who can hold a candle to you."

"Little do you know! She's one reason I feel sure Lieutenant Maybank will get to serve under Papa and will do very well. There must be much more to him than you think or he could have never won the hand of Mildred Maybank. A pretty name, don't you think?"

"Very pretty. How did you find it out?"

"I find out lots of things—without trying. When you meet

13

her, you'll be swept off your feet."

"Where is she?"

"In her stateroom. That's the proper place for a lady on the first few days of a voyage—everyone knows that. By staying there until she gets her sea legs, there's no danger of her throwing up—disgracing herself, I mean—in the dining saloon. I should be there myself, but it does seem sort of silly when I have never felt even a twinge of *mal de mere*——"

"I agree with you."

"Mrs. Maybank is my *ideal*."

With this dramatic statement, Vivian left me. Intensely interested in all she thought and felt, I could hardly wait for my first glimpse of a lady of such promise. I was prepared for a surprise, hardly for real astonishment, a much rarer experience than we suppose. I mused a good while before I could begin to find its source.

I had never before seen a young woman who could so perfectly recall a little girl's lost love of a blue-eyed, golden-haired doll.

I supposed that little girls love homely dolls as well as pretty dolls—there is a place in their hearts for bad dolls as well as good dolls. Mildred Maybank would remind half-grown-up Vivian of her very best doll—her Number One Doll a little Anglo-Indian girl would call her—without a speck of paint knocked off her nose, forever and ever pretty as a picture, daintily dressed and of perfect behavior. The facial likeness was surprising enough—a rather round face, large, bright, innocent eyes with very long, out-turned lashes, pink cheeks, a small red mouth. Her clothes were both proper and exceedingly pretty; you felt that she had never been near any dirt. But it was her conduct that made the comparison so pat. Although that of a perfect lady of the books, it was more than that. Much against my inclination, I could not help but believe she was as good as Vivian pictured her. It was as though the most capable roué in Paris would lift his hat to her and chivalrously draw back.

Such dolls are expensive. My thoughts moved along the same path that Vivian's must have taken, up to a point; how had such an ordinary fellow as Philip Maybank won, as Vivian had put it with sure perception, her hand? There were many runners in that race unless I missed my guess. It was more than a guess, I presently confessed—instead it was an instinct that Vivian could know only by its half-wakened reflex. Around Robin Hood's barn I followed it to a scene of

Mildred's bridal night, when her pretty, proper garments had rustled to her knees like Madeline on St. Agnes' Eve. Vivian's explanation for Philip's victory was that there was more to him than readily appeared. I thought of a likelier reason— one that ill-became a man like me, as though I were breaking faith with my native cynicism. I could not help but grin at myself over the thought that she had married a man of only mediocre powers and prospects because they loved each other.

When I met her, I need pay no attention to her words and could thus devote my mind to her much more revealing actions. The former were what I could expect from a perfect young lady of the decorous middle class—her pleasurable anticipations of India, what a wonderful thing it was to serve the Queen, and how honored she felt to be traveling on the same ship with Colonel Morrow. When I caught myself wondering if this last remark were political, I looked into her eyes and was actually half ashamed. It was noticeable that she always waited an instant for her husband to speak first, and watched anxiously for his approval of everything she said. When he distinguished himself in the least, her eyes shone. When, at our introduction, I tried pressing her hand, she drew it away with what seemed instinctive dismay. And in spite of all what I liked to call middle-class prudery, she was graceful.

"Have you any children, Mrs. Maybank?" I asked, loudly enough for all the deck-sitters nearby to hear.

Her color rose and her eyes darted to her husband's as though for help. Rather to my surprise, he threw her no life line.

"We haven't been so blessed," she answered when the silence grew long.

"How long have you and he been married?" I persisted.

"A little over a year——"

"Why, you've had time for one and have another on the way. You'll do better, I'm sure, in a warm climate like India's."

"It was quite warm last night, wasn't it?" Then seeing that this was an inept way to change the subject, her cheeks burned.

"Warm enough for a good start," I remarked.

She turned her eyes full on mine. "I hope I can present my husband with several children," she said with unimpeachable dignity. "I was an only child."

15

Clearly defeated, I beat a hasty retreat. Thereafter I tended to avoid her, which she no doubt took for a gesture of respect; and I was not sure but that was the fact; certainly I could not escape the conclusion, a smack to my vanity, that she was greatly relieved. I remained as astonished by her as I would be by a completely bad man; adding up a lonely childhood, probably a doting mother and prudish maiden aunts, an over-accent on the word "genteel" and a curiously picture-book prettiness, I still could not make the sum come out a Mildred Maybank. Since the puzzle could not be solved without laborious effort, with many more rebuffs, in my usual habit of mind I put it by.

In the easy pastime of brandy-drinking and sport-talk I spent some oddly uneasy hours with her husband Philip. It was hard to imagine a more unpresuming man, affable, well-mannered, a sound drinker, and with more perception and even more humor than I thought at first; but his restless eyes made me nervous. He was getting on well with Colonel Morrow; I never could, I thought, and saw no reason to cultivate him and be irritated by his excathedra utterances. All this left me leisure for the company of the most engaging passenger on the ship—Vivian Morrow.

Her conversation was never dull and usually dramatic. Her appearance grew on me until I could almost swear it reflected unborn beauty. I became oppressed with the thought of parting with her at Alexandria, where she and her father must lay over on the Queen's business; the journey beyond threatened to be bleak. I teased her just enough to challenge her, showing off my worldliness, and basking in her admiration. Instead of trying to discourage any girlish infatuation she might have for me, surely the first office of a gentleman, I baited it in every way that the open deck permitted. It was pleasing to my ego and pleasantly exciting to my flesh, and I felt I was somehow scoring on Colonel Morrow. Any possibility of unhappy consequences to my lovely little shipmate, I ignored. Since I would not get to see her atop a camel on the desert road to Suez, where again I would take ship, I took all the more pleasure in as charming a view that she gave me our last night out.

The incident was almost altogether by her contrivance. It began with her betting me a shilling that she would be the first to spy the shore lights, which required us to meet on the deck well past midnight. I would have been greatly ashamed to be caught tête-à-tête with so young a girl at that hour; but

Vivian took precautions against it on her own hook. Obviously she had gone through the motions of going to bed. When she made her serene entrance, her hair was done up on her head, and by other rearrangements I could not identify she looked at least sixteen.

She would be in Calcutta only rarely, she told me, and mainly in the small outpost station of Diwanpani. If I went through there, I would certainly call on her father. In a great social demand, no doubt, I would have no time for a girl whose father still treated her as a child; but she was already planning to return to India when she had "come out," and why then she wouldn't be surprised if we should meet again. I would probably be married by then, but we could still talk over old times.

She won her bet, and it was time to say good-by. I looked at her odd face, and the moon invoked something like an aura of her appearance in two or three brief years.

"I dare say it's not proper for us to have a good-by kiss," I told her, "since there's such a difference in our ages."

"Why, Papa's friends never miss a chance to kiss me lately."

"That I don't doubt."

"But if you're thinking of propriety, how young I am, and how old you are, I decline."

"I dare say I was thinking about those things, but my desire is so much stronger——"

"Desire?" she echoed proudly.

The truth was, I longed to press my mouth against hers, and was a little troubled that the unlawful longing came so naturally.

"Yes."

"Not just a casual gesture of friendship?" she asked.

"No. Your first real kiss."

"Well, then—if you want to make it one to remember—I do too."

Her arms tight as a child's around my neck, she put a good deal of enthusiasm into the caress. I could not help but think of Juliet at fourteen, giving her first kiss to a forbidden lover. It could not have been more lovely than this, in spite of her early seasoning by the Veronan sun.

17

Chapter Three

I continued on to India and with my inchoate plans. All of the first two years I gave to seeing the country, listening to its sounds, sniffing its manifold and exciting scents, trying to touch its bare flesh. I was in cities of marvelous names—Amritsar, Rawalpindi, Jodhpur, Allahabad, Agra, Benares, Peshawar. I rode on camels and elephants, in oxcarts and doolies, river steamers and bunderboats. Partly for the sport —and a great part of every sport is self-challenge—I hunted tigers in a swelter of the Ganges Delta and snow leopards in the biting wind off Karakoram. Partly it was a flirtation with Death, passionate at times, and at times queerly sorrowful, but never quite rational, and beyond my power to explain.

The enterprise had two curious consequences. One was that I obtained a rapport with natives that most sahibs never gained in their tarrying here, perhaps because they never ceased to be exiles instead of inmates, and hence they never tried. We did not understand each other—the brown man and I—but we hit it off. The second result was the winning of an astonishing amount of repute with the jungle dwellers not only on shooting grounds I had visited, but far and wide. They considered me a much greater *shikari*—hunter—than the size of my bag would prove. In fact, the fame came too fast to be well earned. Old trackers by distant cooking fires named me among the few elite of the great game. Plainly it was a matter of the emotions of my shiny-eyed companions of the trail, not their well-weighed judgment. For some strange reason I appealed to their sense of drama.

Toward the end of the second year I made a first tentative probing of the vast jungles eastward of Calcutta, toward hell-and-gone Yünnan. The journey took me through Diwanpani and to the great bungalow that General Morrow called home. There I looked in vain in the garden for a head and a heart of fire. Choto Memsahib had gone to school in England, the Mohammedan chokidar told me in the corrupt Hindustani of Anglo-India. When I replied in the full vigor of Urdu, he withdrew his palm and straightway became my brother in bemoaning her absence.

Truly there was no such memsahib in all Hind! The very flowers of the garden had blossomed but meanly, and with scant perfume, since she went away.

What seemed at the time a mere incident of my brief stay at Diwanpani made a lasting impression on my mind. Any travèling sahib putting up at the big, shabby dak bungalow was certain of an invitation to dinner. As the son of a baronet with three thousand pounds I could bet with almost perfect safety on being entertained by Number One of the station, whether civil or military; and that eminence was at present held by Colonel Morrow. In the present muggy weather all the pukka memsahibs—meaning the pure English wives of officers or officials—were off to the cool hills; and I was a little afraid that the doughty old soldier might honor me formally and alone. Happily, he decided in favor of having me at Regimental Mess.

The quarters stood on cool, high ground overlooking a charming garden, and were mellow with age and tradition. The *pièce de résistance* of the excellent dinner was baked fowls, reminiscent of English pheasant but larger and racier; I was told that they were a great, flame-colored pheasant unknown in the aviaries of Europe and as yet unnamed by ornithologists, but common in these hills, "jolly good eating, and affording fair sport when walked up." Then as I marveled at India's lavishness, I considered the servants waiting on our small number—one behind every man's chair besides the streams going back and forth to the kitchen, pantry, and wine cellar. No ducal butler could command his staff better than the regimental khansaman, a Bengali with the common name of Haran Lal and the face of a scholar. But I got the fleeting impression that the officers need not employ faulty Hindustani to speak to him. Watching his face as Colonel Morrow discussed the Sikh Wars, I believed that he understood every word. I thought that he pretended ignorance of English to avoid the name of Babu, meaning in sahib parlance an educated native and held in scorn.

Near the foot of the table sat Philip Maybank, a full lieutenant now, but either as colorless as before, or I was colorblind. His eyes rested easier than when I had seen them last, and the queer thought struck me that Mildred's absence had benefited his nerves. It might be that in her presence he could never quite relax. Quite likely she did not shed her intense propriety even in the bedroom and he had to stand perpetual watch of his P's and Q's. If there was anything to that, there was a great deal more. It was involved with her porcelain-looking prettiness, which must make powerful demands upon him. What these demands were, I could not imagine. When I meditated upon him, she kept rising before my eyes. She was not only his better half, as the saying went: he was kind of an appendage to her. He was not very significant when he was with her, yet you noticed him; he had an identity as Mildred's husband. Now he had become insignificant. He had almost ceased to exist. He was certainly more composed in an oyster-like fashion; although I did not know exactly what "happy" meant, I ventured he was happier.

The rugged regiment of sepoys must make great demands upon him too; and I wondered if he were able to meet them. Sitting next to Colonel Morrow, I approached the matter obliquely and was soon instructed in it. Lieutenant Maybank was one of the best junior officers under Morrow's command. His main fault was the imposing of too strict discipline. His men jumped when he spoke, and plainly held him in the great respect that is born of fear.

I was surprised by my own lack of surprise.

The general talk of the table was more dynamic than at most Mess dinners, and at first I did not know why. Certainly the main subject was not essentially exciting to a civilian—what would happen to the East Guards—the pet name for the Seventh Bengal Rifles—when Lord Dalhousie's policies of Empire were put in effect. Recognizing Russia as the main foe, he looked north and west. Only a few head-hunting tribes menaced the settlements of Farther Bengal and Assam, so the eastern battlements were falling into neglect. It was quite possible that Diwanpani would soon cease to exist as a military post, the regiment barracked in or about Calcutta, leaving only outliers to man the fort.

Although his camaraderie with his officers was quite marked, Colonel Morrow's voice of course remained dominant over the board. However, there was another that rather slowly began to loom large in my hearing. It belonged to Ronald Blain, whose name I had heard occasionally in connection with all that boded good in India. When the old chiefs discussed the youngsters, he was very likely to be mentioned as a "coming man." He was rather young for his rank —in his late twenties—and he appeared to have the quiet power on which women dote. His body was very fine. If I were a woman, I thought I would call it beautiful. It was so well proportioned that it appeared fully a stone lighter than the scales would tell—looking sharp, I guessed him at thirteen stone. His face was as up-to-date as his conversation—

I thought of it as significant of the present middle-class rule in England as the Duke of Wellington's face was significant of the Old Order. It was broader and not as bony as the faces of the Norman aristocrats. His features were larger and more handsome and less elegant.

He had a respect amounting to worship for the amenities. Either that, or his meticulous observance of them was premeditated tactics of a campaign. It was odd to see so big a man so spick-and-span. Over and above this—or else showing through—was an extraordinarily rugged individual. Of course he did not talk back to the regimental commander, but he spoke out. "Colonel Morrow, it appears to me that you've overlooked . . . I think you have failed to differentiate . . . Sir, isn't that statement too broad?" But when I put myself in the Colonel's boots, borrowing his highhandedness, I could not be in the least annoyed by this captain's proposals, or anything but impressed. They showed in the first place a profound attention and understanding of his points, and his amendments appeared to lend them strength. They were never, I noticed, confutations.

Vivian was mistaken in thinking that her father could not stand the company of the very clever men. This man was that and, which in the long run would count even more, desperately ambitious.

"I was sorry to miss the Colonel's charming young daughter," I remarked to Ronald in a suitable opening after dinner.

"Oh, do you know Vivian?" He had an amused look that the Colonel would have liked, but which I thought put on.

"Yes, we were shipmates coming out two years and more ago."

"If she admitted you into her circle of friends, I'll wager you had a jolly time."

"I've never met anyone with more *joie de vivre*."

"I'm not too versed in French expressions. As a plain soldier, the Queen's English is good enough for me. I dare say you mean 'joy of life.' "

"An excellent translation," I said with a sober face.

He colored slightly. "I've never seen a young memsahib with more spunk."

I knew now why he had put on the amused look. He had seen its like on the faces of many big sahibs when the Colonel's spunky, sprightly daughter was mentioned, and it served to mask his feelings. I did not know what the latter were,

21

but they were very strong.

In the morning I continued my journey, and the jungles of the Tripura closed for a time about me. I circled back and traveled on, and all I came to know of India only decried the dim vastness of her unknown. I had dreamed and even started to prepare for a great adventure—no less than an attempt to penetrate the terra incognita of the Hindu Kush—when the pleasant management of my own life was taken out of my hands. This came about through the collision of English and Russian power on the Black Sea.

I cared not a whit for the expansion of either empire, let alone for the Turk, and could find no logical reason for joining the combat. Perhaps it was a reluctant gesture to the Queen, whose arms in India I had declined to bear. I had upspoke rashly before pukka sahibs against England's conquering by force of arms one Indian province after another; and Russia could at least hit back with more than rusty matchlocks and Pathan knives.

The younger son of a baronet, I was straightway commissioned as a subaltern of horse. Indeed it would have been "detrimental to morale" for one of that eminence to serve in the ranks. I was ashamed at first to be over Tommies, who knew how to fight, but was soon sickened to be under officers who did not know how to lead. Actually I was a better officer than three fourths of those above me. There was much I needed to learn but a great deal more they needed to forget, the harder task of the two. At least I had had experience getting in and out of places without the leg irons of regulations, relegation of authority, precedences and orders. I could forage like a pack rat to get food and blankets for my men. It was not this handiness, however, that won me a captaincy. Instead it was the carrying off of my superiors by sickness and slaughter.

Historians will relate the bloody boggle of the Crimean War. They will tell of reconnaissance consisting of the study of two ink sketches of the Peninsula; of a naval attack planned in waters that proved two feet deep; of an army knowing no maneuvers beyond those of a barracks drill field; and of seventy-year-old generals who had not smelled powder since Waterloo. They may remark on a regiment that marched all day to find themselves exactly where they started. I wonder how they can bring themselves to recount how a cavalry brigade, trying to recover guns which courtly Lord Raglan had decreed must never be lost, was sent headlong into the point-blank fire of Russian cannons.

I was one of a freezing, starving, plague-ridden host who passed the winter of '54 in siege lines before Sevastopol. There were thousands more who did not live to see "the angel with the lamp," a most strange and miracle-like reminder of human glory, all of which seemed departed from our ghastly camps. I was of the force that celebrated the anniversary of Waterloo by an assault on the stronghold, only to draw back decimated, in limping, bleeding shame. Even so, the Russian troops were in a worse fix than we. In addition to botch and boggle in their high command, there were spoils and treachery. In the way of soldierliness, the big, blond Muscovite knew only how to die. Our Tommies won battles in spite of our officers, and at last the allied armies found a general, the Frenchman Pelissier, who would as lief pull Louis Napoleon's beard as Palmerston's wig.

The war dragged on and finally dried up. Early in the year of 1856, I resigned my lieutenant's commission—I had been demoted for commandeering two hundred pairs of boots from a bulging depot—and returned to Calcutta.

There I gave over my dreams of crossing the glaciers guarding Kafiristan: the Crimea had been too chilly. I was resolved to miss no meals or meet no avoidable dangers. But I had managed to make friends out there and hoped to make some here. I had been boon-fellow with other officers and comrade to my men. Not satisfied with the compromise, but dreading return to my solitudes, I rented a Number One bungalow on Chowrighee, hired twenty servants for a total of twenty pounds a month, with commissions and baksheesh, and prepared to make peace with sahib society. Indeed I had every intention of shining forth.

That society was willing enough to make peace with me. If anyone knew I had waltzed with a housemaid at a ducal ball, he charitably let it pass. Obviously that bit of rough going I had had at Crimea had done me no end of good! A "rum card" theretofore, I should now go true to form as an English gentleman. The view was so widely held that I was admitted to membership in the Ganges Club, patterned after the Carlton in London, and colonels, commissioners, and sometimes generals and provincial governors dined at my table, knowing that their precedence would be well looked to. Their ladies patted my hand, and made casual mention of nieces and daughters soon to visit India.

But Colonel Morrow's daughter had visited India while I

23

was hungry and cold before Sevastopol.

She had been seventeen then, far more virginal than at fourteen. When I had known her, she had been hardly aware of the condition; it was a word that meant a physical fact which she considered only now and then. At seventeen her virginity had hung over her like an aura. It was an intensely personal mystery that someday would be solved; to young officers clustered about the budding beauty it was an attraction as subtle, as elemental, and as powerful as a needle to a loadstone. Among them was certainly Ronald Blain. The East Guards were still at Diwanpani in those days, and he its most promising bachelor. What chance would the others have? What chance would I have had?

Now the East Guards had been moved bag and baggage to Barrackpore, leaving only one company to man the fort. Colonel Morrow was still there, recovering slowly from a severe leg wound got from a bursting gun, and passing the time snipe-shooting, masheer-fishing, and pig-sticking; but everyone knew that his Brigadier Generalcy was in the machine and would roll out any day. At the start of the cool weather he came up to Calcutta to attend a staff meeting. When I encountered him at the Ganges Club, I requested the honor of entertaining him at dinner.

He accepted with evident pleasure on the supposition that I was making a handsome return for his official hospitality at Diwanpani four Rains ago. I did not think he guessed my real motives, since they seemed strange and a little startling to their very possessor. I wanted to hear news of Vivian. My memory of her had not dimmed in the least and my imaginings of her, twenty-one now, ripe for any kind of kisses she would stand for, were unaccountably strong. In case of her return to India, I wanted all the capital I could make with her doughty sire.

What was I up to in inviting also Major Ronald Blain? It was a pukka-enough act—as the adjutant of the East Guards under the present colonel, he too had been called for some sort of report to the same meeting. He was known as a great favorite of Morrow. When the latter took over the newly formed brigade, no one doubted that Ronald would become his aide-de-camp.

So it looked well to have him, and the Colonel would think it a nice compliment. So would Ronald if he were of open instead of suspicious nature. If he divined I had an ax to grind, certainly he was not such a fool as to think it concerned Vivian, whom I had known only as a little squirt of fourteen.

I had always been grateful for the common sense of others, blinding them to the immensity of my follies.

Sooner or later Colonel Morrow might want to compare me with Ronald. I had not been seen at good advantage that night at Diwanpani, but I intended to be so, as head of the table in my own mansion. Somewhat of a fancier of food and drink, I wrote an excellent menu. The other guests would be well chosen, the accent would be on wealth and position. Whatever Ronald's place and prospects, he was not the son of a baronet, and I did not think he had three thousand pounds a year.

The old soldier came in limping, but like "that old Lord Maurice, not a whit subdued." Beyond and above my position of host I appeared to have won some regard from him I had never noticed before. Ronald came with him, acting as his aide, and in the full dress of the East Guards, he took the eye. His own eye made a quick rove. It lighted upon no pretty young girls out from England, and instead on the somewhat grim faces of the three foremost dowagers of the capital and three official couples of corresponding importance. What I thought was zeal flicked across Ronald's handsome countenance. His gains tonight could be greater than in a major battle.

"What have you heard lately from that dashing daughter of yours?" one of the dowagers asked the guest of honor when the dinner was under way.

"I had a few lines two boats ago," Colonel Morrow answered. "I count that a fine instance of parental respect, if you know what I mean. At the time she was visiting her aunt, Lady Stephens, in Portman Square, and I surmised she was being squired about by a good many young blades. I had no fault to find with that. There's safety in numbers."

All laughed pleasantly.

"Did you ever meet the young lady?" one of the dowagers asked me.

"Seven years ago," I answered.

"Oh, she was a mere schoolgirl then," the dowager told me. "You should have seen her when she came out in '54, with her hair upon her head and wearing her first Paris gown. You were in Crimea, I believe—but Ronald remembers."

"She cut a swath from here to Simla," Ronald said, looking at me.

25

"You didn't fare so badly, Ronald, if I remember well," said the wife of a K.C.B. "It seems to me that your score was at least three to one over your nearest competitor."

"It would have been three to nothing if I'd had my way," Ronald answered. "Colonel, do you think we'll be lucky enough to have her visit us this year?" He spoke rather complacently, I thought.

"It's not unlikely, but I won't know till she walks off the ship."

"Colonel Morrow, I'll wager you ten to one that if she does come, she'll either stay, or go home under some other name than Vivian Morrow," said the K.C.B.

"And I'd lay two to one I could guess the name," a sporting dowager offered.

"We'll see, we'll see." The Colonel's smile about the table gave Ronald his due without skipping me.

That I had risen in the Colonel's estimation became even more patent when the ladies had retired, leaving us gentlemen to some excellent port. He moved from his place and took an empty chair next to mine.

"Just a word, now," he said. "May go deeper into the business later. I've been officially informed of my Brigadier Generalcy, to be gazetted when I return to active duty. I hope it will be in the next thirty days. My brigade is to be made up of my old Seventh and Colonel Dugan's regiment of Gurkhas."

"I'd congratulate you, General Morrow."

"It should be an interesting command. The Gurkhas are nippy fellows, and they'll have only white officers, the same as my sepoys. If we don't see some good action, I'll miss my guess."

"Yes, sir."

"Simon—I'll call you that, since we came from neighboring shires—I of course know your record at Crimea. If I had been your C.G., you would have got a good wigging for lifting those boots, but not demoted. Regulations have got to be obeyed, no matter how damned stupid, but you were new to the military life and hadn't been through the mill. You did a good job against the Redan, and that evened it up with me."

"Thank you very much."

"Well, I've been thinking you've had a good start, so why not finish it? You'll want something to do soon; why not serve in the Bengal Army? I believe I could find a spot for you in my brigade. You'd have to start as a subaltern, of course, but the beggarly pay would cut no ice with you, I dare say, and promotion should be rapid."

I tried to look both grateful and doubtful. If I had shown improvement, the General was mistaken in its amount. I had no burning desire to serve either the John Company or the Queen. If offered a commission in the Coldstream Guards, I would still try to wiggle out of the honor; and I simply lacked the moral strength to lead natives in battle against their own kind for English gain.

"Sir, I'm very sensible to the honor," I replied. "True, I've been thinking of going into some branch of the Civil Service, but I'll give the proposal my most serious consideration."

General Morrow turned curtly away. I had a sense of its not mattering very much—he could not get at me very well unless Vivian returned; and in that case, Major Ronald Blain would get at her first. This dinner party did not matter either, save as an hour or two of self-flattery. A grayness of spirit came upon me. I looked at the plate and the glass, the glossy cloth, the servants coming and going, the well-dressed sahibs talking and laughing, and it was all bleak as a dream when one sleeps cold. Loneliness is a disease, I thought; the person afflicted cannot get a doctor because of the rigidity of the quarantine. If I slipped into the kitchen and out the door and down the road, I would not be missed until time for the people to go home, and then only as the payee of due respects.

I would go down any road that led somewhere. There must be a job for me that would justify my existence, that I was invented for. It could not be one requiring any sort of martyr. I had no ability to submerge myself in a great cause. I was not noble enough to strive for fame, which Milton truly called "that last infirmity of noble mind," and not gifted enough to win it if I were. A younger son's usual choice was between Civil Service and the Military. I would not enjoy either career, for I would always feel cheated of something, and the reward of outperching a greater or less number of competitors did not seem worth the effort.

Perhaps my plan to penetrate Kafiristan was on the right track. The trouble was, I did not prize enough the stuff I would bring back—maps, figures, scientific facts. I would enjoy the adventures, but the Minjan River could flow where it listeth, for all I cared. Although I had no quarrel with hypocrisy, I could not work it on myself, and the game must be worth the candle.

My guns were put away in grease. My expert tracker and shikari Puran was guarding his fields from raiding deer and wild pigs. Well, I would go forth with him again and have intercourse with tigers, and perhaps in the jungle some scales would fall off my eyes. So when my guests had gone on ways I could never make mine, I wrote to Puran in his village in the Sundarbans, and bade him come to take charge of our shikar, and sent him a five-rupee note hidden between two playing cards pasted together, which a native seal-breaker would regard as *pooja* of some sort, and scrupulously eschew.

The letter dispatched, that night I dreamed of Vivian. That did not surprise me: her frequent visits to the gray and silent scenes of my dream world was one of the main mysteries of my mind. On this occasion I perceived her clearly, even with a sense of color. She was coming gaily down the gangplank of a ship with Ronald Blain.

I woke remembering that the week-late P. and O. liner lately calling in Madras had been due in the Hooghly last night. That fact alone could not send me on what would surely be, by any counting, a fool's errand: rather it would be the recurrence of an impression received and, I had thought, dismissed, at dinner last night. There had been a drollness in Ronald's voice when he had spoken of her visiting India again, and his expression had been faintly smug. Suddenly it occurred to me that this impression had caused the dream.

It happened that I had great respect for dreams. No, it did not happen so—it was one of the inevitable results of introspection. I had long ago decided that dreams vivid enough to remember have great bearing on our waking lives, and if we could plumb their dark wells, we would find truth. Suddenly I felt quite certain that Ronald had foreknowledge of Vivian's visiting India very soon. I believed that she had written him to meet her on today's boat. Her father apparently did not share the secret—he had been his usual forthright and downright self—but perhaps she intended to give him a surprise.

Well, I would like to surprise Ronald Blain by beating him to the dock.

I rang for an early breakfast, but revulsion came upon me as I stuffed it down. To go to the ship on the strength of a dream about a girl as remote as she, whose puppy-love was seven years over the dam—I could not be such a silly ass.

It was unthinkable that she was on the ship, inevitable that we would embarrass each other if she were.

In spite of all that, I went. I was driven to it against my will as men are sometimes driven to a silly fist fight. I had to go, to stand up for myself, the peculiar fool and outsider that I was.

There was no sign of Ronald Blain. That relieved me, and I would be even more relieved to discover presently no sign of Vivian. I approached a clerk sorting mail behind a barred window.

"Could you tell me if Miss Vivian Morrow is aboard?"

Up-lighted the little man's peaked cockney face.

"*That* she is!" He gazed at me as though we had bet on the same winning horse at the Derby. "I know she 'asn't got off without giving me a cheero."

My spine had one brief, powerful tingle. I considered sending a note to Vivian's room, then with soaring spirits went to look for her. At fourteen, she had been a good trencher-woman and she would want to fortify herself with a hearty ship's breakfast before disembarking. When I passed from the glaring deck into the shaded dining saloon, its brightest spot was Vivian's auburn hair filled with sparks.

I paid no attention to her beauty as I approached her table. She looked at me without seeing me at first, then sat perfectly still. That the man approaching her was Simon Peeltower, not Ronald Blain, gave her that creepy feeling that all sensitive people know—a perception of mystery all about them ever, occasionally moving in obscure and meaningless ways. I saw it steal into her face, changing the shape of her eyes and mouth, and then watched her deny it. Chance had brought me here, she thought, and Ronald was not far behind.

"Simon," she said quietly.

"May I sit down, Vivian?"

She nodded. I thought she was in the same boat that I was, about talking—quite sure that we should engage in the "well, well" of long-parted acquaintances but not equal to it. There was drama here that we could not expel. The easy conversation of the other breakfasters was a subdued murmur in the room, and the native servants appeared to flit on winged bare feet. Vivian laid her knife and fork side by side on her plate. This was part of the semaphore practiced in India where few servants spoke English and not many masters knew Hindustani: it meant that she had had enough.

29

She rolled up her napkin and put it in a ring. I thought she was giving me a chance to look at her closely, and I did so without amazement, so perfectly she fulfilled the promise that a skinny, odd-looking schoolgirl had made to me.

"You've come out very beautifully, Vivian," I told her.

"That could mean very little—or a lot," she answered thoughtfully. "Will you try to be a little more explicit?"

I could not analyze her beauty if I tried. If beauty is analyzable, it is probably not real. It is not a set of features and our perception of it is certainly a reflex from an unrecognized desire. I thought beauty did not satisfy but reminded us of a universal longing, never to be fulfilled, and that was why it is always a little sad.

Her eyes were so dark blue under their dense sorrel lashes as to appear black in this light, and they were effectively set, as by an old and cunning lapidarist. Her pale olive skin might easily suggest native passion to the mind that lies below thought—a bond with the lusty sun. Her delicate nose and serene mouth enhanced rather than reduced the effect. Even obtuse men would have a troubled awareness that she was a great prize.

"You are very beautiful, Vivian," I said.

"Do you mean that, Simon?" she answered in a troubled tone.

I smiled.

"Aren't there more important subjects to get over with, first?" she went on.

"There couldn't be a more important subject."

"Very well. I've often wondered what you'd think and what you'd say. Is it real beauty?"

"Don't you know?"

"Sometimes I believe it is and sometimes I don't. Real beauty is so rare and strange. Mamma was really beautiful, but that's made me all the more doubtful. I'm much more likely to believe it now, Simon. You wouldn't lie to me."

"Not about that, of course."

"Are you able to see beauty more clearly than most men, because you're so plain?"

"Why, I fancied myself rather stunning." I smiled as I said it, but there was no mirth in the smile, and almost no mockery.

She knew I waited anxiously for her reply. As I had said so lightly a moment ago, there could not be a more important subject between her and me. More than I could imagine depended on our appearance to each other. Unless profoundly appealing, a gate would slam shut. Beyond was a path with many pitfalls: if we passed them all each would have the other's appearance as part of his own, which was an awkward way to say we would possess each other's beauty, the last being a reflection of a recognized desire. It meant that we would lie naked in each other's arms.

"I'll try to tell you how you look. I wouldn't have been sure if we hadn't met again, but I was right all the time. You are good to look at—without being good-looking—perhaps I mean reassuring. You've got a compact body, not in the least imposing but suggesting strength and even some grace. Your features are good but they don't match and the whole effect is plain." She paused and then said, "Now."

"Well?"

"Are you living in Calcutta?"

"Yes."

"I asked for you when I was here before, and you were in the Crimea. Later I wondered if you'd been killed. I thought it very likely but never tried to find out. What do you make of that?"

I shook my head.

"I can't make it out either, because I've thought of you often, and wondered. Simon, did you just happen to run into me here? I suppose so, but you didn't act surprised." She asked the question in a more casual tone than she had employed before.

"The mail clerk told me you were on the ship."

" 'Arry? He's a great pal, but why should he volunteer the information?"

"He didn't. I asked him."

"Then someone told you I might be coming. I wrote of it to only one person—I was going to surprise Dad, pleasantly or unpleasantly remains to be seen. But I told that person not to tell anyone. And I thought he could keep his mouth shut."

"Aren't you expecting him to meet you?"

"Of course. He ought to have been here before now. Didn't he tell you?"

"You ask him."

She pushed back her chair and a servant sprang to help her. "I'm not going to wait for him any longer," she said. "I dare say he was away on duty and has sent me a note. I'll see if it's in my room."

31

She looked there, but I did not know the result until she stopped at the post office.

"I was 'oping you'd come by, Miss Morrow," Harry gloated.

"I wouldn't miss it, and you can make it better by giving me a letter or two from shore."

"Not a thing for you, miss. Maybe a lot of the letters you wrote your friends were delayed like this one." He picked up an envelope from a box and scrutinized it. "It missed the last sailing from Suez, and you've caught up with it."

"May I have it, 'Arry? There's no rule against it, I hope." She turned to me. "Letters go stale so quick."

"No fear! Now you're 'ere, you might as well deliver it in person."

Her eyes were a little narrowed as she took the missive; then I thought she was encountering difficulty in controlling both her countenance and her voice.

"This is the letter I wrote Ronald Blain saying I was coming," she said slowly. "That explains why he's not here to meet me. But it doesn't explain——" She paused.

"You're right. It doesn't."

"What is it, Simon? Your eyes are full of wonder——"

"He didn't get his letter, but I got mine. You didn't use paper—or ink—or the Queen's mails—but I got it just the same."

Chapter Four

There were people around us and she did not speak until we gained the dock. By that time the quick flush was gone from her face. I decided that her wonder at the event and perhaps some mild emotions in its wake had given way to mundane disappointment. Apparently this bit of pooja—what non-Indians called magic—worked by some god of the country, did not repay her for missing Ronald.

"This is India, where nothing adds up just right," she said. "Now I've got to clear my baggage and you might as well *juldi jow.*"

This term meant "leave in a hurry."

"Can't I wait for you and take you in my rickshaw to meet your worthy sire?"

She looked at me curiously. "You have nothing better to do?"

"I've nothing at all to do."

"You toil not, neither do you spin?"

I shook my head.

"Anyway—don't wait. I'll go in a hired dooly. When Papa's in Calcutta he usually stays with Sir Howard Gravestone of the John Company. Is he there?"

"Yes."

"Then until we meet again——"

"When and where? I told you I have nothing to do."

"You know, Simon, that takes away the compliment. Did you do it on purpose? I'll meet you at the Gymkhana. We couldn't avoid each other there if we tried."

It appeared that we parted more as strangers than we had met. That is often true of people who have not crossed paths in many years—the bonds they had put on long ago had worn off without their knowing it in the slow erosion of the years. I made no effort to see her in the next two days—I would let busy, greedy Ronald compliment her with his attentions—and when I encountered her at the polo field I remained only a moment with the cluster of tall officers and sporting civilians paying her homage. I did not become one of them. I tried to make this plain. I had no intention of competing with them, I told her by my over-polite manner. I walked on and watched the game.

At a garden party three days later I saw her in the company of the most sporting of the three dowagers I had lately entertained. The old lady saw me and beckoned; Vivian turned and looked at me with what seemed a becoming and exciting shyness. "I don't want Ronald to win in a walk," the grande dame cried, conspicuously absenting herself. And just as it seemed that Vivian and I were going to find something we had misplaced, a visiting admiral, the affair's guest of honor, came up as though being piped aboard his flagship and claimed her for a promised tête-à-tête.

"Don't forget the ride you promised me, Vivian," I said as she started off.

She faced me. "I didn't promise you any ride."

"You're a liar."

"What?" the Admiral demanded.

"Don't challenge him, Admiral. He would spike your pistol and kill you by treachery. Also—he happens to be right. I did promise him a ride—to get rid of him. Simon, it's for

Monday afternoon, at four."

Monday was four days away. Out of this fertile ground under this burning sun, a bamboo could grow a foot in that time; and a first careless kiss could lead to a lascivious embrace. But I did not know how much or how little of Vivian I truly desired. I was jealous enough of her to have a claim on her, which did not make sense; and my excitement over her was greater than the sum total of all others in my present life.

I was not fighting for her as much as waiting for what would happen to her and me. Indeed I had never fought for anything, except survival for my company and me in the Crimea. I looked forward to the ride with Vivian as to an exciting play.

She was waiting for me, that afternoon, beside a nobly carved statue of an elephant that was not as old as the River but certainly older than the throne of England. Probably a representation of the god Ganesa, it stood on ground that was once holy, probably in the courtyard of a temple, and the people came from afar to worship it and to make it gifts. It was now a rather choice feature of a Company official's garden, vistas having been provided to show it off well. If it thus became symbolic of the new India, Vivian was its symbolic mahout. Indeed she was too fine a representation of India's conquerors to typify them. Yet the clear-eyed natives might find her an emblem pleasing to their hearts. The Moslem kings with all their pomp had come down and there were new gods to propitiate and new times washing over the ancient land like the flood waters of the Brahmaputra, and before those floods receded, she would do as an atavar.

Her riding habit appeared too pretty to be practical. It was contrived to set off her high colors and reveal the small delicate molding of her body. In telling contrast with this, her *sais* led up a powerful hunter well over fifteen hands. It was a very clever idea, I thought, or else it revealed interesting depths of her character. Her bound into the saddle from the sais's hand was free and fine, and she was so fearless that the high-mettled Barb yielded completely to her control and seemed to share her joy. Neither could bear to dawdle on the road to Alipore. We steeplechased it all the way, our two sais lost in dust. The wind painted her cheeks a lovely quince color. Her hair, escaping its pins, flowed from under her helmet and streamed back in flames.

When she dismounted to preen herself, I looked for the

34

schoolgirl who had worn her hair up on a night at sea seven years ago. If I could find her in this great young memsahib, I would fall in love with her. There was a veil between us now, flimsy-seeming, translucent, but hard to draw aside. I was sure she was aware of it and thought that she, not I, had hung it. I began to approach it obliquely.

"Your father made me a flattering offer," I said.

"Yes, and he was very put out with you for refusing."

"He ought to be grateful to me. On thinking it over, he should know I could never be a credit to his brigade. I'm not the military type."

"You're a liar. You called me one in fun—to shock the Admiral—but I call you one in earnest. If you once accepted a commission, you'd make a superb officer—until you were killed. You'd drive yourself to it. You'd be ruthless and bloody. You'd do everything the job called for—those things you would hate the most, you would do the best. So of course you dodged it. If you hadn't you'd have been a fool."

"I'm a fool anyway."

"That's one of your favorite fictions, Simon. No, it's more than that—it's a very cunning trick. You want people to believe it. In that way they won't suspect your motives and penetrate your schemes."

"What are my motives? What kind of schemes?"

"To get what you want out of the world, and not have to take anything you don't want. You don't want power—responsibility—duty. To get out of having to take them, you let people think you're a fool."

"How do you know all that? I should say, what makes you think you know it? You haven't laid eyes on me since you were fourteen."

"I'm not sure I'm right. The puzzle might be a great deal deeper. But don't forget we got very well acquainted on the boat."

"Yes, I gave you your first kiss."

"You shouldn't have. All the excuses we both made still didn't keep it from being the act of a cad."

"That's changing the subject. You told me not to do it—to always look facts in the face, no matter how unpleasant."

"No, it's the same subject. You don't hesitate to be caddish in doing what you want. Dad said you refused the commission because you didn't want your pleasures interfered with, and he was perfectly right. However, there was another reason even more discreditable."

35

"Would you mind telling me what it is?"

"Not at all. Ronald told me something when I was here before. He was not backbiting—he didn't know I'd ever met you or would ever meet you. He said you were a traitor to your class. He said you weren't in sympathy with what we—the English—are trying to do out here. Everyone seems to think you've become pukka since you served in the Crimea, but I think a leopard can't change his spots."

"Is it pretty spotty not to want to fight natives on their own ground in order to take that ground?"

"It's slovenly. Even whores are famous for their kind hearts——"

"Young whores," I corrected her. "Not old ones."

"Anyway, kindness costs very little in money and saves you a lot of disagreeable jobs. My hat is off to the men who do things——"

"The men who win. Ronald, for instance. But you were mistaken in thinking that what Ronald said about me was without malice aforethought. He knew I'd met you—I had told him so—and was likely to be his rival when I came back from Crimea."

"Good for Ronald! I respect him all the more for trying to spike your guns. Someday he'll be Lieutenant Governor of India."

"What will you be?"

"The wife of the Lieutenant Governor, like as not."

"What will I be?"

"The same outsider you are now, unless in a poetic moment you've been killed by a tiger."

"Is my being an outsider important to you?"

"Of course it is. I'm an insider. It raises a wall between us."

"It might be crossed, somehow. A good beginning might be if we kissed again."

"This is not the time to try it. Simon, I'm pretty serious about this. I wouldn't let your renegade tendencies shut you out of my life—I'm not that much of a pukka memsahib—but they may reflect a nature that would keep you out, or shut me out."

She was stroking the gloss of her horse's neck and speaking in clear tones. I knew that this girl was a great prize, far and away beyond any I had ever contemplated. I felt a sense of great good fortune that she was not hopelessly beyond my reach, and it seemed I had only to stand a moment in a wind of feeling to fall in love with her.

"One question more, Vivian, of a practical sort. Does your father suspect that my renegade tendencies—meaning unwillingness to fight natives for whatever reason—had anything to do with refusing the commission?"

"Such an idea couldn't enter his head. I didn't tell him, any more than I told him about your dance with the housemaid. He thinks it was plain self-indulgence and sloth."

"Do you think he'll forgive it?"

"Yes—until you 'find yourself.' "

"Isn't that quite a concession from such a pillar of the Empire?"

She looked at me strangely. "Not when you're the son of a baronet with three thousand pounds a year."

Chapter Five

Vivian's eyes told me to say nothing about that, to let that go. She looked at her cinch—she was a good horsewoman —then mounted and dashed off. We did not speak again until she pulled up before what appeared to be a native's house of the better sort, in a pleasant garden.

"It's still early," she said, a childish eagerness stealing into her face.

"Yes?"

"Do you know who lives here? A real swami. Well, he may be a fakir, but he's not dirty and disagreeable like the ones you see on the streets. He speaks excellent English and wears beautiful clothes. All the women are going to him—either in the open or on the sly. I intended to go on the sly, for Dad wouldn't approve. And this is a wonderful chance."

"I've heard of him. He calls himself Sakta—that means a worshiper of Kali—and I think he's a clever fraud."

"Just the same, will you lend me ten rupees and wait for me?"

I handed her the note. The fact that he charged a pound for his fortunetelling went far to brand him as a mountebank. The real seers of India were simple souls, rarely approaching a sahib in fear of defilement, and content with a little *rôti* from the charitable.

Vivian hastened away, returning in about twenty minutes looking herself like a sibyl.

"He's marvelous," she burst out. "You must go yourself someday——"

"I might as well go right now, if you'll ride around for a few minutes."

"Good for you. You're not as cynical as you pretend."

God knew I had never pretended cynicism, or had a cynical bent of mind. I supposed she meant skeptical. However, the self-styled swami was cleverer than I thought—receiving me in a room cell-like with austerity, with no reek of incense or the least clap-trap. He was simply dressed in white, and his pale-colored countenance could well belong to a Brahman esthete. I did not think he was anything of the kind.

"I see that you suffered a great loss many years ago," he began in a firm voice fit for an Anglican bishop. "Perhaps it was your father—I see now it was your mother. She was very unhappy. You didn't stand up for her as you should."

"If you please, I'm prepared to pay for certain information," I answered, "and won't need any other."

He had schooled his countenance far better than I mine; even so the expression that passed so fleetly revealed a rebuffed feeling. This so-called swami was a sensitive man, easy to rebuff. I began to think that he was not a deliberate fraud, in spite of his looking too intelligent to deceive himself. . . . The expression was one I had seen often in India associated with . . . But the association escaped me for a moment.

"How may I serve you, sahib?" he asked with such dignity that I felt ashamed.

"I want a description of the man whom you told the young lady she would marry."

"That is properly part of her reading, not yours."

"I'll pay ten rupees for your exact words. That's pretty easy money. Also, I'll consider them confidential."

"Then it would seem that you believe in my powers of divination."

"I think that you found out from her, by adroit suggestion, what she wanted to hear, and told her just that."

"That's an old fortuneteller's trick, I know. If I played it —and would be willing to answer your question—your ten rupees would be well spent. It might save you thousands of rupees and much pain and a bitter defeat at last. By nature you are very intolerant of defeat—that is one reason you undertake nothing very important or difficult. If you found out that winning Miss Morrow is of extreme difficulty you might decide it was not very important. Ten rupees is a handsome fee for one question, but I decline it with thanks."

His fine eyes glimmered in triumph. Then the association I had missed a moment ago came clear.

"You felt I had rebuffed you a moment ago, Sakta. I did not mean to hurt your feelings—I took you for a cynical faker, not a fakir. But you must admit your feelings are rather easily hurt. That is true of most half-castes."

He managed a faint smile that did not conceal his great, inward start.

"You have keen eyes, gentleman whose name begins with *S*."

"I should say your name begins with *D*. I'd think you belong to one of the old Eurasian families—De Castro—De Silva—De Vieira—"

"You missed it there, my friend. It's plain Lopez."

"I've heard of many half-castes passing as solid white. It's rather novel to find one going native."

"Extraordinary, I assure you. But like all great strokes— quite simple. As you know, the lot of the half-caste in India is always difficult and frequently painful. You spoke of our sensitive feelings—to my regret I've never quite got over the debility. But it was quite wonderful of you to recognize me. My women and associates never question my nativity. By this simple choice, I become one with India, instead of an anomaly. There are other advantages also."

"Ten-rupee fees, for instance. Say five readings a day——"

"Nearer ten. A few sahibs and memsahibs, but mainly prosperous natives. I don't take half-castes because I can't read them well—their natures are too complex."

I thought of Vivian growing impatient, and quite likely taking off for home. But I could not leave this amazing man this soon.

"I can read you well enough, despite your complexity, to know that you won't betray my innocent deceit," he went on. "To satisfy your mind further—I am by no means a fraud. It's true I haven't a grain of preternatural power, but I can do a much better job than all so-called swamis to whom rich people go for help in their perplexities. You understand that the real seers are not available to them. They are afraid of sahibs and to rich natives they speak as the Nazarene spoke to Nicodemus—'Give away your gold and follow me.' "

"You made a very shrewd guess when I first came in——"

"Shrewd is no word for it. Partially by the sensitivity of a half-caste, partly by long and assiduous practice, I can read

39

the inner nature of a man by outward signs. Often I interpret these signs subconsciously—their meaning reaching me by real inspiration. I knew at first glance that you had been lonely and guilt-ridden for many years. The person who had loved you was dead or lost—your expression when I mentioned your father told me it was the wrong guess—obviously it was your mother. I am sorry you declined a full reading. It would have taxed my powers."

"Can it be, then, that you gave Miss Morrow a true description of her future husband instead of the description she asked for?"

"They were not necessarily two different men. Miss Morrow is the kind to get what she wants."

"I'd give ten rupees to hear what you told her."

"I can't take your money, my friend."

At that moment the scene changed in a strange way. I felt its sudden tension, and as I gazed at Lopez, his urbanity disappeared. It took no second sight to discover fine sweat on his forehead.

"I've spoken very frankly," he said, no longer in the suave, faintly theatrical tone he had employed before. "It isn't customary with me, I assure you. I'm greatly interested in you, not only because you are the first visitor to identify me as a half-caste. You have demonstrated a real interest in me, which no doubt you feel in all men—a quite wonderful human gift. Most sahibs never had it, or else they lose it in India, where people are seen in such swarms as to lose the aspect of individuals."

"Thank you, Lopez." Vivian would say it was mere self-indulgence.

"India is a very bad environment for most white people," Lopez went on. "It could be a very good one for you, if you live here long enough. I'm inclined to hope that you win the beautiful memsahib, for she has a great deal more to her than is readily obvious—perhaps even more than you divine."

His eyes looked haunted, and I knew he was considering saying something important, and was in doubt how, if at all. I stopped worrying about Vivian's impatience, and he saw that. I was afraid the spell would pass off.

"When I decided to capitalize on my sensitivity, I read all I could find on necromantic lore," he went on in a strained tone. "I was particularly interested in why so many of the predictions of native soothsayers and horoscope-casters came true. There were two reasons—one that they could

40

sense the desires and moods of the people, and one because the people believe their prophecies. One such prophecy, made by many augurs over the last decade, had a good deal to do with my decision to go native."

His eyes, black and shining with excitement, had the effect of drawing mine.

"I dislike resorting to what may resemble cheap mystification," he told me. "However, I am forced to do so. Miss Morrow may not marry anyone. She may not live to do so."

"What in God's name do you mean?"

"I'll say one thing more, and request that you neither offer me any money nor make any further remark. It may be that at this time next year there will not be a single sahib or memsahib alive in India."

Chapter Six

I found my way out the door and to the groom who was holding my mare. Apparently I did not smell the same as when I had dismounted, my sweat being of a different sort and temperature, for she shied sharply. The man seemed to expect a reprimand. I called him "sias" and did not know his name; I wondered why such a good rider could appear so servile. I knew the inner life of my mare as well as I knew his.

"Where is the memsahib?" I asked in Hindustani.

"She said to tell you, sahib, that she could not wait for you, and has gone home."

When I reached home, I sent her a chit, apologizing for my long stay with the swami—hinting that he had entertained me great guns—asking to escort her to a forthcoming ball at Government House. I did not know the name of the "boy" who carried the chit, nor had I the least notion of how he spent his time out of my sight. Thinking of her and of him, of the finely dressed, pale-faced guests of the Government-General and of the innumerable servants in the background prepared my mind for confronting Lopez' auguries. There had been talk of mutiny before—it was discussed as a "possibility" and a "menace" at many regimental messes—but I had never before met an intelligent student of Indian affairs who actually believed it was coming.

What use to make of the fact was a hard question. I was inclined to put it by until my nervous shock passed off, in

41

which case I would likely let it slide. There was certainly not the slightest use of reporting to the authorities the unsupported "maybes" of a professional fortuneteller. I knew only one native with whom I could discuss the danger, my expert shikari and gunbearer Puran. He had come a few days before in reply to my chit and was enjoying a good loaf in my compound. I gave him a glass of arrack to loosen his tongue, and sitting alone with him in a cubby—quite as though before a watch fire in our hushed camps in the jungle—took him by surprise.

"Puran, when do the *gurus* say that all the sahibs and memsahibs will be slain, and Hind return to the reign of the nabobs?"

His throat worked once. "On the next moon, sahib," he replied.

"Do you believe it?"

"Sahib, I'm only a jungle wallah. I can show you a tiger's tracks by the water hole and follow the drag of his kills, and you remember how I've taken you in the dawn where the black bulls come out to graze. Let it remain so, sahib."

"No, I cannot. Will the people rise? Give me your true opinion."

"The people have heard the prophecies of the gurus, but I don't think they will arise unless led by the Bengali soldiers. Many of these have gone mad from wearing red coats. If the sahibs leave the guns unguarded—if they put too great strain on the sepoys' faith with their bread and salt—if they don't call the English regiments back from the foreign wars—I think that Mother Ganges will run red with sahib blood."

"Would it be to your heart's desire? Speak truly, Puran."

"No, because you and I have been happy together on the trail and in camp."

"Aren't the sahibs' laws more just than the laws of the sultans and rajahs?"

"Yes, and our hands aren't cut off, and we needn't give bribes to every hanger-on of the court before we get judgment. The people of the little villages where no sahibs dwell see the good the new laws have brought, and I think they'll wait and watch, tilling their fields, until the great storm passes by. The women are glad that suttee is now forbidden. But many of those who deal with the sahibs hate them. Fair dealing and good pay do not make up for the coldness in their faces and hard, scornful voices. I too have seen and heard, and it was as though a cold wind bit me to the bone."

"Must these of such tender feelings knock their heads on the floor, as when they petition their own lords?"

"Nay, sahib. But every little grievance will loom large when the sepoys have taken the forts and cities. The spoil will be rich, and all who have felt the weight of the sahib hand will want to cut off that hand."

"Is the word yet told on what day the sepoys will rise?"

"No such word will come, sahib. Only chapatties [unleavened bread] will be passed from hand to hand to the four winds."

I wished that Sir Henry Lawrence were in reach. He was already alive to the danger of a mutiny in the sepoy armies, and was one of the noblest Englishmen that ever served India, but he was far away in the Punjab. Then the notion struck me of telling General Morrow. He was in a position to act powerfully on the matter if he so desired, and my acquaintance with him, though meager, was closer than with any other ranking officer.

I gave him time to finish dinner, then sent in my card with a request for an interview. He received me more affably than I had expected, perhaps because he expected me to ask for the commission proffered before. If so, perhaps later I would come with another petition, to which he would give due consideration.

"Sir, I've heard some rumors that I felt duty-bound to report to you," I told him after the amenities. "They deal with the threat of mutiny that we've been hearing of. According to my informant—a reliable native—the sepoys will rebel within a month."

I waited for his scornful smile. It did not come; instead he pursed his lips as though in serious reflection.

"Thank you, Simon, for coming to me with this," he said presently. "It was the proper thing to come to some responsible officer instead of repeating the rumor at a club and getting people excited. However, we've heard it from other sources."

"In that case, I won't take any more——"

"Have a brandy with me." General Morrow pulled a cord and spoke in expert Urdu to the tall, impassive-looking Mohammedan who answered. At once, by the genie lamp of such households as this, two crystal glasses appeared before us filled with pale, fluid gold.

"If trouble comes—and it is very likely—it's our own damned fault," the General went on. "We've tolerated incompetence in both the military and the civil government. That pertains, I'm sorry to say, high up as well as down. In the first place, we should never have permitted native troops to have native officers. If we couldn't have found enough gentlemen who could afford to serve, we should have trained some of our yeomen, and paid 'em enough to live on. I abhor snobbery, and we may pay through the nose for it yet."

I made a polite response.

"Simon, you may not know there have been sepoy mutinies before," he went on. "The first incident occurred in 1764 and was properly dealt with. Hence there weren't any more for sixty years. In 1824 another batch of mutineers were efficiently put down, and the lesson lasted another twenty years. But that bad show twelve years ago was badly bitched. No example was made, and the fruit's now ripe. And now some asses in our arsenals have made an inexcusable blunder."

I wondered if it would constitute an excuse for the sepoys to break faith with their "bread and salt."

"It's no longer a secret," the General replied to my look of curiosity. "The new Enfield cartridge has a greased patch, which the sepoy soldier bites off in loading. Those fools used suet and lard, and a low-caste *badzat* at the arsenal at Dumdum taunted a Hindu soldier with the fact—gibing that he'd been defiled. The story spread like wildfire. The officers ordered that clarified butter be substituted, but a good deal of damage had been done."

"I dare say," I remarked, as mildly as possible.

"If there's a flare-up, I expect it in this immediate area—at Dumdum and Barrackpore. But I can assure you, it won't spread. General Hearsey is a very competent officer, with enough iron in his guts to use a strong hand."

"That's good news. Thank you for receiving me——"

"Thank you for coming. I've suggested to Hearsey that he drill hell out of the sepoys for the next fortnight. We can't give 'em any notion that we're worried about 'em. I rather wish that Vivian would put off her trip to Diwanpani —she's mad to see the old diggings and to get at the snipe —until the trouble blows over. Y'understand the natives read meanings in every act of a ranking officer's family, and I'm afraid they'll think I'm sending her to safety."

"I don't believe they'd think that of General Morrow."

"Thank you. By the way, she gave me a message for you, but to save me I can't remember what it was. Wait a few minutes. If you're not rushed. Unless she's gone to bed, she can jolly well deliver it herself."

The General marched out, limping only a little from his leg wound, his fine straight back set off by his tight-fitting evening clothes. I took it that Vivian had at least started for bed, for the wait grew long, and then she appeared in such an easy-to-get-into dress as she might have worn at tiffin. In every dress I had ever seen her wear she had a different aspect. In her riding habit atop her tall horse she had appeared vital as her name, confident almost to boldness; now she looked as though she had never discovered the beauty that instantly lighted the room—a little shy, and very young.

The message that she had for me was that she had accepted Ronald Blain as her escort for the coming ball. It developed soon that she was engaged from tiffin to bedtime every day between, and on the day following she was setting out for Diwanpani, one day by river steamer and one by carriage beyond Dacca.

"I'm evidently a ten-o'clock scholar," I said.

"You could have been a little prompter if you'd cared to. I made two of the engagements after I got home from the ride——"

"You rode off while I was with the swami, or I would have——"

"It's not that I'm so excessively popular," she broke in. "It's only that girls of lighter complexion than a creamy brown are fairly scarce."

Her innocent expression did not deceive me. The goose Gossip flies fast, getting fatter and juicier at every lighting down over Anglo-Indian society. I wondered if some sterling memsahib with Vivian's good at heart had talked to her at dinner, or previous to our ride. That she had come out with it was a good sign, I thought.

"When will you be back in Calcutta?" I asked.

"I don't know. But you mentioned going on shikar out Cachar way. You could hardly miss Diwanpani en route, and could stop for a civilized meal."

"You may expect me."

"You can stay now for another brandy, if you like. Dad has excellent brandy. That is—unless you have an engagement with the lovely countess."

She referred to so-called Countess de Motte, who spoke English with a charming French accent, and was not invited to pukka affairs. Rumor had it that she was an actress who had eloped with a Spanish adventurer, had been dropped in Calcutta, and was seeking passage home.

"I have no engagement with her—tonight," I said.

"I shouldn't mention her, because it would indicate jealousy. Well, the indication is correct. I *am* jealous of such women. They have ups and downs, but they really live. They're not tied hand and foot to English convention. Of course she's far more exciting than I. She's had so much more experience—she can give you so much more."

"Not exactly give it——"

"Sell it, then. I'm sure the price is reasonable. You have to pay in some form for every girl's favors—so-called nice girls as well as the other kind."

"That's a very sophisticated remark to come out of such an ingenious-looking memsahib——"

"I had a Cornish mother. I got this skin from her. She was pure Celtic and something of a witch. Since we lost her, I've had to be a little sophisticated to make up for Papa's innocence. By the way, your stock has gone up a little with him by reporting the rumors of mutiny. You were way behind the Fair—the Survey has been hounding the high command for months—but he was glad you showed that much interest."

"Oh, my God."

"Well, you still haven't joined up. And you must be pretty intimate with natives, for you, a mere sportsman, not in the secret service that I know of, to have heard the rumors at all."

"The creamy brown complexions you spoke of can be quite pretty," I said.

"Simon, won't you at least pretend to be a little—disconcerted? I almost said a little decent. I know many other young sahibs go with native girls—what else can they do? —but they do it on the sneak and are decently ashamed of it and would deny it to their last breaths——"

"By the way, I didn't discuss Indian affairs with any native girls."

"No such dull subject, of course. If you were the Governor General, how would you deal with the mutineers?"

"If it was my job to maintain a conquered empire, I'd deal with them bloody. I'd strap them to cannon mouths as Clive did—or was responsible for—in 1764, and blow 'em to bits. Or else I'd turn the artillery on them as in 1824. That's the way to rule—go the whole hog. Since India still has able rulers, such as General Morrow, there won't be any mutiny. If it starts, it will be put down."

46

"But without your help. I dare say that's all right. I wouldn't want you and Ronald Blain to think the same—it would be too much of a good thing. Let's have some brandy in snifters. It's really voluptuous."

Vivian was too delicately formed to appear voluptuous, but there was a fine swell under her bodice and another beneath the small of her back. I let my thoughts take their coarsest vein in regard to these, which took the edge off caution, as did the brandy. This house belonged to a rich official of the East India Company and was gaudily furnished. The lamps were blue Chinese; the rugs were of that incomparable raspberry dye of Inner Asia; the fumes of the drink heady. I went to sit by Vivian on a great teakwood divan with golden velvet cushions. Her face remained very still and I felt sure she was prepared to surprise me—whether pleasantly or otherwise I could not guess.

"Do you want me to behave differently from Ronald Blain, as well as talk differently?" I asked.

"Yes, but you don't know how he behaves!" She laughed to herself at that.

"I'm going to assume he's a perfect gentleman. His conduct on the polo field is exemplary. I don't think he'd try to kiss you until you are engaged to him."

"I'm not. Are you going to try?"

"Yes."

"You may be sorry. I'm no longer a little schoolgirl idealizing a young man whose escapades got him shipped out of England. You took advantage of me——"

She stopped, and the surprise she had for me was exquisite. Her lips met mine unstintingly and without haste, the kiss fulfilling the promise of the other as her beauty had fulfilled its promise. Indeed it was an expression of beauty, vital and superb. Her life had been intensified and enriched in these seven years, hence its currents were more powerful. Those currents debouched into mine by a mysterious act of intercourse that raised the tides of both.

I thought she had decided on this single adventure to memorialize and round out the other. But it was more than she had bargained for, and her lips were tardy in turning away. As her pupils expanded and a dark glow appeared on her cheekbones, their resistance slowly ceased.

Every instinct told me to make the most of her lowered guards, at whatever risk of her anger. Presently she was lying across my lap, her mouth and throat defenseless, her eyes black pools, and her countenance suggesting a sleeper's in an ecstatic dream. My hand was hard-pressed between her knees, but the tension was easing as my whisperings wove through her fancies. My whispers were of love and were involuntary. I hardly knew of them, but in those moments of exultation they were true.

A door closed with a soft sound in the rear of the house. I gave no sign of hearing it in the hope that would dull her attention to it—and apparently she had not heard it or else ignored it. But my dread of interruption was hard to hide. I think it got through to her slowly, for she suddenly stiffened, her eyes changing shape and glistening, the beautiful mystery of her face instantly vanishing. Then rather slowly but with decisiveness and a definite dignity she resumed her seat beside me.

"I didn't know I was that much of a wanton," she said with every sign of calm.

"I wasn't sure you were that human."

"Human? I said wanton. Almost everybody's human— that's no distinction. I'm not going to make it an excuse for wantonness. I know my nature. I'm a Cornish Celt—we have a devil of a time behaving ourselves."

"How did you find out your nature?" I asked. "With Ronald?"

"That's none of your damned business. Does my letting you go that far at first blush—blush is not the word—entitle you to probe into my private affairs? I meant to have only one kiss—as an experiment—but something went wrong. That flatters you, of course, but it's better to do that than let you think I'm loose. A loose woman. My God, what a fine condition for a general's daughter——"

"A little flattery wouldn't hurt me," I said. "I've never had very much."

It was the right thing to say. She turned, looking at me keenly, and the anxiety went out of her face.

"I don't know why I weakened, if that's the word. I think you somehow suggest unknown and exciting depths—you make people feel adventurous. I can't get it any straighter. You must go now."

"When can I come again?"

"Stop at Diwanpani when you go tiger hunting. We'll ride and shoot and I'll show you the old fort. It too has unknown and exciting depths."

"We'll explore 'em, but in the meantime isn't one of the

48

dinners you're going to a stuffy official affair that you can leave early?"

She tried to keep her eyes from glinting. "As a matter of fact," she said thoughtfully, "the one tomorrow night will be stuffy no end. It happens I'm going in my own rickshaw —Dad will be late—and if I get a headache when the ladies retire——" She stopped and waited.

"I know an interesting bagnio not twenty minutes from your gate. I'll meet you here, you'll get in my rickshaw, and you'll wear a veil. When we get there, we'll go in a certain door, and be put in a snug little room with a table and a divan and peepholes overlooking the dance floor. I can promise you the best nautch dancing in Calcutta and probably as fine as any in Rajputana. There'll be some wonderfully spiced food and drinks. And it will be an experience you'll never have with any other suitor."

"No other suitor would insult me by offering it."

"Shall I meet you about ten?"

"If I get the headache. There's something the matter with my head that I'd consider it at all."

Her brief but eloquent kiss lived on my lips as I made my way through murmuring streets homeward. The waxing moon over the rooftops reminded me of Puran's prophecy, but I could not believe it now; there seemed an upward surge of all my tides of fortune. A street gamin in an alleyway called "*Khuna suar* [literally, eat pig]," then ran laughing with his mates. A man's voice from the dark said "*Kunwari* [virgin]?" in a guarded tone. Once I had taken the bait, and instead of the sordid escapade that I would want to forget, I had met an adventure to remember always. But I knew better than to run the risk again.

If I married Vivian, she would unite me with my kind. I could lay down the inheritance of my mother's exile and her ghostly tears would dry. We would make a home in Hind with white walls and a green roof, befitting the lucid sunlight and the warm, procreant rain; and I would found a house worthy of our finding each other. From thence would issue sturdy sons, bronzed of skin, gay of heart, to be comrades of their darker countrymen, and deep-bosomed daughters. It must be built upon the rock of deeds, which, with beauty's guidance, I would hew.

49

Chapter Seven

After tiffin at the Ganges Club, the talk in the lounge turned to the rumors of mutiny. No one here seemed to expect uprisings in the sepoy army until it was again thrown against such a formidable foe as the Sikh or the Pathan; and the consensus of opinion was these would be quickly curbed. It would be a jolly good thing, however, to recall some of the English regiments at present in Persia and the Crimea. The high command should lose no time in replacing *raissaldars* with white officers.

The group today was made up mainly of Company officials, tea and indigo planters down from their gardens, and junior officers. Except for one long-retired lieutenant colonel, Major Ronald Blain was its ranking soldier. He had been only a few days transferred from his command of a battalion of the East Guards to a staff position under General Kearney and should know the temper of the troops. Even so, he advanced no opinion until an upcountry commissioner asked for it.

"All I can say is what has already been said publicly by much better-informed men than I," he replied modestly. "In the first place, the War Office can't strip other strategic outposts of the Empire to reinforce India. We get to thinking sometimes that India is the whole show, but she isn't. In the second place, it takes time to train white officers to replace the raissaldars. In the meantime, it behooves us all—soldiers and civilians alike—to play ball."

"Be a little more specific as to that last, Ronald," an admiring police officer urged.

"I mean for every man to see to his job, even if he has to miss his sundown chukkar or even his tea. The whole machinery of the Empire must run smooth. Colonel Holley, we know how you've earned your leisure, and that makes us admire you all the more for applying for any post where you can serve. All those who aren't serving should be ashamed not to follow your example."

I had not been very late in discovering myself the theme of Ronald's discourse. The generalities spoken first had been intended to lead to the specific case, being mine. It was plain

50

he had discovered my importance in his affairs, but I was a little surprised by his choice of stroke. He ought to know that the first blow, before my guard was up, should be a stunning one. I could not see what he had to gain other than some dearly-bought face for himself and a public rebuke to me. If I now took a post in the Empire, he might get credit for enforcing it. If I did not, I could conceivably become the by-word for failure of duty, with such terms as "slacker" and "parasite" bandied freely. Still I felt that the thrust was not worthy of this good blade.

"It just occurs to me," I said, "that I'm the only man in this assembly who hasn't a job."

Ronald managed to look a little embarrassed. He glanced from face to face.

"By Jove, Simon, you're right."

"It just happens I'm not living on the sweat of other Englishmen's brows. My grandfather in America paid my fare. That doesn't stop me from being an Englishman."

"Since you're the son of an English baronet, I should think not," Ronald said in a thoughtful tone.

"The question is, how good an Englishman? England lost her American colonies because she tried to rule them by force. Being a good Englishman might mean believing in English principles as to the rights of other peoples and nations. I'm not persuaded that we have any right to take over India piece and piece, as we've been doing for a hundred years."

"I've heard you express those sentiments before," Colonel Holley said stiffly.

"At present I'm a wayfarer in India. I'm taking no money out of the country—instead I'm putting some in it. Later I might see it differently, but for the present I'm going to remain in that capacity."

"I think it's a good thing that you served in the Crimea, Simon," Ronald remarked.

"Otherwise I might be awarded some white feathers?"

"As for me, I'm only a soldier. I obey my superior's orders, which derive from the Queen. It's for wiser men than I to decide on principles."

"For wiser men than any of us here," a junior officer said in clipped tones.

"It's not a case of white feathers," Ronald went on. "It's a case of standing with your own kind. I've nothing more to say except this. When the shoe pinches, those who don't

51

stand with us stand against us. At least we'll have to consider it so."

"Thanks, but my shoes are still comfortable."

With a sense of theatrics that I did not like but could not avoid, I finished my brandy, mouthed a "Good day, gentlemen," and walked out.

The afternoon and evening stretched very long. My pleasant routine of siesta, reading, tea, walking the streets vital with human story, drinking moderately, and dining leisurely with such interesting Europeans or natives as I could cultivate was clouded not with guilt but with anxiety.

The incident at the Ganges Club had started me thinking of my repute before the world. I cared a great deal more for it than I liked to believe. Ordinarily it accounted for ninety-nine human deeds to the soul's one. If I did not fear it I would go up to the beautiful state of Sikkim, buy half a dozen of its beautiful young virgins, hunt and fish, read and loaf, and forget Anglo-India and all her works, including Vivian, her father, and her lover Ronald.

Was I trying to eat my cake and have it? I went to studied lengths to safeguard from gossip the adventure proposed tonight. Engaging a public rickshaw, I posted its bearers on a street corner about halfway between Vivian's lodging and the bagnio. I came in my own rickshaw close to her garden gate and waited in the shadows.

Fool that I was, I began my watch at half-past nine—fearful that some freak of chance would fetch her home too soon —although I knew better than to expect her before half-past ten. Why should I expect her at all? The dinner party where she sat bejeweled and bedizened would not be nearly as trying on her as she had made out. She was too involved with Mrs. Grundy and all the Powers That Be to be bored by official stuffiness; indeed she would be so impressed as to think twice and thrice before taking off on an escapade with me. Young men would be there to pay her pleasant court. My kisses would be cold upon her lips by now; theirs were an exciting promise. I was the younger son of a baronet with three thousand pounds a year, but my rivals were not outliers; they belonged and were not recipients of "a jolly good telling off" at the Ganges Club; some indeed were richer and all were making careers.

As the night wore on, I could think of a dozen reasons for her not to come, not one for her coming unless it be passion's stirring in its sleep. I had waked it last night, and she might

52

conceivably desire its company again. This I could not credit: more likely she would wish to avoid its perilous persuasions. I believed that most young virgins, unlike young men, were rarely self-kindled, rarely sought passion for its own sake. I flattered myself that I had led her further into its delights than my more conventional rivals; but even of this I could not be sure, nor find the least reason for believing she would prefer my guidance to theirs. I could fancy myself waiting bleakly until, toward midnight, she returned with her doughty sire, then taking inglorious flight lest I be seen.

At a quarter after ten I made out her rickshaw ghostly moving down the moonlit street. You would think that after my doleful forebodings I could hardly believe my eyes; instead a revulsion of feeling deprived me even of joy. It hadn't been worth all that, I thought. Fool that I was . . .

I stepped out of the shadows and she called *"Bankay"* to the bearers. In case any of them understood English I mentioned a late supper "at the commissioners'." She dismissed the men and took her seat beside me. And instantly her beauty, like her body's warmth, touched and enveloped me; and all my little devils sped away.

"What about the General?" I asked, my voice vibrant with joy.

"I told him a whopper."

General Morrow would be easy to deceive. He had not a cunning hair in his head. I took him into my now bright, heart-warmed world.

"How was the dinner?"

"Dreadful. I wouldn't have come if it wasn't. I had no business coming. It was just the awfulness of it—like jumping off a cliff—"

"Well, I'll try to make it as awful as possible."

"You always say the wrong thing, and it spoils me a little bit for people saying the right thing. You do it deliberately. It's a very clever cheat. You're probably really a pretty dull fellow inside. Or else you've fought something so long and so hard—even before you danced with the housemaid— that you attack everything in sight like a mad dog."

"Are you a fighter, Vivian?"

"As I told you once before, you're changing the subject. Why don't you fight for the right things—anyway, the things that will benefit you and not harm you? To answer your question—I'm a live-and-let-liver. I know what I want in life and I won't get it by fighting either myself or other people. I'll

53

get it by keeping my head, no matter the temptation to lose it. I won't be tempted to swap what I want for something I don't want. You're thinking I didn't keep my head very well last night. Actually I was taking what Papa calls a calculated risk—to find out something."

"I can almost believe that."

"Coming tonight looks as though I'd lost my head pretty badly. But I reasoned it out—decided I wanted to know you better and that the danger to my reputation was too slight to bother about. If it gets out that I visited a bagnio, of course I'll say you took advantage of my innocence."

"Do you think anybody would believe that?"

"Simon, don't you know by now that the important people —the people who can help you or hurt you—believe exactly what they want to believe and nothing else? That's the way they became important. It wouldn't do for Anglo-Indian society to believe that a general's daughter knows what a bagnio is. It's in my favor that I'm a member of the upper middle class instead of the aristocracy, because Anglo-Indian society is likewise. We're all pushing ahead together. In a choice between you and me, even the spiteful women have to stand by me. They wouldn't, of course, if you, on the bare verge of being an aristocrat, went along with them, but you don't. They'd readily believe that you deceived me and took me to a bagnio for the devil of it."

"What would happen then?"

"Nothing very serious. You're still the son of a baronet with three thousand pounds a year. They'll gladly believe everything bad that can be said about you, but you're still forgivable."

"I don't suppose you heard about the incident at tiffin——"

"You don't suppose I did? What do you think that poisonous old Colonel Holley talked about all through the fish course? For the first time in a long time he was the sinecure —that's not the word—of all eyes."

"No, it isn't the word, but I know what you mean. Well, what did you think of it?"

"I was greatly flattered, of course."

"What?"

"What could it mean but that Ronald is trying to do you down? If so, why?"

"You must have known he was that keen on the hunt. But you didn't know that he regarded me as a dangerous rival."

"Oh, yes, I did. I told him you were. Ronald becomes much

54

more intent on a prize if he thinks someone else wants it, especially someone he respects. You may be just the other way, and it's a mistake to tell you about him. I want you to keep on paying me attentions, if only to arouse his competitive spirit, and this may be the wrong tactics. You may not like competition."

She was speaking in a low, blithe, intimate voice. It was charming me, and I had trouble keeping my head clear.

"You said 'someone that he respects.' I didn't know he respected me." And what was I fishing for?

"He does, intensely. All Calcutta—the little part of it we know—respects you but doesn't like you. The sahibs at the Ganges Club were delighted to mob you and get rid of a little of their spleen, but Ronald's the only one who dares to make you an enemy. You represent too much that they worship. You ought to have heard the excuses made for you by the people at the dinner—even by old Holley himself. It turned my stomach."

"What you've just said is—the most important thing you said—was that Ronald's attack failed."

She looked startled. "That's true. It was bound to fail."

"Why did he make it then? He's a long-headed man. I would say he's a terribly able man."

"Of course he is, but he started out with a wrong premise. It was that public repute is as important to you as it is to him. He couldn't imagine anything worse than being mobbed by the Ganges Club. To be called a slacker would kill him. He doesn't know it runs off your back like water off a duck. He wouldn't take me to a bagnio, not because I might be caught, but because he might be. He is always careful——"

"Turn your face and put on your veil."

"How ripping! Are we there?"

"No, but we're going to change rickshaws, and the bearers have sharp eyes and long memories."

I instructed my own bearers to be at another corner, not far from Vivian's lodgings, at midnight, and to wait there until further notice. Only when they were out of hearing did I give orders to the head bearer of the public dooly.

"The place must be something awful," Vivian remarked, herself awed at last.

"It's a Moslem bagnio, owned by old Chatta Dass, a Bengali. The upper rooms flutter with little brown ladies of pleasure. But you won't see any of them, or anybody getting knifed. It's a Number One den."

"May I smoke some opium?"

"Not while you're with me. Maybe that's inconsistent. The English sahibs forced the Chinese government to let 'em sell opium by the ton—but of course the buyers were poor coolies, not memsahibs."

"And you're never inconsistent when it comes to sahibs versus natives. I wonder what you'd do in case of a real mutiny——"

"I wonder."

We entered an arch into a dark alley. There was no danger of our being bludgeoned and robbed—we were now on the premises of Chatta Dass. One of his servants met us in the court and guided us through a dimly lit passage into a *kamra,* this term meaning almost any kind of room. Ours was one generally reserved for adventurous Europeans or opulent natives and was the most elegant in the establishment. The walls were hung with gaudy silk tapestries; there were gilt mirrors at each end; the knee-high table was rosewood inlaid with ebony and ivory; the divan was authentically Persian, being a lavish heap of rugs covered with cushions. A slit in the walls, over which a curtain could be drawn, afforded an unobstructed view of the dance floor thirty feet distant. This was for looking out, and I made a careful scrutiny of the walls to see that there was not another aperture for looking in. Blackmail was a fine art in the Far East.

"You can remove your veil, Vivian," I told her when I had shot the bolt on the door.

"You speak like a Turk to his brand-new virgin," she replied—rather boldly, I thought, considering the kind of kamra this was. She bared her face and sniffed long. "What a marvelous smell!"

"I don't know how it's done. It's an ancient art known only to people who make a cult of voluptuousness. Frankincense —myrrh—spikenard in a devilish medley. I dare say it covers up a lot of other smells not so pleasant."

" 'All the perfumes of Arabia will not sweeten——' " Vivian quoted thoughtfully.

"Of course they can't. This is a bagnio right on."

"Well, that's where you invited me."

Vivian made herself as comfortable on the divan as though born on one. As she gazed through the wall slit I was caught up with wonder at this conjunction of East and West. Evidently the dinner party tonight had called for utmost propriety in the way of attire, for her dress would win the approval of our prudish Queen. It was not nearly as graceful or as beautiful as the attire of an Indian princess; on the other hand, a skirt is by the nature of things more vulnerable raiment than the pantaloons, gathered at the ankles, worn by many women of the Orient. Bizarre riffraff could look freely upon Vivian's face. If she were a Mussulman's daughter above the grade of peasant her own male cousin would be denied that intimacy, and she would be compromised to be alone with him "while water may run out of a broken jar."

The power of Vivian's beauty over me was moving me toward momentous action. The intuition, almost an intimation, was that I would never marry her otherwise. But there was an even more startling possibility: that consciously or subconsciously she realized this, and that was why she had come.

A bell tinkled, and I unbolted the door to receive a tray. On it were spice cakes, preserved ginger, sugared mangoes, dates stuffed with bitter almond, rice balls flavored with caraway and cloves, and a flask of heavily spiced cordial that I thought was a distillation of fig wine and certainly no beverage for True Believers. The perfume that filled the room must have been like that Porphyro sniffed as he waited in the closet for Madeline to disrobe. We ate and drank, and while we were hardly conscious of the droning music from the dance floor, it was subtly exciting us. Every time we stirred there was a fresh insinuation of perfume in the warm air. No doubt it rose from the rugs and cushions and of course was one of the accommodations to seduction provided by Chatta Dass.

Various nautch girls danced to fifes and kettledrums, but these were run-of-the-brothel performers whom even the Mohammedan bhang-eaters in the hall outside hardly bothered to watch. Presently a roll of drums and rattle of calabash announced the main event of the entertainment. Chatta Dass had promised me what he called "Dance to Nandi," performed only rarely, and by the best dancers money could buy. Even so, I had not known what I bargained for.

I began to have an inkling when a turbaned crew erected in the middle of the floor a realistic ten-foot imitation of an image seen all over India. Devout Hindus of the Naga and other cults regarded it with reverence—it was one of the most ancient of religious symbols—and Chatta Dass would not have dared perpetrate the blasphemy of their gods if his customers were not almost altogether Mohammedans. Otherwise he was on rather solid doctrinal ground so far. Nandi is Siva's sacred bull, the symbol of procreation, and he was often represented by this image.

"If you look, you're going to be shocked," I told Vivian.

"That's the idea, isn't it?" She gazed through the slit and her expression did not change. "I think it's in bad taste, but everybody in India has seen *linga*. If the dance is good enough——"

The music stole out, very soft and with slow measures, punctuated by far-off-sounding throbs of a tom-tom. The dancers appeared to be from Rajputana, with aquiline, not especially pretty faces, and their movements appeared slow to a nerve-racking degree. It dawned on me soon that I had never seen a dance anything like it, unless it was a strange ritual to Shaitan performed by Arab girls at Suez. That it was superb and ancient art I had no doubt.

Perhaps Vivian and I were among a very few Europeans who had ever seen it; perhaps Marco Polo was another. Patently Chatta Dass had intended not only to give me my money's worth, but to pay some due to the fellowship we had established. The dance must be extraordinarily difficult, putting great strain on the performers. I was not aware of the music and their harmonic movements quickening, only of a growing tension and excitement. My scalp crept; there was a pleasant tingle on the sides of my neck that stole down my spine and raised goose flesh on the calves of my legs. I tried to remain detached from the magic to study its makings, but drifted off again and again as one fighting sleep.

No movement or attitude of the dance appeared lewd, and probably no spectator had ever been able to explain its impassioning effect. Oddly enough, this effect was most powerful in periods of the dance in which the music suddenly stopped and the dancers stood perfectly still, as though transfixed. In the first of these periods I turned my face instinctively toward Vivian to discover her mouth leaping toward mine. Yet we left the greedy feasting as the rhythm was resumed and until the next pause remained as in an exquisite trance. Thereafter we found each other without seeking, almost without knowing, not making love to each other as much as participating in the rite, although with but a small part as yet of the rapture beginning to transfigure every dancer's face.

As though with aching labor, my brain brought forth not

58

an explanation of the spell upon us, but an identification of it among recorded human experiences. In some Indian cults the worship of Durga and perhaps the Sivan linga is observed in the early summer with an orgiastic feast. It is supposed to invoke fertility in the womb of woman and of earth; after various rites are performed every woman receives the embraces of any man desiring her. They come to the temple with that intention; and I did not doubt that the final prelude to the orgy was this very dance performed by the temple priestesses. It had been perfected through the ages until, through appeals to the senses that the wisest swami could not trace, it functioned to undermine civilized restraint and incite blind lust. Even free from its spell, I could not have analyzed its lecherous suggestion. The dance was indeed a sacrilege in this iniquitous place, but it had the beauty of the dream of Cythera and Isis, and no matter how wicked, it was fine art.

The garments of the dancers fell away. They began to utter gasps and sobbing cries, which I could not believe were deliberate, their meaning otherwise all too plain. Like worshipers to the feast of Durga, Vivian and I had invited these transports. My hand was deeply searching her glowing body; hers did not resist and presently cleared its way; her limbs entwined with mine. The music had stopped at another period, I thought, as she sank into the hollow of my arm. . . . But immediately I began to have the impression that it was a longer pause than before.

I was keyed to the music, but it did not resume. I yearned to love Vivian to its rhythms, and now felt inward discord. The sudden silence became instinct with stealth. The gaudy trappings on the walls, the gilt-framed mirrors, and the sensuous perfume in the hot, heavy air told me a tawdry story of bought embraces and goaded lechery. This was to be the scene of my union with Vivian—this was where my path, wide of my kind, had led. Tonight I had gone native and taken her with me, and we must find our way back.

I know nothing more than this. I felt that there were other forces brought to bear upon me, perhaps inciting all the rest, but I did not know what they were.

"Vivian, that was real pooja," I said in a wonder-struck tone.

The desire darkening and dimming her eyes swiftly vanished.

"I dare say the music stopped just in time," she replied with a wonderful simulation of dignity, if indeed it were not real. "Our veneer of civilization must be mighty thin."

"I have an idea that everybody's so-called veneer of civilization is mighty thin."

"At least I'm glad that whatever is between us—or whatever may be in the future—was stronger than we were."

"I think we had a strange and wonderful adventure, although not the right beginning for a bridal adventure."

"Well, let's get the hell out of here before they bring us in a love philter or some other stronger pooja." With quick movements she pulled down her veil.

"I'm not going to take it off again tonight until I'm locked in my own room," she told me when I had called a rickshaw.

"I hope you'll relent——"

"No, it's a sign I'm withdrawing from the world to meditate."

When the wheels were turning on the hard-baked smooth clay road she stopped meditating to yawn. "Have you a good, strong shoulder?" she asked.

I fixed her in the hollow of my arm, and thought how I would like to have her there, in lovely sleep, a thousand nights. She appeared to doze off; and afraid of more words veiling truth, I did not speak to her till we came in sight of my rickshaw. Like a sleepy child, she changed and took her place, her fragrant head on my shoulder. We were nearly to the gate before I spoke.

"How soon may I come to Diwanpani?"

She stretched luxuriously. "When the spirit moves you."

"It's going to move me in a very few days after your arrival —in fact, as soon as I can wine and dine a messmate arriving from Crimea."

"I'll be so glad to see you, Simon. And as for taking the veil——"

She raised it and gave me a drowsy kiss, which I thought prophetic of many good-night kisses on nights that we did not part.

Then I was alone in the alien street. I looked about me, as though I did not know the scene, but I knew it full well . . . The nameless coolies running as mechanically as the wheels turned, their livery destroying their last aspect of individualities, their cries without human likeness. Highlights cast on skins by flaring rush torches, briefly glimmering and vanishing. People asleep in the streets and gutters and doorways; others standing in forlorn clusters, others moving briskly on unimaginable errands . . . I had got back here safely, the thought itself serving for harsh laughter. I had been in great danger of being bound to someone, but I had escaped.

What I thought was a night jar flushed from a wall; more likely it was a bat. It went winging off, and my brain jumped, and I was back where I belonged. This new scene was imaginary, perhaps some sort of sorcery, but I must have dreamed it a hundred times for it to be so familiar. I was alone in the middle of a wide, wind-swept field. I had an office there, an easy one performed by merely standing still. It was to scare birds from corn. I could not myself help garner it and eat it because I was a manikin of straw.

A sleepy chokidar admitted me to my silent house. My *naukar*, wakeful as an owl, handed me an envelope that had no doubt arrived on today's steamer from London. It bore our family crest and at first I thought it was my carefully worded Christmas letter from my father, actually mailed to arrive in time for the holiday. A closer glance at the writing revealed that it was from my half brother Howard.

It read:

MY DEAR SIMON:

You will be distressed to hear that our father, ailing since last spring with a kidney trouble, died peacefully at the Hall Thursday last.

The Queen has sent condolences, and the county nobility and gentry have been profuse in their expressions of sympathy and regret. Enclosed find a copy of the obituary notice in The Times. *In his will he left you some articles belonging to your mother, which will be forwarded as per your instructions.*

He was buried in the parish churchyard with a very impressive service by our vicar. I will raise a small monument there, and give a window to the church in his memory. He asked for you the day before his death, forgetting that you are so far away, but on being reminded of the fact, appeared reconciled.

Life must go on. The summer has been excessively warm, but the wool crop does not appear to be short, and the pheasants have brooded well.

Your afftnt. brother,

PEELTOWER.

P.S. Our solicitor is writing you presently in regard to the money your mother brought our father. The gist of it, which you should know as soon as possible, is, in her haste to provide for you while you were a minor, she got Father to assign to you the income off half her fortune. But the words "in perpetuity" were left out, the principal sum was never entailed or gone out of his possession, and as it is now willed to me, I have decided against continuing the remittance. I trust this will not be a severe blow to you and you will easily recoup the loss in "Golconda."

Chapter Eight

My first impulse was to conceal the disaster from everyone. I was as dizzy as though trying to stand up after being knocked flat, but aware of the empty-looking eyes of the valet—seeming as inhuman as a camera lens but as sharp—I tossed the letter with a careless gesture on the table. Then I pretended to yawn. As yet I did not trust my voice.

"I trust the sahib has not heard ill news," the man remarked.

"Yes, I did," I replied. "My father, long ailing, has gone to his gods. But I have been parted from him for so long—the black waters spread so far—and since he favored his older son, I was never as close to him as most sons with their sires." This last, I thought in increasing panic, was a mistake.

"But as the sahib was his duly begotten, though not his first-born, surely he will come into great riches."

"We will see," I said with a shrug.

"Sahib, it was in my mind to ask, tonight, a trifling favor. I reconsidered, on hearing of the sahib's loss. But, again, there is the old saying, 'Tears shed for the dead do not blind, while the cattle are being counted.' My father ails also, and unless I buy him medicines, he will shortly die. Will the Protector of the Poor lend me five rupees?"

I started to reach for my wallet, but my sick will moved, and my hand came out empty.

"The sooner he dies, the sooner you'll count the cattle."

His quick fawning steadied me until I could get shed of him. Then I carefully burned the letter, as though it held evidence of some damning crime. It did, in a sense—an unforgivable crime in Anglo-Indian society, and deserving instant exile. It must be concealed until compensated for. To that end, I must strike hard and at once.

I had no feeling of weakness as I sat down on the edge of the bed. My sensations were curiously like those of rage—my face felt hot and my neck swollen and my pulse throbbing.

Perhaps anger is a very frequent reaction to danger, and my danger was imminent and very great. My brain was clearing rapidly and I drove it with all my will.

I had often thought of ways to make money, should I want to increase my fortune. There was more of the stuff heaped up in India than in any country in the world, and I had marveled over the rectitude by which capable sahib officials kept hands off. The treasure vaults of some of the sultans and maharajahs were comparable to the genii hords in *Arabian Nights*—jam-packed with gold and jewels past counting. Such kings as had let incidents occur displeasing to the British, and thereby lost their thrones, often received "pensions" of ten lakhs of rupees—a hundred thousand pounds. There were still images in the temples whose eyes were rubies or diamonds or emeralds as big as walnuts. But the days of a poor adventurer making off with the Kohinoor were all but gone. "To him that hath, will be given" was more true in India than in England. Rajahs gave handfuls of pearls to their sahib and memsahib friends, not to their pinch-bellied secretaries. If I lost face in India, my chances of "recouping my loss in Golconda" would be dead as a dead cat on an Indian dunghill.

I had enough money left from my last remittance to wear a false front for a few weeks more. And those weeks promised a crisis in Indian affairs, of the kind in which bold, unscrupulous men in preferred positions could feather their nests. I no longer believed that a mutiny could possibly succeed. But there would be sound and fury to frighten the English and terrify the degenerate native princes who had become their cat's-paws.

It would be a time of easy openings and for swift promotion. Young inexperienced men would be given responsibility to tax their powers. At the first alarm I could get a captain's commission hands down. But the plum I must pull out of the mutiny pie was some sort of political agency to a native court. The duties would be to soothe the rajah's nerves, encourage his loyalty to the White Rani, and in general look out for English interests; the necessary qualifications were primarily a name with some prestige and the *savoir-faire* of those to the manner born. If in addition the appointee possessed a degree of boldness and ingenuity, and no concern whatever for the morals taught at public school, he should be able to scare his royal highness out of several lakhs of rupees for Number One.

Many such offices would be created in the next few weeks.

Positions of trust calling for no great talent or experience, they would go to sons, nephews, and favorites of the bigwigs. I could not land one of them on my own hook, despite being a baronet's son with, presumably, three thousand pounds a year to keep me honest. I needed immediate and powerful backing of the kind that General Morrow could furnish his prospective son-in-law.

I had better work fast! The ring must be on Vivian's finger, the announcement widely published, and a bond between us not to be lightly broken, before the next new moon. All this would be in the bag by now, save for my high folly and sorry weakness of an hour or two ago; and now Vivian was out of my reach for several days. Then happy circumstances would take her to Diwanpani, a small, lonely station where we could ride, shoot, and explore the old fort. There opportunity would knock again upon my door.

There was only one thing more to decide before I slept— and sleep I would. My dear brother Howard would not believe it, but the power of the blow he had dealt me had enforced in me a degree of self-command that had never before seemed necessary, and hence slacked. It had knocked off a great deal of fat from the muscles of my will.

It was common knowledge that General Morrow had no wealth other than small accumulations from his pay. I would certainly not be following, at least directly, in my father's footsteps. Was I in the least honor-bound to confide my financial collapse to her before I asked for her hand? I had no intention of putting that much confidence in either young romantic love or carnal appetite. I did not think General Morrow could ask any questions that I could not parry. True, there would be wrath to come, but that was a mere cloud in a distant sky compared to the lowering rack of poverty and defeat.

I tested all this thinking before I undressed. If I won Vivian's promise, but failed to win a fortune, I would give her a chance to jilt me before the knot was tied—a stituation of novel interest. If despite my sharp practice she decided to keep the bargain, surely I would do all I could to prevent her repentance.

The ladder was a long one with every rung an "if." But that was true of most great adventures that had won, true of many a piddling deal, and I could think of no short path to fortune less steep and perilous. I had two great prizes to win, and nothing that I valued to lose. I could not ask for a more exciting challenge.

I wakened afraid of the clear light of morning, but on careful examination the structure showed no more flimsy than the night before.

Among some curios picked up in India, I found a pair of anklets made of hair-thin threads of gold intricately woven, and bearing little golden bells. These I sent to Vivian with a cheerful note. In the next two days I crammed on the political history of all the Indian monarchs. It seemed to me that Cooch Behar, on Bengal's northern frontier, might be a fertile field for a quick coup. It was a small state, but rich; its maharajah lived in deadly fear of the Bhutanese; and its small-wigged political officer was at present vacationing in England.

Forsaking my plan to entertain a former messmate arriving soon from the Crimea, I set out for Dacca, on the road to Diwanpani, two days behind Vivian. Here I picked up enough of my hunting gear to make a show of shikar to the hills beyond, but the game I sought was much bigger than a royal tiger. On the second evening out of Dacca I arrived at the sleepy station, as perfect a scene for whirlwind courtship as I could wish.

It lay on a pretty tributary of the Barak River, against the first rise of the Tripura Hills. Time was when it had been projected as the great eastern bastion of all Bengal. Now most of the officers' houses stood forsaken and anteaten in their rank-grown gardens; fire had swept some of the lines; and only one company from Morrow's old regiment served as a garrison of the big, stone, half-dismantled fort. This company, its white officers and their families, some half-caste artisans and their pretty wives and children, and a motley crowd of natives made up the post. But it was still a post; and the Union Jack was flown from the flagstaff on the Queen's birthday. General Morrow's bungalow and the other married officers still boasted liveried servants. I had to move quickly in making my arrangements with Vivian; otherwise I would be invited to dinner by the present commandant of the station, none other than Phil Maybank, now a captain. It was his reward, I thought grimly, for being such a praiseworthy junior officer. Although his pond was small and well-nigh stagnant, while his seniors were away he was its biggest frog. All this had come from marrying a walking doll named Mildred. I seemed to hear the laughter of the gods.

Arriving at sundown, I put up in solitary grandeur in a big

65

dak bungalow infested with wood rats, probably snakes, and possibly ghosts. The latter were known to frequent lonely resthouses off the beaten paths, where they might meet old comrades and go about their dim affairs without troubling the living. The ancient chokidar appeared to look at me twice before he was certain that I was of the quick, then tottered away mumbling. Perhaps he went to tell his shadowy guests that they must not show themselves tonight or make any more noise than they could help. Otherwise their trespassing on government property might be reported to the authorities.

My bearer carried a note to the big bungalow at the head of the row fronting the drill field. He returned with Vivian's orders that I was to present myself for dinner in an hour. I appeared in full evening dress, to find her the like. The word "stunning" is so freely and loosely used by the English as to lose most of its meaning: tonight the most careful lexicographer would not hesitate to apply it to Vivian's appearance. I was stunned enough to forget my clever opening address.

Her gown was no doubt Parisian, definitely bolder in design than those seen at the table of the Queen. It had hung in her closet in Calcutta instead of kindling the eyes of old duffers and narrowing those of their wives. That she had worn it tonight for a tête-à-tête dinner with me was an exciting portent.

There was a subtle excitement charging the whole scene. As we stood on the veranda to watch the immense kite-like moon clear the Tripura Hills, there was no perceptible sound but the clack of locusts in the dusky trees, which appeared to accent the elemental silence. The lights of the other bungalows looked dim and distant. We could not hear the servants moving about the shadowy interior because their feet were bare, and by that token we could not know them as human beings, and so it did not matter if they knew what we were up to out here in the dark, or in the garden later, or even in Vivian's warm, sweet-scented bedroom. Their conspiracy of pretended ignorance about us would feed our lasciviousness. I thought of the Dance to Nandi. Delicate, lovely, virginal-looking in the moonlight, Vivian could hardly be less obsessed by the memory than I, or less moved by it.

"I shot snipe with the Maybanks today," Vivian remarked with a show of calm.

"How did you do?"

"It's of no interest how I did. Do you suppose I could be

66

General Morrow's daughter and not shoot well? The interest lies in how they shot. They weren't born out here. They were born in some stuffy English town or city. They never saw a snipe till they came to Diwanpani."

"How did they do? I agree it's of very lively interest."

"Phil made a few brilliant shots, but on the whole was a dreadful dub. Mildred behaved with awful propriety. She was dressed so properly I could hardly stand it. Phil waited on her hand and foot and paid no attention to me, in spite of my being General Morrow's daughter. When she had to go to the privy, all the bearers knew it because she went to such tremendous efforts to find a big enough bush. I thought if she fell down she'd break into a thousand pieces and sawdust would run out. But do you know—she shot better than any of us."

"What do you make of it, Vivian?"

"Nothing. Up would fly her gun, down would fall the bird. She fired with a kind of fury. Do you know who I thought she might be firing at in the inside of her soul?"

"No."

"Ronald. He was responsible for Philip and her staying here in this moribund station. Dad was in the hospital with his blasted leg—Ronald was adjutant of the regiment and actually made the decision. Mind you, I don't know that she bears the slightest resentment. To hear her talk, she loves every minute of it. She's everything a soldier's wife should be, according to the book. And of course she's ten times better off than she would be in England."

"Aren't we all?"

She gave a start of urprise. "All except you, Simon."

"Why am I an exception?"

"You know how it is with most of us. We like to pretend we're the same here as we were in England—as though we grew up having servants all over the place—dressing for dinner every night—eating off gold-leaf china and damask cloth. But you really did have all that. You're the son of a baronet——"

I interrupted her. I did not want her to say "with three thousand pounds a year." If she did say it, later I would have to explain why I did not correct the mistake . . . Anyway— and the pure sardonicism of the joke made me smile—to talk of money was not good form.

"We lived like most country gentry," I said. "Nothing very grand."

67

"Since we're all playing the same game, no one dares expose anyone else," Vivian went on. "Dad's father was a mousy little major of an irregular regiment at Waterloo. My mother was the beautiful daughter of an obscure Cornish M.P. Now look at me—dressed like the lady mistress of a French marquis. I felt so queenly—not a middle-class queen like Vic but the real Bourbon or Hapsburg—that I could go with you to bagnio."

"Not typical Anglo-Indian behavior, I assure you."

"How many of those pukka sahibs at the Ganges Club keep native women? How many lieutenants' wives get in wrong beds on the officers' row? It's partly the climate, but it's mainly a sense of power. When one's ego is inflated, all his whims became imperious. We white women are scarce out here—middle-aged tabbies are surrounded by doting bachelors—moderately pretty girls have their pick of half a dozen men with good careers. Of course it goes to our heads."

"I repeat that mighty few would go to Chatta Dass' elegant establishment."

"If so, I'm more spoiled than most, or more realistic. I know I can do about what I damn well please, provided I don't do it openly, and still make a good marriage. If Dad hadn't come to India to command natives—if he'd been able to get in one of the aristocrat regiments—he'd be about a major instead of a brigadier general. If I were in England, I might have my pick of several solid middle-class boys, and I might have even attracted a baronet's son, but how I'd watch my P's and Q's! I wouldn't yield to my unlawful impulses. I wouldn't think, 'Well, if I lose him, there's plenty more on every bush.' Here I can be a real adventuress."

"You've changed your tune since you talked to me about the fake French countess."

"That was before you sat down beside me on the divan. I couldn't put over so much after that. After the bagnio, I can't put over anything on you, so I might as well be honest."

She might as well be honest, but I doubted if she were doing so. When the General's butler announced dinner, she lay her fingers on my arm and escorted me into the big dining room with a queenly ceremoniousness. A thrill started along my spine as we took opposite seats at the glimmering table. There were enchantments being woven, the purposes of which I thought I knew, but I could not be quite sure.

All prosperous residents in India accumulate treasures in the way of glass, china, plate, and cloth. Even in the most remote stations they live in a rather formal style with a good deal of luxury. But it seemed that Vivian's servants had combed through the chests for the eggshell-thin goblets and old, worn silver that glimmered magically in the candle-light. The white wine that sparkled and the red that glowed came out of odd-shaped bottles mysteriously projected from the shadows behind me, and if these were not of rare and ancient vintage, my excited fancies fooled me. The fish were fresh from the brooks; the wild duck long hung.

It seemed to me that the candles had been placed deliberately to disclose Vivian's beauty. Their glimmerings on her bare arms and shoulders shifted and changed, and drew my eyes to the half-revealed swell of her ripened breasts and the narrow pale shadow cast between. Her beauty was a variation of an old Celtic type still found occasionally in Cornwall. My imagination kindled, I thought of the first Vivian who had cast a spell on Merlin. Doubtless her skin too had been olive-hued, and her hair, like her name and her heart, held sparks of fire.

"This is not a dinner, but a feast," I told her.

"I wanted to do you well."

"What is the occasion, Vivian?"

"Well, let's see. What could it be? Have you heard any more about the mutiny?"

I was surprised by her mention of this subject as we sat sipping wine. When I could, I made a brief, sharp study of her face. Her color was higher than usual, and movements and brilliance of her eyes and her restrained gestures indicated suppressed excitement.

"Not a word."

"That doesn't mean it won't come. So perhaps we'd better eat, drink, and be merry while we may."

"That's ingenious, but I don't think this is the ball at the eve of Waterloo. By the way, the trouble is supposed to start on the next moon. Where will you be then?"

"In Calcutta, I suppose. Maybe off on a visit. I dare say I won't let it affect my plans."

"No, we can't pay natives that much respect."

"That's quite true. After all, we're just a handful out here and they're how many hundred million? We've no right to be here, perhaps. That's your opinion, and I don't blame you. But don't you think it's rather—magnificent?"

"Yes, I do. The English are a magnificent, amazing people. I'm proud to be one of them."

69

She was looking at me steadfastly and the brilliance of her eyes changed to a warm, lovely radiance.

"You're in a hard fix, Simon, feeling as you do."

"There won't be any mutiny to speak of. You know that, and of course it has nothing to do with this feast."

"Where are you going to be on Christmas, Simon?"

"I don't know."

"Aren't you going on shikar? You certainly won't get back by then. Perhaps you can count this your Christmas dinner, a few days in advance."

"I could, but I don't. Vivian, I've got a troubled feeling that it might be a kind of consolation prize. Have you become engaged since I saw you last?"

She shook her head.

"Well, that's a relief."

At that point the butler brought champagne. He poured a little in Vivian's long-stemmed goblet and waited until she tasted it; at her nod, he filled mine.

"To you, Simon," she said, raising her glass.

I remarked on the excellence of the vintage and its chill. Surely there was no ice at Diwanpani.

"It's kept in a very deep cellar. A secret cellar that no native knows about. You mustn't mention it to anyone."

"I'd like to go down."

"Well, we can't—tonight."

Her talk became more lively as the butler kept filling her glass. Most young ladies in Victorian society would not dare drink so much champagne. It would surely lower her guard and promised to put her in my hand before midnight. The Celtic blood that had darkened her skin and was now glowing through it was the most fiery on our cold island. Even so, champagne in her father's house was a more respectable aphrodisiac than a nautch dance in a perfume-drenched bagnio. The same outcome would have an entirely different aspect—being not quite lawful, but at least a frequent and forgivable prelude to honorable marriage.

Perhaps this feast was in farewell to her virginity. Its quittance has always been an occasion for feasting in all lands, and Vivian might desire it with an extreme desire. The thought was more intoxicating than the wine. Perhaps to give it way and give way to it was the real motive of her deep draughts—a motive not so furtive that she herself remained unaware of it. Apparently she believed that the bad air of our last meeting alone had prevented our coition and betrothal—

70

I had wanted her to believe that—and tonight she set her own stage. Actually there had been other obstacles which even now I could not understand, since I had wanted her then hardly less than tonight. Certainly they had now disappeared or been rendered impotent.

This presupposed the existence of what was still, to me, a tremendous wonder—that Vivian loved and prized me enough to choose me as her capturer and mate.

As Lopez had said, she had depths I could not plumb. I would never know her very well, and that made her all the more desirable. If my life became linked with hers, it would be ever an adventure of exploration and surprise.

Chapter Nine

We ate the fruit of paradise that Englishmen call mangoes and laid our dessert silver on our plates. Again she took my arm, and I felt a momentary thrilling pressure of her fingerends. She led me to the veranda and I led her on to the steps. At the top of them she stopped.

"I'm sure you don't want to walk in the garden," she said.

"No, but I saw a stone seat by the old well——"

"It's a haunted well, and the seat is in a dreamy, secluded place. Do you think we ought to go there?"

"I'm sure of it."

"Will you take the consequences, if I will?"

I looked at her big eyes. "Yes, Vivian."

When we were seated, I started to draw her across my lap. She appeared to hesitate.

"Do you want me to lie in your arms?" she asked.

"Yes."

I felt her breast yield against the hard bone and muscle of mine.

"What now?" she asked in a low voice.

"This." But her lips were motionless against mine.

"You want me to respond to your kisses?"

"As you did before."

"You mean—until I lose my self-control?"

"Whatever the consequences, we agreed to take them."

"We both agreed to that," she said, then waited with parted lips.

In spite of this strange insistence on my being the wooer,

71

there could be no doubt of the swift sweep of her passion. Soon I was making love to her in a way at once primitive and exquisite.

"You didn't do this before," she said wonderingly.

She did not want me to answer.

"It's a delicious sensation—I suppose for you too," she went on, between her deep breathings. "After all, it's just another approach to the same thing."

The thrilling throb of my pulse paused and changed. I knew then that I was frightened, but I dared not stop and seek the cause; my instinct was to undermine as quickly as possible her last resistance.

"Wait, Simon," she breathed, in the height of a caress. "Remember, we both agreed to take the consequences."

"Be still."

She breathed deeply two or three times. Then she held her breath a long while, as though to give full way to an ecstacy, her lips immobile against mine. But I knew the instant that she pitted herself against its further advance. A few seconds later I knew that she had balked and depotentiated it by a feat of will. With no strain she thrust away my arm and rather leisurely sat up.

"This is about the point we reached at the bagnio," she said, not trying to conceal her troubled breathing.

I could not speak.

"It was where you stopped," she went on. "I was not sure I could stop when we got there again, but I tried, and I did. It gives me a good deal of satisfaction."

"It didn't give me much, that night. And now——"

"Now you want to go on, don't you?"

"Terribly. I did the other night, but——"

"But not enough to do so, under those conditions. They were very bad, and were partly—a small part, anyway—what checked you. They wouldn't have checked me. Nothing could, but your rejecting me."

"Good God, I didn't reject you——"

"Not exactly. You withheld yourself from me. You wanted to fall in love with me, I think, but wouldn't let yourself. Do you know why?"

"If that's true—no."

"I think I know. It's an awfully sad thing, but the sooner you know it, the better. You've proudly and almost fiercely rejected not only love but friendship, not because you don't want it, but because you didn't credit it—you didn't think

72

you were worthy of it, and so it couldn't be real. You'd done nothing to deserve it, so you wouldn't be put in the position of taking it. You felt yourself a figurehead, representing a baronet's son and three thousand pounds a year."

"Not a figurehead," I told her. "A manikin of straw."

"So when the dance ended and you suddenly realized that in a moment more we would go too far to come back—that you'd have to marry me—you stopped. You were very polite about it, to me and to yourself, when you blamed it on the gross surroundings. Mainly they just gave you an excuse not to take the leap. You didn't feel equal to having me marry you. With that same dark pride, you stood back."

She was speaking in low tones, slowly and clearly. Perhaps that enabled me to realize every word, and not be confused or made obtuse by amazement. My brain remained clear, and I knew now how much I wanted her, as though I were sick and she would make me well. I nodded to her and waited.

"But I wanted to marry you, and I didn't give you up. You see, I hadn't got over being in love with you in all the years we were parted. You may not think a fourteen-year-old girl can fall deeply in love. She can. Shakespeare knew that, as he knew almost everything else. Usually girls that young have crushes that save them from the real thing—but when it's real it's perhaps more desperate and painful than any love that comes afterward. When you broke off that night I was in great pain—the physical pain of frustration and terrible disappointment. In the little talking we did, I had to fight myself to keep from saying things that would part us forever, cruel things that even then I knew. On the way home I pretended to be asleep. Really I was thinking hard—I began to see that your cowardice was honorable in its way—an honorable coward won't undertake any enterprise whose failure would hurt others. I thought it might be curable—and I wanted you in spite of it. So I decided to try again. You'd come awfully close—next time you might win, win being the right word."

She looked at me in inquiry and I nodded again.

"Here—Diwanpani—would be a good place. Papa would be away and I intended to have every condition favorable. I planned a wonderful dinner. I brought this dress especially to wear tonight. As you discovered, it was more convenient for a lover. Now you must be wondering what went wrong."

"Very much."

"It would seem that everything had gone right, wouldn't

73

it? You came here to propose to me—I knew that in five minutes after your arrival. You were going to seduce me—that's not the right word—and propose immediately afterward—the moment I was almost certain to accept. There was not the slightest danger of your getting frightened and stopping. Maybe you would have picked the moment just before—when I was aroused and aching to be possessed and needing justification. When you first decided to propose to me—about the day you sent me the little anklets—you didn't know that none of those devices were necessary. That I was so in love with you that I would have become engaged to you on the day you met me on the ship. You couldn't know that I played 'indifferent' only until I saw it was the wrong play. You couldn't believe that anybody loved you."

"You keep using the past tense. I still don't know what worked the great change."

"I want to ask you something, Simon. It's not very important, really, except to fill in the picture. Suppose *I* hadn't stopped. Before the engagement was really settled—when we had cooled down a little and were talking about it—you of course didn't expect me to ask what might be called a practical question. Young ladies aren't expected to ask practical questions. Nevertheless, they expect to be informed of the mundane facts—they almost always are well ahead of time. Were you going to say anything about how we would live? I mean, the money to live on?"

"No."

"I was to assume that you had three thousand pounds a year?"

"Yes."

"If it was a wrong assumption, you weren't going to remove it?"

"No."

"Well, that's all right. You'd be proposing to me under false pretenses, I suppose, but if you wanted me or needed me enough, I'd admire you for it. After all, if I didn't investigate your financial position—through Father, of course—it would be my own fault. Well, you do want me—I knew that at the bagnio—and I believed when you became sure that I loved you, you would love me. I think you needed me then, and since then something happened to make you need me in a different way—an immediate, vital need. You needed me to survive even if you were—as you see yourself—a manikin of straw."

74

"Why was that, do you think?"

"I heard of your loss the day I arrived here. Papa sent me a message by special bearer: he had heard it from his banker. Of course I wondered what you would do. The news must have come on the last mail boat, and your first act was to send me that beautiful pair of anklets. You arrived two or three days before I expected you. Still it would appear quite a puzzle, since you knew I hadn't any money. But we talked a lot on the ship to Alexandria—you were flattered by my adoring attention—and since I was in love with you, I remembered everything you said. You'd read a good deal about India—especially the native courts. You told me that if you wanted to make a fortune quickly you'd try to get a post at one of them. You'd stir up trouble between the rajah and the English, and, by playing both ends against the middle, shake him out of several lakhs. Now would be a good time to make such a coup, for all Anglo-India relations are greatly strained. But to get the position you'd need powerful influence."

"That's a fine piece of reasoning."

"Don't give me too much credit. I really didn't believe it until tonight—I can believe it now only because you are an outlaw except for your own laws. But all through dinner tonight I thought you might confide in me. I don't blame you for not doing so—you wouldn't trust anyone that far—and you had no reason to expect the bad news would leak out. It was in character for you to conceal it. I don't mind, really."

The scene had visual drama. This was no doubt heightened by the dramatic action, and yet the two might interact in some degree. The moon hung near, and gave the effect of intimacy with the silvered landscape. The latter did not appear moonlit as much as both seemed rapt in the same enchantment. The fort appeared as a monolith raised by a race of giants to a gigantic god long passed from heaven and earth. The moon looked down on Vivian as though they were sharers of secrets and of immortality.

The need came upon me to break the spell and come down to earth. I wanted to feel its hardness under me and take refuge in its brutal facts.

"Your father's estimation of me was not as generous as yours," I said. "Quite correctly, he decided I'd conceal the disaster, and by acting quickly he warned you in time."

"Your estimation of my father is lacking in generosity," she answered. "He's stuffy, and he's a martinet, but like so many other Englishmen, he's sentimental. It never entered his head

75

you wouldn't confide in me. He wanted me to know in advance so I could weigh the whole matter before you came. I'll recite you his last sentence: 'Sweetheart, if you love this young man enough to marry him, don't let this misfortune stand in your way.' "

"Do you mean——" I stopped and wiped my face and drove my will to the most fearful question I had ever asked. "Is it true that if I *had* confided in you, you would have married me? By that one act, I'd killed your love——"

"Certainly not." She spoke quickly and, I thought, with compassion on what she saw in my face. "I doubted if you'd tell me. I didn't even want you to—in you it would have been weakness. Dad's sentimental, but I'm not."

"What did kill your love for me? You said it had lasted for seven years, and it's certainly dead now."

"It isn't dead. I'll always have it for a keepsake. But it's no longer an actuating force. I was quite sure yesterday that I wouldn't marry you—and I'd stay out of any fix that might make me. I arranged that beautiful dinner as kind of a tribute to you, before we broke up. I wanted the best possible background for our farewell—after all, it's quite an occasion. I didn't want it to be slipshod. It *was* a nice ceremony, wasn't it?"

"When did you become absolutely sure?"

"Perhaps not until you came."

"It's a rather odd thing to say—however, it seems to me you've already said it—in plain words, when I lost my money, I lost you."

"I lost you, Simon. The man you were before, and that I fell in love with. Your money had shaped your whole nature. It was like an extra arm—no, it took the place of an arm you'd lost. To you it didn't—you felt like a straw man—but it did to me. You hid your cowardice—I don't know any better word—wonderfully well. You're a sensitive man, and I think the money made you a coward—a habit of thinking it was all you were worth until it *was* about all you were worth. It made you appear brave, but not in a reckless way. You didn't conform, but that was all right—it didn't weaken you —in fact it became you, like your plainness. It was all right for you to speak up against English conquests in India— everybody knew you had nothing to gain, and knew that you weren't a fool because you had nothing to lose. Ronald tried to make capital of it, but didn't get anywhere."

"Then why did it even ever appear brave?"

76

"Achilles appeared brave, didn't he? We know he wasn't —very—since he'd been dipped in the Styx and was invulnerable except in one spot. People admire the appearance of bravery much more than the real thing. The real thing worries them—it's too noble. Achilles was the most entrancing figure in all romance. He's thrilled the ages until very lately, when so-called moral notions began to interfere with our hearts. You too were invulnerable, I thought—you could go with native women—appear in the most public places with the fake countess. You were almost a renegade, but that made you all the more attractive. You'd danced with a housemaid in front of a royal duke. Well, what did Achilles amount to, when he was struck in the heel? What did you amount to, Simon, when you'd lost your money?"

"A comic figure," I answered, "that no girl like you would waste your time on."

"Not comic, exactly, but freakish. Do you think I'm a heartless jade? I don't want you to—I don't think I am. I'm not being realistic—I'm being human."

"I salute you, Vivian."

"My God, I'm glad. You've got wonderful resources if you'd just use them. It wasn't necessary before. Do you think you will now?"

"I'm too dizzy to think straight."

"You won't blame me for not waiting to see?"

"Of course not. It's too much of a gamble."

"I was already involved with Ronald. He has no money either, but he doesn't need it to win. Simon, shall we kiss each other good-by? One passionate kiss as though we were still lovers?"

I thought upon the act in its every lascivious passage.

"I wouldn't miss it if I thought it could possibly lead to your seduction," I answered, "but you're too strong. You'll be seduced only when you damn well please, and not before. You're the strongest woman I've ever known."

"Oh, come on, Simon. Be a good little fallen Achilles."

"You really want it, don't you? One big, last, free thrill. Well, I do too, but I'm going to deprive myself to deprive you. It's not easy, I assure you. Perhaps it's my first real victory. You won't ever be satisfied now—absolutely. No triumph will be quite complete."

"Good for you, Simon. You make me almost sorry I can't wait for you."

"You misunderstand me, Vivian. If I could seduce you,

77

I'd leave you flat. I wouldn't marry you now to save your soul from hell."

It was the last word, strange-sounding in this warm, soft silence, under this fateful moon. But I denied what the moonlight seemed to betray—a shadow falling across her face like the pain of a grievous wound.

Chapter Ten

If ghosts of travelers forgathered in the old dak bungalow they must have wondered what had happened to the time. It had run down; and yesterday, today, and tomorrow are all one. To the living, Time is a tide on which we move here and there in our little boats of being, seeming to go fast or slow according to our exertions, but which ever sweeps us, at its own implacable pace, out to sea. When I had got out of Vivian's sight, time appeared to go slack. I was a little drunk, I thought, and had better walk it off. Perhaps the real trouble was I did not want to accept my own identity and so my acute realization of it became dimmed.

It was a strange experience, alike to the delirium of fever. It passed when the cocks began to crow and I returned to my rooms perfectly sober and sane. Then there was a sound of nearing, shuffling feet, and I opened the door to find the old chokidar standing there, making up his hazy mind whether to knock.

"Sahib, there is an old jungle wallah waiting to see you," he said in Hindustani. "I told him it was very late and you must sleep, but he would not heed me. Such monkeys from the hills do not know sahibs as I do. I have served them for fifty Rains, and know their due. He has plagued me to admit him to the Presence, and he is so wearying——"

"Did he tell you what he wants?"

"Yes, but—I forget. Doubtless it is some trivial thing that he, a *jangli*, holds of great weight. Shall I tell him you will beat him?"

"Has he newly come down from the hills?"

"Only an hour after the sahib's illustrious arrival. He heard of it from his son, a Tame Kuki, one of some score who have built huts two koss from the fort."

"Tell him I will receive him."

The chokidar salaamed and shuffled away. Wanting no

78

more truck with myself tonight, and too excited to sleep, I would welcome the hillman's visit. I hoped he would prove an "Old Kuki," with headhunter Naga blood riot in his veins —of a tribe of animists in whom I had once taken an academic interest. Cattle-runners and wife-stealers, they made a good deal of trouble for the border patrols. However, they had once offered to become blood brothers to the White Queen—a pleasant ceremony of lightly pricking her vein while she pricked theirs and sucking a few drops of one another's gore. Victoria had not seen fit to comply, and so they had never acknowledged her as their overlord.

Suddenly my visitor was in the room as though he had flown in. Actually he had come on feet as silent as a leopard's, and instinctively had advanced like one under cover of shadows. Undoubtedly he was an "Old Kuki" of the true breed. The design of his tattoo and the snake teeth worn in his ears revealed him as a village chief. Small, he stood very straight; past middle age, to judge from his thin gray mustache, he looked leather-tough; facing a sahib, he did not salaam except for touching his forehead.

His Mongoloid countenance was of a kind hard for Englishmen to read, but I had not the least doubt of the earnestness of his mission. Perhaps because I had so few interests now, I was eager to find it out.

"Do you speak Hindustani?" I asked.

"Yes, sahib. Many of my people do, whereby we may trade with the people of all the hills." He spoke it fluently, although with a juicy accent. "I am Toto, headman of a village two days' march in the Tripura Hills. I came down to seek aid of the Captain Sahib—Be-lain Captain Sahib—of whom my son had told me, but he has gone to lead a host in Barrackpore. Then my son told me that Peelh-tow Sahib had this day come to Diwanpani, so the good auspices, when our guru threw the chicken bones on the floor of the magic-house, might yet come true."

"That will be seen. Speak plainly."

"It had come to us two Rains ago of how Peelh-tow Sahib shot tigers in the Sundarbans."

"It is a long way from the Sundarbans to the Tripura Hills."

"Yes, but the salt sellers travel far and tell many tales on the threshing floors. Now in our hills Bagh cannot be driven. The ground is deeply gullied and he may slink away in the ravines, or perhaps break back through the lines, killing as he goes. But he may be shot from a hiding place, or even tracked to his lair. And it chances that a very large bagh, to afford the sahib good sport, and with a skin such as the burra sahibs covet, dwells near our village."

"I have not time or money for sport, Toto."

"Heed me, sahib, for the love of your gods! This bagh is indeed large, but his pelt is mangy from old age. In his youth he was an honest tiger, catching deer and wild pig in his own jungles; and in his middle age he became a cattle and buffalo thief, raiding our byres. But a year ago he caught a buffalo that he could not master. We lay listening to the battle, until Bagh crept away, roaring in anger and pain. But though the buffalo died, Bagh did not die."

The story was beginning to shape like some I heard before. Toto touched an amulet on his naked breast and his eyes looked haunted.

"That was on the eve of the new moon," Toto went on. "On the rise of the full moon Bagh caught and carried off a child playing at the brushy edge of our barley field. In the dark of the moon he slew a woodcutter of a village four koss distant; and then in the twilight, an old woman who had lagged behind her sons returning from the harvest. Since then he has killed four times the count of my fingers of my people and our kinsmen in nearby villages. Only in the heat of the day may we walk safely on the roads, or even the footpaths from field to field. We have come to call him Kharab-Bagh [the Wicked Tiger]. He mocks our weak arrows, and will not enter the traps we have built, or fall in the pits we have dug. When we elders sat in council, we spoke often of one of us going down to Diwanpani to seek help from the rich hunter sahibs, but the police sahibs had bade us never again set foot on the plains, lest they hang us for the sake of some wrongdoing long ago. Then it came to me that I, headman of my village, must go down even though I be caught and hanged, and the auguries were good, and so I have come."

I felt a prickling sensation at the back of my neck, and an intimation of good fortune.

"Toto, I'm not a rich hunter sahib. All my treasure has been wasted or lost. The skin of Kharab-Bagh would not bring ten rupees. What will be my wage if I free your people from this affliction?"

"Sahib, we will give you of the remaining cattle and buffalo to the worth of ten times ten rupees. Also, when our young men may again go abroad in the forest, we will gather for you those things that sell to the ships at Chittagong—cutch, and herbs of certain sorts, and horn—to the same amount."

I had held and refused commissions in the service of the Queen, but this was the first workingman job ever offered to me. Coming so swiftly upon my fall, it seemed to me a stroke of kismet rather than blind chance. What might I find in the dim, silent jungle? Perhaps a new orientation, perhaps death, perhaps myself.

"I'll be ready to start when the sun is four hands over the hills. My servants will return to Calcutta, and an oxcart of my hiring will carry my gear to the village of Tame Kuki, where your son lives; from thence on your kinsmen shall bear it to your village."

"Yes, Protector of the Poor!"

I had been called this every time I tossed an anna to a beggar. For the first time it did not make me faintly ashamed.

I went straight to sleep, to waken when the sun shone through cobwebbed glass of my window. The old chokidar served me curried eggs; then ten minutes' sorting made an amazing reduction in my baggage. Since I had not expected to go on shikar, I had brought to Diwanpani only a part of my hunting gear, but like all affluent sahib travelers in this land where face counted so much and bowed backs so little, I had laden my servants down with bedrolls, a quilted mattress, clothes for every kind of function, chests of tinned foods and bottled drinks, medicines, cigars, a favorite saddle, a spirit lamp and accessories for brewing tea, a water boiler, a fumigator, and—God save the mark—a collapsible commode. Actually the boys connived in this extravagance—the more baggage, the merrier my rupees jingled in pay and commissions. But I was a poor man now. Such face as I had left required no furbishing.

I was troubled over having only one heavy rifle—a reliable .600 double, fired by percussion caps. Puran's waiting with an extra gun had been no small comfort when driven tigers had broken from the thickets toward my stand. Then I remembered that Kharab-Bagh could not be driven. He would come and go on his horrid business at no man's bidding, and I would not choose the ground for our encounter, and if two bullets would not suffice, I would have no time for a third. Anyway, I thought of a more important post for Puran, the only native in my train I could fully trust.

I sent for him, and behind a closed door gave him his instructions. He was to remain in the native town of Diwan-pani, and if the chapatties began to pass to the four winds, each recipient making and dispatching four more, always the sign of a breaking storm, he was to seek me at Toto's village in utmost haste.

One bullock cart stowed all my gear. Toto took the reins; and without a single attendant, I led the way up the dusty road toward the Tripura Hills. I meant to ride when my feet tired, but just now I was doing penance for pride that had gone before a fall. I wondered if Vivian, perhaps mildly curious as to my future fate, now and again glanced out the window toward the dak bungalow. If so, she could see a fine sight.

My heart felt a little lighter than it had any right. I blessed the small, brown, almost naked man shouting in an unknown tongue the unspeakable ancestry of the cart beasts. The roof of the finest bungalow in the officers' row slowly disappeared amid the foliage of the trees.

At the Tame Kuki village, Toto's son provided another cart, this time drawn by buffaloes, whose steps were slow but of great power. The wheels creaked and complained on the sharp steeps, but they did not deign to grunt. I passed the night in the house of a grain dealer in a Tripura village in the cool of the foothills, sleeping on a rosewood bed, as soft as a rock, of which he was very proud. In midmorning, where the road was two dust-filled ruts and we were halfway up the knee of the mountain, we came to the mouth of a footpath, and here a dozen small brown fellows, naked save for a belt flap, waited to carry our baggage up dizzy heights to their village. Toto's son, Ambibat, had run ahead of us to inform them of our coming.

The cart-road dust faded out of the air and it became crystalline and fragrant. Ambibat sniffed it, and its effect on him was like a puissant drug. A younger replica of Toto, he had neither stood nor looked so straight. Now that he had returned to his native hills, out of the sultry plains and far from money-lenders and earth-shaking sahibs, he no longer seemed a Tame Kuki but truly an Old Kuki. The damp path wound upward through a magnificent ancient forest, open enough that we need not worry yet about Kharab-Bagh. I breathed deeply from the exertion of climbing, my head grew strangely clear, and my soul asked the green silence to give me a sign.

Most men awake to the mystery of their own beings sometimes ask for signs. My spirits lifted by the adventure, grateful for the interlude before I must again set a course, I found myself believing that the tide that had turned would now rise well. I had learned my lesson; I had been punished; perhaps Fortune would now be as extravagant with favors as of late she had been with blows. I could hardly hope for a lost legacy from my long-dead grandsire in America. I would not expect my brother's family to be wiped out in one painless catastrophe so I might become Sir Simon Peeltower, Bart. No, that would be childish, but perhaps I would be given a sign of a great change.

Now I walked with little brown men who did not know one English word. They were not my kind; much of my befriending of natives might have been only skin-deep. Partly it had been a gesture of defiance to those who had denied me their regard. But I would make pooja to the gods of the hills, if they would draw back the veil of the future to afford me one brief glimpse. I would be content with the verifying of one vision. The desire that conjured it up was one that the old gods, driven from on high to these steaming jungles because they served men's lusts, could well understand.

No presentiment of the future was vouchsafed me. Instead I was shown a jungle scene of austere beauty, and what I could read in it of my kismet depended on my own imagination. In the open grass under the canopy of intermeshed tree boughs loomed a black, solitary form. It was a bull gaur, fully nineteen hands at the shoulder and weighing three quarters of a ton, his male powers declared by his massive head and neck, his heavy horns and dewlap, and low-hung scrotum. He had been banished from his herd, I thought, and must roam the wilderness alone. No doubt a younger bull had battered him to his knees and stolen his cows . . .

But as the light cleared a little more, I saw that his horns were tapering instead of blunt, and were blue at the tips. That meant he was a young bull, newly come to his full strength with which to avenge his banishment by the herd leader, hardly aware of it yet, not yet putting it to trial.

He raised his head and sniffed . . . He made a lowing sound, deep-throated, ominous . . .

Chapter Eleven

My eyes and heart began to open to the inexhaustible wonder of the jungle. Many birds had protective coloration, as the bird books put it—meaning that they hid in green feathers amid the gush of greenery. Generally these were sweet, quiet birds with subdued pleasant voices. But many birds flaunted gaudy colors, red and gold and silver and burnished black; and these flew up with raucous cries. They lived dangerously, taunting the prowling cats; they were tough and ungenteel; it struck me that they were immoral too, since the Law of the Jungle ordered subservience to its lords. They were a low-born lot, I thought, akin to English jays and jackdaws; and the safer their perch, the more ribald their outcries. Not so the princely devilish peacock making vain, vulgar display on the bloody ground.

We could never see far. Screens of vines like green water-falls pouring out of the trees to the thickets below concealed stratagems going on behind. Further off the light became virescent, then bluish as it dimmed to a dreamy dusk. We felt the presence of things we could not see, as of sounds we could not quite hear. When we stopped to listen, every man with his head cocked, the infinitesimal noise quite disappeared, as does that made by ghosts in the old dak bungalow at Diwanpani when the sleeper lies breathless with straining ears.

Toto, a few feet in my van, found three-toed tracks as large as my hand in the moist earth. He bent to gaze at them, and all the porters stopped with strained faces. They knew when he straightened that this was not the mark of Kharab-Bagh, only that of a great deer hunter and wild-hog slayer, no enemy of the people. Bursting with laughter, they paced on.

Toto's village hung on a steep sidehill and was mainly mud-walled huts with thatched roofs, enclosed in a paling of bamboos sharpened and hardened in fire. The men's house, where young, lusty bachelors lived and entertained girls of marriageable age, stood half hidden in the woods. In the byres, milk and plow beasts were indeed few, and the small fields looked forsaken. Still I did not expect the people to be so thin and hollow-eyed.

Toto looked about him in a deeply anxious way, as though he noticed a falling-off in the two or three days he had been absent. That could well be true; native peoples may subsist on very little for a long time without apparent loss of flesh, then quickly melt away. The Old Kuki were tireless hunters, but they dared not enter the jungle save in broad day or in big parties, both unfavorable conditions for finding game.

An abandoned hut had been swept and garnished for my use. The porters had hardly stored my gear there when one of the village girls brought me a bamboo flagon of green coconut juice and a basket of mangoes. The same compliment would have been almost unthinkable in a Hindu village in contact with white people. The villagers would have been ashamed of so paltry a gift to a strange and presumably opulent sahib, and on no account would it be delivered by a young woman. The great Indian institution of purdah—female seclusion—was unknown to almost all hill tribes. The girls never thought of veiling their faces, usually they married their chosen lovers, and their husbands did not own them body and soul.

Perhaps because she was rather tall for a hill girl—an inch or two over five feet—she looked skinnier than the most. Her skin, about the color of a hazelnut, was tightdrawn over her facial bones so that they appeared very prominent, but I was struck with their delicate fashioning, not at all unusual among the Tibeto-Burmese people occupying the hill tracks along the Brahmaputra. With a little more meat on her, she would be very pleasant to look at by a man like me, not as moral as most Englishmen in the scientific meaning of that word, more skeptical of tribal concepts of beauty and truth, and as unprejudiced against a dusky skin as would be a man from Mars. Her black eyes appeared lifted at the outer corners and of great depth and luster. Besides a looped and tucked-in waistcloth that served for a skirt, she wore a chudder-like robe such as I had seen the women donning as we approached the village, but I thought that she bared her breasts at ordinary times. Judging from outward signs, they were fine examples of that feature of which young, shapely hillwomen were justifiably proud.

"What is your name, Joy to My Sight?" I asked in Hindustani.

"The name that may be given"—this meant that she had a secret name, like so many animists—"is Latah."

"A gift for a gift." From my food box I gave her a hand-

85

ful of sweet cakes.

The ravenous look on her face startled me. Her hand lifted toward her mouth, then fell.

"Taste one of them, Latah," I suggested.

"Not in your presence, lord."

She took quick leave, and I watched her as she walked rapidly and then ran down the village road. No doubt she had little brothers or sisters with whom she must share the gift. She entered the long-house at the head of the row, indicating she was a daughter or close kinsman of Toto.

My first job was to provide the villagers with a hearty meal. It would raise their morale, now so low that I could not expect courageous help from them. If I knew hill people, they would stuff enough to strengthen them for several days, in case the main undertaking interfered with further food garnering in that period. So I summoned Toto and asked him the most likely place to shoot a big sambur bull or a couple of barasingha.

"The sambur come to our brook to drink in the evening, only three hundred paces below the men's house," he answered. "They have learned they have naught to fear from us of late, and naught to fear from Kharab-Bagh, who can no longer catch them even if he did not shun their horns. But, sahib, Kharab-Bagh often lurks by the footpath close to the stream on his own business."

As the sun began to pitch, I went there alone with my heavy rifle. Toto had offered to go with me, but his quavering voice had told me he would be of no use. I did not like the look of the rough ground, and the shadows that began to creep felt cold. Once my flurried heart turned cold as I thought I smelled tiger rank on the breeze. I flung the rifle strap across my shoulder and shinnied up a tree, only to discover an old mink exploring the creek bank. I dared not be abroad after sundown, and was getting discouraged over finding any deer, when three samburs, a large stag and two hinds, came stealing into view. I shot quickly, the bull and one of the hinds falling as though poleaxed by the heavy bullets. The other hind ran off before I could reload.

Toto had instructions that in case he heard me shoot to bring a dozen of his men, making all the noise possible to scare Kharab-Bagh. I heard their din at once, and soon watched their faces as they looked down at the fat deer. This hunting had been a different thing from shooting stags in the great preserves at home, and my heart warmed to the shouting and laughter. If Kharab-Bagh was lurking near, and if he were a were-tiger as some of the villagers no doubt believed, the human soul inhabiting his terrible body must have quailed.

The carcasses were carried to the village in noisy triumph. Cooking fires were built around the threshing floor, and the women and girls dressing the meat behaved very properly, no quick hands jumping to mouths with fatty tidbits. When the meat was broiling, Latah stood rather close to me, as though the acquaintance we had made gave her special rights.

"Mother," I addressed an old woman with bared breasts, "when you were young you needed no help from the milk cows to nourish your lusty babes."

When she looked blank, Latah translated the Hindustani into the Tripura vernacular.

This was a sociable occasion, the air was savored by meat broiling in abundance, and the Terror out in the dark seemed not as irresistible as before. The crone made a grinning reply.

"My grandmother bids me prove to the sahib that I am her granddaughter," Latah interpreted shyly. "But I will disobey her."

"Surely you are not ashamed when so many of your sisters——"

"The daughters of the Old Kuki are not ashamed of their shaping in the sun," she told me proudly. "But, sahib, this is a time of drought."

"I think it will rain tonight," I told her, sniffing the meat. "Latah, you speak Hindustani well."

"My father Toto taught me a little, and I have stayed long with my brother among the Tame Kuki, who speak it well."

"What does your name mean in Hindustani?"

"The name of a bird with a white breast that can run very fast. Is it not Lawa?"

"Can you run very fast?"

"Yes, sahib—when I try." Her eyes sparkled.

She was certainly of the age to visit the men's house. There, according to Kuki custom, she would share various beds and in time enter into a quasi-marriage with a favorite. If this proved lucky and happy he would pay her bride-price; otherwise both would choose again.

"What name shall I call Sahib?" she asked. "The one Toto calls you by, I forget it because I cannot see it."

"You may give me a name, little hen."

She looked at me big-eyed. "It is a great honor, sahib. Then I shall call you Shikra [hawk] Sahib. Shikra too is a hunter, and your nose is humped at the top like his beak."

The meat was now ready, but the people still stood back. Then Toto spoke to his daughter, who proudly brought me the buck's heart on a palm leaf. I gestured for all to fall to, and in two minutes there was not a face in the assembly ungreased from eyes to chin. It did not seem possible for less than two hundred men, women, and children to devour every crumb of a five-hundred-pound buck, including all his inwards, leaving only gnawed and marrowless bones; and I was a little afraid some of them would be sick. Instead they were made at first childishly happy, then sleepy.

"At that rate, the mango tree will soon be in good leaf," I told Latah.

She gave me a greasy smile, then, sobering, she showed me a piece of leg bone from which the marrow had not been sucked.

"This I will hang in the chief's house for our *nat* [household spirit] in thankfulness that Shikra Sahib has come."

In the morning I sat on the threshing floor with Toto, the elders, and the best hunters, while the others stood thick about us. Patiently I went about separating the wheat from the chaff of all that they could tell me about Kharab-Bagh. All testified to his heavy ruff, massive neck, and large but gaunt frame indicating a senile male. All agreed that since he had been wounded by the guru's buffalo he had never attacked the villagers' livestock, although he occasionally ambushed barking deer and wild pigs in the dense undergrowth. This was the worst of news, because it meant that my plan of tying up an animal to attract him to my ambush must go by the boards.

There seemed no pattern of behavior in his man-killing, except that he had never raided in the full heat of the day. His range embraced three or four villages in an area of about ten miles square. The buffaloes came home from their wallows, every animal in his place in the long, slow-moving file, without their herder. An old woman who had climbed a tenfoot platform to scare wild pigeons from a pea field was seen there one minute, missed the next. A mother who had left four children playing outside the paling while she borrowed fire from a neighbor returned to find three of them scattered, each with a crushed skull, and no sign of the fourth.

"Did Kharab-Bagh return there the next day?" I asked, my skin prickling.

"Yes, sahib, in the cool of the afternoon. Doubtless he remembered the great killing of the little ones, and was seeking their cold meat. But we had buried them, as our gods and our hearts decreed."

"When a villager is carried off, do his kinsmen follow the trail, shouting and beating gongs, and bring back what flesh and bones remain?"

"Yes, sahib, if the trail is not quickly lost. When Kharab-Bagh carries off a grown man or woman, the feet drag and leave marks, but when he takes a child, he carries it clear of the ground, and his own pugs are hard to follow on grassy ground. Yet we and our neighbor villagers often bring back Kharab-Bagh's leavings, which he would surely devour the next day. Moving quickly, we have sometimes cheated him of the first mouthful of his feast."

"Then mark me well. At midday a runner will carry my message to each of the villages he raids. My word is that the next time Kharab-Bagh kills, a runner must start out that very moment to bring me word. Also, the kinsmen of the slain shall swiftly follow the spore with gongs and shoutings, but when they come upon the kill, they are not to carry it away, nor lay hand upon it. Instead they are to build a great fire close by, and remain there until I come."

"Sahib, it would anger our gods if the torn and bloody dead be left aboveground," Toto said with a drawn face.

"The dead will take no harm therefrom, but it comes to me that Kharab-Bagh may take great harm."

Toto did not look at the elders or at the village guru before he spoke.

"Yes, sahib."

It would not be easy to wait patiently for some man or woman or child in this or a nearby village to be killed. In the meantime I played a long chance. The same messengers brought word to every village that an old and decrepit buffalo be led to the edge of the fields and slain. Very few Bengal tigers, especially if old and wary, will eat found carrion, but Kharab-Bagh's conduct was unpredictable, now that he was a cowardly killer of defenseless prey. If one of the carcasses was dragged away by a big-pugged tiger, I was to be summoned at once.

Days began to drag by. I welcomed each in hope, only to see it close with no advancement of my quest. The villagers fed well on deer and wild pigs that I shot about the neglected fields, but Kharab-Bagh would not come to my bait, and Toto's men, searching far and wide in the midday hours, could not find his spore. One night I heard him roaring in hungry fury not half a mile below the village. I rose, and the hunters assembled at the threshing-floor, and we listened with stifled hearts.

"He will kill soon, sahib," Toto told me, "even if he must burst down our paling."

Kharab-Bagh was moving a little eastward when we heard him last. When he bethought himself and hushed, he turned south to a place he had bloodied about six weeks before. This I learned from a panting runner just before noon of the following day. When he had blurted out the main tidings, I heard what he knew of the detail while completing some last-minute preparations impractical before then.

When the sun had been two hands high, a villager had sent his son, Parro, who was about thirteen, to collect some jungle produce gathered the day before. The forest there was open, and the boy rode a buffalo, such as Kharab-Bagh feared. However, open-looking country where villagers could not creep up on a tiger was not necessarily one where a tiger could not creep up on a villager; stalking was Bagh's trade. In the rage of hunger of many days, the man-eater had dared run beside the buffalo long enough to scoop once with his great paw, or perhaps the boy had dismounted for some reason. In any case, the buffalo had galloped home green-eyed with terror and riderless.

The runner had started at once to bring me the news, and a dozen or so of the men had rushed shouting and beating sticks to backtrack the buffalo to the scene.

"I am the headman of my village," Toto told me, stammering, his brown skin appearing to be tinted gray. "So I will go with you to seek Kharab-Bagh."

"You have no gun, and my chance of killing Bagh is better if I seek him alone." My chances of survival would be better too.

"By Sahib's leave, I will run at his side as far as the paling," Latah gasped.

This and Toto's offer were novel to my experience; and I was already undermined by the story of Parro. Still the swell and smarting of my eyelids were a curious and perhaps meaningful sign. Latah said "Sahib" several times as she trotted beside me, obviously wanting to tell me something more, and since I could not stop for her to get it out, I thought I would miss hearing it. However, she managed it on the run, and it indicated a great leap of her imagination.

"Sahib, I am named for the bird like a little hen we call Latah . . . She is a good runner and hider . . . She and I are of the same *nat,* and if our guru could put my spirit in her body—I—I will run and hide beside Kharab-Bagh—and bring Sahib word of his coming and going—and warn the sahib."

I did not take time to kiss her dark, trembling lips, although sure that I could well afford it and perhaps prosper by it. When I glanced back she stood at the gate of the paling, her hand raised high.

Chapter Twelve

From the runner's village we backtracked the buffalo to the scene of the killing. The search party had not returned defeated; but I looked in vain for the smoke of their watch fire, signaling that they had followed the tiger's trail to his feasting place. I remembered that his kill was of light weight, which, if he held it midway, would hang clear of the ground, leaving little sign of his passage.

It turned out that luck had been with us in this matter— and, by that token, with little Parro. I had done battle with nightmare all the way—a vision of Kharab-Bagh running off with his prey without first taking time to kill it. Instead the blood pool indicated that the boy's skull had been crushed with one blow, and there was enough sign to mark the beast's course to the edge of the thickets. Here bent or broken vines and what looked like rubies on the leaves had guided the keen-eyed shikaris. We heard them and their fellows yelling and shouting a few furlongs farther on.

Two of the search party came running to our call.

"Are the bones cleaned?" I asked. If so, the day was lost.

"No, sahib. Kharab-Bagh fled from us before he had half finished his meal."

The cluster of terrified men fell silent as I came up, and one of them led me to a clump of ground-palms. I looked upon what was left of Parro, he who had felt the surge of inchoate manhood such a short time ago, and I was glad of the savage coarseness of my mind whereby I could hate an irresponsible beast.

Clearheaded now, I went about my undertaking. It was bad luck at the least that only saplings grew about, none of which would bear my weight. This was somewhat mitigated by the broken thickets, affording a fair view of the area about the bait. The wall of the ravine was near enough for shooting in bad light, but the soil on its steep base was too thin to permit the digging of even a shallow cave, above which rose thirty feet of precipitate naked rock. The best I could do was have the boys level off the slope under the cliff, affording me a seat that could not be surprised from above. My elevation was about eight feet higher than the palm clump, and my view covered a semicircle of about sixty feet radius.

I brought there my tea flask, an unlighted lantern, and my rifle. The hillmen departed shouting, the receding noise intended to assure Kharab-Bagh, waiting close by in the thickets, that the coast was clear. I sat with my rifle across my knees, watching for a tawny glimpse in the farther thickets and listening, now that the silence had closed in, for the first furtive sound.

In half an hour the common slow traffic of the jungle was resumed. A jungle cock and his hen scurrying through the thickets, stopping now and then to scratch, made me think of Latah. After a while, a lizard crawled up the cliff; and when he had long gone about his business, a mongoose came looking for snakes on the warm rocks. He found none and went his way; and then a pretty barking deer stole into view. My scent was carried off; so why did she suddenly stop, her head pointed forward, her ears erect, her legs braced? I could not doubt that she had sniffed Kharab-Bagh, and my stomach churned when, uttering her hoarse cry, she turned and bounded away.

I cursed the king vulture that glided down from his sky-watch and lighted, with outstretched wings, a few feet from the palm clump. If others followed in the custom of their grisly kind, I would have to shoot one to serve as a scarecrow; and the roar of the piece would long delay the return of Kharab-Bagh. Instead the great bird took off and lighted on a tree sixty paces distant. Perhaps he knew that Bagh was close by, watching his kill. When other vultures lighted in distant trees, I no longer cursed them and wished that they would light down and attack the carrion. Their clamor would be sure to reach the watcher, and likely he would rush out to protect his waiting feast, giving me a clear shot before the midday light began to fail.

I had a sense of it failing while the sun was still above the trees. I could watch the shadows' slow creep; the little puffs of breeze felt cooler than before. I fought in vain against a deepening disquiet. My fancies began to be tinged by something like delirium: it would be like this if this were the world's end, its last dying drift through time before Time died, and of all its creatures only three still had solid form—carrion in a palm thicket, a great tiger licking his bloodied paws in a hidden place, and I. The Hindus thought that Kali, the "dark mother," wife of Siva the Destroyer, took a tiger's form. She must have been the first aspect of Brahma, and after she had devoured all the people, she would be the last.

The sun shone in the treetops and I thought it would glimmer through the boles for a good while yet, but I had not reckoned on some low hills beyond. The light was suddenly reduced, and my pulse as abruptly quickened. It slowed again when nothing happened but a barely perceptible dimming of distant scenes and what seemed my snail-pace drift into deeper solitude. If I killed Kharab-Bagh—and I did not believe it now; my intimation was of his killing me—I would like never again to be alone.

I must soon light the lantern and hang it over the bait. I must not wait till I could no longer see to shoot before venturing down. It should not keep the tiger from his kill. He had once carried away a charcoal burner from the fireside. Still I delayed the act, fearful that he would take alarm and deprive me of my last chance for a daylight shot—fearful, too, that the oil would not last until tomorrow dawn. Suddenly I realized that my eyes were being adjusted to the failing light, and night was a great deal nearer than I thought. The shadows massed and darkened; the effect was of a dim lamp slowly turned down.

With stealthy motions I was reaching for a friction match when I thought I detected a faint taint in the evening freshness of the air.

It faded out, then returned. It slowly spread and intensified until it was rank in my nostrils. Kharab-Bagh had left his lair and was coming back to his kill. Any one of the myriad shadows to windward might conceal his form. His bright colors were now extinguished; he could be differentiated from the shadows only by his movements; he was a living shadow. I fixed my gaze on the cleared space between the palm clump and farther thickets. Both barrels of my rifle were cocked, my finger on the trigger guard. My terrors sped away and so did all fantasy, and I was at the highest pitch of life I had ever known.

A twig cracked . . . Kharab-Bagh's injuries from the buffalo fight had made him a little clumsy . . . Then the profound silence was ruffled by a continuous rhythmic sound, halfway between a rustle and a swish. My scalp tightened with a creeping sensation as I realized what it was. Kharab-Bagh had approached to the edge of the thickets to survey the scene, and sense or instinct had warned him that there was a barrier between him and his desire. He was lashing his tail in fury.

The sound ceased, and a moment later his rank smell began to thin out. Obviously he had drawn back, and I could not believe he would come again. Hoping against hope, I sat motionless for perhaps ten minutes more, until the dusk began to close the openings around the kill, and I could not trust to shoot even at ten yards' range. In haste now to light my lantern, I broke the stem of the first match; and the second crackled and flared. I lighted the lantern but had no intention now of hanging it over the bait. I meant to keep it beside me for protection.

Reaction setting in from the intense excitement and exhilaration of a few minutes ago must have dulled my mind, or I would have perceived more quickly what a treacherous friend the dim light was. I realized it only when I stopped to wonder at the sudden blackness of the night. My furtherest probing vision stopped at ten feet—and Kharab-Bagh could cover twenty in one bound. I picked up the light with the intention of setting it about that distance down the slope. At that instant the brush rustled in a different direction from before, upwind from me, at about the same level, and not more than sixty feet away.

Kharab-Bagh had come back, but not for the broken meats. He was creeping along the foot of the cliff to make a fresh kill.

I set down the lantern and snatched up my gun. As I leveled, the end of the barrel thrust into blinding shadows. My brain bursting with terror, I acted either with great resource or in animal panic—with a thrust of my arm I upset the lantern and sent it rolling down the hill.

The flickering light and shadow may have given Kharab-Bagh a few seconds' pause. I became conscious not of better vision, only of less helplessness. My terror was trans-

94

muted to power as I heard the tiger's leap and saw a blackness that rushed in through paler shadows that seemed to recede. I fired into its middle, so dynamized by my escape from impotency that I could not miss.

Chapter Thirteen

Any greater victory that I might win in my life to come would certainly be less elemental. It could have more human ecstasy, but not as much natural glory.

I fired my second barrel into the stone-dead tiger; howling, I reloaded and blasted the air. Then I poured lamp oil on a rotting log and set it afire. Furiously piling on fuel, I soon had a bonfire that lighted the whole ravine, turning Kharab-Bagh's hide into royal vestments of cloth-of-gold. I could not think of the pitiful human remnants lying only a few feet away in the ground-palms.

The high flames soon brought the villagers and pandemonium. Little Toto seemed to be Pan himself. Ordinarily rather dignified, he was leaping about in heathen transports. My sanity was restored by the sight of an old man and a young one, both with drawn faces, wrapping something in straw matting, oblivious to the riot around them. My shout of "Khamoshi!" stilled the uproar until the mourners could complete their task.

These left shortly with their nearer kinsmen carrying torches. Ten men with fleshing knives peeled off Kharab-Bagh's skin, and Toto would yield to no younger man the honor of bearing it home. Shouting and waving firebrands, the entire party of celebrants started across country to Toto's village. That orgy was in store for them there, I had little doubt.

But I had misjudged the tribesmen, or the state of their hearts and minds. All the village gongs resounded and every log drum thundered, but the store of palm toddy was politely shared with the women and children, and no runners were dispatched to nearby villages for more. By the time a wild boar that I had shot was spitted and set to roast, the dancing and prancing had ceased, and the people went about patting and sniffing one another's faces in grave, childlike joy. They did not gorge tonight, and although they hung on my words, they seemed shy of expressing gratitude. I thought I knew why: it was beyond their power to express.

Toto made bold to tell me that their visitors would presently return to their village, and, by the sahib's favor, they would like to carry with them the tale of the death of Kharab-Bagh. Completely refreshed, I related the story, and I had never seen so much human happiness in one assemblage. Mine too was near zenith tonight, the past and the future curtained off from these present glimmering moments. Not a cloud upon it, only a little troubled question, was Latah's keeping her distance instead of standing close to me with big luminous eyes. I saw her in the crowd, but could not get her to look at me. Perhaps she thought I had neglected her on my first triumphant return. I would make peace with her before I slept, I thought.

The visitors departed with flaring torches. Our villagers were glad to have them go so they could rejoice in their closeness. Then I saw Latah do a rather puzzling thing. After wiping her throat as though overheated, she slowly removed her chudder-like garment and hung it on her arm. None of the other young women had bared their breasts tonight, and none followed her example. Indeed all of them seemed to be looking the other way.

I knew now that her grandmother had not spoken entirely in jest. Latah was the best-formed of all the village girls, whose slim symmetry would be notable in any land. A moment later she disappeared, only to enter Toto's house at the head of the row. It was an inconvenient place to talk to her, and I saw no way out of waiting until morning.

Toto noticed my first move to go to my hut, and hurried toward me. Rather to my surprise, he salaamed.

"By the sahib's favor, I would speak to him of a matter," he said.

"You have my leave."

"If I speak too freely, the sahib will not be angry, because he knows my heart yearns to serve him. I am a hillman and I do not know the ways of the sahibs, and what to them is seemly, and what is not. The sahib has spoken many times to my daughter Latah and, watching his face, I thought she found favor in his sight."

"Truly she did."

"Will Sahib honor her and me, and truly all my people, by taking her for his handmaiden tonight, and for as long as he remains in our hills?"

I did not reply at once, my heart beating too fast for me

96

to trust my voice or my impulse. Toto's usually impassive countenance could not conceal his anxiety.

"It is a great honor, chief," I replied. "But it comes to me that Latah might not take pleasure in the pleasure I would take in her. Tonight she shunned my company."

"That was only shyness, sahib. She knew I would speak to you of her."

"Then she is not unwilling?"

"Unwilling, sahib? She has made pooja to her *nat* to find favor in your sight."

I tried to steady myself. After all, the proffer need not surprise me, considering Kuki customs. Unmarried girls of Latah's age felt free to give their favors to whom they pleased, and temporary unions were a commonplace here. Indeed Latah might gain face with her companions by sharing the couch of an honored visitor.

"Toto, you have pleased me greatly by offering this precious gift. If you will ask Latah to come to my hut, we will talk together, and see what befalls."

Toto gave his neck a little twist, a sign of Kuki satisfaction. His eyes twinkled as though quite certain what would befall.

I went to my quarters determined to keep a solid sense of values. A jungle child whom I had defended from Kharab-Bagh, very little if any older than Parro, must not become in any way a victim of that victory.

I lighted and hung my lantern. Its light was muddy and sickly, then became charmed by what it shone on. Latah had put on weight since my coming a week ago—only a pound or two making a marked difference in her appearance. She was no longer hollow-eyed and a very thin layer of flesh between her facial bones and the skin gave her countenance a smoother moulding. Knowing I must deal with it soon, resolved not to let it play tricks on either my conscience or my judgment, I opened my eyes wide to what she promised in the way of a maid with a man.

Her dusky skin appealed to profoundly primitive instincts. I fancied that Eve, always pictured by Renaissance artists as glimmering white as a fair-haired Piedmontese, had been of about this shade. Its perfect harmony with a primeval background was good evidence that it was the first human color. Too, the shape of her head and face was what we English call primitive—giving the effect of a continuous sloping line from crown to chin. I had trouble, though, applying this fine theory to her form. It looked as though it had been bred for the

97

harems of voluptuous Indian princes. Such femininity in miniature, all the curves that men like in proportion, excited sensuous imagination. The same thing was true of the daughters of a great many hill tribes. Latah was the belle of the village, I thought—probably in most demand at the men's house—but two or three other girls must give her a close race.

I offered her a seat beside me on my cot. She accepted it shyly, and gracefully enough, considering that she had sat down not fifty times in her life, her ordinary easy posture being to squat on her heels. I had smiled at her entrance, but neither of us had spoken yet. This would have been embarrassing to both of us if she were an English girl visiting my room with these intentions. Here it tended to relieve embarrassment. Her sitting there in silence, her gaze moving from one of my possessions to another, might be primitive stolidity, but it gave the effect of poise.

"Would you like a sweet cake, Latah?" I asked.

"Yes, sahib."

I took one from the tin, and she munched it with grave enjoyment. Throughout the Orient, ceaseless and often meaningless conversation is not a social necessity—periods of quiet seem to enhance sociability.

"Your father, Toto, promised me good payments and rewards if I slew Kharab-Bagh," I said. "It comes to me that his giving you to me, to take pleasure with while I stay at his village, is in keeping with that promise."

She turned her eyes on mine in puzzled wonder. After thinking over what I said, she shook her head.

"No, sahib. The kuki men may not give their daughters as they give cattle, nor can they sell them. When a village boy and girl decide to make a house, he brings to her father cattle and other things of worth, a great store if he is rich, small if he is poor, which reveals the joy he takes in her, and which comforts her sire for her absence and makes easier his old age. But no cattle are given when a boy receives a girl in the men's house."

"Toto did not bid you come to me?"

"No, sahib."

"He did not speak of it to you, Latah?"

"Not until I had spoken to him."

"You wished to pay me honor for slaying Kharab-Bagh?" I was sure this was not the answer.

98

"No, sahib. To win the honor of being your hand-maiden."

Latah employed the Hindustani word *izzat* for "honor," which was synonymous with "face." Since she was translating the best she could a Kuki idea into another language, I was still not satisfied that her motive was entirely the gaining of prestige among the villagers, although it appeared the main factor. I was, and would be for a long time, longer than I would live, perhaps, a village hero. That she had a strong conscious or unconscious desire for me, I could not believe. She did not give the least sign of it, and its spontaneous awaking was almost unthinkable, considering my alienship from her. Then I was struck by her use of "handmaiden" —literally, "female servant"—instead of "bringer of delights." It seemed to mean a relationship covering more than the other. It gave me a clew to her silence and immobility. She would not presume to address her lord in word or act until he addressed her. Yet that extreme humility seemed proud.

"Latah, I will remain here only long enough to collect some jungle produce to sell at Chittagong."

"That I know."

"If you lodge with me for those days and nights, will you be to the young bachelors the same as before?"

"No, sahib."

"Do you mean—for I must make sure of this matter—that they will not invite you to the men's house, or be as willing to take you to wife?"

She looked dumfounded, then her lips seemed hard put to it to stay straight.

"They will invite me as often as before, and have the same willingness to make a house with me. I meant, sahib, that if Sahib has looked upon me with favor, they will hold me in higher honor."

"Suppose, Latah, that by lying with me you get with child. How would that bear upon your dealings with the people, young and old, and what would happen to the babe?"

"Sahib, if my belly swelled from your seed, the unwedded daughters of the village would stick out their tongues at me, so many of the bachelors would want to take me to wife. Those who have wives already would likewise pay court to me, for good hunters and corn raisers among us often take more than one wife. Fear not that the seed would not come up well. Though I am thin now, I am a hearty eater, and my

99

nat has ever driven off the sickness-devil, and no girl in the village can gather more barley from sunrise to sundown. When the babe would be born, think you he would go hungry? We Kuki women are not *thuu* [literally, a dried-out stump]. By your favor, look at me, sahib."

"I see now that the babe would grow fat and lusty."

But I saw more than that. I saw her pride in the womanliness, not only in its beauty but its function. The beautiful forms of the Kuki girls could be, I thought, a consequence of a similar pride throughout the generations. Beautiful was another name for desirable.

"Sahib, would he not become in time a great hunter and chief?" Latah asked. "When good seed is planted in barren soil, the stalk is better than by the planting of poor seed, but what if the soil too is good? Sahib, forgive your handmaiden for speaking of such worths as she has. It would have been more fitting if my father Toto made them known to you. I am not the least of the village girls, either by birth or by accomplishments. Both of my grandsires were headmen of good villages, wherein the people fed well and lived long. No other girl learned Hindustani so quickly or so well, and few may keep pace with me in the field work, or in butchering game, or in handicraft of the houses. The people would not forget that he was the son of Shikra Sahib—all of them have come to call you so—and although he would hunt with bows and arrows and spears instead of the thunder-guns, yet he would slay many deer, and perhaps tigers and leopards."

Latah was speaking in deeply earnest tones. That earnestness gave warmth and, I thought, lovely meaning to her countenance and caused a real and startling beauty in and about her eyes. I had been failing to listen earnestly enough. I had taken a superior attitude toward her claims and hence toward her and hence toward the reason she was making them. Conscious of my white skin's contrast with hers, of being English while she was a hill girl, I had failed in fellowship with her. My mind had been about to object to such a fate for a child of my loins—a half-caste, so called, to start with, at best a chief of a village of illiterate semi-savages. I was thinking that the danger of having a child by her should make me send her away. That was what an English sahib was supposed to think.

Well, I was not going to send her away. That might be weakness, but suddenly the strange inkling came to me that it might be strength. Why should I call the chance of Latah's

100

kindling a danger? To whom was it dangerous? Not to her or to me or to the fruit of our mating, save for the danger that pertains to life itself. Was I sure that English life was better than Kuki life? The brat would be loved, and for the rest, he could take his chance with the other children. Life in a hill village surrounded by tiger-infested jungles, in hair-raising intimacy with ghosts, goblins, and all manner of baleful or beneficent gods, might be a superb adventure. If God were willing—and a last flutter of English prudery made me change the name to Kismet—who was I to deprive him of it? I had met only a very few people who sincerely wished they had never been born.

Latah sat beside me, a beautiful specimen of the human race, giving me reasons why I should not deny her favors. She had told me that the sickness-devil had never laid hand on her. Suddenly I knew that if I denied her body's union with mine for any reason other than lack of desiring it, I was not a humanist or a freethinker, but a prig.

"How old are you, Latah?" I asked.

"I have seen fourteen Rains."

Vivian was fourteen at our first kiss. But Latah had also seen fourteen ardent Suns.

I leaned toward her and gently sniffed her cheeks. Her only response was a little sigh that I took for happiness.

"Latah, when a woman of my tribe takes joy in her lover's addresses, she returns every one."

That opened Latah's eyes. "Even at the beginning she makes so bold?"

"With a little urging. If you take joy in mine, it is commanded, not urged, that you so respond."

She sniffed long at my cheeks and throat.

"Latah, I shall woo you as the sahibs woo their sweethearts —the boldest and not the more bashful. The wooing will be of a new sort to you, and if any passage does not bring you joy, let it be known to me."

"Your servant will obey your commands."

Coming so swiftly upon the aching loneliness of my watch for Kharab-Bagh, mere physical communion with this pagan girl was no small boon. It was far more than that—with our first kiss it became superb adventure in dynamic life. Other white strays in native villages had had similar opportunities, but few so great a need or as receptive a mind. I could not, if I tried, reconcile it with Occidental morals, at least those

101

taught instead of practiced, but feeling no guilt, I refused to consider them.

It was literally Latah's first kiss. A caress all but unknown among the animist tribes, it took her by agreeable surprise. There was a question in her eyes that she was shy at putting in words.

"In Hindustani, it is called *bosa*," I told her.

"And many young men do so to their handmaidens?"

"Their handmaidens do to them likewise."

"It is permitted of me, also?"

"If it was a joy to you, Latah. Have you forgotten?"

"A joy to me?" she asked, when she had kissed me with shy ardor. "Bosa is sweeter on my lips than wild honey. I have never felt such joy."

I did not remind her of her experiences in the men's house. She would have not come, I thought, except for the tribal sanction, or, no matter how agile my mind in justifying my desires, could I have invited her. But I rejoiced in her innocence of the wooer's art. Instructing her was more than a sensuous delight. My imagination was wildly aroused; the little hut at the jungle rim was the perfect scene for a prehistoric idyl. Never having been taught shame of the flesh, and no longer afraid of committing an impropriety in my sight, she became completely responsive.

"This is a wonderful thing," she told me, quivering. "I will make gifts to the guru of dressed skins and eggs."

"No, set the eggs and hoard the skins. We have only started to play, and when we are in earnest, what harvest after the Rains?"

"I will make thankful offerings to my *nat*," she burst out a few minutes later.

"The little hen with the white breast that can run very fast? Is the white breast good to eat?"

"I may not eat it, but the others find it so. I will throw corn in the woods——"

She grew breathless then, and I began to marvel at the virginal aspect of her love-making as well as its intensity. Each sensation seemed completely new to her, relished as though she could not get enough and thought it the ultimate. Apparently she had yielded to the bachelors in the men's house without adequate wooing and had never been wakened. Young men of the Kuki were by no means a brutal lot, but the use of narcotics such as bhang and opium was often associated with their entertainments.

Then my marveling turned to solemn wonder as I made a breath-taking discovery.

In a few seconds I rose, on the excuse of sharing with her a glass of arrack. I measured it slowly, trying to steady my hands. She gasped out a Hindustani word.

"Latah, did you say 'Jaldi' [quickly]" I asked.

"I should not have said it, lord. Forgive your handmaiden!"

"There is no fault, but the waters are sweeter after long thirsting."

"But after lifting the cup, it is not good to have it snatched away. Have mercy on your servant for her presumptuous tongue! When the venison you had brought the people had been cooked, and its savors filled the air, what if you had forbidden us to eat? I do not need the arrack to warm my blood. It is even now on fire. Do not blame me for crying my hunger, when you have spread the feast."

"Is it a new hunger, Latah?"

"Yes, and a new aching, so sweet I cannot bear it any longer."

"You felt the like in me."

"Has it passed away?" she asked. "Is the stomach turned against me for some fault? If so, I will go quickly——"

"Latah, you didn't tell me that you have never gone to the men's house."

"No, I did not. I thought that my father Toto told you. I bade him tell you, thinking it would win me favor in your sight. I would have bade him tell you I had been there moon waxing and waning if I had thought it would raise me in your regard. But you would have found out the cheat just the same."

"You have seen fourteen Rains. It was lawful for you to go there one, perhaps two Rains ago. Latah, why didn't you go?"

"It was not because no young man invited me," she told me, her eyes on mine.

"Why was it? Will you tell me? My hunger is greater than ever, but it is my kismet to ask the question, and to bid you answer it in truth."

"Lord, I did not want to go. There was no better reason."

"Then why did you want to come here? It was not to gain face with your companions."

"No, lord. I would gain face, but that was not why I made so bold. I yearned to lie with you, sahib, and give you joy in me, and take joy in you. And the cause of that yearning

103

was your killing Kharab-Bagh."

I was slow in getting any sort of grip on this. Instead of a seemingly difficult thing that turned out simple, it was a seemingly simple thing that turned out difficult.

"Latah, you spoke fair words with me on the day of my coming and stayed close to me at the feast."

"Yes, sahib."

"If then, or at any time until tonight, I had invited you to lie with me, would you have done so?"

"No, sahib."

"As I went forth to meet Kharab-Bagh, you kept pace with me to the paling, and invoked your *nat* in my defense. If time had permitted us to linger in a bower safe from interruption, would you have accepted my embrace?"

"No, Shikra Sahib."

"Was I not the same man then as when I returned?"

"No, sahib. You had not yet killed Kharab-Bagh."

I tried to make this out a savage concept. "That made me as a godling in the eyes of the people," I suggested.

"No, sahib. No godling, but a strong, cunning, and lucky hunter. I felt bravery in you to go, but most men are brave, and what good would it have done us if Kharab-Bagh, not you, had won the battle?" She scratched her head vigorously to think better. "For such a hunter, I had saved my maidenhead. Perhaps my *nat* told me to—that I cannot tell. For him to untie my knot would give me great joy and great hope, and the planting within me of his strong seed, a great satisfaction." (For the latter, Latah had employed *razamandi,* which could mean either the gratification of a hunger or the happy outcome of a deal.) "I knew that you would soon go back to your own people; still it would have been Shikra Sahib who first sowed me; and perhaps my first-born would be of that sowing. When you were gone I would seek the most brave, cunning, and lucky hunter who would make a house with me."

Suddenly I was thunderstruck by this dark savage girl's link with Vivian. The English beauty had rejected me because I had lost stature, Latah had accepted me because I had gained it. Money had been at least my brace and Vivian had sensed my weakening at its loss; Latah had found resources in me making for survival in her world. Perhaps both girls were more elemental than most, Vivian descending from the aboriginal Celt, and Latah an animist. I thought that more natural would fill the bill, or even more feminine. That I wooed two so alike was no great wonder; a man usually woos the same kind of woman again and again, and I might be more moved by femininity or more aware of its adulteration than many men. The real wonder was I had got both of them to talk. That was the consequence of a probing mind, engined perhaps by a kind of courage.

" 'When the meat is done, tongues should taste and not wag,' " I quoted.

Latah laughed raucously as natives are prone to do when a stranger comes out with one of their own sayings.

"What is your will with me, sahib? Shall I go, or stay?"

"What of the fires that were lighted? Have they burned out?"

"They will blaze high, sahib, at the lightest touch of your hand."

I looked with elated eyes at the kitten-like grace of her posture, the dusk of her body accented by the white spread. I could have her, and by a law old as the jungle I was entitled to her, because I had killed Kharab-Bagh.

"Then we will make a great feast, Latah, to bless the planting. Open your arms wide."

Chapter Fourteen

Spent by her bridal adventure, Latah fell into the silent, warm, lovely sleep of the truly young. I lay awake awhile, rejoicing in her head on the thick of my arm, her breast and belly and limbs sinuously conjoined with my side. A condition of my life heretofore, often as unnoticed as the air I breathed, like the air in being a medium in which I had my being, no longer existed. It was loneliness. Latah had driven it off like a bad *nat*.

I was deeply concerned with her. Bodily near or far, she was in my life to stay. This was partly the effect of her surrender to me, but partly mine to her in a sense impossible to grasp. Among the Kuki as many other semi-civilized tribes, a girl's virginity did not count as a great treasure; but I had found out that Latah's was, and hence its winning a great triumph. It had become so in a mysterious way—somehow connected with her own prizing of it, in turn the measure of her self-prizing which derives from the soul.

I knew that our union tonight had meaning and beauty

that we both could feel but never understand. Latah's lack of what we call civilization had in no degree reduced these, and indeed added to their wonder. Her fears, rising sharply at one moment, had given way to a quite lovely ecstasy. The dimly lighted hut had become the scene of advent; from henceforth Latah and I shared a secret greater than the sum total of those we could confide, one that could be realized only in poetic feeling. But I need not have been incredulous— Cythera is a very ancient goddess. Christian beatitudes had given us nothing to take her place.

But if Latah had become her priestess at one mysterious moment, at dawn she appeared only a delighted little bride. She wakened me as delighted brides have wakened their brand-new spouses since time out of mind, and with the same consequence. Perhaps she was more gusty in her love-making than most primly raised English girls, being a down-right pagan who knew no word meaning lewd.

It occurred to me that Kuki civilization might be just far enough along to make life the most worth living. Life here might have the gusto of pre-Homeric days in Greece, or of those of David, when he and his people were nomadic shep-herds. It was certainly more exciting to hunt deer with ar-rows than with rifles, and to fight tigers than political enemies. In Latah's civilization women had been neither trampled down nor inordinately elevated. Carnal love was seen as the thing it was—a delightful gratification of an appetite which was not their fault, a delicious bait to catch babies, not too solemn to joke about, and, with the right partners, a deeply human and often illustrious adventure.

The lantern had burned out, but Latah rose and opened the door to a morning freshly perfumed by the jungle breeze. Her skin rubicund in the morning light, she knotted her hair and put on her waistcloth.

"Shikra Sahib, do you trust your servants to clean and care for your great gun?" she asked. Evidently every good Kuki hunter looked after his own spear, bow, and arrows. That was part of the moral code.

"No, little hen."

"Then, while you see to it, I will prepare the morning meal."

She went away down the village row, and returned with some rice flour, a piece of wild pork, and a cooking pot. With unhurried movements pleasant to my sight, she went about making a fire, chapatty-baking, and meat-broiling. We ate together without breach of Kuki manners, then I talked with Toto about the jungle produce promised me for shooting Kharab-Bagh. The amount already in the village was collected and stored for me, and about twenty of his people went into the jungle to gather more. I told them that if crops were large enough to bring two hundred rupees from wandering traders, I would cancel their debt of cattle and buffalo.

The harvesters went forth happily because Kharab's skin was off his carcass and the vultures were on it.

I thought that the party would gather about ten rupees' worth a day. With what was already gathered, the harvest should take sixteen or seventeen days. In the afternoon, Latah and I went deer hunting. By my agreement with Toto, his young men were to bear the kill to camp, prepare the skins for me to sell in Chittagong, and smoke the meat for themselves, paying me in jungle produce at the rate of five rupees per hundredweight on the hoof. The animals were thick and tame from lack of hunting, and in spite of sparing the hinds and fawns, I shot three sambur and two barasingha. Happily the old people and the children could smoke and sun the meat.

Latah and I could not count ourselves relentless nimrods. On that first afternoon a grassy bower pale gold with sifted sunlight caused us to relent, and I was all but alarmed by the witchery making there, in the warm silence and flower scent. There were no apples and no figs in this later Garden, no guilt and no shame; and instead of the end of the world that I had dreamed at the death watch I could vision the beginning of another, where I had caught a nature goddess with whom to found a race. There were no eyes but hers and mine to perceive beauty, no knowledge of good and evil save our own.

Naked amid the greenery, small, slender, pale brown with pit-black eyes and flowing black hair, she was moulded as I fancied Lilith, or Demeter's daughter, or perhaps Artemis before she whitened to become chaste Diana. Perhaps I was the Boar in what would be, in ages to come, a cult like that of Adonis.

I thought to tell her of the myths that wakened these fancies, for she would understand them far better than I, let alone a dust-dry don at Oxford, but instead she instructed me.

"Shikra, if we meet what seems a small brown man, hairy

as a monkey, give him some tobacco," she said as we walked on.

"Who is he?"

"He is the shikari god, who herds the deer and the wild cattle, and since you are now his namesake, he may appear before you."

"I shall be most polite to him."

"If we anger him, there will be a veil cast before your eyes, and you won't see any more game."

"What does he do with the tobacco?"

"He smokes it or chews it, I don't know which. Anyhow, he is very fond of it."

That was the nice thing about pagan gods—they were so extremely anthropomorphic. They could not be too hard on human beings' frailties, when they possessed them in godlike measure.

"Shikra, I wouldn't be surprised if I'm with child," she went on cheerfully.

"So soon?"

She nodded childishly. "Just now. Before Kharab-Bagh began to eat us, couples who could not get a baby went to the jungle to make one. It's a very good place for everything to grow. And what do you think I saw at just the right time?"

"I couldn't guess."

"Not my *nat*, but her close kin. A jungle hen, and she stood and looked at us. Do you think that was a sign of good luck?"

"It could very well be."

"But, sahib, you must eat lots of deer meat. The stag deer, not the hind. The meat is very rich right now before his horns fall off."

"I will eat some wild boar, too, and some goat, and some roast peacock."

She nodded, understanding the part each played in sympathetic magic—the same as in our myth.

"The great black bison gaur is good too," she said.

"I may not eat him, Latah. I think he is my *nat*."

When we returned to the village, Latah looked shaken by the amount of jungle produce that the harvesters had brought in—worth nearer thirty rupees than ten here in the hills, and at least twice that amount in Chittagong. The easy explanation was that only the bare edge of the jungle had been cropped since the Rains. At that rate, I would have my

108

wages in seven days.

"It may be that when I have sold it I will return to buy more," I said quickly, to take a shadow off her face and one, quickly and strangely falling, off my heart.

"That would be good," Toto replied. "The police sahibs have forbidden us to go to the plains because of a trouble long ago, and we have had to sell the goods to the salt dealers, whose scales lie in our teeth."

Latah took a little walk down the village road, frequently scratching her head, then ran back to us.

"Shikra, I know how you can make heaps of rupees," she burst out.

"They would be most welcome."

"Do you know that pods of musk bring three times their weight in silver at Chittagong?"

"I've heard so," I answered, staring at her.

"The reason it is so dear is traders are afraid to go among the Mishmi peoples who gather it in great store—lest their heads be cut off and stuck on posts. Only a little trickles out through Bhutan. Is it not true, my father Toto? You know how the traders always yearn for musk."

. "It is so." Toto's eyes were alight with pride.

"But the Naga people may trade with the Mishmis, because they are kinsmen. Now the Naga people also take heads—it is a great shame—and the traders durst not go among them, either. But we Old Kuki are kinsmen of the Nagas. Our men may go among them safely, and the Naga fathers lend them their daughters to make their visit pleasant. Is it not true, my father Toto?"

"Truly, the Naga Hills was once our home, and when my father's cousin went there as a youth—he had done not well in the sight of the sahibs—it was even as Latah says."

"The Naga Hills are seven days' march," I said.

"Ten days, without heavy sweat, by the old path that doesn't touch the plains, through Cachar and Manipur. But, sahib, there be salt of wisdom in Latah's words, which were no doubt whispered in her ear by her *nat*. If my young men went there with bags of rupees, they could buy the musk pods from the Nagas at half their weight in silver. A bag of them could pass for a sack of corn."

As far as I knew, the scheme had never been tried. The Marwari were bold traders but not rash enough to trust capital and goods to penniless, unbonded jungle men who could come and go like crickets. The fact remained that travelers about the world were constantly reporting the honesty of a great many primitive tribes. Their itching fingers could resist sweets no better than children's; liquor left about appeared in the same quantity but weak-tasting, and tobacco was in danger; small, shiny things were likely to become misplaced, only to show up' when their owner cursed and carried on. But his more important belongings could be left unguarded months on end.

I did not think the Kuki men would steal from me. The danger of their being murdered for their goods could be warded off by appearing as poor as usual. The tribesmen along the way almost never committed murder: they merely cut off strangers' heads so that the good spirits thereby freed would stay with them, receive high honor, and help guard their fields against evil spirits. If the Kuki travelers touched only their kinsmen's villages and stuck to the hill paths not worth a footpad's watch, I thought they could go and come between their hills and the Naga country at only reasonable risk. They would delight in the adventure; travel expense would amount to only a few pice per day; and if Latah's figures were anyway near correct, I could afford to pay them well.

She and I discussed the project off and on, when we were not stalking deer or playing honeymooners. Also I projected plans for cheap and safe transport of my goods to Chittagong, and for dodging, if it were worth the risk, export duties. It occurred to me to establish a depot not far from the crossroads of Diwanpani—perhaps at the Tame Kuki village. A large number of bales and boxes could pass for a hunter sahib's baggage.

On the night before our first parting, Latah wept on a strange unworldly peak of passion she had never gained before. I was afraid she would take these unaccountable tears as an ill omen, for hill girls rarely cry at all, let alone in ecstasy. Her sleep was soon deep and serene. I found myself dreading tomorrow's departure—so many little kismets could prevent my return. But to wish to shed my white skin as well as my sahib attire was a silly wish. I could not become a member of Toto's tribe, a spear thrower and bowman in the jungle, and a maker of pooja in the magic-house.

Latah escorted me to the cart road, walking properly behind me. I decided against kissing her wistful lips in front of her tribespeople, since the alien caress would accent the exogamous character of our love affair. In the end I did so, and it appeared to make both of us proud. At the village of Tame Kuki I need not ask for news of mutiny: the composure of the people told that there was none. Here I wrote two letters, one of instructions to Puran, and the other to my intelligent and fair-dealing Parsi landlord in Calcutta, authorizing him to close my house there, cancel the lease, and make various disposals of my property.

The jungle produce, including my deerskins and antlers—the latter, ground up, being greatly prized in China as an aphrodisiac—brought six hundred rupees from a Chinese broker. It amounted to sixty pounds, once my week's spending money, but I was not in the spending business any more. Returning to the Tame Kuki village, I found Puran, bearing good but not surprising news.

"Some chapatties were passed in and about Barrackpore when the moon was rounding," he told me. "Fires broke out in the sepoy lines, and the soldiers were sullen and pretended not to understand their orders. But General Hearsey Sahib took a firm stand, the punishments were swift and sure but not overly severe, and the trouble died out like a ghat fire in heavy rain."

A mountain labored . . . This was the lame and impotent conclusion of the gurus' soothsaying . . . The Indian swarm was lucky that its malcontents were so easily subdued, yet I could not help but feel ashamed for them. Probably there would be other stirrings as efficiently put down, and recorded in the court-martial registers as "insubordination."

Nothing had happened to prevent my return to Toto's village! The scheme I still toyed with, of getting by hook or crook a post in a native court in order to swindle a terrified rajah, must go by the board; and other coups I had contemplated had better wait until I could accumulate enough capital to brighten their chances. Vivian had followed her nose to her usual profit. It did not seem likely that she would ever have regrets.

After bargaining for a well-built native house to serve as a depot, I sent Puran to the northern Tripura to round up jungle produce. Then I made homesick haste to my now beloved hills. Toto's son ran ahead to announce me, and every villager able to walk or light enough to be carried met me at the footpath.

"Have you thought of me in this long time?" I asked a demure-looking lass, only lately a child, who had pressed her mouth against mine.

"Now and then, Shikra Sahib," she replied. "As one thinks of mangoes when they are not in season."

"Can it be that you have already taken another lover?"

"No, sahib. Nor will I take one until the Rains break and pass. My field, if you do not plant it, shall lie fallow. That is the bidding of my *nat*—I don't know the reason—but it is also his bidding that when the Rains have come and gone, I shall make a house with a youth of my village, even if Shikra Sahib would pay me ten rupees for one lying in his arms."

She was walking behind me, speaking in low, calm tones. I found myself believing her utterly, her *nat* in this case being woman's imperious instinct toward survival and obtainable happiness. Meanwhile there was a look in her eyes comparable to one I had seen when broiling venison had perfumed the air, and I wondered what measures she would take. I could not resist the glowing enjoyment of leaving the problem to her.

My little pagan did not disappoint me. The men had hardly housed my baggage when she spoke in businesslike tones.

"Shikra Sahib, I have found out about the musk buying and will stay here to tell you now. Then you may talk to my father Toto and the others at the threshing floor."

"I am eager to hear, Latah, and to give thought to it in quiet and seclusion."

Toto repeated this to his tribesmen, solemnly tapping his own head to indicate weighty thought. He and the others left, and Latah closed the hut door. Then she dropped her eyes and a distinct flush enriched the hazelnut brown of her face, throat, and breast.

"Sahib, I·have made too bold," she murmured.

"Why, it is dutiful of my handmaiden to instruct me in the business forward."

"The sahib knows what business I was on and mocks me for my haste. Truly, sahib, the fever came upon me and I spoke as one does in the raging fever, with no mastery of my tongue."

"Isn't it strange, considering you have thought of me only now and then, as you thought of mangoes when they were not in season?"

"Sahib, I am the daughter of a chief, and a good field worker, and no few of the young men want to make a house with me. It is not well that Sahib fear he has weakened me by his joy-giving, whereby I cannot longer walk erect and

112

must lean on him. Truly he has strengthened me."

I believed that I would think of that, and wonder over her saying it, many times throughout the years to come.

"We Old Kuki women are slaves to no man, and our hearts, instead of weak, are very strong," she went on proudly. "We do not waste their yearnings on what we cannot have. When they are broken, we bind and bandage them up the best we can, so we may go on living good until we die. I worked very hard while Sahib was gone. He will owe me many rupees for jungle produce I have gathered, and I cut up and smoked much meat to be eaten when the crops are lean. Tired at night, I went quickly to sleep, and when my eyes opened at dawn, I got up quickly."

"Did you never waken in the dark?"

She hung her head. "Yes, sahib."

"What then?"

"I thought of the cold pool we call Hilna-Dant [literally shake-teeth] where we go to bathe in summer, and I threw in my spirit and made her swim about until the fever broke."

"I've caught the same fever, but I know a better way to break it than throwing my spirit in Hilna-Dant."

If not a good sahib, I was proving quite a good pagan. Even so, I had not known how much I had parted with until this regaining.

When we were both satisfied for her to sit quietly on my lap, I thought again of what she had given me. I thought of it now in a clearer way than before; and so an impulse that had come to me again and again during her absence, and which I had rejected as preposterous, now returned as a solid idea to be sensibly weighed. To do so, I had to discover why I had shut my mind to it before. I had been afraid of the opinion of others. If I did what I wanted to do, the pukka sahibs and memsahibs would ostracize me. Vivian would be gladder than ever that she had cast me off. I would play the fool . . .

But I had become ostracized already. The halfhearted operation had become decisive when I had lost my money. I had better not go on living my life according to how it would affect Vivian. I was an associate of Toto and his tribesmen; I was a friend of Puran; as a man, I was involved with all mankind; but in this world there was only one soul bound to mine, and that was the soul of Latah.

I came to my decision as she was talking about our musk-trading project. The young men would vie for the chance of a journey to the Naga Hills; and she had picked out four that appeared the best fitted for the post. They were neither timid nor reckless, she said; when they ate bhang or drank arrack, they did not tell secrets; they were lucky in all their enterprises and got along well with strangers.

"I will send those you have named," I told her. "Each may carry a sack of salt on his back and a small bag of rupees hidden in his armpit. Latah, is it not true that the Old Kuki may go as far as the village of Tame Kuki, where the hills begin, without breaking the White Rani's law?"

"Yes, sahib."

"I have taken a house there in which to store my goods as they await transport to the ships. It affords room for one or two to reside in comfort, and there I will stay when I am not on the roads. But it is needful that someone remain there in my absence to count the stuffs that Puran and your tribesmen and perhaps others will bring in, and pay out wares or silver. It comes to me that you could fill the office well."

Her brown throat worked once.

"For how long, sahib?"

"I thought until the next Rains are done, when the cart roads will be as buffalo wallows. Then you may return to your people, bearing good gifts to please both Toto and the youth who will make a house with you."

"Will you still abide with the Tame Kukis?"

"No, I will go to dwell among my own people, as is my kismet."

"Truly it is your kismet, as it is mine to make house with a youth of my village. But speak truly, Shikra Sahib. What if then I am big-bellied with your son or daughter? Do you swear by your gods that when the time is out you will not take the babe from me, or do aught to make him be as a sahib instead of an Old Kuki?"

"He shall be as my gift to you, in remembrance of the house we make together and of the great joys we have shared."

Chapter Fifteen

My plans began to work out in a reasonably close accordance with their shaping. When the four young men took up the dim trail toward the Naga Hills, Latah and I, with the

114

help of Toto's son, transferred ourselves and our baggage, including her housekeeping equipment and presumably her *nat,* to our new house in the Tame Kuki village. From the rooftop we could make out the fort at Diwanpani, and when the wind was right we could hear the company of sepoys at rifle practice; but I paid no heed to Vivian's comings and goings, and when I could not keep an old wound from smarting, I knew where to go for balm.

The weeks drifted by like pearly clouds across a summer sky, one so much like another that we were hardly aware of its passage. Our business prospered but did not even start to make me rich: I had never thought it would, and of the capital I was accumulating, the main could not be counted in rupees and annas. Although the musk brought from the Naga Hills sold at four times its cost, yielding a clean profit of six hundred rupees, I did not try to hasten a second venture, for the travelers were enjoying their home-coming, their own cooking pots and thatch, and it was not for me to turn them into money-grubbers, when I too made pooja to pagan gods. On my bi-monthly trips to Chittagong, I sat and talked and drank with men and women of my own complexion, greatly enjoying the interludes, but when I came in sight of the Tripura Hills I made haste "like to a roe or to a young hart upon the mountain of spices."

Latah was happy—and I had never before considered that old apt saying—as the day was long. I did not make her so, save as a satisfactory companion in her pursuit of happiness —and not an aggressive pursuit either, rather more her own harmonizing with scene and event. She was of a happy disposition. She was a Midas of a kind—everything she touched turned to joy. If I had tried to make her unhappy, I could not—she would have simply shut me out of her life. She did not pass, but took pleasure in, the days I was absent from her—cooking herself good meals, running our store, smoking and chatting with the Tame Kukis. That pleasure was many times multiplied when I was with her because she found a more complete expression of herself, a greater sense of harmony with life, in loving me. It was never a destructive love, rarely even painful. She was the best-oriented, most perfectly poised person I had ever known.

She had only one disappointment—that the gentle curve of her belly did not grow. She did not blame me, herself, or her *nat*—the trouble lay in my failing to sow seed in the precisely right stage of the moon. She could have plenty of time

115

to raise a good crop when she made a house with a village boy; but our time was short. I thought that she was yet too young to conceive readily; I had noticed that very few of the early matings at the men's house bore fruit, and took it that Nature did not often smile on them until the girls were fifteen or more.

Late in March, Puran brought further tidings of the great world beyond the Barak River. I had taken leave of that world until some day of return but was not divorced from it, and what I had learned since my departure caused me to be more troubled by the report than if I were still its habitant. There had been some more teapot tempests in the sepoy army. A regiment of Bengal Rifles stationed at Berhampur had refused the new greased cartridge in fear of defilement; and as the men were being marched to Barrackpore for disbandment, a mutineer had killed an officer and wounded a European sergeant major. General Hearsey's courage in attacking the fellow had alone prevented a serious outbreak.

"Are there any signs of trouble at Diwanpani?" I asked Puran.

"No, sahib. The sepoys there march and drill as one man with two hundred legs and arms."

"What of the stations up Mother River?"

"There is some thunder but no rain. It is my belief that, now the regiments of Tomi are being brought from Burma and from Persia, the gathered storm will blow by."

My own opinion, got by sniffing the air, was that the danger was real but, if it could be warded off until the Rains, it would then pass. The Rains not only lay the dust of the old year and raise the young grass of the new. They are a new marriage between the ground and the sky, the copulation that kindles the earth's womb to new fecundity. In spirit they are related to the northern spring, but spring infiltrates the ramparts of winter; she plays hide-and-seek; when she finally invests the land we do not know it until the news is stale. Not so the rainy season in India. The heat mounts day by day through April and May. The earth bakes hard and breathes no more and all its voices are still; and hope flutters in the heart and there is a sadness over all the land. Later the clouds gather, but whisk away. Then one day they roll in dark, unbroken ranks, piling up and packing the whole dome of the sky. A wind rustles and presently roars, and the heat breaks in an instant. Then all Creation thrums with the

116

choral music of the Rains.

Then the mind of man contemplates life, not death; and he feels reborn.

Happily for both of us, Latah did not share these troubles with me. She was too good a fatalist to be frightened of the future, too serene to worry over events beyond her power to shape. The day had come that we met; a day would come that we parted; in the meantime we had found joys we could never lose. She never spoke of our coming parting, and apparently thought of it only rarely. I was sure that our love affair would enhance instead of reduce her happiness in another lover when I had gone; and that assurance came to me in a surprising way. I had simply compared her with myself.

It was an incident of the road that settled my mind in this regard, indeed throwing light upon the whole episode. I had bought a horse to shorten my absences from Latah; and as I turned from the village lane into the cart road, I saw another equestrian from the direction of Diwanpani. The figure was small compared to the big beast; the gait was fine and fast; and what looked like flame flared back from the rider's head.

I stopped and waited. Vivian pulled up, and as she was steadying her horse I had a good look at her. No person's appearance is quite real; it is as many reflections as there are eyes to see it. My eyes had not changed toward her. I was immediately moved by her beauty, so brilliant and rare, and the only reason that my desire for it was less sharp was that a great deal of beauty had been given me, easing my hunger, since I had seen it last. I was unable to compare it with Latah's beauty although there seemed more similarities than differences. Each was a condition of harmony with a different scene and a different age of man.

"How are you, Simon?" she asked when she could ease her reins. "I must say you're looking Number One." The latter was a byword in British India.

"So are you, Vivian."

"Do I? I was afraid I'd begun to fade. You're brown—a little leaner, I think—lithe as a Tartar. I thought your plainness wouldn't become you any more—but it does."

"It stands to reason it would become a plain man better than a toff."

"I think your plainness is only skin-deep. Simon, I didn't just happen to ride out this way. A letter came for you on the Diwanpani post, and it gave me a good excuse for a call on you." She groped in her duster pocket.

117

"Our acquaintance has always been involved with letters. One you wrote to Ronald that didn't arrive. One from my brother to me—one from your father to you——"

"Maybe this one will have happier—consequences—than any of those." She handed me the missive.

"Will you pardon me a glancing at it? It's quite an event for me to get a letter these days, and maybe you can carry a verbal reply."

"If you look at the back, you'll see it's from the Ganges Club."

"Then I'm afraid it isn't an event after all." I opened the envelope and read its enclosure. "In fact—if you look at it the right way—it's a mere formality," I told her. "Just a polite note from the Board of Governors requesting my resignation."

She drew a deep breath. "For not paying your dues, I suppose. Couldn't you ask for a temporary——?"

"I'm paid up till the end of this year, but I am informed that the balance will be refunded me."

"Oh, my God!" After this outburst she sat still, an unmistakable pallor on her face. "Simon, if you think I suspected that—and brought it out here to try to shame you——"

"Such an idea couldn't cross my mind. However—you should have suspected it. It came a little sooner than I thought——"

"Simon, I didn't think anyone in Calcutta had heard about the hill girl. No one in Diwanpani has mentioned it yet—it's not the kind of thing most natives tell the sahibs and memsahibs. I found it out from Ida, with whom I'm unusually close. I didn't tell a soul——"

"You didn't tell about my dancing with the housemaid, either—a sporting thing."

"I doubt if I was so sporting—in this case."

"Anyway, this was certain to get out," I went on when she stopped with compressed lips. "As you know, I didn't try to hide it. And that made it a major crime against Anglo-Indian society."

"I said—a minute ago—I wasn't trying to shame you. Shame was the wrong word. I knew you wouldn't be ashamed to be kicked out of the Ganges Club."

"But don't you think I was stupid not to have resigned?"

"I'm afraid I don't think it was stupid. You considered it none of their damn business. Since it was nobody's damn business but yours and hers, you didn't try to hide it, and you

118

didn't publish it either. I wonder if you're one of the few real aristocrats I've ever known."

"God forbid."

"I'm not flattering you. Mark you, Simon, I'm a very careful observer. I'm very sharp, like so many women on the make. In spite of the many mistakes I made about you, I admit another. I thought that losing your money would teach you a lesson. I didn't see how you could afford any longer not to conform. But you took a wild hill girl and lived with her openly. After that, you ought to have had the grace—they'd use that term—to resign from the Ganges Club. Instead you let them kick you out. Simon, don't you know that people *can* hurt you now?"

"They always could."

"But you go right on your own sweet way." She looked off, then back into my face. "I suppose the little barbarian is lovely."

"She seems so to me."

"Do you want to know how it affected me? You might be polite enough to say yes."

"I would, very much."

"You expected me to rejoice at what most memsahibs would think your fall. You thought it would make me much gladder to be rid of you. You didn't know me any better than that—no one does. But you went ahead, anyway, living with her four miles from Diwanpani. Only one thing that ever happened to me has ever stung me more."

"I'm sorry about that."

"I think you are sorry it stung me—instead of glad—and I don't like that either. Are you going to keep her always? That's none of my damn business——"

"It's hard to say where our businesses start and leave off. Latah is going back to her village to marry one of her tribesmen after the Rains. That was her own decision. She knows it's best for us both."

"Well, when the Rains come—and it's cool enough for me to sleep with him in comfort—I'm going to marry Ronald Blain."

There was only one reply to that that I knew of.

"The heat doesn't stop Latah. She's not as civilized as you are, and under these circumstances—this hot weather—of course I'm glad."

"You're saying she's more of a woman than I am. It was nicely put—you wouldn't mind if I were stupid enough to miss it—but I'm not. No, I didn't miss it."

She was not pale now, but white—two different things.

"I'd still kiss you if you'd let me," she went on. "I'd like to have you think about the kisses I give Ronald. But for the rest—we're now in the same boat."

"I'm missing that."

"I wouldn't marry you now to save your soul from hell."

Chapter Sixteen

I completed my errand and returned to my dusky bride in the Tame Kuki village. There the days sped too fast for my content. Soon the Rains would break, and shortly they would pass.

"Shikra Sahib, if the sipahis turn against the sahibs, what will you do?" Latah asked as we sat in our doorway in the light of an April moon.

"If it is a great uprising in which many sahibs and mem-sahibs will be killed, I will go and fight the sipahis beside my own kind."

"You would not go back into the hills where the killers could not find you?"

"Not. It would be against my *nat*."

"Would you take me with you when you go to join your kinsmen?"

"No, I would send you to Toto's village."

"I would rather go with you. Perhaps, if they killed you, they would yet spare me, because I am not a memsahib. But even if they killed us both, I would still rather go with you."

"There's no sense in that."

"There would be none if, after we are dead, I would go to our Land of the Spirits and you would go—what is the name of the place?"

"It has two names. Heaven and Hell. I think it's the same place."

"I would not be allowed to go there, and perhaps you would not be allowed to go to our Land of Spirits. Still, I think we might go someplace together. There must be many places that the dead go. We could find one to suit us."

"It is idle talk. Have we no better use for our mouths?"

"Yes, sahib." She turned and laid her lips gently on mine.

At the close of the first week in May, clouds began

to catch and hang on the crests of the Tripura Hills. Thunder dunted one evening, a hot wind rolled up the dust of the plains into a lurid cloud, and a few warm drops of rain spattered in the trees. It was too early for the southwest monsoons, but not too late for another storm, brewing a hundred years in India, to break in screaming fury.

Hardly a week later I gave up a horn-buying trip into the Cachar because of loneliness. If I had been a few hours earlier, I might have fallen in with exciting company on the road to Diwanpani—no less than General Morrow and his daughter Vivian. According to bazaar report, they had been visiting tea-planter friends on the Barak River and had been recalled by special bearer from Dacca. They traveled in great luxury with many bags and boys, and by making a little haste, I could no doubt overtake them. Instead I dawdled on the road until I was within four miles of the Tame Kuki village. It was there that a special messenger came to meet me.

It was Puran on a hired pony, and his face was gray and drawn as though with fever. He wheeled and rode beside me, telling me his news above the clump of hoofs in the dusty road.

I could wonder, if I had room for it in my brain, at the amount of detail. One of the wonders of India was the swift spread of rumor and report, rather like ripples running out in an ever-larger circle from a swirl in a pool, or the wind's waving of tall wheat.

On May 10, in the great military station of Meerut just north of Delhi, a cavalry officer had ordered rifle drill with the new greased cartridge. Nearly a hundred of the men refused and were summarily court-martialed and degraded and put in irons on parade. On the following evening, all the sepoys of the garrison mutinied, freed their comrades, and killed every European officer they could get hand on. Joined by the ruffians of the bazaars, they then slaughtered the women and children in the English quarter and mysteriously disappeared.

It was thought that they had scattered through the countryside. Instead they had marched to Delhi, followed by a howling, swelling mob, and here were joined by sepoy regiments at the great cantonment. Shooting down the officers, the bloodthirsty rabble swarmed into the city, and such Europeans or loyal servants not yet hacked to death by street ruffians were butchered en masse. Brave young artillery officers and sergeants blew up the arsenal to keep it from falling into the mutineers' hands, but the main powder magazine of three thousand barrels was seized.

The deposed Mogul of Delhi was proclaimed ruler. Up the Mother River a thousand miles the small and great cantonments were in flames, officers and their families murdered, while the rebel sepoys and riffraff gangs rioted in the cities, looting, burning, and butchering. Guerrilla bands swept through the countryside to the outlying stations, killing all Europeans and half-castes in their reach, and seizing ferries and roads to cut off the escape of those who fled.

I did not interrupt Puran's outburst. It might deflect his mind from some important fact. Only when he stammered, beholding visions of the great events he had reported, did I ask my first and most immediately urgent question.

"Is Diwanpani under attack?"

"I do not know, sahib."

"Did you meet the General Sahib and his train on the road?"

"No, sahib. I came by an old footpath from Argantala, where I heard the news. A runner had brought it from Habiganj."

"Did you hear if Calcutta had fallen?"

"The runner thought not, because of the regiments of Tomi newly come there."

No doubt there were many citadels in the path of the storm that still held, offering temporary refuge to any white people who could gain their gates. But I thought how few English regiments stood guard in India now, most of them in the far northwest, and wondered where they would strike back.

Perhaps the company of sepoys at Diwanpani had not yet heard the storm. Even so, they might have kept faith with their bread and salt, for they had stood well at Chillianwalla and were still in holy terror of General Morrow. They had white officers and had been cut off from the general disaffection. At least it was unlikely that they had taken their officers by surprise; at almost the worst there was a good chance for some of them and the other white people of the station taking refuge in the fort. Although partly dismantled, it was still a strong fort, well provisioned, with a well behind its walls.

"You don't know whether word has reached the Tame Kuki village?" I asked.

"No, sahib, although the news ran in all directions from Habiganj. But, sahib—even if the looters and killers come, they will not harm the Tame Kuki. They are not in league with the English and have nothing worth stealing."

"Are there looters and killers on the westward plains?"

"Yes, sahib. I heard they had reached Dacca, swinging eastward from the Ganges. The runner had seen many, led by redcoat sepoys, crossing the river. Their numbers swelled at every bazaar."

If they had not reached Diwanpani yet, they certainly would soon.

As yet there were only purposes in my mind, not plans. Happily, I saw no difficulty in safeguarding Latah. Her brother could take her to Toto's village before the guerrillas ranged eastward from Diwanpani, and they would not penetrate the steep, hungry hills for such poor loot as could be found there. I would see her on the road, then set out for the fort. If it were already seized, I did not know how or where I could join my kind. To do so was not a choice but a compulsion.

At the edge of the village I gave Puran plain orders. In our few minutes' stay here he was not to tell the news to anyone. He could account for my bringing him here by saying he had suffered sunstroke on the road—certainly he looked the part. I did not want to risk one of the villagers inflaming the sepoy garrison at Diwanpani before I could warn the officers.

In a moment more the precaution was proven useless. All the Tame Kukis were clustered on the village road, struck dumb with excitement. There were only about sixty of these —it was almost instantly apparent that my Old Kuki was not among them. There was not the slightest reason, I considered, to be dismayed. She was no doubt in our house, hiding the gear that marked it as a sahib's. She might be away, caching it in a safer place. Certainly she would be taking calm, intelligent steps in the behalf of both of us.

Before I could go to look for her, the chief of the Tame Kuki spoke to me.

"Sahib, your handmaiden is not here."

"Do you know where she is?"

"When the word came of all the sahibs and memsahibs in the north being slain, she went to Diwanpani."

That was not true, I thought. It did not fit in with any-

123

thing. She might have told the Tame Kuki so, to hide some other errand.

"Does anyone here know her errand there?"

No one spoke for a moment, but that did not mean that no one knew. It came to me swiftly that they all knew. I looked at an old woman with wasted breasts standing close by, and her dim eyes lighted strangely.

"I will tell you, sahib," she said quietly. "Latah did not tell me, but I know what business she went on. She asked the bringer-of-the-news if it was yet known to the sahibs at Diwanpani. He said it was not, but they would find it out soon when the people came to kill them. He said it was a good thing they did not know, for they would run into the fort and lock the great doors. When I looked again for her, she had gone."

The old woman paused, and then, looking me in the face, she spoke more quietly than before.

"Sahib, you also are a sahib."

Chapter Seventeen

My watch stood at four minutes before three. The old woman told me that Latah had set out for Diwanpani when the shadows "crawled from under the elephant's belly"— about one o'clock. The distance was four miles, which she could have easily covered in the meantime. The Tame Kuki had heard no shooting from that direction as yet, but there had been scattered shots up toward Brahmanbaria.

My preparations required only a few minutes more. My heavy rifle was already in my saddle scabbard; from a locked chest in our house I took what powder and balls and caps I had in store and put them in my saddlebag. From a cache under a board I took a hundred silver rupees of our hoard, leaving fifty and a roll of fifty five-rupee notes for Latah's use. The coins would probably buy more than ever before, while the paper might soon be worthless. If Latah spent them, she would get good value for them.

I gave Puran some of the coins and recalled his mind to a grass thicket where we had lately seen a barking deer, less than a mile from the fort. He was to make his way there after he had rested his almost exhausted horse. I set out for Diwanpani at a brisk gallop, resisting a hard hunger to go faster. The heat of the day was intense and this gait was the mare's best to get her alive to my destination with some run left in her. My moves thereafter depended on how many of our people could reach the temporary, fair safety of the fort. I had good hope that Vivian and her father had already gained it and that Latah could look out for herself anywhere on the countryside. I was the latest on this road and presumably in the greatest danger.

There was more traffic than on a feast day—orderly as yet, curiously quiet, and purposeful-looking. The people were moving as might sea gulls before a gale, in varied directions; each had his dream of riches or of vengeance or of merely peace. An old Parsi dressed in rags and driving a sleek pair of oxen might well be a moneylender with a rich hoard under his shabby goods; a band of young Bengali making toward Diwanpani might have long knives or even pistols in their bags. None moved to get out of my way; it was the sahib who turned out of the road. Most of them did not appear to glance at me; a great number scowled; one threw a stone that went wide of the mark. I wondered how many of them would be looting and burning before sundown.

I had gone less than a mile when I began to hear what appeared to be rifle fire in the intervals between the clumps of the mare's hoofs. It was somewhere near the station and had no clear meaning yet. Before long the bursts became frequent and unmistakable; then over the plain rolled the heavy peal of cannon. There was no longer any doubt that the station was under attack by mutineers of armed mobs, and that the fort still stood.

The intervals between the big guns' boom indicated either a very small garrison or a weak siege. Still I would assume for the present that all our people had been warned in time. I would not as yet contemplate the possibility of Latah's errand being discovered and her falling into the attackers' hands. It remained a heavy shadow across my mind but hardly conspicuous among other shadows of the unknown.

The rifle fire was so sporadic that I could picture the attackers taking cover, occasionally popping up to waste powder and to draw fire from the loopholes in the walls. A score of smoke clouds in a row told that the company line had been fired; and the yet clear sky beyond the drill field showed that the mobs had not yet set fire the officers' bungalows. The servants in those houses had either joined the mutineers, joined the garrison, or were dead. At this moment the big house at the end of the row might be a scene of such destruction of property and perhaps life as General Morrow had never visioned there in his darkest dreams.

The road curved near the swampy grass thicket where, if we both lived, Puran and I might meet. No travelers were in sight as I turned in, and the ten-foot grass instantly concealed me. I pushed through it until the mare began to plunge in the boggy ground, then tied her to a stump. Taking my rifle and bag of rupees—I carried forty rounds of ammunition—I made my way out the far side of the grass thicket into thorn scrub along a watercourse. In a few minutes I had gained a peepul tree almost at the edge of the drill field. With my rifle across my back, I climbed into its densely foliaged top.

The bare ground made conspicuous some small objects scattered about. At one end of the field there was a cluster, giving the effect of a design of red, white, and brown blotches. I could hardly believe they were human bodies, but of course they were. The red ones were sepoys, perhaps loyal members of the garrison killed by mutinous comrades, or, as I hoped, vice versa. Some might have come from nearby posts. The other dead were no doubt rioters and rabble.

Gangs of natives who yesterday had saluted or salaamed to every sahib in sight were rifling the storehouses and depots —going in every door and window out of sight of the guns. Hundreds more ran in and out and around the officers' houses beyond the field. Fully a hundred and fifty were red-coated armed sepoys, too many not to include deserters from this garrison. Their late comrades fired on them from the loopholes, but the range was too long for many hits. The cannons were silent, being shotted and primed for a time of greater need.

Similar scenes on a smaller or greater scale were no doubt being enacted throughout the Ganges Valley. My thoughts ever shunted off this immense fact, speeding back to the immediate moment and event. Had the officers and their families been warned in time? Was General Morrow watching the wreck of a great part of his life's work? Was Vivian in the fort, perhaps firing at bigger game than snipe, or was she dead in the looted bungalow? And where was my bride from the hills?

I did not believe the rioters would lay any extended siege. When the storehouses and bungalows had been stripped and burned, they would move westward in search of easier killing and richer loot. Meanwhile I knew no safer place to wait than this dense treetop. My only fault with it was that the patch of thorn scrub was the nearest and most likely hiding place for fugitives from the station, and the mobs might comb it before they rolled on.

So rushed my thoughts during my first, sharp scanning of the scene. This occupied only a matter of seconds. Only a few seconds later—I had held my perch not one minute by the watch—there was a sudden ragged burst of rifle fire from or near the fort. It was as though the riflemen at the loopholes had discovered an enemy party in some sort of maneuver and had fired en masse. There were no answering shots, and I looked in vain for its target. Indeed the sporadic fire from the mutineers had abruptly ceased.

"The garrison's reloading after the volley," I said in an undertone to myself, in reply to some great anxiety I could not yet explain.

I waited, it seemed confidently, for the quickest reloader to discharge his piece again. The time of silence seemed longer than it really was; yet it ran on, it did not break; second after second it held, until too many seconds had gone by not to indicate some change in the situation. It could be only the commander's order to the men to save their powder. Certainly they were no longer firing at will.

That could not account for the cessation of the return shots. The mutineers were no longer firing at the loopholes, and suddenly I perceived they were all more or less involved in a widening, quickening activity I had not yet grasped. In fact this had been going on ever since the volley, but because it was not very near the fort I had ignored it. Now I saw that its center was the big bungalow at the head of the row —Vivian's home. The crowd there was rapidly thickening. The looting of the storehouses had stopped and the red ants and the white ants and the brown ants were all scurrying in that direction. They came from every part of the field. More and more went in the door and none came out.

Then I could not watch any more, because someone was coming through the scrub behind me.

I had heard it rustle, and then very slowly, good hunter that I was, I turned my head. At once I caught a glimpse of a man's form moving cautiously toward the rim of the field about fifty paces away. Although he would not pass very close to my tree, I felt sure he would discover me. Very carefully I began to unsling my rifle. By its threat I might be able to keep from firing . . .

Then the thinning brushwood gave me a better view and I saw that the newcomer was white. Although he wore no coat, his trousers and boots indicated that he was an officer. At such times the human mind does not wait for revelation— it leaps to probabilities. In one surge of thought I took him for an officer of the garrison, somehow separated from his men and trying to get back. Like me, he had crept into the only cover affording a view of the drill field.

Now he raised his head to peer at the officers' row beyond. Although his face was bloody, I instantly recognized him as Ronald Blain. In the same instant I was sure that his business here concerned General Morrow and Vivian, who had been headed this way when I had last heard of them. But there was a dreadful strain in Ronald's face, and I looked away to gaze again into the field.

There were still no shots. Of the several hundred rioters I had seen at first, about a hundred milled about the door of Colonel Morrow's house, and all the others had disappeared.

I spoke quietly.

"Captain Blain."

His hand shot back to his right thigh. When in the field he wore a pistol there. He arrested the gesture because, I thought, he had recognized a white man's voice. Then, his arms out from his side and his fingers spread, a posture significant of intense distress, he lifted his gaze.

"Who is it?" he gasped.

"Simon Peeltower."

"What's going on at the Morrow house? Can you see?"

"Almost the whole mob's gone inside."

"Oh, my God!"

"What's the matter, Blain?"

He did not answer, only stood staring into the field. With my rifle over my shoulder, I swung down from the tree. He walked rapidly toward me as though to be in striking range of me in case I unslung the gun, but the act appeared instinctive, impelled by a great disorder of mind. I thought he tried to rally.

"Are you sure they've gone inside?" he asked, his voice shaking. "Haven't they given it up for a bad job and moved on?"

"Ronald, I saw them."

"How many?"

"Hundreds."

128

"Then they're lost. The garrison's lost."

"They went in Morrow's house——"

"There's a tunnel leading from the wine cellar to the larder room under the fort. Only a few officers knew it—Vivian, of course, and I suppose Sergeant Gray. The entrance was hidden in an old cistern——"

"Could they get from the larder into the citadel?"

"Yes, when the garrison could no longer hold the stairs. Well, I've got to go too. Give me a boost over the palisade——"

I started to tell him what I knew and save him from throwing his life away on a lost hope. The meaning of the volley was quite plain now—at that very moment the mutineers had burst into the citadel. The reason that the guns were silent now was that there was no one left alive to fire them. Instead of saying all that, I had only to say, "Look!"

Some looters were beginning to stream out of the Morrow house. At once a reverberating roar of triumph rose as the great door of the fort began to open. Out poured the conquerors, shouting and dancing in exultation. When they had gone in, only about one man in five had a rifle. Four out of five carried rifles now, and many more than before wore red coats.

Ronald stared at me with wide eyes. "They're all dead."

I nodded. But before I could ask who "they" were—whether he knew how many had put their trust in the deathtrap—if any I loved were among them—his expression changed and he spoke tensely.

"Where were you when this happened?"

"Steady, Ronald."

He caught his breath and nodded. "Forgive me, Peeltower. You didn't stand with us before, but you're a gentleman——"

"I don't believe being a gentleman has anything to do with it."

"A white man. That's what I meant to say. I was half out of my head, but I'm getting hold again. Look at 'em! Oh, the red-handed, murdering——"

"Let's back up a little, Ronald. We'll need more room to maneuver if they come this way."

He followed me into the heavier brush, from where we could keep a fair watch without so much danger of discovery. I saw the dangerous brilliance in his eyes diminish and knew he was in shape to question.

"Do you know how many there were?"

"All the officers but Phil—Captain Maybank—were killed in the field. Two thirds of the company mutinied at a given signal—shot them down without warning. Phil escaped and led the loyal men into the fort. The artisans and their families were there, but thank God all the memsahibs escaped."

Vivian was a memsahib, but Latah was a hillwoman. In all probability Ronald would not know if she had been with the doomed garrison, but anyway the time had come to ask. I had held back the question too long.

"A Kuki girl named Latah who lives with me came to warn the people. Do you know what became of her?"

He looked startled. "Was that the girl I saw? It must have been. Yes, a Kuki girl came to the Mess just as the attack started. I don't know what became of her, but I'm sure she didn't go into the fort."

"Thank heaven. You said all the memsahibs escaped—of course you included Vivian."

"There are only three station at Diwanpani, and two of 'em were in Calcutta. Phil's wife Mildred was in the Mess when the shooting started, and ran into the garden. I saw her and helped her slip out to join the General and Vivian——"

"Where are they?"

"Hiding out. You see, they were cut off from the fort by the mob. The General has been called back to active duty and I was appointed his aide—I came out from Barrackpore to escort him to Calcutta. He and Vivian and I all got here just too late——"

"Just late enough, you mean."

"No, I mean just too late. I'm not thinking about our luck in not being in the fort. If we had got here a little earlier, we could have stopped the mutiny—no one would have been killed but a few traitors. A runner was here with a confidential chit from Dacca—he'd missed me on the road. It said that traitors were busy at Diwanpani and there might be an outbreak. But there wouldn't have been one if the swines' eyes had lighted on General Morrow! He would have cowed them so quick—" His voice fell away, and his eyes, gazing vaguely off, wheeled swiftly to mine. "Have you seen Sergeant Gray?"

"I've seen no white man but you."

"Then he's gone too, poor devil. I hope he kept his head and fought 'em to the last, but he was excitable——"

"Have you anything like a weapon, in case we have to

130

fight our way out of here?" For I had noticed his empty pistol holster.

"Nothing but my hands. I lost my pistol climbing down a bank. Are you a good shot, Peeltower? If not, I'll take your rifle."

"No, thanks."

"The mob ought to move on shortly. They're robbing the houses now—as soon as they've got all the loot they can carry, they'll set fire to 'em, then probably head for the Assam Valley to raid the lonely plantations. You can be sure they won't make toward Dacca or any military post——"

"Ronald!"

My sharp tone startled him, as my instincts had impelled.

"What is it?"

"Are you making the terrible mistake of thinking this is a local uprising?"

"Oh, there may be other flare-ups. This was a bad show, because the sepoys' discipline had cracked. Poor Phil was not the man to leave in charge—I recommended him and will have to answer for it to the high command. I was deceived by his martinet ways, but I know now they covered up—I'll have to say it—incompetence. The sepoys had nothing to do and began to think they were lords of creation. Some of 'em conspired with the badzats at the bazaars; and the whole post looked like easy pickings. But as soon as we can bring up the rest of the regiment, we'll tie 'em to cannon and blow 'em to kingdom come. Every looter will be hunted down and hanged. Our loyal sepoys won't sheathe their bayonets until the shame's wiped out."

I had let him talk to the end. Maybe it was for his own good. Maybe I thought the medicine would take hold better.

"Delhi has fallen."

"*What?*"

"I said that Delhi has fallen."

"You lie!"

"Don't bother to apologize. We'll both be too busy. The whole Bengal Army is in rebellion."

I was watching his face and I saw his passionate incredulity break before the truth he knew I was telling. Still there was no terror in it. This was one of the strongest men I had ever known. But there was something worse to see than terror. It was that awful soul-shock that comes to men when their long-worshiped and seemingly impregnable idols begin to totter. Ronald had had only one god, I thought, and just now

131

he had found out it had feet of clay.

"Give me your rifle," he said after a terrifying, breathless pause. "I've got to go to General Morrow."

Chapter Eighteen

I told Ronald to wait until I scouted. A quick glance at the field revealed the mobs occupied with looting—big bands sacking the Mess Hall and the dead officers' houses, and small parties rifling the cottages of the half-caste clerks and artisans, who with their families lay butchered in the fort. I did not stay to watch the traffic there, but went as quickly as I could to the exact spot Puran and I had seen the barking deer. Puran was due to be at that exact spot now or very shortly. I did not see him at first, but that did not signify his absence.

"Sahib!" came his low voice.

Then he came out of his ambush in the high grass.

"Have you seen anything of Latah?" I asked.

"No, sahib. But I did not come by the cart road."

"Have you heard of many with guns on the roads east and north?"

"A great many between here and Dacca. Runners have brought word that all the ferries and fords of the Surma River have been captured and are being watched. They will slay all the white people except the General Sahib, also their servants and the half-castes. The General Sahib is to be taken alive."

"What do they want of him?"

"He is to be taken upriver, even to Delhi. He is one of less than a score of great sahibs whom the new Mogul will put in cages for the people's mirth."

I had no trouble believing that. Morrow's fame in Bengal was far greater than his rank: in the native mind he was the archetype of the British officer.

It would be better for me, I thought, if Puran and I stole away, united with Latah, and lay doggo in the hills. I could not do so on account of four of my kind in hiding about the fallen station and others of my kind dead on the field and in the fort. Returning to Ronald, I found him in what a sportsman would call better form. He had recovered from the worst of his shock: obviously he was a man of great resiliency and native optimism. The signs of this were in his face and

132

posture and particularly his bellicose challenge of Puran.

"Who is this man?" he demanded.

"Puran, my servant."

"Was he with you when the killing was going on?"

"I stand responsibility for him."

"Still, you shouldn't have let him see me without my permission. Does he understand any English?"

I shook my head.

"Anyway, be sure that you don't mention my chief's name in front of him, or the ladies. I won't trust any native until he's proven loyal."

"Except for native help, we'll never get back to Calcutta."

As he thought this over, I took note of a white smoke cloud rising from the lower end of the officers' row. Obviously the rioters had begun to set fire to the houses.

"Ronald, can they fire the citadel?" I asked.

"Well, it's stone, but there's woodwork inside——"

"Then they can and they will. How can we scare 'em out? Puran, do you think any of the looters would know you're in my service?"

"No, sahib. We have passed this way together only once."

"Puran, it isn't meet that the dead should be burned when friendless and alone. Can you follow the road to the gate of the drill field and mingle with the throng, and when they bring torches to fire the fort, tell them that there is powder hidden in the walls and surely they would be blown to such small pieces that they can never be gathered up at the burning ghats?"

"Wait a minute, Simon," Ronald broke in in English. "I know how you feel—I feel the same—but the mob can't hurt those people now, no matter what they do. Somebody might recognize your man and start looking for his master. He might be seen leaving this ground."

"How do you know all our people are dead? Some might have hidden—others might have played dead."

Puran had waited patiently for the alien talk to end. Then he spoke with a semblance of his old cheer.

"Sahib, I will tell the badzats that my mother's brother was once a sapper eating the White Queen's salt and he himself had helped hide bombs and devil-dust."

Puran vanished in the grass behind me. He became one of the ant-like figures running about the swarm, and evidently his rumor of hidden petards and mined walls spread fast, for the zeal to set fires suddenly passed away. No other houses were burned, and it seemed to me that the last looters made haste to vacate them. Not long after that the ants paused when they met and appeared to smell one another, as when going back and forth to a dead cockroach. Another rumor was on the wing, I thought, for presently booty-laden gangs streamed through the gate to the west road.

The place cleared with a progressive swiftness. The last-built fires had only begun to die down when no one remained to watch them. The scene was no longer terrifying but had an eerie horror, an effect of the great empty field with its scattered dead and smoking ruins and its last monument, still tall, still with the aspect of a citadel guarding its silent garrison.

Puran walked boldly through a maize field to our hiding place. Ronald spoke first in fluent Hindustani.

"What news do you bring?"

"The people in the fort are all dead."

"We know that already. Did you find out how many sahibs are among them?"

"I heard talk of only one."

Some great emotion blanched and drew Ronald's face.

"They'll pay a thousand to one," he cried. "Was it May-bank Sahib?"

"I heard the badzats speak of him as the Captain Sahib."

"Then there's a possibility that Sergeant Gray is still alive. You were right, Simon. We've got to see for ourselves. He might have found a hiding place."

"Puran, where are the looters going?" I asked.

"Sahib, runners came with word of great riches and much killing to be had at Dacca and in the Delta towns."

"That will complicate our journey to Calcutta," Ronald said thoughtfully in English.

I could not restrain an ironical answer. "I dare say."

"No fear, we'll find a way. Now we'll look at the fort."

He spoke in the manner of command.

We withdrew into the grass, then ventured into the road. Ronald had no horse and could not keep up with Puran and me if we rode ours, still I did not think that was the reason that we too went on foot. We could cut back to them if need be, and we had better leave them concealed for a time of greater need.

"This is rather a risk," Ronald said thoughtfully. "They might have known we'd try to look after the dead, and set a trap for us."

134

I was realizing now a great and growing respect for Ronald. For one whose house had fallen down in treachery and murder, he had borne up wonderfully well.

"What should we do?" I asked.

"I don't know—except to take care. I think we'd better scout the mouth of the passage before we go in the fort."

We went up on the veranda of what had been the big, impressive residence of General Morrow and his daughter Vivian. The boards were slippery because a native had bled to death there. It was a bayonet wound, I thought, and I wondered how and where he had got it in order for Death and him to settle their account at this spot. I wondered if he were loyal or a mutineer. Maybe it made no difference now, since he would not go to the burning ghats in either case. The drawing room, where the least speck of dust had been forbidden, had been looted and then savagely wrecked—the chairs broken to pieces, the rugs desecrated, the lamps smashed, and the pictures slashed. I thought that a "boy" who had once served in the house, perhaps an old retainer, had led the wreckers.

The door to the wine cellar, from which the passage led, opened in a big pantry. At the entrance lay a dead sepoy, likewise bayoneted, and there were three other bodies lying near the head of the stairs. Two were natives, one of them shot in the head and the other knocked in the head by what might have been the barrel of an empty rifle. Between them lay a white man. He had been a powerful man, about twenty-five, who had fought a mighty fight before he died. Since he wore military trousers and boots I thought he must be Sergeant Gray. His coat had been removed, but his shirt made up for it in the way of redness—I could not see a white thread. He had been hacked to death by many swords and knives.

"He was either trying to come out or go in the passage," I said.

"He shouldn't have done that. He should have known those devils would see him and find the way through. That's the way it must have happened."

"Didn't you say you thought he went into the fort with the rest? Through the gate, I mean."

"I didn't know what became of him."

"If he didn't go in with the others, he would have tried to hide out. A trained soldier wouldn't risk being followed into a hidden passage unless ordered to do so or in an extreme emergency. So it stands to reason that he was inside the fort

135

and something happened to make him go out through the tunnel. What could it be?"

"If you're inferring he deserted his comrades, I'll ask you to chuck it. He was a humble fellow but a real soldier. I think he came out on some desperate errand. Maybe he knew General Morrow was in the neighborhood and tried to help him. I'm afraid it was the fatal mistake that lost us the fort, but it wasn't cowardice. I'd bet my life on that."

"How did he happen to run into a band of mutineers in the cellar of the General's house? It's as though they were laying for him——"

"Rubbish. A gang of them were in the cellar, looking for booze. They heard him or saw him, and rushed him and killed him."

We had spoken in low tones. Even so, it seemed in reckless disregard of what we had come for—to take precautions against a trap. The truth was, I had stopped worrying about a trap. It was almost unthinkable that a portion of the mutineers would linger about the scene of their butchering. Even if they did not fear vengeance they would want to take part in the next kill. Also, I had caught a feeling of temporary safety from Puran. I did not smell danger on him or see it reflected in his face. Ronald had apparently arrived at the same conclusion.

We went out of the house and walked boldly to the gaping door of the fort and entered the dim dusk of its ground floor. Its smell was a familiar one to veterans of the Crimea, and there was no sound but the excited buzz of flies. I stopped suddenly.

At the foot of the stairs lay four who must have been among the last to die. Three of them were sepoys without coats or sidearms, and the other was a young white woman whose bloodied hair was once brown. All lay face downward and had been shot in the back, apparently as they tried to flee from the butchery above. I heard myself speak in deep-throated fury.

"I thought you said all the women were saved."

"My God, Simon. I'd forgotten that Sergeant Gray was married. It was only recently——"

"You couldn't have helped her."

We climbed the winding stairs toward the citadel. There were no dead on the landing, indicating that the invaders had come up from the passage in stealth, assembled on the lower floor, and by rushing the stairs took the garrison entirely by surprise.

We went through the iron door at the top of the flight onto a stone floor strewn with dark forms. The nearer were bare-footed natives and two fully dressed sepoys who had no doubt been shot by the garrison; the others lay nearer the walls. The brilliant tropic sunlight through the ports and loops cut through the gloom, weirdly lighting a few of the dead, and appeared to obscure the others. About twenty of the bodies had been stripped naked, and these I took to have been loyal sepoys, their uniforms and arms stolen by the attackers. However, I had to look closely at each one in search of my fellow sahib, Philip Maybank. Dead men look curiously alike. The differentiation of dark skins from a white skin was dulled by the dull shades of death, and all of these skins had been almost completely bathed in blood. All the bodies bore almost countless wounds.

"Do you see the officer sahib?" I asked Puran.

"Here he is, sahib."

There was a bench along one wall for holding emergency tools, fire buckets, and other articles to be needed in a hurry. On this, fully dressed, lay the Captain's body. There was a little blood on the left breast, probably from a bullet wound. The legs were composed, and the right hand grasped the hilt of a sword.

My first thought was that it was some sort of ghastly joke. But when I looked for its point, I could not find it.

"Is it a sign of respect to the officer sahib?" I asked Puran.

"I think not, sahib, but I don't know what it is."

The rest of the bodies were those of houseboys, half-caste clerks and artisans, and, what was so awful to my soul, the latter's families.

For my soul's sake, I moved among them and counted them. Among them were grandparents, young wives, and children. Almost all had been killed by steel—the mutineers not wanting to waste powder. Some had run about, and I found where a little girl with a memsahib ribbon tied in her hair had tried to hide.

"Sahib, the mutineers were mad with hate," Puran told me in a tone of bitter shame.

"What of the rabble from the bazaars? Were they also mad?"

"They caught the madness."

"What is to be done, Puran?"

"God knows. For there is a worse thing than you yet know." He spoke so softly that Ronald, nearer the door, could not hear.

"Tell me quickly."

"It may be only an evil dream. Aye, that is what I think. I dreamed that the passage was betrayed by one with a white face."

Chapter Nineteen

I did not hear what Puran said. Hearing is a process of reception of sound by the brain: these sounds were told to wait in the anteroom until I could give them my attention. For the moment I was bothered by another matter—one not very important according to what are called the realities. I came to a decision and imparted it to Puran.

"All of these here except the Captain Sahib and Gray Memsahib are sons and daughters of Hind, whether of mixed blood or not, and all have Hindu forefathers who went to the burning ghats."

"That be true. The forefathers of some may have been Mussulmen, but before that, long ago, they worshiped Brahm."

"This fort has been stripped of its stores, and its secret surprised. There are none to garrison it for the remainder of the war. After we have seen that there is no breath in any of these bodies and we have removed the sahib and the memsahib who would wish to be put in the ground, we will bring fire and make this place of their death their funeral pyre."

"There is no breath in any of these bodies, as Sahib can see, and it is a fitting thing to give them to the flame."

I told Ronald of the plan. With one blast of gunpowder we could dig a grave large enough for Philip, the Grays, and the officers killed in the field.

"There must be two graves," he said quietly.

"Why two?"

"The officers in one. Sergeant Gray and his wife in the other. You won't understand that, Simon. You're not a soldier. The sergeant would want it that way too."

This was like a drunk man taking off his shoes by habit before he goes to bed. It was a profound habit of thinking emerging through the fog of shock. Ronald's shock was

138

greater than I had perceived.

"You'll have to attend to it, Simon," he went on. "I must join General Morrow and get him back to Calcutta at the first possible moment. That's why I need your rifle."

"I need it too, Ronald."

"May I ask what is your next move?"

"I'm going to look for my hillwoman if I can do so without too much risk. I'd better explain that she's pretty good at looking out for herself. Then I expect to work my way to some military post where I can serve."

By now we had walked out of the fort and Puran was searching for a canister of powder.

"That's the proper thing, Simon," Ronald was saying. "You can make it without great danger if you take your time. But General Morrow and Vivian and I must travel fast. I hope we can be on our way by midnight."

"For the present, you'd better draw back in the grass," I proposed. "You'd be hard to flush there if another gang comes along. Puran and I will join you there as soon as our job's done."

"Thanks, I'll stick it out with you."

"You needn't. We've a plan of retreat if we run into trouble."

Visibly reluctant to seek any safety that I did not share, Ronald withdrew into the grass jungle. Puran reported that the mutineers had stripped the post of powder, but he had found a ready means to bring the white dead to the funeral pyre. This proved to be a team of oxen that had wandered off the road, their Hindu driver hanging headfirst out of the cart. For which side he had died, if either, we did not know; but as hire for the cart Puran would bring his body too to the cleansing flame.

Standing in the sunlight, Puran pronounced Hindi words of farewell. I invoked Allah, which was merely another name of God, and quoted from the Christian burial service, all this with no thought of its being an empty form, since my kind had seen fit to perform it these thousand years. The flames rose swiftly and in a few minutes burst from every loophole and port. Presently they leaped through the roof, higher than the tallest trees.

"Now we can go from this place," I told Puran.

We could not go far for the present. I knew of no safer place to lie doggo than the high grass behind the fort. Ronald too showed no haste to depart—I thought that the light but steady traffic on the road had persuaded him not to try to meet his party until after dark. That would not be long now. The sun was beginning to pitch. Calling to Ronald that we would join him presently, I followed Puran to the horses. When we had watered them and changed their pickets, we paused in the cool shadows of a tree-grown watercourse.

"Puran, your dream of a white face betraying the fort makes no sense," I told him.

"I have forgotten it, sahib."

"It will return and haunt all our days until we bury it. What made you dream it, Puran? It is true that the secret of the passage was a sahib's secret. But perhaps a sweeper in the General's house, going into the old cistern to hide his thievings, came upon the trap door. Little by little he probed the passage and discovered its purpose. One day he heard of a rajah, a guru, or one who seemed a beggar in a bazaar, who would pay much silver for the information."

"It could be so, sahib, but it was not so."

"How do you know?"

"From the talk of the looters as I ran among them. Not one sepoy knew of the passage when they rose and shot their officers. It was found only after the battle had begun."

"That's no indication of treason. Ronald Sahib—Blain Sahib —says it was found by looters in General Morrow's cellar when Sergeant Gray came forth. Is it a lie to hide his own guilt? He is one of the most pukka of all sahibs, and one of the bravest. More than once he has proven to all who fought beside him his willingness to die for the Queen. He and I are enemies. We have coveted the same maiden and stand far apart on many things. But would you have me believe that he would sell the secret of the fort even for his own life?"

"No, sahib. He would die like a sahib."

"What other white face is there to betray its fellows? All the officers but Maybank Sahib were killed on the field. Maybank Sahib was killed when the badzats came into the fort, and so was the wife of Sergeant Gray. Gray died at the tunnel mouth, leaving alive General Morrow, his daughter, and Maybank's wife hiding in the grass. So what truth lies in your dreams?"

"Doubtless it was the prompting of an evil spirit, so brush my words out of your ears."

I wished it were possible. The best I could do was put them by for now.

"Puran, I'm troubled in my mind about where to go," I

told him. "I will tell you of the two roads, one of which is easy and the other hard. After I have made my choice, you may choose to go with me or to go your own way."

"Aye, sahib."

"The easy road is to make toward the hills. We would be hard to catch there as two jungle cocks. We would get word to Toto of our hiding place, and if Latah is alive, soon she will come to us. I have great confidence in her aliveness. She will walk wide of Death's traps and he cannot have her except for what she deems a just price. I think she will stay alive until I meet her again."

"I think so too, sahib."

"From those hills I can take byways and jungle paths to some army post where I may serve with my kind against the foe."

"I could go with you to the plains, then turn back to my village in the Sundarbans."

"The other road is toward Calcutta with the four white people."

"It is truly a rough road, and unless there are rich gains for you, there will be poor scraps for me, not worth the pains."

"These four are my own kind. At the last ditch I must stand by them. It is in my heart that the memsahibs live, and not die by the knives of the badzats. Now while the General and Blain Sahib are excellent soldiers, they are not good stalkers of quarry. While in this chase we would be the quarry instead of the hunters, still our skill would stand us in good stead. They are not practiced at covering their tracks and at lying out; also, because they are such pukka sahibs, they are not skilled at making friends with poor folk along the way. So I think if we join their party the memsahibs' chances of getting to Calcutta alive will be increased."

"What then, sahib?"

"Speak out like a man, Puran."

"If you save the red-haired memsahib from quick death, what will be your reward? Will you have her for your woman for her whole life, for a year, for a month, or even for one night? You say that the Major Sahib is her lover. You used the word *ashiq*—one who enjoys her. Will you share her with him and have her for your own, while he wails about the door? If there is good sport to be had with her, there is good sense in your helping her. But if not, it seems to me a buffalo calf would have more sense."

141

"It does appear so, yet I cannot stand for her to die."

"Then it must be that you too are her lover, with all the pain of love without the gain."

"That is what I fear."

"What will be your gain in helping the General Sahib and your enemy Blain Sahib?" Puran asked as I started back to join Ronald.

"Blain Sahib may sink or swim, but the General Sahib is needed at the council table. More than that, if he is caught and put in a cage for the people to mock, it would be a bad thing for all men everywhere."

Puran spat lightly in the dust.

"At least there would be good hunting along the road, we being the hunted instead of the hunters," he remarked cheerfully. "Truly the sport might be as good as going into the long grass after tigers."

"I think it might be better."

"Then by your leave, I will follow you a little way."

Of none of this was I sure in my own mind. As yet I did not want Puran to guess my most immediate uncertainty—whether we would be able to join Morrow's party. I did not think Ronald intended to invite me. His outward reason, that he did not have the authority, masked his inward reason, that he did not want me along. He had great faith in his own ways of operating, small in mine. He desired the unshared responsibility—the importance, I could well say—of escorting two memsahibs and a lame general through enemy lines to Calcutta. There was nothing wrong with that desire: strong men —I could well say real men—loved responsibility and importance. He looked forward to the dangerous, difficult undertaking. But I was quite sure that he underestimated the danger. Likely General Morrow would do the same. Anyway, I did not know how to reach General Morrow.

"It is true that you and Blain Sahib are enemies," Puran remarked as we hastened through the grass. "And I don't think he will want you sleeping in the same camp with the memsahib you both desire."

"If he knows what I know, it wouldn't worry him. Anyway, he is too great a sahib to think of such things in times of danger."

"Sahib, men will think of such things at the very gate of Gehenna."

The present most outstanding fact in regard to Ronald was his sudden absence. Puran and I discovered it the same second—as though by the feel of the air. The tree where he had perched was now the roost of wild pigeons. There was not the slightest rustle in the grass.

"He did not want us to join his party or to know their hiding place," I said.

Puran looked at the grass and the ground. "I think he stole away as soon as we were out of sight."

"Where shall we pass the night, Puran? Twilight sets in fast."

"Let us go far from here, sahib. There is nothing here now of your people but a stone shell that was the fort, some looted houses, and black bones. There is a taint in the air—let us get out of it."

"That is my wish also."

"I know a place where we may build a small fire, cook a meal, and then lie down in peace, where all that has happened will become as a dream in the night. Lord, I am not a mutineer, nor are you one of the oppressors. I have stood against my kind today and you have taken a dark woman instead of a memsahib. Let us wash our hands of the matter and get on to our horses and ride into the hills. We can get corn from the hillmen's fields and meat of many kinds from the jungle. Only when the storm has blown by will we come down."

"That would be a wonderful thing."

"Then let us go for the horses."

"I think it is a forbidden thing. It comes to me we must ride the storm out, for the only peace to be had is the peace of those yonder in the fort. But we will go for the horses and then look for the road."

The grass was still thick between us and the picket ground when Puran took a quick stride forward, then stopped.

"I do not hear the horses plucking the grass, nor the sound of their tether rope drawn across the stubble," he said.

His eyes were fixed on mine. I nodded as though I had expected it all along. We went on to the empty picket stakes, then I waited while Puran looked for sign.

"They had only started to eat when they were taken," he reported. "The one who took them had followed us into the grass and saw us change their pickets."

"Who was the one?"

"He wore military boots and was a good horseman, to judge from the ease with which he saddled both horses,

143

then rode one off, leading the other. He took hardly a wasted step——"

"There is a piece of paper lying in the grass. I think it was left fastened to the stake but fell off."

Puran handed it to me. The page had been torn from a notebook and bore a pencil note written in a small, clear, precise hand:

Simon Peeltower, Esq.,
Diwanpani, India.
DEAR MR. PEELTOWER:
I have seen the necessity of requisitioning your two horses for her Majesty's Forces in the present emergency. Claim for compensation may be made in due course.

Your obed. svt. etc.
RONALD BLAIN
Major, Morrow's Brigade

"The sahib is a burra [great] sahib," Puran remarked.

"That I don't doubt. But we won't need the horses to get into the hills, for we could walk even to Toto's village before dawn. Also, they would likely neigh when we most need silence."

"But sooner or later we will need swiftness more."

"The hoofprints are plain in the soft ground. We might follow them until light fails."

"I think they will be lost before then on the road."

We followed the tracks with increasing difficulty to a rude causeway crossing one corner of the swamp, hard-packed by buffaloes going back and forth to graze. They would be hard to follow in bright daylight, so I saw no point in Puran's straining his eyes in the now thick dusk.

He was about twenty steps ahead of me when he suddenly ran down the embankment on the other side and disappeared in the grass. Five minutes later I made out his returning shape in the shadows, and then what I thought was a grin on his dark face.

"I have found the horses, sahib. The burra sahib had hidden them for a greater need."

"Why didn't he take them nearer the hiding place of his friends? Do you think there was no other grass jungle between here and there?"

"There are many along this road. I think he intends to turn off this road very soon."

"There is an old cattle path turning off not two hundred paces. It is the way the sahibs take to go snipe-shooting by the jeels left by the floods."

"Does it not pass close to the great jeel that sahibs sought to drain?" Puran asked.

"Aye, but the great jeel is now a swamp abandoned to the wild buffaloes. It may have islands of solid ground where sahibs could lie doggo, but how would they get to them? No man could wade a furlong through the muck without exhaustion."

"Sahib, there are some inches of water above the muck. Morrow Sahib's shikari—Dasa is his name—told me so. This water is alive with crocodiles. Also, there is an island in the middle, no larger than a tennis court, over which the waterfowl pass in great flocks. Morrow Sahib told none of his officers about the island, lest the sport be spoiled, but sometimes he took there great official sahibs who visited Diwanpani and who loved fowling. All this Dasa told me when we came to Diwanpani four years ago and I had boasted to him of our good sport in the Sundarbans."

"No doubt he keeps a flat-bottomed boat hidden not far from the cattle track. Dasa goes with him everywhere, and it would be a natural thing——"

I stopped because I had to make a decision.

"The cattle path would be easy to follow by starlight," Puran remarked.

"Then we will see if we can overtake Blain Sahib. We must go on foot, for it there were a good place to hide horses, he would not have left them here."

Puran nodded and swung into his long tracker stride.

The set of his head was cheerful; he had nothing to do for a while but work his legs. I had to keep on working my head. Ronald had less than an hour's head start, I thought, and we were probably traveling faster in the now solid dark than he had dared travel in the dusk while there was still the quiet traffic of the farms. If the boat was at the island—and General Morrow would not like lying doggo in a cul-de-sac—Ronald would have to signal for it. However, Dasa might have been told to expect him at nightfall and would be waiting on the shore. Ronald was both capable and bold—he had a habit of succeeding in his ventures, one of which was to give Puran and me the slip. In that case, Puran and I would have to retire from the scene. Any further attempt to join the General's party would very likely expose them to danger.

145

Would that not be the easy way out of my dilemma? Instead of unwelcome heroism to four people, some of whom wished to avoid me, I would demonstrate my common sense by hitting for the hills. That was what would happen, I told myself. My mind would soon be at ease as to Vivian, her lover, and her father. No doubt that was what I wanted, and only a die-hard sense of duty, the dread of not doing my part . . .

"Liar!"

I pronounced the word fiercely under my breath. My very expectation of being too late was full proof that I ached to be in time—that was the way my mind worked. My heart thumped with anxiety, but it was not a hero's heart. It was only an unspeakably lonely one.

"Puran, you can set a faster pace."

"Aye, sahib, but there is no need."

"Then we are too late to overtake Blain Sahib?"

"No, sahib. I have just now seen what looked like a firefly on the shore of the great jeel. But it burned too long."

"I wish I knew what to say to him——" The words slipped out in Hindustani.

"Speak boldly, sahib," Puran answered with great dignity. "Do not let him think we need him. For although the world has turned upside down and I fear we have not long to live, there is still a thing to look to, and that is izzat."

Chapter Twenty

Most English boys know the screeching cry of our little barn owl, its like unheard in India as far as I knew. I imitated it the best I could as we approached the jeel and soon received Ronald's reply. Then we made out his tall form.

"Is that you, Simon?" he asked in an undertone.

"Yes. Puran is with me."

"Well, what is it?"

"We've come to help you get Vivian and General Morrow to Calcutta."

At first he did not quite know how to answer. I began to perceive that the special pains he was taking had to do with one of three occupants of a big punt drawing in to shore, in easy hearing in this kind of silence, glasslike in its fragility. At first I had assumed that all were native boatmen. Now I was quite sure that one of them was Vivian.

146

"That's very good of you, Simon," came Ronald's pukka reply. "But if I had felt we needed help, I'd've asked for it."

"You didn't need to ask. You left such an obvious trail when you hid our horses that we became worried about you. The fact that we've followed you here within a few minutes of your arrival indicates your position is not as safe as you presume."

"Then you knew of the General's retreat?"

"I didn't, but Puran guessed it."

"Do you think your coming here has made it any more safe? How do you know you weren't followed?"

"Stop it." It was Vivian's voice, low but sharp. "It's very handsome, but it makes me think I'm having a nightmare." She rose from the thwart and sprang to shore.

"Forgive me, for God's sake," I said. "I doubt if any of us are in our right minds—I know I'm not. Of course you haven't heard——"

"Yes, I have. We heard the guns, and Dasa scouted ahead. Ronald sent him back with Mildred, with word to go to Dad's old stand in the big jeel. Later he sent his own bearer to signal from the shore that the fort had fallen. Ronald, how did they get in? Did the last of the garrison go over to the mutineers?"

"No, the mutineers found the underground passage."

Ronald had tried to speak firmly, but his voice trembled and I liked him the better for it.

"Oh, that's impossible. Nobody knew it but Dad and you and Phil and I."

"Sergeant Gray knew it. We found his body in your house, close to the entrance. He had died fighting, but the mutineers found their way into the fort and slaughtered every one, including Gray's wife."

"Sergeant Gray wouldn't have left her there unless—I can't think of any reason he'd leave her. All I know is, it wasn't to save himself. Could Philip have sent him to try to find and save Mildred? He didn't know you'd found her and hidden her."

"That seems the most likely."

"Don't say anything about it to Mildred. She couldn't stand to think that Phil had risked the safety of the garrison—and lost—to try to help her. She idealized his soldierliness. Her consolation is that he died a hero."

"He did, Vivian. Whatever mistake he made."

"It was quite a mistake—one for the gods to laugh at.

147

Trying to save her, losing his own life and all those in his charge, when she was already saved. Well, what now? I dare say we'd better put out for the island. The boat can carry five."

"There are six of us, but it can carry us easily," I said.

"Ronald's bearer isn't going back with us. Ronald, Dad wants him to scout the fords on the river—he knows the country well—and report tomorrow night. He said it was to be by your consent."

"That goes without saying."

"Well, what about Simon and his shikari? You're in command."

"Simon, if you and Puran are in need of a hiding place, you're welcome to come with us," Ronald told me with great courtesy. "I'll relinquish the horses if you choose to go elsewhere. But I'll have to repeat my opinion that I don't believe you can help General Morrow and the two girls to Calcutta. I believe that the smaller the party, the less the danger."

Vivian started to speak, then thought better of it.

"By your permission, I'll talk to the General about it," I answered.

There were three poles aboard, one in charge of Dasa. Puran took one of the remainder, and I the other; and with the three of us thrusting in turn, the big flat-bottomed punt shot through the water with a singing gurgle. The fresh air rushed against my face and dried its sweat. So heavy was my mind and heart that I could hardly recognize the effect as one of mild pleasure. Perhaps it was only a stronger sense of being alive. This boat could hold seven people without foundering. With the wide jeel on which to maneuver, we could outdodge and outrun a considerable number of cumbersome native dugouts, even if the mutineers could find and assemble them. The retreat itself was one not likely to be suspected by the mutineers.

Then I thought that something more than this had refreshed my spirits, and that jump of my mind brought me straight to Vivian. A good deal of starlight beat up from the dark water and showed me her profile, delicate, beautiful, and strange. There was no use to deny that she was a vivifying force in my life. Her name was Vivian, I mused, no doubt after the Cornish witch who betrayed and enslaved Merlin. Suddenly I discovered that I had been prey to an illusion. It was that I had surrendered Vivian to Ronald. When the stunning effect of today's disaster began to wear off men's

148

brains, many illusions would be found dead. Almost always they are false paths of retreat. When a man's back is to the wall, he comes to scorn them.

I had lost her, but I had not surrendered her, and if the time came round, I would try to get her back.

"You mentioned some horses, Ronald," Vivian said. "I had understood you to say you had lost them."

"I did lose my own. These I mentioned are Simon's horses that I'd requisitioned in the emergency."

Vivian uttered a little laugh. "Forgive me, all of you," she said quickly, "but maybe we'd do better to laugh whenever we can. I started to say, Ronald, you have quite a way about you."

Ronald had no great amount of humor. Perhaps that was his main lack. It might be also one of his main sources of strength. Humor is a deadly enemy of fanaticism, one form of which was Ronald's driving force. He was a fanatically pukka sahib with a fanatical belief in a pukka sahib god.

"Thanks, but I'm so dull-witted that I don't quite see the joke——"

"It's on me. It's on us all who ever dared smile at the pride and glory of British India. You'd requisition the harem of the Nizam of Hyderabad if you felt it your duty. Forgive me for my frivolity. I'm not in my right mind. Ronald, I know perfectly well that, except for you, Dad and Mildred and I would be dead this minute. We'd've never thought of going to the big jeel——"

"You're not safe yet. All of us are far from it. You don't know the worst, Vivian. I didn't either until Simon told me. I don't know how I can bring myself to tell General Morrow. It makes the trouble we're in seem insignificant. The pride and the glory have suffered more than you can dream."

"Do you mean—Delhi?"

"How did you know?"

"In bringing Mildred here, Dasa had to hide her in a thicket while he fraternized with some natives. They turned out to be peaceful cultivators, but they gave him the news from the runners."

"I'm glad I'm spared the telling. The only comfort is, if the other commander had been like your father, it would have never happened. Well, we'll win it all back. Every score will be paid. Believe me, Vivian."

"I do believe you. Now let's not talk about it. Simon, he requisitioned your horses. I didn't know you'd ever be that

149

co-operative. I can't laugh again, but——"

"He requisitioned 'em when I wasn't there. Later we found where he'd hidden them. But I'll turn them over to yours and Mildred's use."

"Won't you need them yourself? I'd think you'd have to get the hill girl out. Dasa said that any native who stayed faithful was to be killed." Vivian stopped and caught her breath. "Oh, great God, if you tell me she's already dead——"

"She's alive as far as I know, and I don't think she needs my help to stay alive."

"Oh, good. And there's the island. There's Dad and Mildred waiting at the landing. We're still alive—if you say we'll win, Ronald, we will. I feel more hopeful."

We drew up to what appeared to be an island of about two acres grown to low sedge. In daylight it would be hardly distinguishable from the numerous brakes of high reeds. Dasa pushed the boat into what appeared a ready-made berth enclosed with rushes. General Morrow, on the higher ground, gazed at me with no ill-mannered suspicion, although I was sure he had not recognized me yet. When he spoke it was in low, calm tones.

"Ronald, I am glad you got through and Vivian found you. You brought someone, I see——"

"I'm Simon Peeltower," I broke in. "I wanted to talk to you, and Ronald and Vivian were kind enough to ferry me over. The boy is my old shikari, Puran from the Sundarbans."

"Why, certainly. At least we can pool information—maybe help one another in many ways. Come with me, please."

He led us up a narrow path, then down a short flight of steps into a round pit, four feet deep and perhaps fifteen feet in diameter. It was obviously dug by men, and I thought it might be the cellar of a vanished Moslem tower. This explanation would not hold after General Morrow had lighted with a friction match a lantern sitting on the floor. The meager glimmer revealed roughly timbered sides, a wooden floor, and four big homemade chairs with backs and arm rests. Baggage was heaped at one side.

"The lantern itself is invisible from the shore," Morrow explained. "What little radiance it throws into the air would be taken for the lights often seen over marshy ground."

"Thank you," I replied.

And now I could explain the excavation. It was a rather elaborate shooting stand for waterfowlers. Comfortably seated, their eyes just above the level of the hedge, the gunners would not be seen by the incoming flocks until in gunshot. In this weather it was a comfortable retreat, but it might not be above suspicion by the mutineers. Many hands had worked at the digging and timbering not many years before.

The weak light showed what might have been a life-sized lady doll that had come to life. Her hair was golden and her eyes were blue and her flesh was almost as bright as porcelain. She looked wildly from Ronald's face to mine, but bit her lip and did not speak.

"Ask them, Mildred, and get it over with," Vivian said, her voice pitched low to conceal its nervous rasp. "You can be sure it's not good news, and it's hard enough to tell bad——"

"I didn't ask them because Phil wouldn't want me to until General Morrow could find out what he needs to know," Mildred replied in her rich voice.

"Tell her, Ronald," General Morrow ordered.

"Mildred, we found him in the fort. He had only one bullet wound. They had laid him in state with his hand on his sword."

The girl drew a sharp breath. "I didn't know the beasts could be that—decent."

"I don't believe they were. I'll tell you what I think. I believe Phil was killed by a bullet coming through a loophole before the fort fell, and the loyal men laid him out. That counts a lot more than any kind of tribute from the enemy. In either case, it showed what they thought of him—what a splendid officer he was."

I saw Mildred lift her head, tears rolling out of her eyes. I had not meant to glance at either Vivian or General Morrow, but my gaze brushed their faces. Morrow looked dumfounded. Something like horror was on Vivian's face.

"I'm not good enough for him," she said. "That's why he was taken from me."

"Don't say that," Vivian cried. "You were a wonderful wife to him—everyone knows that. You've nothing to regret."

"I agree with Vivian, Mildred," General Morrow said. "You've been brave—you must continue to be brave."

In the silence that fell behind his words, Dasa, waiting on tiptoe, spoke cheerfully.

"Din ka khana, sahib?"

"Jaldi, Dasa." Then the General spoke in English. "We

must eat to keep our strength up."

Dasa served us cold chicken, chapatties, and hot tea in dishes from one of the bags. The General supplied brandy and cheroots.

"Is Puran an old retainer?" the General asked me when the brief rite was over. "Please pardon the question."

"Yes, sir, my old shikari, and if I can't trust him——"

"I know what you mean. If we can't trust someone, we'd all better die. Tell him to help Dasa get ready for the night. You take one of the chairs, Ronald, to keep an eye out for any sign of a boat. There may be one or two somewhere about the jeel, and we can't afford to be spied on. Although they couldn't attack us without assembling a fleet of boats, bringing them overland from the river villages, our plans for a quick break for Calcutta would have to be changed."

This last was for my benefit, I thought.

"General, if I may, I'll repeat to Simon your orders in case a native boat does come up," Ronald said. "We're to lie low and let him land. If he doesn't land, we're not to let him escape with word that we're here. Our plan is to set out after him in the skiff. We'll fire the General's buck rifle only as a last resort. Its sharp crack won't carry as far as the report of your heavy express."

"Very well," I answered.

"I'll take one of the chairs, in respect to my older bones," the General went on. "The rest take the others or sit on the floor as you please." And when we were settled, "Simon, I assume that you heard of the uprising and made for the fort and in that way encountered Ronald."

"In general, that's right. A hill girl, Latah, whom I live with, heard of it first and went to warn the garrison."

"Did she, by God!"

"I followed her there, intending to be with the others, but arrived too late."

"I wonder if you've heard anything that we haven't. I'll ask for Ronald's report in a moment."

"I've heard that the mutineers and mobs at Diwanpani are moving toward Dacca anad the Delta towns. Some bands that knew you were coming from the east told Puran that they were going to take you alive."

"For torture?" The General spoke quietly after a brief pause.

"Worse than that. The leaders of the mutiny have ordered that you be brought to Delhi to be caged and exhibited

152

with about twenty other great leaders in British India."

"We'll see about that. Thank you, Simon. Have you anything to add, Ronald?"

"Only this. I think you'll be glad to hear it. The fort had been rifled and would be of no more use to us, so Simon and his man brought in the officers dead on the field and set it on fire. It was the best disposal of the dead we could think of. He did it at some risk and deserves credit for it."

"I thank you, Simon, from the bottom of my heart," Mildred said, not seeing my flushed face and sweating hands.

"Was Sergeant Gray's body brought there too?" Vivian asked.

The question startled me, although I could not think why. "Yes."

"We'll go on," the General said. "Vivian told me that your purpose in coming here is the one I would expect from a sahib—to help her and Mildred—and me too in my official capacity—get to Calcutta."

"I want to go there myself, too," I answered quickly.

"Of course you do—to serve with your own people. But of course you know that when people have to travel by night in utmost stealth there are advantages in keeping the party small. Will you tell me in what way you hoped to help us?"

"I've no reason to think I can be of any special help, but Puran can. He is a good tracker and scout."

"We could use two good outliers. Simon, I remember well the night you brought me rumors of the coming mutiny. Did you hear them from Puran?"

"Some of them."

"You've been alert to the danger—waiting for it to strike. Is it your opinion—based on what you've heard—and seen —and felt—that it's going to be widespread? For instance— do you believe that Delhi has fallen?"

"I see no reason to doubt it, or that the whole Ganges Valley is in revolt." I repeated all the detail that Puran had told me.

"I must say, General Morrow, that I'm not convinced of it yet," Ronald said stoutly. "If it should be true, vengeance will fall so fast——"

"It may be worse than we dare dream. We may meet unimagined difficulty in getting to Calcutta. I wish we could start tonight."

I wished so too. I was thinking of how many natives must

153

know of General Morrow's shooting box in the big jeel.

"Ronald's bearer should return from his mission just after dark tomorrow night. We'll be ready to set out at once. Simon, I accept your proffer with many thanks."

While we had talked, Puran and Dasa had cut and gathered a large quantity of dry rushes. These they heaped on the floor and covered with a tarpaulin, making a rude bed taking half the floor of the pit. I smiled to myself over Morrow's observance of the proprieties—Mildred assigned the place nearest the wall, Vivian next to her, then the General, Ronald fourth in line, and I on the outer flank. It would have satisfied Queen Victoria, I thought.

When we had separated from one another about the island, we three sahibs lay down in a row. Mildred gained her place in a quick modest flutter of white. But Vivian dallied with her arrangements and did not flinch from the dull yellow glimmer of the lantern. My eyes, rolled up, as she knew well, found her hair flowing, her shoulders and feet bare, and her limbs free in a *robe-de-chambre* taken from her bags. She came so close to me that the skirt almost brushed my face. I had a rude impulse to lift it and look up. The lantern behind her revealed the slim, voluptuous moulding of her thighs. She was glad to have me aware of this as she made her addresses to Ronald. She crouched a little behind him and bent down.

"I know you didn't want to miss our good-night kiss, Ronald," she said in low, jubilant tones. "I'm sure I didn't——"

"Darling——"

Her face descended to his. Her luminous hair dropped down like a curtain. Their kiss was long and her wan shoulders grew tense with its ecstacy.

She crept away, and a few seconds later I heard stifled sobs at the end of the row. Mildred was weeping bitterly— Vivian trying to comfort her. Staunch General Morrow made a diversion with some final orders to Dasa, who had the first watch.

"You need not call me, Dasa," Ronald added in his expert Hindustani. "I'll wake up."

"Yes, sahib."

The crying ceased. Ronald yawned and made me a philosophic observation that I hardly expected.

"Strange bedfellows, eh, Simon?"

"Right."

"Well—good night."

154

All my dreams darkened and sorrowful, I slept through Ronald's watch and wakened only when his hand fell lightly on my shoulder.

"You asked me to call you at two. But I'm not in the least tired, if you'd like a wink or two more————"

"I'll get up, thanks."

The watches were only two hours long, and I passed mine in thought. Actually its keeping was not much more than good form—the sky had turned murky, restricting my vision to a stone's throw about the island, and an almost incessant low rumble of thunder, presaging the soon break of the Rains, concealed the soft sounds of the night. Puran had no watch, but on the minute—almost the second—of four o'clock, he rose up beside me.

"*Nohin bagh* [no tiger], sahib?" he asked, his grin barely discernible in the dark.

I lay down and drew an imaginary cool sponge across my brain. It was followed by the first haze of dreams. I was aware of sleeping about an hour through the continuous rising and falling rumble of thunder. Then again there was a hand on my shoulder.

"Will you come with me, sahib?"

I recognized Puran's touch and the low murmur of his voice. There was no appreciable thinning of the darkness, yet I fancied I could see his face more plain than when he had taken the watch. I rose and stood beside him, looking out at nothing but variations of darkness that were the shore of the island and the waters beyond.

"Listen well," Puran whispered.

I did so, then shook my head. "I hear nothing but thunder."

"Wait for a little break between one peal and another."

Again I listened in vain. "What do you hear?"

"A low, steady splashing of waters."

The peals were continuous for a long minute all around the horizon, then as one died out the next was slow to sound.

"I thought I heard it then."

"What could it be, sahib?"

"A great herd of gavial fishing in shallow water?"

"Come to the other side."

I did so, and heard the sound from the opposite direction.

"What do you think it is?" I asked.

"I don't think it is made by many boats being poled through the water."

155

"I'll waken the others."

I had only to say "Wake up, everybody," in a low, urgent tone. Ronald was instantly on his feet and came to me silently and quickly, the effect one of implacable grimness. The white cloth that enfolded Dasa like a cocoon rolled aside and he appeared to shoot straight up. General Morrow instantly threw off sleep but not its lethargy in muscle and bone, and to save him a violent effort I gave him my hand. We five men lined up against the curving wall. I saw Vivian move swiftly behind us and knew she was putting on her clothes. Mildred had slept in most of hers and waited to fasten buttons and buckles before she withdrew her sheet.

"We've been hearing water splashing all around the island," I said. "Can you hear it?"

I thought the peals would never cease.

"I hear it, sahib," Dasa answered.

"What is it?"

The thunder concealed it again, and Dasa had to hold it in his memory, pinning it there with his will, while he listened to its echo-like ghost.

"It was like many wadings blended together."

"Men couldn't wade in that muck," General Morrow said.

"No, sahib."

"Horses would plunge and founder."

"That is true, sahib."

"You're sure it isn't boats paddled by natives?"

"I am sure of it, sahib."

The thunder sank to a low mutter.

"I don't hear it," Ronald said.

"No, sahib. It has stopped."

"We'd better get in the boat. All of us. The light's beginning to clear."

"If this is what I think, it is too late."

Each of us made his first moves toward the common end of flight. As General Morrow picked up his rifle, he asked without loss of time, yet in a tone that did not appear hurried:

"What do you think it is, Dasa?"

Dasa did not answer, for a voice over the water answered for him. It rose from the thinning dark about a hundred paces from us. It spoke in what we called Babu English—the English spoken by educated natives. It was high-pitched and carried well above the thunder.

"General Morrow, you will please stay where you are, oha yess!"

"Who are you? What do you want?"

"I am Commandant of a force serving the Mogul. I have a hundred men, each with rifle and bayonet. We have surrounded the island at approximate-lee ninety yards, standing at intervals of sixty feet, and you would have a deuce of a time, I tell you, getting your boat through, for we would blow her out of the water. If you fire on us we will bake you all over a slow fire. Now we will send an envoy with a white flag to receive your surrender."

The unnatural-seeming sound ceased, and we waited for General Morrow's reply. In between the thunder muttered and rumbled.

"I don't believe you!"

"You do not? You think I am alone, making a great bluff. Sipahis, *chillana!*"

"*Din! Din!*" The cry rose fiercely from a hundred throats ringing the island.

"You believe me now, I bet you," came the Babu's voice.

"Are your followers sepoys? If so, what regiment have they betrayed?"

"Some of us are sepoys from disbanded regiments rearmed and united in glory under me. We are foot soldiers, oha yess, but now you would take us for irregular cavalry! Most irregular, I tell you." And his shrill giggle carried well.

General Morrow turned his face to Ronald and me. It was white, and I thought he was stunned with amazement. But no terror was on it that I could see, and there was none in his low voice.

"Are they in boats? I tell you no horses would wade that mud."

"Look," Vivian answered.

We had been gazing westward. Vivian pointed east. There the sky was paler, and against it stood a row of dark shapes. Rather slowly they took meaning in my brain.

"What are they, Vivian?" the General asked. "I can't make them out."

"Water buffaloes brought from nearby villages. There's a boy on the neck of every one with an armed native behind."

"Then we're caught like rats in a trap."

Chapter Twenty-one

General Morrow turned back to face the leader and, cupping his hands at his mouth to save all the breath he could, called clearly:

"Send your envoy with a white flag. If anyone else comes nearer, we'll shoot him dead. Tell your envoy that if he touches our boat we'll kill him. Give us good terms, or we'll fight you to our last bullet."

"Then you must have ver-rie few bullets," the Babu replied. "We have a hundred rounds each, and every time one of you shows his head, by Jove we will give him the whole volley! But my terms will be generous, no fear!"

"My terms!" Ronald growled. "Listen to the filthy swine! General, as your aide-de-camp——"

"Wait, Major Blain!"

We waited while the envoy's buffalo trudged slowly toward us. The short thick legs moved with a maddening drawl but with irresistible power. Not once did the hoofs clear the water: that was why they had made so little sound. Long before the bull had gained the island, the light had cleared, revealing his hundred fellows, each with a short and a tall rider, a living wall. As the Babu had told us, they were about sixty feet apart. For us to try to break through in the boat was death too plain to question.

The message bearer was a young Jain wearing a blood-stained green military jacket over his dhoti. The master of the big beast was a skinny village boy of about ten, gray with fear.

Touching his forehead with both hands, the Jain handed General Morrow an envelope. I expected it to contain a pompous document written in an elaborate script. But both the handwriting and the text proved to be plain and strong.

In respect to the dim light, General Morrow handed it to his aide to read aloud:

"GENERAL MORROW:

"I will accept only unconditional surrender.

"The slightest resistance will result in the immediate death of all of your party except you. You will be caged and exhibited throughout India.

158

"If the English people with you obey my orders implicitly, they will be treated as prisoners of war until they can be judged by the proper tribunal in Delhi.

"Your surrender will be declared by your party's emergence into the open, dropping your weapons, and raising your arms. If this has not taken place by 6 A.M. we will attack.

"Committee for the Restoration
of Indian Freedom,
Lower Bengal Branch,
"Haran Lal, Chairman"

Ronald's voice broke off, leaving his lips parted and his eyes wide. His face had been flushed a few seconds before. Suddenly it was white.

"That can't be the same man——"

"You mean the writer of this ultimatum can't be that silly ass on the buffalo?" Morrow asked in a firm voice. "I don't doubt it for a moment."

We all knew what he meant. Babus rarely had a good presence in front of sahibs. Nervousness often betrayed them into a grotesque imitation of English mannerisms. But administrators soon learned their great capabilities.

"I didn't mean that, General. This document is signed— Haran Lal."

I too had heard the name before but could not remember . . .

"Our regimental butler? Oh, no. That's a common Bengali name——"

"Dad, it *is* our Haran Lal. I thought his voice was familiar when he first spoke."

I remembered now . . . The regimental khansaman who had stood close to Morrow on the night he had entertained me at Mess. I had thought he understood English. I had been moved by his scholar's face. When the regiment had been sent to Barrackpore he had remained as a kind of caretaker of the all but abandoned Mess House.

"It seems the tables have been turned." General Morrow spoke with a great dignity of despair.

Ronald glanced at his repeater. "Sir, it's my duty to tell you that it's twelve minutes to six o'clock."

"What choice have we but to meet his terms?"

"General Morrow, may I consider that permission to give my opinion?"

"Yes, sir, you may."

"Sir, I think we have another choice, and a better one. I consider surrender no choice at all—natives have already shown us what their promises are worth, and we would be killed by torture without striking one blow for our cause. I request that you lend me your buck rifle. It won't glimmer in this light and I'll take a careful aim at their leader. I can make him out distinctly and I don't think I'll miss. It is at least possible that if he is killed the others will lose heart. If not, we will do what we can to make them lose heart. With Simon's rifle and yours we can fire many rounds before they can gain the island and overwhelm us. My opinion is that they won't like the medicine we'll give them and withdraw. But if they don't, we'll have given a good account of ourselves. There will be that many fewer mutineers to fight our countrymen."

General Morrow passed his hand slowly across his forehead and down his cheek. Vivian looked at her lover and tears welled in her eyes.

"Ronald, I didn't know you were so brave. I can hardly believe that anyone can be so brave."

"It's not bravery, Vivian. Our backs are to the wall."

"Ronald, more than half those men are sepoys," General Morrow said firmly. "They are not going to break because some or many of their number fall. Also, they are good shots. They will hold their fire till one of us stands up to shoot, just as the leader said. You and Simon may survive one volley, but not two—or three—or five. Neither will I or the two shikaris. That would leave the girls alone. They might hardly have time to load last balls for themselves. The offer may be treachery—I fear that it is—but there's a chance that it isn't, and none at all in my opinion, no chance at all that any of us can live, once we have fired the first shot."

Ronald stood stiffly at attention. "Sir, I await your orders."

"This is not wholly a military matter, Ronald. We have no power of life and death over Mildred, Vivian, Simon, or the two natives."

"You have over me, General," Mildred said quickly.

"Mildred, you've heard our opinions. Would you vote to surrender or fight?"

"I'd vote to surrender. While there's life, there's hope."

"Vivian?"

"I know Haran well. I don't think he'll butcher us."

"Simon?"

160

"I saw the dead at Diwanpani, but I think we'd better surrender."

General Morrow turned to the two natives and spoke in vigorous Hindustani.

"Dasa! Puran! The sepoys have sent a note promising to take us alive to Delhi if we yield peacefully, but if we resist, to roast us over slow fire. Which course would be the best?"

"Wait a moment, General," I broke in. "The letter didn't promise any mercy on our native followers. Unless Haran will include them in the promise, I vote to fight."

General Morrow cupped his hands over his lips.

"Haran Lal!" he shouted.

"General Sahib!"

"If we surrender, will you treat our servants as you treat us?"

"They will live as long as their masters."

"Then we surrender in trust of your written word."

Ronald turned his face from us. I thought it might be to hide tears. Haran Lal called an order to his followers, and their burly mounts went into ponderous motion. Their muzzles thrown forward, their long black horns laid back, they took one strong stride after another, each so slow that it seemed the piston stroke of some massive engine. We watched the big ring slowly contract. The boy drivers took joy in keeping abreast of one another. Without waiting for orders, Dasa and Puran began to roll up the bedding and shut the bags.

Vivian, standing between Ronald and me, spoke in low tones.

"Ronald, I think you were right and we'll be butchered."

"Perhaps not."

"I think it was Haran who led the mutineers to the tunnel. He could have discovered it somehow——"

"Was he thick with Sergeant Gray?"

"I don't think that had anything to do with it."

"Gray might have tried to find Mildred and trusted Haran. Anyway, Vivian, don't let Haran know that you suspect him. He's unstable, and it might throw him into a fury."

Certainly Haran was in capital spirits now. Well in advance of the line, he waved and smiled and salaamed as though he were a bringer of good news, and then struck a jaunty attitude as his buffalo hauled out of the water not sixty feet from us.

"Good morning, one and all!" he called jovially. "By Jove,

I make a good target, sticking out like a sore thumb, but we have made a gentleman's agreement, and I will trust you as you have trusted me. My word, Mr. Peeltower, I didn't know you were of our jolly number, but I should have deduced it, oha yess! I caught a glimpse of your handmaiden, the pretty little Latah, only yesterday!"

"Is she all right, Haran Lal?"

"I've no doubt of it. If need be, she could fade into the grass like a jungle hen. Pardon me, General Morrow! To you I owe first my respects! Also the charming memsahibs, and the best officer of his rank in India, Major Blain!"

"Thank you, Haran Lal. But compliments are bitter in defeat."

"Peeltower Sahib, you are something of a scholar. So the officer sahibs said of you after your visit with us four years ago. Do I remind you of a figure in the Hindu pantheon?"

"There is one who always rides a buffalo. Is it Yama?"

"That is damned clever! Yama was the first mortal to taste death, and so was made a god. He is green and red-eyed and four-handed—and I could have told you what that meant if you had sat down with and talked to me while visiting our Mess." Suddenly Haran was speaking gravely, deep sorrow in his face. "If you had—if something like that had happened only two or three times in all my life—I would not be here. I might even have been one of your party. No, I would be among the dead in the fort, perhaps the first to die. Well, it is too late."

He smirked again and gave General Morrow a frivolous salaam.

"Now, sir, will you kind-lee have your party emerge from the box and stand in line? The guns are to be laid gently on the floor. And please take care that neither of them goes off by accident—my men have not had their morning tea and their nerves are on edge . . . Maybank Memsahib, the gentlemen are waiting for you to lead the way. Thank you, oha thank you.

"Morrow Memsahib, you may leave room for one of the gentlemen between you and the young widow. Major Blain, you may have the place. You, Peeltower Sahib, may stand on the other side of the General's daughter. Take the other end of the line, please, General Morrow. Now stand at attention, please. Chests out—you will pardon me, ladies—heels together, arms at sides, and count off, beginning with General Morrow."

162

"I don't appreciate this horseplay to prisoners of war," Morrow said quietly.

"Prisoners of war! It is quite an admission from one of your status, General. Only an hour ago you would have called this whole shooting match no better than foul insurrection!" His voice changed sharply. "Please obey my orders without hesitation."

"One," the General answered without a shadow of feeling in his voice. Mildred called "Two!" With great dignity Ronald spoke in an almost exact imitation of his chief's tone, and Vivian sang out "Four" with great verve. My own "Five" was businesslike. Meanwhile I was thinking hard. I thought it very possible that in the question of surrender Ronald had been right.

"Including the two lackeys, all present and accounted for," Haran remarked. His large brown eyes, handsome and wonderfully expressive, brightened with an idea. He began to speak in Hindustani.

"Dasa! Puran, I believe your name is! I have just now spoken of you two as 'lackeys.' I would not have used the term two days ago. Countless numbers of us Indians served in menial capacities to the English—it was part of the tribute India had to pay to her conquerors. But today *we* are the conquerors. You two have been set free. You need never again fetch and carry—burden your backs with their gear—lick their boots. I tell you, not even a sweeper need ever again empty and clean their privies. It may be you do not know this. Perhaps the change has come too suddenly for you to grasp it. But the time has come for you to make up your minds whether you are men or jackals. Now I will give you the choice."

Both Puran and Dasa stood perfectly silent, and Haran Lal's eyes grew glassy.

"Dasa, you shall decide first. If you wish to be free, prove it by spitting in the faces of all these sahibs. Then you may either join our company on the journey to Delhi or go your way. If you wish to remain a body servant, we will consider your body part of your master's body. Whatever fate is meted out to General Morrow will be meted out to you."

"I am too old a dog to change masters, Haran Lal."

"I told you, you would have no master in the new day just breaking. You would be free."

"I am too old a dog to learn new tricks, Haran Lal."

"But not too old for a dog's death! No, it will not be soon,

163

Dasa. It is in the mind of a great pandit in the north that General Morrow will be among the last, perhaps the very last sahib, to die. Puran, you may make your choice."

"I choose freedom, Haran Lal, if I may signify it in a way that will not shame me."

"What do you mean?"

"I had nothing to do with sahibs until I took service under Peeltower Sahib when he came to my village in the Sundarbans on the way to the tiger grounds. Of all the sahibs, he is the only one who has ever spat upon me, and if I spit in the faces of the other sahibs and the mensahibs, it would not be in fair payment. In his face only do I wish to spit."

"You are a true Indian, Puran, and it shall be as you say."

Puran came and stood in front of me, his dark eyes burning.

"Peeltower Sahib, you will remember when I broke the whiskey bottle in Latah's village and you spat on me."

"Puran, I had but lately lost my money, and I had drunk too much already from that same bottle. Why don't you remember the many favors——"

"Favors, sahib? The gift of an old belt you did not want, or a few pice baksheesh? To you I gave my back and my legs, and it was no mercy of yours that I did not die of fever or in the claws of a tiger."

With that he spat violently in my face. Out of the corner of my eye, I saw one of Lal's men clasp the hilt of his knife. My only movement was to start to raise my hand to wipe away the spittle.

"*Stand at attention!*" Haran Lal shouted.

I obeyed.

"Will you come with us, Puran? We need men like you."

"No, Raissaldar. Let me ride to shore on one of the big bulls and I will go my way."

"Prisoners of war! File right, and quick-step to the boat."

The men on the buffaloes laughed loudly at the sight. One who had dismounted threw out two of the three poles; and as Dasa picked up the third he knocked it out of his hand.

"Haran Lal, we would like to see one of the memsahibs earn her bread," he said.

"Are you a fool? They earn it with *puttha*, not *pasina*." It was a way of saying that they were harlots, and again the men laughed.

"The red one does so truly," someone shouted. "I've seen her steal away to the Major Sahib's bed, and doubtless he

164

gives her three annas. But Lal Pandit, let us not sully the name of the golden one. If all the memsahibs were like May-bank Memsahib——"

"Bah, she's not a woman," another called. "She's a china doll."

"No, but she's not for sale in a bazaar," Haran Lal broke in in a firm voice. "I was at fault for including her in my jest." Then in English, "Maybank Memsahib, I pray your pardon for my slight to your virtue. You were the fitting wife for the great Captain Sahib, and you will be treated as an honorable prisoner of war. If you were not safer in our hands than if you were free, I would set you free."

Tears rolled slowly out of her bright, blue eyes. "If you felt that way about my husband, why did you kill him?"

"I, memsahib?"

"Men like these you lead."

"The fortunes of war, memsahib. Truly I am sorry. Now we will cross the jeel toward the market road. The boat is to keep between two ranks of my followers. Whoever poles the boat——"

"I'll do it," Vivian said. She picked up the pole and stood aft.

"Then shove off."

Although heavily laden, the boat moved lightly before Vivian's quick, skillful thrust. Her hair was luminous in the sunrise light, her face wonderfully alive.

I rose to spell her.

"A few strokes more to show that barnshoot," she told me in a low voice. The latter was bazaar invective, with an obscene connotation.

"All right."

"Simon, I always seem to be present in your darkest moments. I think I may be a Fury sent from hell to you alone. You didn't say anything, but I saw your face."

"Better men than Puran have broken faith."

"I could hardly believe you spat on him once. It isn't like you, you know—you're so damned gentlemanly. I like you better for it."

There was only one thing wrong with that, and I started to tell her so. On second thought, I kept silent. There were too many forces operating here that I did not understand.

What was wrong with it was that Puran had made it up out of whole cloth.

Chapter Twenty-two

A surprise was waiting for us on the bank of the jeel. I knew it by Haran Lal's strangely boyish eagerness as we disembarked and marched to a cluster of buffalo carts under the mango trees. In one of the carts were about a dozen prisoners' irons of antique type.

"You recognize the pretty things, oha yess," he said to General Morrow.

"Quite."

"You have seen these very ones, and no doubt ordered them for some of your sepoys. We got them from the arsenal at Diwanpani. Who do you fancy will wear them now?"

"I know who will wear them now, but who will wear them a year from now? Have you thought of that, Haran Lal?"

"Not you, my friend, I'm sure. You will be in an iron cage drawn by four buffaloes."

He smiled a queerly radiant smile, then quickly sobered and spoke Hindustani in a tone of command.

"Hosain!"

"Lal Pandit!" The response was made by a stalwart young Mohammedan whose handsome *anga* and headdress as well as his countenance indicated a better social station than most of the men.

"Your squad shall have the honor of ironing the prisoners. But you may pass by Guriya Memsahib." Guriya was the Hindi word for doll. "Leave free the left hand and foot of Dasa the slave."

Hosain gave his orders in a very low voice. Six sepoys leveled their rifles on General Morrow, Ronald, and me as the work went forward. The ironers crouched close to the ground, giving their companions plenty of room to shoot if any one of us made the slightest move to resist. While our shackles were being fastened, none of the squad approached Vivian, and instead the idle men waited with what seemed to me growing anticipation and excitement. The eyes of human beings are almost always a prime mark of humanity; but these eyes had a sheen like those of beasts of prey. I was quite sure that Hosain had told his squad not to put irons on the redheaded memsahib because he would attend to the duty himself.

166

"I'm afraid we're going farther and farther into a cul-de-sac," I said in a low voice to General Morrow, the back of my neck prickling horridly.

"What do you mean, Simon? We've surrendered and must bear the shame those devils put on us. But they'll pay for it in the end."

"The time to fight was when we had guns," Roland said.

I had not told them what I meant, but Roland knew well. The irons had been cunningly contrived to cripple. We had become so crippled that we could no longer even die how and when we chose.

But a cold thought coiled and uncoiled in my brain that some of us might be dead in a matter of minutes.

"Lal-Bal"—literally, Red Hair—"I will now put on your anklets and bracelets with my own hands," Hosain said.

When he had shackled on one of the cuffs, he gathered her hand in one of his and held out her arm, pretending to admire the effect.

"A big bangle for such a small wrist," he remarked. The men laughed excitedly, as though this had hidden meanings. "Now the other must match it so you will be fit for the ball . . . A great ball, where all the sahibs will vie with one another to dance with Lal-Bal . . . Oh, yes, my children, that is the custom of the sahib-log. They do not guard their women from lustful eyes and hands; even young wives may whirl about in the arms of their husband's messmates. But if a native gardener attends to his natural needs in sight of the bungalow, he is discharged.

"Now we will see to the leg irons. The band is much too large for this little ankle—if it would bend the slightest, she could get her foot through it . . . But see, my children, it would fit better farther up. It swells out round and fine as a pineapple . . . But have I fastened it securely? It must not fall off and shame Lal-Bal when she goes dancing. Look well, my children."

Hosain drew Vivian's skirt halfway up her thigh. Ronald stiffened like a towering cobra about to strike. A drop of blood left a red track down General Morrow's chin. Mildred had turned paper-white and her eyes and mouth became round. Dasa turned gray and looked away. I knew that he was the wisest of all and I tried to benefit by his wisdom.

Vivian stood straight, with her hair aflame, and said only one word:

"Steady!"

167

"Now for the other band," Hosain went on, his voice trembling. "Why, the shackle is a little rusted. I must look closely at it to fasten it. I cannot work from outside this tent——"

"Stand where you are," she said. "Don't move. Don't do anything."

"I can't," Ronald said in a choked voice.

"Leave it to Dad. Hear me? Both you and Simon. Dad, you must be calm. If you raise your hand we'll all be murdered."

"Haran Lal!" General Morrow's voice was well controlled, as were his hands at his side.

"What is it, my good friend?"

"Hosain Jemadar shames his office. Bid him show more respect to the prisoner."

Jemadar was a military title of honor. Hosain got quickly to his feet, and until I saw his face, I thought the stroke might have told. It was flushed and evil.

"Haran Lal, when have the white men showed respect to our women?" he demanded.

"Now that's to be thought of."

"India is full of half-castes, and how many of their mothers bear their fathers' names? You are a Bengali. How many little virgins of your faith have sat in the water pans with swelling corks to be made fit for the white lechers, gross as donkeys, at ten rupees for the first breach?"

"And after that they cast them by," a sepoy shouted in a high-pitched, shaking voice.

"Oh, yes, the sahibs are too fine to drink after a native or lie where one has lain," Hosain cried in bitter hatred. "But we Indians are not so haughty with our fellow men. We will obey the 'Isai mocking to do good for evil, and not abjure the white bed because Blain Sahib has lain there. Aye, and we will take our turns like brothers while the sahibs look on."

"But we won't look on, Hosain," I said in Urdu, as quietly as I could.

"How can you help yourselves?"

"We will fight with our chains, and you won't be able to subdue us until we are dead. The General Sahib, whom you wish to bring to the Great Pandit in the north, will be the first to die."

"How do you know?"

I stepped closer to him. "I will warrant it."

In the momentary hush, in which a last coin seemed to spin, Mildred gasped and then spoke.

"Haran Lal?"

He turned to her quickly. "Memsahib."

"You are an educated man." She was employing Hindustani so corrupt, actually an Anglo-Indian dialect, that I had to guess at her meaning. "I always thought you were, but it was against the rules for memsahibs to speak familiarly with the Mess House attendants, and I never mentioned it. Educated men must set an example for the ignorant. Especially they must act with self-control. I believe you are a brave man too, although you have been misled. So you must protect Morrow Memsahib even at the cost of your own life."

These sentiments, expressed with bastard grammar and barrack-room pronunciation in a stilted tone, gave the starkly evil scene an aura of nightmare. If I did not know the speaker and were blindfolded, I could believe that this was meant for an obscene parody mouthed by a native jester. Its barely veiled superciliousness, the very essence of stupidly smug memsahibism, would surely infuriate such an intellectual man as Haran Lal. What could he do now but give his men full license to rape and butcher?

He was speaking now. My heart stopped . . .

"Memsahib, we beg your forgiveness for the evil in our hearts." He spoke in English, his voice ringing with sincerity. Then he leaped up on one of the bullock carts and began a fervent address to his men.

"Hosain Jemadar and comrades! Maybank Memsahib —to us she is Doll Memsahib—has saved us from a great evil. It comes to me that she was spared from death in the fort at Diwanpani by the great gods, that we might not shame ourselves before them and all men. It is right that there should be fury in our hearts at those who have wronged us. We will kill them all. Every sahib shall die the death that he deserves, and his women and children shall follow him to the dungheap. But Doll Memsahib is not like the rest. I think she is a very *farishta* in mortal flesh. Although she has not told us so, I think that at times she speaks for a Devi, perhaps one of the very great. On the journey north, we will pay her every honor in our power.

"Not again shall we let the righteous wrath of our spirits turn to evil lust of the flesh. Now we will take the prisoners to their doom."

Watching Haran Lal and Hosain, I had hardly glanced at Vivian. Even now I dared not fix my eyes upon her face and only caught glimpses of its changes. Throughout the crisis

169

she had never succumbed to terror. She had never ceased to be intensely alive, intelligent, and pugnacious. As the immediate danger passed, her gaze stopped for a fraction of a second on mine. In that iota of time I could imagine her eyebrows raising slightly.

Haran Lal began to shout orders. Mildred was escorted to the foremost cart and seated on sacks of fodder. Here she could ride comfortably, ahead of the dust. General Morrow and Roland were hustled into the next cart, to be guarded by a file of riflemen and two riders armed with Gurkha knives. Vivian was put with me in the rearmost cart, and only one shamefaced Jain, apparently unarmed, came aboard to guard us.

While this was going on I lost sight of Puran. When again I searched for him he had disappeared.

Haran Lal, Hosain, and a green-coated Bihari with the stripes of a daffadar mounted horses, and with much shouting led the column. The boys riding the buffaloes headed in a long file toward the village. All of the marching men pushed ahead of our cart without a glance at us: I thought this was something more than a reflection on our importance as prisoners compared with General Morrow and his aide. A good half of the troops were reasonably honest farmers, joining the expedition for adventure and loot, and it seemed likely they were greatly ashamed of themselves. Each had lost face by his tacit acquiescence to a monstrous act. Now they tried to exorcize some of their shame by shaming Vivian. As I had been her open defender, they had left us together, birds of a feather, in their dust.

The badzats from the bazaars were not in the least shamed, only resentful of being thwarted, but they dared not run counter to their more respectable comrades. We might hear from them later, I thought.

We made down dusty wheel tracks over the sun-baked plain in the direction of the river. Except for the driver and one guard, Vivian and I were alone in the jolting cart. I could never remember a greater need to speak or so tied a tongue.

"Thanks," she said at last, almost under her breath.

"I don't doubt that Haran Lal has supplied us an escort who can speak English."

"That's all right. I'll try not to shock the barnshoot. Well, why have you grown so mealymouthed? You want to say something to relieve my terrible humiliation, but you don't know how to start. An English memsahib, barely missing be-

170

ing the victim of general rape. Hadn't I ought to wish that I were dead?"

I felt a great renewal of hope and capacity for joy. "Thank God you don't and never will."

"Perhaps I never will. I'll cling to life like a wounded cat. Anyway, I don't feel in the least humiliated, only wonderstruck at my escape. Lots of women haven't escaped—you can be sure of that. Two lucky chances saved me, one of them the presence of a non-pukka Englishman whose actions they couldn't foresee. I mean you. You'd taken a hill girl and lived with her openly. You'd killed Kharab-Bagh and been expelled from the Ganges Club—the local men knew about it and told the rest. They thought it just possible that you would kill Papa—defeating their main goal—in some kind of protest against their raping me—it seemed just senseless enough, just as aside from the point, for them to believe it. Ronald might have told them he would kill me. I think he might have done it as a last resort. They might have understood that and gone ahead anyhow. Simon, how did you happen to hit on it? Are you really smarter than the rest, or do you follow your nose?"

"I suppose I sensed from the first that it was their only vulnerability. The leaders have convinced all hands that General Morrow's delivery alive is of utmost importance."

"The other piece of luck—incredible luck—was the presence of a model Queen Victoria."

"That's not quite right, you know."

"It's an approximation. At least a simile." Vivian shut up and her eyes for a few seconds looked haunted. "Pardon my frivolity—and be as frivolous as you can, will you?"

"I don't think I can pull it off."

"Well, be thoughtful then—about non-essentials. Play at intellectual curiosity. That and frivolity are both forms of the *danse macabre*—the only screaming civilized people are allowed to do when they're frightened almost to death."

"Stout fella!"

"Let's play we are in England and it happened twenty years ago. All the danger's over—we're just speculating on the pros and cons. I don't think you could have saved me, Simon, by yourself. They wouldn't want to show that much fear of your threat. Remember that nine out of ten of an Oriental's actions are determined—at least influenced—by face."

"Orientals only? How about our actions? Face before the

171

world—face before oneself—rather, the face we like to believe is our own and must live up to at almost any cost."

"All right. Yes, we've gone a degree beyond the Indians and Chinese—we fear we'll lose face if we are caught keeping face. Anyway, you scared them and gave them a moment's pause. And they really didn't want to do it in the first place."

"You couldn't make any Englishman believe that. You said yourself there'll be many cases——"

"They were driven toward doing it by its awfulness—the strange, terrible lure of profitless evil—I don't understand it any better than that. But they longed to get out of it, and when Mildred gave them a maudlin justification, they jumped at it."

"Why didn't you give the—I was going to say devil but I shall say angel—her due? It took courage to say anything, and she meant every word that she said."

"Don't I know it! Simon, of all the people in the world that I'd least rather owe my life to—it *was* my life, and that's no joke—I'd choose you and Mildred. In your case, you know why. I want you to crawl just once, instead of crow. Mildred is everything I'm not. I told you once she was my ideal, but even then I hated her to hell. She's not beautiful and she's not bright, but she can do far more with men than I can. She could take any man away from me except Ronald, and he would stay only as a matter of duty. I can see them at their chaste farewell—kissing each other on the forehead—both of them too noble to hurt me. And to make it worse—I say to make it worse—she's too good to try."

Vivian had been speaking with increasing rapidity, and her eyes had become too bright. Although I had suspected from the first that it was a form of hysterics, only then did I know that she had deliberately given way to it to save herself from some more dangerous form. All the time she had been fighting with high intelligence and a dauntless will to live.

"Could she take me away from you?" I asked, grinning. The half-asleep guard saw the grin, came wide awake, and watched us suspiciously.

"That's too hypothetical. I wouldn't have you in the first place, and couldn't get you if I would. But she couldn't take you away from Latah. I mean all your Latahs, this one and those that come later—if you live. You've gone native past recall. Do you know who I think will take us all, and very soon?"

172

"I know, and I want to take one stroke against it right now, for what good it may do."

The hysterical brilliance of her eyes changed to a trenchant gleam.

"Very well."

"At present we are being flattered by some alert attention. You remember Baron Munchausen?"

"Of course."

"I'm sure of one thing," I said slowly in a lower tone than before. "If your father suffers any more shock he won't live to reach Delhi." I lifted my chain and touched my left breast.

"His heart? I didn't know you knew. He's tried to keep the secret so he could go back into service and die on the battlefield."

"It's *mirgi,* isn't it?" That was the native name for apoplexy.

"It's worse than that. Enough excitement, and his heart will stop like that!" Vivian snapped her fingers.

"If you told Haran Lal, don't you think he'd be careful?"

"Do you think General Morrow would let me beg mercy from his capturer? He's a real pukka sahib."

We were both getting a little flicker of enjoyment out of the grim jest. But neither of us believed it would do much if any good, and this was still the danse macabre for all I knew, and the music was the low, intermittent rattle of our chains.

Chapter Twenty-three

Haran Lal parted company at the river landing with fully half his men, who promised to go overland and rejoin us at the mouth of the Brahmaputra. I guess that they were attracted to the plunder of Dacca. The rest of the force and ourselves were to travel in a fleet of river boats with square sails and auxiliary steam engines turning paddlewheels. These had been confiscated from the John Company and were manned by the original crews. I looked at the men in desperate search of any hope that might lie in them. In reply they gave me a dull, uninterested glance and turned away.

A few years before the John Company had contracted with a Malabar rajah for some thousands of hands to be used in irregular river transport. They were to receive so many annas to live on; after so many years' service they were to return to their native shores with a certain number of rupees. For this they toiled and waited. A sort of headman received Company instructions in Hindustani, gave orders to the boat captains in a Malayan tongue, who in turn, with kicks, blows, and shouts, drove the crews. Since these were low-caste Dravidians who had their own customs and gods, they lived utterly apart from the people of the land; and they never knew or never cared what river ports they touched or the why and wherefore of their endless journey.

Haran Lal had no doubt dealt with an under-foreman in charge of the flotilla, probably bribing him with loot. But although we could expect help from them no more than from the epileptic adjutant storks on the sand reefs, they would not harm us either. They were only barely aware of our existence.

We prisoners were put in the largest of the boats with two armed guards. Since it was built to transport a score or more of enlisted men's wives and children, we were better billeted than we had hoped. With our captors' boats on our bow and stern, the flotilla made down the sluggish waters. We were given food by our guards, and at the end of an unearthly long day we slept. When we wakened we were little dots on a wide flood.

Before the second night we came on a western-flowing river that was one of the maze of waterways of the Padna, the greatest of the Ganges' giant mouths. Thus began a journey that for length and oddity might have equaled those of the prison ships to the penal colonies. As miles went, it seemed much longer than it was. The prevailing winds blew from the southwest, whereby we tacked interminably from bank to bank when we could sail at all. During calms and headwinds our ancient, single-cylinder engine, shipped out from Glasgow, clattered and coughed and wheezed with an unbelievable waste of effort, while the fireman and tenders shrieked at one another, running about as though in terror of an explosion. At full speed ahead, with the smokestack belching smoke and flame, we ran four knots an hour. A good part of every day we lay stranded on mud reefs; since the Company woodyards were usually stripped to feed the busy burning ghats, we tied up while the crews went into the river jungles to cut fuel. At this rate we would not make Allahabad short of a month.

The great fact remained that we were all still alive.

Our food was plain but adequate. Our guards remained respectfully aloof. The boat wallahs ignored us completely, turning away their faces when we looked at them; they ate apart and slept in hedged camps on shore. Most of the mutineers spent the nights on the village landings while we remained on our boat under guard, but we were allowed to lay our mats on the breezy deck. We were forbidden to speak to the villagers, and I could see little sign of disaffection among them. It appeared that they tended their fields and cared for their buffaloes the same as this thousand years.

It was noticeable that we never touched the larger towns and cities; and one of our pastimes was to try to identify them. Ronald's confident explanation of our wide sailing was they were in English hands and Haran Lal feared that we might be rescued. I thought it just as likely that they were infested with mutinous sepoys who could very easily take us in hand for disposal. What that disposal would be was becoming clearer every day.

The great river had always been a highway for both the living and the dead. The latter came down from the ill-fed burning ghats of the innumerable poor, half consumed or sometimes barely charred, but usually the journey was short because of the crocodiles waiting on the mud reefs. In former days the white people journeying up and down took care not to see the horrid, blackened blobs that sometimes bobbed alongside, but after a chance view of one bloated shape that had not been passed through the fire I began to keep watch for them. Unknown to my fellow passengers, I looked at them as closely as I could and kept count of them.

There began to be more burned or scorched slough from the Hindu burning ghats than usual, and as yet I had not confessed the obvious reason. With this addition, there were fully as many remnants of white men, women, and children. Most of these appeared to have been attacked by crocodiles and discarded, but I knew soon that the mutilators too had once been human beings. Above the city of Bhagalpur, about three hundred miles from Calcutta, they became suddenly more numerous. From their appearance, I judged that they might have drifted from Benares or Allahabad on the main river, or perhaps from Lucknow on the Gumti, or from small stations along the Son. There must have been twenty or fifty that passed unseen for every one I saw. Then the numbers thinned again, and I thought that all of these had been butchered by surprise on the day of the uprising, and only

175

those who had found refuge in the last of the great far-scattered forts were still alive.

The reason there were more from the burning ghats than usual was that the crocodiles had gorged to satiety.

But we were given greater proof of mounting danger.

As late in the afternoon we came in sight of the great city of Patna, one of our guards ordered us to lie flat on the floor of the deckhouse. For more than an hour our flotilla hugged the opposite bank, while we prisoners carried on a muttered but largely immaterial conversation.

"I think this is to prevent our rescue by loyal forces from Dinapore," Ronald said. "They've come in to keep order in Patna, and Haran Lal is trying to sneak by. Catch him going to all this trouble to dodge his own gang! I know Babus, and they're not that kind of stuff. They're all weathercocks."

"Did you see the dead people in the river?" I asked.

"I saw two or three. I don't doubt that the mutineers surprised some lonely posts such as Diwanpani, and it may be that Delhi and Meerut have fallen as the runners say. But what about Cawnpore—Umballa—Allahabad? There was at least one battalion of Tommies at Dinapore, and the sepoys were among the best in the Bengal Army. I wish there was some way that we could signal——"

"Ronald, I think you're wrong," Vivian said.

"I'm afraid so, and anyway, we must wait for a better chance and brighter hope," General Morrow added.

"Dad, I don't think it's coming. I think that Ronald was right back there in the pit—when we could have killed a good many and maybe—one chance in ten—scared off the rest. But the little chance that's left still hangs on Haran Lal. I don't think he likes murder but is in love with glory."

"Anyway, we're still alive," Mildred said. "While there's life, there's hope."

I still believed Ronald had been wrong before, and was sure of the danger of leaping from the frying pan into the fire. But that danger could not be much greater than continuing on as Haran Lal's prisoners. Certainly we must seize the first chance that by any reckoning was favorable to our escape.

At sundown we sailed boldly past the old military post of Dinapore. There was not a white face on the John Company docks, the warehouse doors were gaping, and the sentries gone. There was no sound of a sunset gun from the post, and no bands played.

"It's in rebel hands," General Morrow said heavily.

"Sir, it may have been abandoned to the mutineers," Ronald replied, standing at attention in spite of his irons. "The troops have likely been sent where they're needed more, and the civilians to some place of safety."

"What place of safety do you suppose?" Vivian asked. "But thank heaven, Ronald, for your guts."

Night was falling as we started to put in to a village on the next reach of the river above Dinapore. It was a quiet scene, with cattle lowing and cooking fires glimmering, and the only alien note was a bunderboat moored in a creek mouth. I wondered if Haran Lal saw it in the heavy shadows. My question was answered a few seconds later as the lead boat in our flotilla suddenly changed course and continued upriver.

At once there was great activity in the little inlet. At least a score of riflemen in red coats and shakos rushed out of shadows, loosened the mooring lines of the bunderboat, and sprang aboard. While some of the feverish crew rowed her into midstream, others unfurled her lateen sail. Catching the land breeze, she slanted across the river to intercept us.

"I don't see a white face," General Morrow said, peering into the dusk. "Ronald, do you think they're friends or foes?"

"See their black bandoleers! They're from Hotchkiss' Regiment of Native Foot stationed at Dinapore. It's one of the best——"

"They're outnumbered. We'll bide our time."

The bunderboat drew within stone's throw of Haran Lal's budgerow. What appeared to be a subadar-major standing in the bow called across the water:

"Who are you, and what are you doing with sahib-log?"

"I am Haran Lal—known in our book as Failsuf of Bengal—and I am taking important prisoners to our great chief."

"We've never heard of you—anyway, you've brought them far enough, and we'll come alongside and take them off your hands."

There fell a brief pause. Then Haran Lal spoke in a high-pitched voice, not altogether steady, but his meaning was quite plain.

"I am under the orders. We will fire on you rather than disobey."

"You had better sing a different tune, fat Babu from Bengal. We are under orders of Kuav Singh."

177

"Who is he, General Morrow?" Ronald asked in low tones.

"I think he's a Sikh general."

"Then he's surely on our side——"

"Shere Singh wasn't. Wait."

"Then the old lion must be General Morrow," the subadar-major was saying. "I thought I knew his gray mane. You can keep him, Haran Lal, and we'll relieve you of the two young sahibs and their pretty wives."

"Haran Lal," a big voice called from a boat behind us, "give them all but Morrow Sahib and our pretty doll. I am sick of their smell."

"How do we know they have come in with us?" Haran Lal replied. "They may still bite the grease patch and serve the sahibs."

"I think it's possible," Ronald said under his breath.

So far the conversation was in Hindi. Now one of the bunderboat crew began to speak in fluent French, in the hope of one of us knowing the language unknown to our captors. No doubt he had come from Chandernagor, the last remnant of French rule in India.

"Sahibs, we are true to our bread and salt. We have been sent by our sardar to rescue you, and we only pretend to be among the mutineers. Ten boat lengths ahead and one to the left is a big mud reef. Attack your steersmen and run up on it. We can fire on your guards and take you off before the others can swing around, and their bullets will fly wide in the gloom. It is that, or die by torture in Delhi. Quickly! Quickly!"

"Does anyone know what he said?" General Morrow asked in an undertone. "It's some dialect I've never heard."

"Behudgi," I answered quickly—the Hindustani word meaning nonsense.

The light revealed a discoloration of the water where the shoal stretched. Our steersmen and guards were too intent upon newcomers to pay heed to us. In one vision of the dying day I saw all this and then what a more pious man might have believed was a sign from heaven.

At one side the mud reef rose above the water, littered with dark shapes. These had drifted there, and the river, falling rapidly now in bitter end of the drought, had left them there, looking a little like half-grown crocodiles. Instead they had spread a feast that the gorged saurians rejected, and the vultures were either likewise replete or had flown to roost or had not dared light in the silt. They had been cast naked into the river, and the waters had washed their wounds and there could be no doubt of the color of their skins.

The shoal came alongside and began to glide by. The bunderboat that had dropped a little behind the leader and nearer to us began to edge away. The hope, perhaps the chance, for life that I had seen had died in doubt and fear.

"Come any closer, and I'll order a volley," Haran Lal shrieked, sensing his victory.

Fearing a whistling hail, the bunderboat cut back toward shore. The faces of my companions had brightened during the brief adventure; now they dimmed again as we saw nothing ahead of us but the dark river and the hot, black night. Vivian turned her back on me with a suddenness I thought deliberate. Mildred's hands being free, making no jangling sound every time she moved them, she brushed tears from her eyes. The silence grew long, and finally Ronald broke it with his old stoutness.

"I believe they were on our side but were too badly outnumbered to try to help us."

"Suppose we had been sure," Vivian said slowly, still looking away. "Could we have done anything?"

"Nothing except fight with our chains. I think they would have helped us. We could have run the boat on the reef. It would have been a poor chance though, and maybe we'll have a better later on."

"Maybe we won't."

"It won't be long before Lal will be outnumbered. The great concentration of sepoy troops is from Benares to Delhi. If the loyal ones reach us first, we'll have a good chance."

"You're not as hopeful as you were, Ronald," Mildred said.

"No. I dare say I'm not."

"You saw those people on the mud reef. But you mustn't get discouraged in the least. All of us depend on you. The General counts on you—he told me so." Mildred paused, then went on in a strangely beautiful voice, "It didn't just happen that you were with us, Ronald. It was Providence. And the ways of Providence are strange."

I was still overcome with that beauty of tone and its reflection in her face, when Vivian stepped closer to me and murmured in my ear:

"Meet me tonight. I've got to ask you a terrible question."

179

Chapter Twenty-four

The boats made upriver for two hours more, in grave danger of grounding on the mud reefs, then moored beside a village. It was the custom of our two guards to take turns standing night watch, the relieved man in easy call and those off duty sleeping on the shore within one bound of our rail. Tonight the shore guard was doubled, but the watch over us was less strict. The sentinels patrolling the shore gazed up- and down-river. Patently they were afraid we prisoners would be taken from their hands.

It was a curious fact that lately we had slept the sleep of slaves—profound, abandoned, somehow gross. I supposed it was a half-voluntary attempt to escape from the fears and ignominies of our journey. In ten minutes after we had lain down on the deck, I heard from all my companions except Vivian the deep, long-drawn inhalation and the short heavy sighs of dreamless slumber. Chains rattled but rarely in our nights, so little we stirred. I took pains with my chain as I crept to the bow of the boat. A moment later Vivian joined me. The guard looked at us—I made a gesture of wiping away sweat. When I offered him a cheroot, he shook his head but paid us no further attention.

I looked at Vivian with her hair down and thought of other rendezvous we had kept, and so many, potential in our fate, that we had failed.

"Do you know why we're still alive?" Vivian asked.

"That's not your terrible question."

"It will lead up to it, I think. The answer is one man's vanity."

"More often, that's the reason millions of people are dead."

"Yes, from Rameses the Great to Napoleon. That's the big side of it. This is just a little side. Haran Lal hasn't had many feathers in his cap, in spite of being a well-educated and deeply thoughtful man. He planned and organized and carried out the capture of General Morrow, who's more famous throughout India than his official record could account for. I suppose the natives regard him as the sahib archetype. Lal intends to deliver him personally to the pandit—evidently the real leader of the mutiny—or die in the attempt. I think

180

that's literally true. He'd like to deliver us too, a kind of setting for the main prize, but he won't hold out for it. The first good-sized determined party of mutineers that we come across can have us almost for the asking."

"That's all obvious," I said, yawning.

"As Ronald said, there's still a chance that we'll be rescued by the English or faithful sepoys, but we're getting more and more into the hotbed of the mutiny, and I think it very likely we missed our last chance tonight."

"Do you believe for a moment that those sepoys were on our side?"

"Don't take that tone. You believed it for more than a moment. You almost halfway believed it at the time and ever since. Simon, since the first time I heard you talk French —it was when we were shipmates—I've kept mine under cover in your presence. It never has been any good. Dad said it was fol-de-rol to start with and he had forgotten I had ever studied it. But I understood well enough what that French-speaking native said. And I more than half believed him."

"Then why didn't you speak out?"

"I'd like to know myself. I had about ten seconds to do something, but I did nothing. Of course I too was afraid of a trick, but I should have put it to Dad and Ronald instead of trusting to your judgment."

"I think you knew what Ronald would do. He would have let the wish be father to the thought, believed the fellow, and tried to run us on the mud reef. I don't think you trusted my judgment; instead you distrusted his. I think you're still glad you did."

"Maybe it was only woman's instinct to dodge a fight. But the fact remains, Simon, that Ronald's judgment on the whole seems to have been a good deal better than yours. You've done nothing but make mistakes as long as I've known you. One was not to pin down that three thousand quid a year before your mother died. One was to miss the chance you had at the bagnio, and a third was trying to retrieve it as you did at Diwanpani. You took a native woman in the open. That couldn't be considered very sharp. Meanwhile Ronald was taking one sure step after another. He thought that the mutiny at Diwanpani was an isolated instance—caused by Philip's incompetence—but you would have too if you hadn't had news from the north."

"He wasn't at his best when he had you and the General and Mildred hide in the shooting box."

"You've played into my hands, I think. I'll show you why in a minute. We were surrounded, and he wanted us to fight. Whether he was right or wrong, we won't know till we're either sent to safety or to heaven—I'm assuming Mildred can get us all in—but I'll wager we were right. Now I'll say something pretty awful, but I needn't worry about it hurting you— I've stopped all that. The shooting box did not prove a good hiding place, but I don't think his judgment was at fault. I think yours was."

She was speaking slowly and in calm tones, partly to avoid exciting the guard. She sat leaning against the rail, both hands dropped over one thigh, her chain resting on the deck; and the star-limned water showed me the outline of her form and the beautiful shape of her face. The continuous ripple of water had become unnoticed verity of our existence. Suddenly I felt very close to Vivian. I would love her as long as I lived.

"Where did I go wrong?" I asked.

"He didn't want you to come there. In fact he tried to give you the slip. He never doubted your courage and faith, but he distrusted your judgment—and why not?"

"He should, of course."

"And he did doubt—and only too rightly—the faith of your servant Puran."

"The terrible question now becomes plain. You're going to ask me if Puran betrayed the hiding place to the mutineers. I'll tell you he didn't."

"Do you mean to say he wouldn't—or couldn't? He spit in your face. That's the acme of native insult. I say that he would if he could. Did he have any chance to do it?"

"He was out of my sight only long enough to find the horses——" I stopped then, not because of the least doubt of Puran, but because I must play a part. I was not willing for Vivian or any of my companions to know how greatly I trusted Puran, lest he fall short of my highest expectations. I was intensely jealous for his repute far beyond the utmost I could say in his behalf, so I had decided to say nothing.

"Dasa told Papa that Puran knew about the shooting box in the big jeel. Dasa had told him, when as shikaris they had bragged of their masters' kills. Ronald said you sent him to mingle with the mutineers at Diwanpani—they were looking then for Papa and me, and he could have told them a likely place to look for us."

"He could've, but he didn't."

182

"I don't see how you can be so sure."

Looking at her as much as listening to her, suddenly I felt deeply depressed.

"Vivian, you know that Haran Lal had every chance to find out about the shooting box. As the regimental butler, he had talked almost every day with the General's bearers."

"Yes," she murmured.

"And you didn't come here to reprove me for a closed mind."

"No, I came to relieve my own mind, if I could. Of course that's impossible, but I thought I might lay a ghost——"

There was nothing of the willful, self-confident memsahib about her now, and her lightness had all gone. I wondered why I had never surprised this side of her before.

"I'll help you all I can."

"Simon, I tell you again Sergeant Gray didn't betray the fort. I knew him well, and it's unthinkable. We both thought that Phil might have sent him out to look for Mildred, but if so, I don't think he would have been caught at the tunnel mouth. He would have reconnoitered like the good soldier he was. If there were looters in the cellar looking for drink, he would have heard them before they heard him. But this is what might have happened. Among the sepoys or natives that went with Phil into the fort, there was a traitor who intended to wait his chance and open the main door to the mutineers."

"That's quite possible."

"Then Phil lost his head and his nerve and sent this man through the passage to look for Mildred. I think it was Haran Lal, who could easily fool Phil. Too late Sergeant Gray realized the awful risk and ran after him to stop him. But the traitor knew that Gray suspected him and laid in wait for him, with some of the mutineers, at the tunnel mouth. Even a good soldier can fall into an ambush."

"That theory acquits Sergeant Gray of blundering but still indicts Captain Phil Maybank of betrayal of duty."

"It's only a theory, but there's an awful lot to support it. Phil was the poorest officer that ever served at Diwanpani. Because Dad adored Mildred——"

"What?"

"She was the kind of daughter he wanted instead of my kind. He's always been disappointed in me. I don't think he can hardly stand to look at me. He knew that Phil was in-

183

capable of command, but kept behind him for Mildred's sake. Phil did what Dad told him—the only thing Dad could tell him—to be strict. To punish the men for every little breach. Phil couldn't put authority into his voice, he could only bluster. I saw him break and run before a charging buffalo and leave a bearer to be killed. He worshiped Mildred—and that day she was not with him. She was somewhere about the post—her beautiful throat to be cut any second. He didn't think of Martha Gray and all those half-castes and their families in his care."

"That's a pretty grave charge, Vivian."

"It's lighter than some I might make. You wouldn't like to have me accuse Mildred, would you? Yet she knew of the passage—Phil couldn't keep it from her. What was she doing before Ronald found her at the Mess? Did she give the secret away by trying to sneak into our house and go through? Or was she caught by the mutineers—and told them as a price for her life?"

"What a horrid thing to say! You deserve to be——"

"Slapped. Why don't you do it? I'd rake your face with my nails. It would do me good. You too think she's an angel from heaven. Papa does—Ronald does—of course she does herself—and that makes it unanimous except for me. I don't, because I hate her. Maybe it's the other way round—I hate her because I do think so. A woman without a fault except for being dim-witted. Oh, I grant you it was a dirty thing to say. I could as well say it about Ronald——"

"Certainly you can. He was outside the fort. He may have tried to get in——"

"What would have been his purpose? To save his own life? He's risked it again and again in battle—he wanted to fight to the last ditch at the shooting box. One thing he's not is a coward. I'd as soon accuse Dad."

"Why not? Were you with him all the time?"

Her body flexed and I could almost smell her fury.

"That's a very poor joke, Simon," she said in a low, trembling murmur. "From you, of all people——"

"I wasn't joking, I assure you."

"I said, you of all people. You've never raised your hand for India. What faith have you ever kept? When the pinch comes, who keeps faith with you?"

"You've suggested that Phil betrayed the fort, or Mildred. I can just as well suggest General Morrow did it. You say he loved Mildred—better than you. He wanted her, not you, for his daughter. It had come to be an *idée fixe*. She was in desperate danger. He took a desperate chance——"

"Why not you yourself?" Vivian broke in. "I believe you did it."

"I was waiting for you to get to me. I think that was the purpose of the meeting."

"Certainly you're the best suspect. I wouldn't know how you found out about the tunnel——"

"I might have guessed it from something you said once. That the fort had unknown and exciting depths."

"I ought to have had my tongue cut out. You see, I didn't know you so well then. What was your motive, Simon? Had your native woman been captured by the mutineers and that was the price you paid for her life? It was your life too, in a way. She gave you all you had until then—you were a straw man. And you wanted the mutineers to win. You hate all the white people. You pretended you didn't mind being kicked out of the Ganges Club—now was your chance to get back at them. I think you didn't know that only Philip and Martha Gray were in the fort—you thought Dad and I and Ronald were there, and the other officers. The mutineers could make a clean sweep——"

I let her stew in her own juice for a few seconds, meanwhile preparing my reply.

"That's clever, Vivian—in fact it's too clever. It's a common thing for the guilty one to make wild accusations."

"That's cheap, Simon."

"You've become frightened, haven't you? Well, you've given yourself away. I see now what your motive was in betraying the secret to some sahib-hating native. You admit you hate Mildred. The reason is you were madly and desperately in love with Phil. Such a weak man was very appealing to a strong girl like you. He rejected you, and you thought you saw your chance to kill them both. The only price you asked for telling the secret was that Phil not be mutilated—that's why he was laid out in state. Of course you supposed that Mildred too was in the fort, and when you found out the truth you went out of your mind. You're still out of it. I've never seen a crazier woman."

The silence held a good many seconds before I knew its cause. Vivian was weeping and could not wipe her eyes without a betraying rattle of her chains. Suddenly my own eyes stung with compacted tears. I had thought that of all the people left alive, only small, dark Latah with her child's pride

185

could cause such a thing again.

"Simon, we're mad," she told me in an intense murmur. "Both of us have gone mad. No sane person could have said what we said. That awful treachery really happened—Sergeant Gray and Martha and Phil and all those people who kept faith with us, women and children butchered—and yet we turned it into an evil joke. Those were nightmare stories."

"Perhaps that's why we told them," I said.

"What do you mean? We're supposed to be decent human beings——"

"I mean we told those stories in evil jest to keep from telling them soon in crazy earnest. The brain works that way, I think. There's a nightmare behind us and one in front of us. We could very soon begin to distrust one another——"

"You mean we're trying to exorcise devils—to lay ghosts that aren't real. But the ghosts are real and you know it. That treachery was so close to us all that we can smell it on our hands. And it may be creeping up on us again."

"Vivian, why did you have me meet you here?"

"Because I'm so afraid. The thing may strike again. I kept hoping it was Puran. You loved the man, and he spat in your face before all the natives and decamped. Maybe I wanted you punished for getting so thick with natives—that went back to Latah."

"Was that the only reason you chose me for your confessor?"

"Who else was there? I couldn't talk to Dad. He's convinced himself it was Haran Lal. Ronald believes it was Sergeant Gray, in error or terror—he couldn't bring himself to suspect an officer, and I don't want him to. That complete devotion to his religion is his greatest strength. It may be our last hope."

"Why did you have to talk to anyone? I think I know, but I'd like to have it verified."

"Because it's not over with. If Phil did it, or even Sergeant Gray, there were forces behind it that are still alive, still able to work. I believe they're with us on this deadly journey. All of our fates hang on what happened at Diwanpani. Until the atonement is made, we can't hope to escape."

"That's superstition."

"All right, but I feel it in my bones."

I thought upon Vivian in all her aspects—all that was between us either as a bond or a barrier—and I believed what she felt in her bones.

I was feeling something in my flesh and blood that had no business there, but it was too real to deny and I could not pretend even to myself to be surprised. Her chains and mine did not retard it and indeed made it seem more reckless and imperious, for tomorrow we might die. I perceived her beauty here in the almost-blackness of the night more strongly than ever before; I came closer to knowing what beauty was and its pricelessness.

"We'd better go now," she said.

"For any other reason than it's late?"

"The guard's been very patient with us. I suppose he's half asleep. No. I don't want to go. I'm very wide awake."

"I suppose you know what's come over me."

"Was any woman ever unaware of that? A man's voice gives it away immediately. I think I'm a little gratified. That's natural enough. But I'm especially pleased by my own complete lack of response. You might think I would say so anyway, but it ought to be apparent in my voice."

"Quite."

"Women are more monogamistic than men. An astonishing number love only one man all their lives. Most of us take the sickness harder than men do, but the cure—if it comes —is more complete. There's not the slightest echo in my body of our love-making. All it knows and remembers is Ronald's love-making. I feel no guilt over what was between us, you understand—it's just ceased to have any meaning. Men are more inclined to polygamy. Their former passions are like malaria fever in their bones. When the weather's right, they come back."

I did notice something about her voice—an irrepressible blitheness. It evidenced nothing more strange or important than a brief remission of her terror and woe. I wished it could last a while longer. She had baited me staunchly, her eyes glimmering in the dark, but I could not play.

Just then the shapes of three late-traveling natives, all with bundles on their heads and one with a fire pot, appeared on the river path. I heard the word "sahibs" repeated in wonder-struck mutterings.

"Who are you?" our guard called.

"Honest men on the way home to our village after selling some fowls in Dinapore," the man with the fire pot replied. "Who are you to accost us?"

"Pass on, before you wake our captains, who will break your heads."

187

"But are not those sahibs in the bow of the boat?" another asked. "A sahib and a memsahib, wearing irons like felons? It is more common to see them cast up on the mud reefs."

"We have many more, whom we take to Delhi," the guard boasted. "One of them is Morrow Sahib, a great sardar of sepoys, and if you were not dull-witted as your own buffaloes you would have heard of him."

"Think you we haven't? It is well known that he is of the twenty to be borne through India in cages. Your captains will be allowed to pass with him when you come to the bridge of swords."

"What fool's talk is that?"

"See with your own eyes if you don't believe me. Too many of the sahibs have escaped in boats, and the sepoys have seized all the ferries of Allahabad and moored them at a stone's toss from one another clear across the Mother River. Every boat is stopped and searched. Outliers watch the bank for hideaways. Only the General Sahib will be passed. The others will be thrown to the badzats of the bazaars. It is the order of the Great Pandit. It will be lucky for them if they die before they come there, for then death will be certain and of no kind sort."

The guard spat on the deck.

"You don't believe me?" the man persisted. "Then you are a fool. In my own village I am called the Jackal because my ears are so keen. It is their jest that when they hear me bark the tiger is nearby."

The natives walked on and the faint glow of their fire kettle soon disappeared. Lingering still was the thrilling echo of the native's voice. It was a little changed since I had heard it last—I thought by a pebble in his mouth—which might be his way of warning me that the happy secret should be his and mine alone. Much against my heart, I decided against telling Vivian at this time.

Puran could imitate a jackal's bark so well that he could call them, drooling for a feast, from the rubbish heaps.

Chapter Twenty-five

All the next day I took joy in the thought of Puran being near me. Whether he journeyed by land or water was a question that entertained me until I arrived at the more reasonable

188

answer. If he rode a horse up the old river road he could gain enough when our wind was foul to make up the distance he had lost when it was fair, but he could not keep close watch or count on being on hand when we needed him the most. The fact that we could camp on either bank while a horseman could not cross except at the guarded ferries would make him go to great lengths to obtain a boat. He had money for her hire and to pay a small crew: I had put thirty silver rupees of my hoard into his charge at Diwanpani—a number that I had thought upon with a strange haunting when only I still believed he had kept faith. Now I could imagine him around every bend in the river.

What I could hardly bear to contemplate was the task he had set himself. At this point he was still its conceiver and sole executor. We prisoners had no money to bribe with or any more direct weapons—all these had been taken from us —and our strongest limbs were chained. And Time that is a gentleman, according to the Oriental saying, was to us a miser and a thug. With good weather, the boats would make Allahabad in three more days.

True, we had plenty of time to think. The trouble with our thoughts was they either thinned out into daydreams or bumped into a wall of fatal fact. However, every shadow of hope that I had visioned and which my common sense denied, I could now reconsider in the light of Puran's return. That much I did on the following day's journey. Also—to the mirth of an old perverse inner man—I complained of a bellyache.

Our two guards were instantly interested. Apparently it was a touch of nature that made the whole world kin. Assured that it was not cholera, they told me of similar pains, often with dramatic consequences. When at sundown we put into an idyllic-looking village, they offered to get me a *jullab*. This I pretended to take, and so had a good excuse to visit the shore well after dark. The guard who accompanied me was too interested in my symptoms to keep a suspicious watch.

Before long an ugly chuckling sound rose from behind the village. I began to question my guard as to various medical matters. During his discourse no twig cracked or shadow crept, yet I was sure that Puran had drawn within easy hearing.

"Would opium be a good medicine for my sickness?" I asked.

"Opium is good for all sickness, save a binding," the fellow answered in a wistful tone. "At this time of year, a pellet or two is worth its weight in gold. The Rains may start at any hour. Sahib knows how the sudden break in the heat will waken fever. Sahib, have you any in your bag?"

"I had some pellets there, but assuredly they were borrowed by some sick one, for I can't find them."

"More likely some badzat stole them to dream sweet dreams."

"I wish I had them to use the second night after this night, when the tertian fever will come back upon me. But by then we will be close to Allahabad and it will be too late to get any. The best time to get them would be late tomorrow night. By then we will be near the villages that trade with the Gonds. The opium there is good and cheap. But I have no money."

"Nor have I."

"Still, if a peddler comes by, I think you could buy some with a gold pin I will get from one of the memsahibs. Then if you and your comrade Bahadur keep half the pellets as a tax, it will be a secret between you and me."

"It may be some jungle wallah, new from his hills, will trade good opium for a gold pin. But the bazaars are glutted with gold pins, now that all the sahibs' houses have been sacked and most of the memsahibs are dead."

"The best bazaar this side of Allahabad is at Hara Maidan. Do you think we will stop there on the second night after tonight?"

"It is not very likely, sahib. Haran Lal will want to push on to the great city."

"The wells are very good there, our doctors say. To drink of them will drive off the poisons of all the bad water that one has drunk for many days before."

"I did not know that, sahib."

"There is an old John Company warehouse. It used to contain many wonders to attract the attention of visitors. It had fireworks from China such as the country people had never seen. Much can be done with bamboo and tiger-dust." This last was Puran's jocular word for gunpowder.

"Sahib?" The guard's tone was puzzled.

"It can sound like many rifles going off, to divert their attention. Isn't that true, Indra?"

"No doubt, but——"

"The shackles must be loose by then, for which I'll need

190

the opium. You said so yourself, Indra."

"Sahib, have you a fever?"

"My head swims a little—it is nothing. For many reasons, Hara Maidan would be best, if we can get there. We will try anywhere on the south bank, come what may. Would you call that fever, Indra? Have ready a report of cholera if we put in for the night on the north bank."

"Sahib, did you say cholera?" Indra asked, his voice shaking.

"I said I haven't it. By now I would be melted away. Only my head swims a little. I don't want the opium early tomorrow night because it would be used up too soon. I want it just before dawn, when the day's work is about to begin, to be kept for the great night. You understand that, Indra. It is very important."

"Yes, sahib." Indra was not excited at being alone with a man in what seemed in light delirium. He was sure that it was caused by an evil spirit.

"If I hear that jackal again, I will hope to get well on the second night. Let us go back to the boat."

We were hardly aboard when there was a perfect likeness of a jackal barking boldly twice in the distant dark.

After that I was appalled by how little I could do. Alone with the secret in my troubled dreams, at waking I could not decide with whom to share it. It was a rude wakening in another sense: for the first time I was face to face with my distrust of at least three of my companions. I doubted Ronald's ability to follow my leadership in any endeavor—even to approve any plan that he himself had not shaped and would not captain. Vivian was Ronald's woman. If he did not possess her body—and I rubbed its likelihood into my face—he held the greater share of her allegiance. She relied on him far more than on me. If she found out the plot, her first impulse would be to share it with her lover.

I did not want Mildred to know it until the last minute. This was a definite conviction in my mind, stronger than any reason that I could put to its support. It seemed to me that she was too good to be trustworthy. Her obeying one noble impulse at the wrong time or place could easily wreck the venture. I was sure that she would be terrified of any attempt to escape, preferring to trust to the mercies of our captors. As far as she herself was concerned, she was probably on the right track. Who could be wicked enough to break such a beautiful doll?

So all the next day I kept the plan to myself. To only one person did I hint of its existence—this the fall of the cards, it seemed, rather than my choice. I needed a gold trinket of some kind. Instead of to Mildred, I went to Vivian.

"Knocking around in the bottom of my bag—my idea was to take them out to look at now and then, and thank heaven for my narrow escape—are the anklets you sent me," she told me in a spirited mutter. "What do you want of them?"

"I think I may have a chance to buy some opium."

Her eyes widened. "You've gone mad."

"Will you get the anklets and slip them into my pocket before dark?"

"Forgive me a good deal, Simon, and I'll forgive you a good deal. They'll be in your pockets before dark."

I looked at Vivian again. As always, it was as though I looked at her anew. There were graces in her face I had not found before, reflecting the graces of her mind and what could fairly be called her spirit. One of them was a capacity for exquisite passion called carnal, although it was perceived only through the flesh and, like other raptures, was realized in the mind. It was more evident in her face than ever before, and suddenly I was dizzy with desire. We would forgive each other much, but I would never forgive myself for letting her escape me. Not even Latah could make up that loss.

The next day was a muggy one, and the shouts from boat to boat were often high-pitched, and short, fierce quarrels were frequent. That evening brought a violent thunderstorm, its winds damp-feeling on the skin, and a few big, warm waterdrops dimpled the river. When the stars came out, I went and spoke quietly to Indra.

"My head is not dizzy and my fever has gone down," I told him.

"It is so on the second day with the three-day fever. Tomorrow night it will rise again."

"I fear I talked much folly on the bank last night, but I think there was grain mixed with the chaff. Didn't we speak of buying some opium?"

Indra drew a long, yearning breath. "Truly we did."

"What is the name of this village?"

"Sahib, it is Kala Khet."

"Then it was one of the villages that our police sahibs watched for smuggled opium. The Gonds bring it down from their hills, and they would not be as scornful of gold pins as

192

the river dwellers. If a peddler comes by the boat, here is a trinket that may take his eye." I put into Indra's hand one of Vivian's hair-gold anklets bearing little golden bells.

Then there was nothing to do but put myself to sleep. I had learned how long ago, at the cost of a half hour's concentrated drudgery and then a flight of dismal dreams. At four o'clock I came awake. This was the last day of the river journey, I thought; the flotilla would probably make Allahabad before dark, and I could not doubt Puran's warning. That meant that in all probability this was the last day of my life. The project of our rescue was too complicated to be very feasible. I would not like to know the chances of my living on. It was only a fake jackal laughing and sobbing out in the dark, but there were plenty of real jackals waiting in hungry silence along this river of death. Puran, old companion, I am sorry to tell that I'll bet on them, not on you . . .

The sick-to-death moon, a yellow horn far out on almost her last sail, revealed a girlish shape on the river path . . . A young village girl, I thought, likely starting early for a distant market or gathering fuel for the cooking fire, a task she had shirked last night. But I watched her intently. Her movements appeared uncertain and afraid. There was just a chance that Puran had recruited her for a dangerous mission. Perhaps she had spent most of the night in his strong arms.

She made her way to the point of the bank nearest the bow of the boat. Indra squatted there, his cheroot glowing in the misty darkness.

"Will you be gone when the sun comes up?" she asked. Since I had lain as near as possible to Indra's perch, I heard her plain.

"Who are you, and why do you ask?"

"I'm a woman of the Gonds. My husband came down from our hills with our whole harvest of opium to sell. The sahib who was to meet us here did not come and the folk say he is dead. But my husband sold a little to a Marwari trader and gave the silver to a harlot and now lies drunken in her arms. Now I too have taken a little, and if I can sell it for enough to buy my boat fare to Hara Maidan, I'll never look into his swine's face again."

I had heard all this above a throttled heart. I had marked the low, clear tone, meanwhile taking note of the girl's costume as the pale moonlight revealed it to my sharpening eyes. I observed her short, graceful skirt, the tightly bound bosom, the head scarf covering her hair and sweeping down her back, and the copper bracelets on her arms, all of which marked the Rewah Gond women down from their hills. The more clearly I perceived her, the more calm I became. Having heard and seen so much, I could await the rest with undimmed eyes and still-believed ears.

"How many pellets have you?" Indra asked in an excited mutter.

"Twenty I have myself roasted, of the purest *dawa*, without chaff or cheat. My husband will storm to find them gone from our saddlebags—and perhaps that will be not a twentieth part of the loss—but you will be gone up the river, and with the help of my *nat*, I the like."

Indra was not surprised or greatly shocked by her words, unthinkable in a Hindu wife. He knew that the Rewah Gonds traced their families through the distaff, and the girls chose their own husbands and kept or discarded them at will. What he did not know was that *nats* were a Tibeto-Burman instead of a Dravidian concept. It was an idea and word beloved by the Old Kuki.

You made a mistake that time, little hen, but on the whole you have done well.

Chapter Twenty-six

Indra brought out the anklet of gold threads. "It is worth sixty pellets of opium," he told her, "but you may have it for twenty."

"How can I tell its worth in the dark?"

"I will make a little torch. Look quickly and well."

Indra puffed hard on his cheroot until its lighted end was a brightly glowing coal.

"What can I· do with one anklet?" Latah asked. "Can I stand on one leg like a stork? Bring forth the other——"

"I haven't it now."

"We are both going upriver, you in this great ship, and I in a bunderboat. If I trade you my opium for this anklet, will you have its twin when you put into Hara Maidan?"

"Why, it might be so, but what will you give me for it?"

"Some more opium? It may be I'll have enough to bend a back strong as yours." Suddenly there was honey on Latah's tongue. "What else would you ask?"

194

"Oho, you like the little anklets very much?"

"In all truth, I've taken a fancy to them. No maiden of the Rewah Gonds was ever known to wear their like—but I am a chief's daughter! And when we Gond women take a fancy to a thing, we will pay a high price."

"Enough to pay your husband back in his own coin?"

"It could be so. You are younger than he, and perhaps stouter of limb. Here are the pellets, and you may slip the anklet into my breast cloth."

"Wah, but it's a tight fit——"

"Take care that you don't tear the cloth . . . You've had ten times time enough to hide the trinket . . . At Hara Maidan I'll have many hundred pellets, as well as silver to buy food and drink for a guest. It may be I will meet you when the stars come out."

She disappeared in the darkness before dawn.

At once I was beside Indra, holding out my hand. "The jackal waked me in time to see a pretty vixen from the hills," I told him.

"You told me, sahib, that I could keep half——"

"You may—and all that you can win at Hara Maidan." I spoke as one man-of-the-world to another.

"You heard her, then! That is the trouble with these shameless women—they won't guard their voices or hide their faces——"

"You wrong her, Indra. The young Gond women are children of the jungle. When they are taken with a man, they have thought for nothing else. Nor do they dally in their choice—there is a saying in their tongue that 'among the daughters of the Gond, love and lightning strike alike.' One of them is worth a dozen plains' girls when it comes to ardor. But truly I have never known one to show her favor as quickly as this moon of beauty. What did you do to win it?"

"Why, nothing but look into her eyes——"

"All knowing natives and many sahibs would envy you for the joys awaiting you at Hara Maidan!"

"But, sahib, we will not stop there! Haran Lal is in great haste and will drive us all day and half the night to make Allahabad."

"Perhaps you will find some means of delaying the journey for such rich reward. If not—you still will have ten good opium pellets to ward off fever in the Rains."

He counted out the other ten into my palm. I went to the

water bucket and through the motions of taking one of them, then lay down on my mat.

Puran and Latah had played their parts inordinately well —the former a master hunter and my little hill girl a born actress—and in me the danger had brought out what seemed a brilliant cunning. But there was danger of overplaying our game. Also, I remembered the last time that I had prided myself on my subtlety. I thought of it every time I looked at Vivian.

I did not think Indra would take any of the pellets until the day's journey was almost over. Also, I was quite sure that he did not intend to share them with Bahadur, our other guard. It would not help us much tonight to have one sleepy guard and one angry alert one: there was nothing to do but borrow danger from Peter to pay Paul.

In midmorning, while Indra slept and the flotilla sped too fast down the giant river, I let one of the pills roll out on the deck in Bahadur's sight. Seeing my seeming dismay, he retrieved it quickly.

"What dawa is this?" he asked.

"Don't you know good opium when you see it?"

"Where did you get it? Haran Lal will want to know. I'll keep this pellet to show to him."

"Friend, your own friend got them for me, to fight my fever. I gave him half of what a golden trinket bought, and I'll give you half of what remains." I put four more pellets into his palm. Then in a low voice inaudible to my startled companions, "In truth, Indra may have a hundred times this many before midnight."

"Why, at Jansi, where the plague rages, they'd be worth their weight in precious jewels! How may Indra come by such a trove? For your own good, speak truth."

"He cannot, unless the flotilla spends the night in Hara Maidan. The hillwoman who sold him these has fled there with her husband's whole harvest, and Indra has promised to meet her there. I heard them talking just before dawn. Now I have spoken truth—will it save me from his wrath as well as yours? If you would share in the loot, it would be better to feign ignorance of his plan until the moment to act."

"Now that is good cunning, but there is not a chance in ten that we'll tie up tonight at Hara Maidan!"

"I think Indra will try to better the chance. If he proposes a stratagem, such as a broken rudder chain, promising you a handful of opium balls, fall in with it that far. And if you

196

make a great haul, speak for me and my comrades in our hour of trial."

"I'll do what I can. I'll let him gull me with the promise of a handful instead of a bucketful—and help him, if it is in my power, to land at Hara Maidan. And if you can keep a closed mouth——"

His tone and expression revealed no concern on that score. Evidently he expected it to be closed permanently by this time tomorrow.

"My eyes will be closed also," I answered quickly. "I will take my first pellet at sundown, to ward off the fever that strikes in the twilight. Tonight it will strike with ten times its usual force, our doctors tell us, for this is the last night of the old moon, and truly it is rife along the river so soon before the Rains. Another pellet, taken at first dark, will afford me refreshing sleep." \

I turned away, sick to my stomach. The word for me was glib. I would bear it with honor if glibness could win; instead I had talked myself and my friends into a trap of death. Indra and Bahadur were not fools: they would settle with me for the implication. They would compare notes. They would report to Haran Lal. All except Mildred, who had put herself on a pedestal, and General Morrow, who would be put in a cage, would be killed grotesquely . . .

But maybe we were to die at Allahabad on any count and we had nothing to lose. There had been a ring of awful urgency in Puran's warning.

Vivian had had a deck of cards in her bag, now ragged and limp with wear. General Morrow and Ronald began to deal bluff, an American game which we played for enormous imaginary stakes, in the narrow bow of the boat. At the General's commanding glance, I took a hand with them. The guard, ten feet away, watchedly idly.

"I saw the opium, Simon," the General said under his breath, dealing skillfully. "What's afoot?"

"An attempt to escape."

The General laid down the deck and looked at his cards. "All, or just you?"

"All."

"I pass the bet," Ronald said. "When?"

"Tonight."

"A fighting chance?" the General asked. "I'll lay twelve shillings."

"A desperate chance."

197

"I'll raise you, General," Ronald said. "Stealth or force?"

I threw in my cards. "One, and perhaps both."

"I'll call you, Ronald. Outside help?"

"Yes."

Both faces expressed such incredulity that I became alarmed. We played in silence until the guard turned his back and sauntered down the deck out of hearing.

"Who?" Ronald asked tensely.

"My hillwoman, Latah, for one."

Incredulity in his face gave way to an excitement quite intense. I thought it was greater than he wanted us to know, and my mind leaped to the theory that it concerned Vivian. This was a pleasing theory. It gratified my vanity, which I would no doubt retain and pamper until my last breath. When under closer scrutiny it became difficult to believe—that Latah's appearance on the scene could in any way affect Ronald's love affair—I still could conceive of no other. Ronald appeared relieved when the General spoke. It was as though he did not trust his voice.

"Where did she come from, for God's sake?"

"She's had money to ride in boats and has followed us all the way."

"Good for her!"

"Good for you too, Simon," Ronald said with what seemed complete composure. "Such fidelity isn't won for nothing. I mean it."

"I don't doubt you mean it, Ronald."

"What can she do?" Morrow asked. "If she could enlist white people—but that's too much to hope for——"

I could hardly stand the ill-concealed prayer in Morrow's soldier eyes.

"There are no white people, but she's more resourceful than you would expect and has Puran to help her."

"Puran!" Ronald marveled. "You don't mean he's come back! Then he has some scheme of his own. He wants blood money, that's what he wants. I wouldn't trust him——"

"I wouldn't say he's come back. He's never been gone."

"Why, he spit in your face——"

"My hope began right then. Until then I hadn't realized his stature."

"Well, what is the plan? Tell us briefly as you can. Unless it has a substantial chance, I don't think we should try it."

"I can't tell you what it is, because I don't know. Indra and Bahadur both have opium, and I hope they'll start taking it

198

about sundown, in native fashion. I hope we'll spend the night in Hara Maidan—if we do there's a chance of a ruckus to create a diversion. I hope we'll get shed of our irons and can make a clean break for the jungle. But it's all hope rather than likelihood. I can't calculate the chance. My guess would be, instead of substantial, it's pretty frail."

"In that case, we'll be shot for our pains."

"I think it very likely that those who attempt the break will be shot, and maybe it will bring an all-out killing."

"What are your orders, General?" Ronald asked. "I'm under them from first to last."

"I have no orders to give. This is Simon's enterprise. He's planned it and worked it out with his two staunch allies, and he's in full command. Simon, when the time comes, tell me what to do. I'll do it if I can. Whether it hits or misses, I thank God for the chance. Because I know—and you too know it, Ronald—we have no other."

I nodded to him in lieu of a deep bow. His eyes glimmered.

"Then, General, you believe what Vivian heard from the native with the fire pot?"

"In case it would affect your answer, General," I broke in, "the native with the fire pot was Puran."

"Were you with Vivian that night?" Ronald asked in an easy voice. This was a curious interlude, I thought.

"Yes."

"To answer your question, Simon, it doesn't affect my answer in the least. Yes, it does—now I know it was Puran, I believe it more firmly than before. I am sure now it was not merely native rumor. Unless your plan succeeds, none of us—with the possible exception of Mildred—will be alive at this time tomorrow."

"I believe it too," Ronald told me after a slight pause, his face white. "I've tried to shut my eyes, but I'll chuck that."

"Thanks."

"The General said you were in command. That amounts to an order with me. Sir, I report to you for duty."

Chapter Twenty-seven

Indra woke in midafternoon and Bahadur engaged him in a long, earnest, and occasionally heated conversation. Their manner at the end indicated an amicable agreement of which each believed he had got the better.

By six o'clock the eyes of both were shining with the first excitement induced by opium. I was sure that they would keep on until the sweet dreams woke and at last died in almost death-deep sleep; but our own hope of escape from death lay in the timing. Although neither was an addict, highly resistant to the drug, there could be a great difference in their capacities. I could reasonably expect them to be increasingly light-hearted, high-pitched, and bold to the point of recklessness—an effect of an illusion of grandeur—until well after dark. By the same token, they might become so satisfied with themselves and their rose-colored world that they would not bother to try to make for Hara Maidan.

Hoping that one stitch would save nine, I made an opportunity to put the remaining anklet into Indra's hands.

"Give this to the Gond woman and bring me a twentieth part of her gift to you."

"I know not what gifts will be given and received, but I think these little bells will ring tonight," he answered knowingly.

The town of Hara Maidan could not be more than half an hour's sail in the present local breeze; Allahabad lay about ten crow-flight miles beyond. That half hour stretched mercilessly long. General Morrow, Vivian, and Ronald played cards without hardly a glance in my direction. Mildred made a five-shilling picture on the forward deck, her bright hair prettily wind-blown. Bahadur whittled on a piece of rotten driftwood, then gave Indra what appeared to be a peg about finger length and breadth; a moment or two later the latter disappeared below. He was gone about ten minutes. Meanwhile the twilight set in fast. Buffaloes trudged in single file from their wallows to the village byres. If this was the last daylight I would ever see, it was a measly ration. I would take with me into eternity a final, dismal scene of gray water and gray sky.

The roofs of Hara Maidan rose around a bend. It was a dank, fever-ridden hole from which young Company collectors had prayed to be delivered; and their prayer had come true in a way they never dreamed. Perhaps Indra had prayed to his gods that the flotilla would put in here tonight, but he had raised no hand himself, I thought, and now the first warm daze of the drug would drown his disappointment . . . You stupid fool, didn't you know that opium is an

200

aphrodisiac to women and a lust-quencher to men? I had known it, but had let it slide . . .

The sick flow of my thoughts checked, and I no longer taste bitter slime . . . I was watching the steersman. He wiggled the wheel, staring at it as though it were bewitched; with a perplexed expression he gazed overside. Presently he called a name. One of his wooden-faced crew replied. He spoke in their Malayalam gobble, and the man took his place at the helm. Every step faster than the last, he went down the ladder to the cabin.

At once rose up his high-pitched yell. The boatmen gaped, and before they could recover from their initial shock, he had bounced out of the hatch and was striking them right and left with a wooden cleat, meanwhile shouting full-blast. One of the less stupid rushed to the pump. Others tumbled down the hatch with frantic cries. The helmsman sped wildly to the stern, shoved his alternate off the stool, and turned the helm hard over. The boat limped toward shore.

"Haran Lal!" Indra bawled through his cupped hands.

"Ten thousand devils!" Lal shrieked.

"A plank's sprung from a rotten peg, and we're taking water."

"Fools, man the sweeps! She'll founder in a minute more! Row for your badzat lives."

It could well be that in his fine, large, devil-may-care humor Indra had clawed a plank too far from a rib and we would be scuttled in deep water. If so, this would be my most distinguished failure, I thought with acrid mirth—the gorged crocodiles spurning the swimmers, Mildred surely rescued by several heroic mutineers, while Vivian, the General, Ronald, and I sank like stones. The river brim was edging perceptibly up our sides. The frantic efforts of the crew rocked the boat and agitated the waters, but apparently left the glooming shore as distant as ever.

This was an optical illusion. Suddenly we were in the stone's toss of some startled washerwomen on the dry edge of the bed, and the next lurch of the boat grounded our bow on a sand bar. The current slowly wheeled our stern until it too was fast. We were in easy wading distance of the shingle, and there was one thing that I knew well. Our attempt to escape would surely be made tonight, come what may. I could see it signed and sealed in my companions' faces.

There ensued the inevitable confusion. Amid general shouting, our water-soaked baggage was fished out of the

201

cabin's hip-deep flood and heaved on deck. The rest of the flotilla gathered about us, and several mutineers, either more officious or more curious than their comrades, waded or jumped aboard. Two boats collided, one of them narrowly escaping being overturned. Haran Lal stood on the bow of what we called his flagship, shrieking commands.

While this was going on, Indra and Bahadur remained wonderfully composed, carrying out Lal's orders with efficiency and aplomb. Happily, the deepening dusk dimmed their shining eyes. Once when Indra passed close to me he gave me a sly dig in the ribs with his elbow. Away on the gloomy shore a jackal barked . . .

Haran Lal was soon persuaded that there was no possibility of beaching the boat and repairing the leak in her bottom before daylight. His boat and the others went in search of the nearest mooring waters adjunct to the shore. To my sharp disappointment, they did not have to go far, and one of the flotilla lay just across the sand reef, not more than twenty paces from us. Our further preparations for flight must be made in deep silence.

Guards were posted and most of the mutineers went to shore for their evening meal. The greater number of these preferred to sleep there, and their stick fires flared in the dark when the cooking was all done. The camp noises died away. We prisoners lay down on the deck, and our two guards, squatting in the bow, babbled softly and continuously. They were quite happy now, darlings of Kismet, and caring less and less whether the Gond woman kept the appointment. I thought they were already forgetting the object of their great coup. Still there was no telling when they would go to sleep.

I kept a close, patient, and largely confident watch overside. The moon had long set and big stars blazed in the deep purple tropic sky and the coppersmith birds in the trees had stopped their ding-dong when I saw a swirl of water by our stern. A dark head appeared and then a sinuous form swung over the rail to the deck. For a second or two I thought that Latah was naked. As she passed in reach of my hand I saw that her sopping-wet skirt and waist cloth clung to her skin, revealing every lovely moulding of her form. Without a glance at me, she crept along the rail toward her prey.

Indra saw her first and gave out a muttered "Wah!" Latah's arm moved and I thought she touched her lips. Both guards rose and hurried toward her. By moving back a few steps, as though seeking deeper shadow, she led them within a few feet of me.

"Have you brought the anklet?" she asked Indra in a very low but somehow sprightly undertone.

"Yes, Evening Star——"

"Then let me hide on your boat until a fat *bannia,* who covets my opium, goes his way. He swears it is stolen—and may his old bones ache for the great lie! I have plenty for you, Indra—all your heart desires. There will be a good share for your friend if he will keep our secrets. And in earnest of the sum——"

She handed to each of them what I did not doubt were pellets of opium.

"Lie down there among the sahibs and memsahibs," Indra answered. "When you think the coast is clear, come to me."

The two guards returned to their squatting places. Indra began to boast in a low, excited singsong of his powers over women, but was quickly silenced by an angry complaint from the nearest boat. Three of my companions—Vivian, Ronald, and General Morrow—lay and breathed as though they were asleep; I knew that they were waiting in extreme tension for the next stroke. The stray inkling came to me that Mildred alone was prey to great terror. If so, it was because she alone had much to lose by the venture. She had pawned more than the rest of us—a good hope of being spared and even deified by our enemies—and perhaps God would be angry with his pretty doll for seeming ingratitude . . .

The two guards fell silent. I thought that they were enjoying the first warm, pleasant waves of their newly swallowed pellets. Latah had begun to creep toward the stern of the boat. Her movements, faintly perceptible against the white rail, indicated that she was recovering something she had left hanging overside on a cord. The slightest knocking sound became magnified in my straining ears; then she crawled to my side with two tools in her hand. These were spanners, of course: I had never doubted that Puran would provide them for the attempted break and had only wondered how and when they would appear.

"Give one of them to Dasa," I whispered. "He has cuffs only on his right wrist and ankle and can remove them himself."

Latah hated even a moment's delay in unshackling my irons, but her love for me drove her to obey. She returned in a moment and began the terrifying task. It would terrify the stoutest adventurer, I knew—to loosen the hard-tightened

203

shackles in patient, perfect stealth; and what if even one of the boltheads had jammed? Her hand against my flesh felt cold but did not appear to tremble.

She began with my right hand. Mine and hers were soon drenched with sweat. She drew long breaths, and when a Herculean tug on the spanner loosened the nut, she gave an all but inaudible grunt. After two more wrenches, her fingers flew. Now the nut came off, the bolt lifted readily from the link. With my left hand I opened the broad iron cuff and my right hand came free.

A monkey, trapped for the jugglers' shows, can be held fast by any one of his four small hands. The mighty elephant may become a slave by a chain made fast around one of his mighty feet. Man is like both in having four members—I had never thought of that before and thought of it now in the attempt to think of anything that would ease in the least the fixation of my whole being on Latah's task. It was a concentration of my whole life that became exquisite torture. Not even my left hand was free yet, and my right and left foot remained in adamant iron.

I tried to remember that I had nothing to lose, everything to gain . . . Liar, you can lose your life in the next second, and what other treasures have you, and one hour of life is worth an eternity of death. I had half despised myself, but now a violent self-love was turning me into a coward. The pit of my soul into which I gazed swarmed with monsters. I could see them plain at last, it seemed, but I would embrace them all for mere breath.

My left hand was free. The cuff lay beside the one from my right hand, but the chains ran to my ankle rings and any sudden movement would make them jerk and rattle. I moved my feet an inch at a time into Latah's reach. Meanwhile Indra got his heels from under him and his back against the rail, but he still made boastful replies to Bahadur's remarks, and these, although somewhat muddled, were still vigorous . . . A flock of night herons winging upriver started to light on our masthead, then rent the night with their raucous cries . . . Bahadur moved as though to rise, paused, and eased his limbs.

"Wah, but my mouth is dry," he declared to all in hearing.

With her heavy iron spanner and then her light fingers Latah removed the screw cap from the bolt of my right ankle band, but the bolt itself would not come out. She worked with it in vain. In trying to force it, she dropped the chain, and it rattled with ferocious loudness on the boards. I was watching Latah's head in the dark. It did not raise—her eyes did not seek my face to ask forgiveness for the fumble—she paid no attention to it. Instead she tapped the bolt with the spanner head, harder and harder taps making louder and louder noise, until it fell out of the shackle and my right foot was free.

The like, it seemed, was my soul. It was no longer shackled to self-love. Of the lives of all of us here, including the life of my spoiled darling, myself, I cared the most for Latah's. Above all of us, I wanted her to live. She became the world, not as an adornment but as an inmate, better than anyone here. I thought that she came nearer to fulfilling God's design. Taking love in its greatest meaning and dimension as far as my mind could grasp and inspiration reveal, I loved her the most.

The bolthead of the last shackle would not give to Latah's strength. I thought to take the spanner from her hand and apply my bigger muscles, but I stood by for her to try once more. Grunting, she tugged her utmost, and the nut loosened. Then I waited in an ecstacy of vision, only my eyes half blinded with tears, for her to finish her task.

My limbs were wonderfully light as I crept back into the deeper dark to help my companions. With mounting hope and hard-to-believe joy I found Ronald almost free. Surely after removing his own less-crippling irons, Dasa had gone first to his master, General Morrow. Just as surely, the old soldier had ordered him to free the younger, more active man. Ronald had had precedence over Vivian at this affair according to General Morrow's moral code, bound up with his religion—more than that, in the ascetic and celibate deeps of his mind. At the worst and last, Ronald could put up a better fight.

At his master's command, Dasa began to liberate Vivian. Ronald crouched beside him, removing the bolt caps with his strong fingers after their loosening by the spanner. I knew that Ronald too was in great distress over making General Morrow wait: the conflict of his loyalties was inevitably dire. They were not love versus duty. It came to my flying mind that, if these two are real, they cannot be opposed. Instead they were one passion of his heart counteracting another. I realized his joy when Latah and I came to his chief's help.

"If the alarm's raised before you can free me, shove me into deep water," General Morrow whispered.

205

"I'm not the man for it," I replied. Perhaps Ronald was!

"Believe me, Simon, I mustn't remain in their power. The cage thing must not occur—the blow to English honor would be too great. I'll find my own way into deep water, but don't pull me out."

"I agree to that."

Suddenly there was a newcomer in our midst. He had slid through the shallows and wormed over the rail, and his presence enhanced the strength of us all. He crouched beside me. I could make out a glimmer at his side that was no doubt a knife, and now and then what seemed surface lights on his eyes.

"Sahib, the firecrackers I have made will go off in the fourth part of an hour," Puran murmured. "We must be in the water by then, below Haran Lal's camps, and close to the shore. I think all those on the shore and any of his men sleeping on the boats will run toward the sound. I don't think there is any danger of Indra and Bahadur being wakened by it. I crept along the bow and listened to them breathe. It was the slow, heavy breathings of opium dreams."

"Tell the others, and when all are free of irons, lead the way."

In five minutes more, General Morrow was free. One bolt cap on Vivian's irons resisted Ronald's and Dasa's strength, and the time grew long and our hearts frenzied before Puran's hammering the wedged spanner with ours forced it loose. Now that all of us were unchained, Puran went overside and gave a hand to Mildred. Dasa followed her, helped the General down, and was reaching up to Vivian when Ronald spoke in a clear, collected whisper.

"I'm going to get those rifles. If we have to swim for it, they'll dry out and be useful."

Puran had told me that the sleepers would not waken. If a risk remained, Ronald wanted to run it for future gain. He was a soldier and I should not stand in the way of his functioning as such. So my brain told me above the curious balking of my instincts.

"Do as you think best."

"If they start to waken, I'll be ready for them." Then he leaned over the rail and addressed Puran. "Lend me your knife," he murmured. "It is the sahib's orders."

I had given no such orders, but I must realize the point was only technical. I must remember that silence had meant assent.

Puran handed up the weapon, and Ronald advanced swiftly and noiselessly up the deck. He all but disappeared in the mixed starlight and shadow, and then my straining eyes made out an indefinite dark shape between me and the sleeping guards, the wanly glimmering rail and the starlight river beyond. The shape bent and shortened. Ronald was bending down, busy at something. Then I heard a most strange and, at first, puzzling sound.

It was like water being thrown forcibly against wood at intervals as rapid as a clock's tick.

I had only barely grasped its meaning when the sound appeared to change to another, louder than the first. Actually there were two sounds now, very similar to each other, but they were not superimposed, and instead they had mingled. Each was like water being thrown against wood at equally rapid but not simultaneous intervals of time.

"Did Ronald cut their throats?" Vivian asked in a strange harsh whisper.

"Very expertly, I think."

Ronald returned with the two guns. The splashings were already slowing up and dying down. "Hurry now," Ronald muttered.

Vivian did not move. "Ronald, why did you kill those men?" she asked in the merest undertone.

"I didn't want them waking up when the rumpus starts. Anyway, the poor devils are better off dead than living to stand trial before Haran Lal."

"That's all right, then." Vivian had addressed this to me, I thought, as much as to Ronald.

Little fingers caught my hand and gave it a tug. We four who remained aboard—Vivian and Ronald, Latah and I—went swiftly overside into the warm waist-deep water where the others crouched. It shoaled swiftly as Puran led us in a slanting course toward the starlit shingle. We came out on it fifty yards below the boat.

"Walk lightly," Puran murmured, leading us on. The night still sheltered us.

Chapter Twenty-eight

As we were stealing along a water-bearer path toward a black spot in the night that indicated thickets, we heard a rifle-like crack about two furlongs up the riverbank. A louder bang re-echoed in a series of explosions, running or bunched, as though an ambushed regiment was firing at will. The main uproar lasted half a minute, then died away to intermittent reports as from hidden sharpshooters.

Puran's firecrackers had gone off on schedule, and in the way of a military diversion, the operation was a remarkable success. The roused-up mutineers ran about, milled, yelled, repeated rumors of battle and sudden death, and fired at imaginary enemies. An attempt was made to form a line of battle—we could hear Haran Lal's frantic commands. Meanwhile the fire that Puran had set to explode the bamboo bombs spread fast through the old warehouse, and by the time we had struck a cart road eastward toward Mirzapur, it threw a lurid glow over the whole reach of river. We had a clear coast for rapid flight, and the chances were fair that we would not be missed for one or more hours.

If some of our other plans had gone awry, the device might have saved the day. As it was, I wished to high heaven I had never proposed it. With our clean start, we would have had no trouble circumventing the sleeping mutineers, and in that case our empty cage might not have been visited until daylight.

Puran's preparations continued to amaze me. Certainly they had filled many furtive hours, which meant that he had traveled most of last night, taking advantage of the vagrant east wind in the teeth of the advancing monsoon. We had hardly started when both he and Latah picked up bundles cached in the river reeds. When we came to a crossroad, he had me stop the party and have all us white people remove our shoes and stockings. Putting their neat and sinewy feet into our clumsy footgear, Dasa, Puran, and Latah were to continue up the Mirzapur road while we took the crossroad south, our tracks instantly lost in the maze of naked footprints in the warm, deep dust.

"Sahib, we three will turn off after a while into a grass jungle," he told me, "then we will remove the shoes and, fas-

208

tening them well around our necks, we will cut back to meet you at the bridge over Badbu Stream, two koss up the road."

He spoke rather anxiously, as though I might disapprove of the plan.

"The old vixens of the Kuki hills could do no better," I replied.

We pushed on through the dimly starlit night. The main road was easy to follow: in a little over an hour we made out a wooden bridge. The stream identified itself by living up to its vulgar Anglo-Indian name. Our three stalwarts arrived shortly, their skins glistening with sweat, their breathing deep and even, our precious footgear jouncing on their shoulders.

The road followed the stream, along which we could surely find bush and grass jungles in the lack of better retreats. So far I had not given much thought to the question of where we would lie doggo during the day, but it would soon become an urgent one. Meanwhile we three sahibs pooled our knowledge of the area. We were twenty-some miles north of the border of Rewah, a semi-independent state, with vast hill tracts affording us likely refuge from the mutineers. General Morrow thought the next twenty-four hours would tell the tale. If we survived that long, we would be at the edge of Gond country, famous for tiger and nilgai that like heavy cover. He did not think that we should consider, at present, entreating the protection of the Maharajah. Ultimately, perhaps, we might make our way to the Son River beyond the Kaimur Hills, the road back to the Ganges, or on to Central India.

Not Latah nor Puran nor Dasa had ever set foot hereabouts or knew the country's name. However, I did not think they would take long in making themselves at home.

A swift recounting of our resources revealed ourselves as somewhat richer than we thought. Latah had retrieved all the money I had left at the Tame Kuki village. With the little leavings of what I had given Puran, we now had twenty silver rupees and forty five-rupee notes. The latter were noisily rejected in the public bazaars, Latah told me, but could be traded five for one with Parsis, Jews, Marwaris, and other merchant and moneylending castes who were not quite sure that the English were quite beaten. Latah's pack contained also a fine Russian revolver I had brought from Crimea, a pair of Lemiere field glasses that she thought I prized, opium for plague, quinine for fever, candles, lucifers, a cooking pot, a fleshing knife, soap such as sahibs used, a razor, salt, and a lump of *ghee*. Puran had a canister of gunpowder left over from his fireworks, twenty cartridges of the greased-patch sort that had helped start the mutiny—he had found them in the bandoleer of a dead policeman—a short-handled ax, a coil of rope, and a good-sized oilskin. Ronald had had more than one use for Puran's knife back there on the boat. He had taken time to slash off a bandoleer likewise containing twenty rounds of ammunition. All the rest of us were paupers except Mildred: she had a small Church of England prayer book and a brush and comb thrust into her bodice. I thought of them jostling against her breasts that were small and shapely—I had seen them outlined by sweat-drenched muslin—and seemed to glimpse an equation expressing Victorian society. It was a vagrancy of the night and soon faded away.

The night would not last much longer. The jackals had stilled and the jungle cock tuned their horns for their early matin. Worse luck, the road had turned off from Badbu Stream across what appeared a vast plain, with no shadow of forest to hide the low-hung stars. We pushed on, ever hopeful of finding rougher country, but found only cultivated ground, thickly peopled to judge by the many intersecting footpaths, barking dogs, and lowing cattle. Instinctively we quickened our gait.

"Simon, we'd better go back," Ronald broke out bluntly.

"It's too late," I answered. "We've come four or five miles from the stream, and dawn will break soon."

"There's a chance that we'll be seen, but not as big a chance as we're taking."

"Puran, can we get back to the thickets along Badbu Stream before day?" I asked.

"No, sahib."

"I still think it's our best chance," Ronald said. "But you're in command."

"I don't think that holds any longer. My part was back there on the river, with Puran and Latah."

"Well, you pulled it off, and what none of us could believe has come true. You've demonstrated real leadership. So unless General Morrow wants to resume——"

"You handled it wonderfully well, Simon," General Morrow said. "I hope you'll continue to lead."

"Just the same, I think in this particular instance, Ronald's right and Simon's wrong," Vivian said.

"I'm going to risk it," I replied, then spoke to Puran. There

210

were many Jats in this part of the Ganges Valley. We had passed one of their villages on Badbu Stream, and I had seen them in the river-town bazaars on previous journeys. Although their main stronghold was the Punjab, they had overflowed into the Allahabad. They were a very large caste of cultivators of Rajput stock, stolid, rather dour, and almost never known to dishonor a debt. Devout, conservative, and never fly-by-night, they had prospered under English laws of landholding and tenure, and I could not imagine them as partisans of the mutiny.

I instructed Puran to run ahead and look for a Jat house, the shape of which he could easily identify in the dark. If he found one that looked promising, he could sound out the householder and, on his pledge of good faith before his gods, offer him two rupees for our food and concealment until nightfall.

"A rich house, or a poor one?" Puran asked.

"One of the middle sort, rich in children. One glimpse of his compound will tell you whether he is worthy of his clan. But if you do not find a likely one in the next mile, choose us a hiding place if it is only a dry ditch, and lead us there before the cows are milked."

"I hope it turns out all right," I heard Ronald tell General Morrow as Puran fell into his swift trot and disappeared. "I don't trust any native in this pass."

Before my worries had made their first long, boomerang loop, Puran returned. He had come on a Jat farmhouse two furlongs up the road and had found the farmer half awake beside his plump wife. To Puran's shrewd questions he had made assuring replies. He had no quarrel with the sahibs and had once won a suit in a sahib court.

"Still, I wish I had promised him only two annas instead of two rupees," Puran told me. "He would not expect runaway sahibs to be heavy-pursed, and now you have been in the river, you do not look the part."

"Considering his risk, he will well earn the sum."

"If we live, sahib, we will have many calls."

The Jat farmer, big and solid-looking as the prototype, was waiting for us in the road. He led us into his clean kitchen, where a lantern gave forth a mellow light and a homey smell, and there he made for me a picture heartwarming as some by Vermeer or Delft. As he stood pouring milk into wooden bowls for our refreshment, his burnished skin bespoke the genial sun over his fields. His wife came hurrying to give us chapatties saved from last night's supper. Children of all ages, with their clothes half on, gathered big-eyed.

I rejoiced that I had acted on my own beliefs instead of on Ronald's doubts. The Jat would have more than the two rupees Puran had begrudged him, if I lived long enough.

Vivian and Mildred were close to exhaustion from their late watch and long march, and for the last few miles had been going on their nerve. The Jat's wife was spreading mats for them to sleep on when she noticed their swollen feet: at once she fixed pans of hot water to give them a good soaking, exactly as might a Devonshire farm wife. Gray and drawn, General Morrow made no apology over his inability to stand watch. Bright-eyed and flushed in contrast, although perhaps from the poisons of fatigue, Ronald offered to take a four-hour turn at a point of vantage overlooking the road. I agreed to take the second, and sent Latah and Dasa to scout our back trail. Puran and I went instantly to sleep.

I relieved Ronald at midmorning, and Puran took Latah's place. When the farmer returned for the midday meal, all of us feasted on curried chicken, rice fried in ghee, and fresh lentils. No wonder his children were glossy and well grown.

"How many have you?" I asked as we munched sweetmeats.

"Six by the last count."

"I thought I counted seven by lantern light."

"It may be Sahib saw a vision of a little one inside his mother's lap."

I went back to my lookout up and about a banyan tree. There was almost no traffic on the road and little to see on the gray, parched plain, and I would have had trouble staying awake except for the growing drama of the weather. The air was heavy and dead-still except for a few small, far-scattered whirlwinds that started up, raised dust high as the vultures' wings, and suddenly collapsed in falling palls. The clouds behaved oddly. Sometimes they moved purposefully through the sky, only to stop and mill about like sheep. Once they massed and darkened and the light dimmed, as though the sun's wick was being turned down, and a few warm drops of rain plopped in the dust and crackled like fire in the dry grass.

The cattle fed nervously, often lifting their heads, and the buffaloes lowed. What must be thunder dunted at the outer edge of hearing.

I longed for the dark so we could resume our march. I

212

thought our long day would never end.

Our whole party was awake and alert in midafternoon. Ronald came out of the house and, making sure there were no strangers in sight of him, moved furtively among the outbuildings. Presently he stood beside me in the root grove of my banyan tree.

"Simon, when the Jat came in for his forage, I almost, but not quite, waked up. You were talking to him, and something you said wove into my dreams. I think you said it—I don't believe I dreamed it. You asked him how many children he had."

"Yes, and he said six."

"You replied that you thought you had counted seven. Well, so did I."

"What do you make of that?"

"There were seven. I'm too used to counting noses of guard details and the like to make a mistake. The missing one is a youth of about sixteen."

"He could be working—but if the farmer lied——"

"I think he lied. I believe the barnshoot sent his son to find who was after us and make a deal with them. We must have a lot of rupees to pay him two rupees for food and a day's hide. That was what worried your man Puran."

"I can't believe it——"

"I didn't want to either. If we hooked it, we'd be seen by scores of natives and they'd cry our trail from now on. But the day's getting dark and there's just a chance——"

"What do you want to do?"

"First, to take a look at that low embankment running beyond the old byre. It's a dry irrigation ditch, I think. If so, it leads from a reservoir somewhere near the village and has got to run out somewhere, and with any luck there'll be a big grass jungle watered by the overflow. I want to go and see."

"All right."

He stuck out like the sore thumb of a giant for a matter of a hundred paces, then there was no sight of him except his head over the embankment. This moved swiftly, occasionally disappearing, until I lost sight of it in the murky light. About half a mile below the farm was a cluster of sal trees, and I could almost see him climbing one of them. My vision failed in the changing light, but I found myself waiting in growing suspense and dismay.

I was in the top of the banyan tree when I saw Ronald's

213

head again. It was on visible shoulders and moving very fast. Plainly he was running erect and at his best middle-distance gait. After one swift, fruitless scanning of the horizon I swung down and ran to meet him. We met by the old byre.

"Get 'em out and going, Simon," he told me, still in good wind. "The bastards are coming."

"How many?" I asked, running beside him.

"They're in three gangs taking different roads—about forty in all, I think. The idea is to surround us. Some are on horses."

Our shouts rang ahead of us. Our whole party was out the door or in it by the time we reached it. The farmer's wife and smaller children hung back, frightened. From the fields came running the Jat and two of his sons. Ronald's eyes narrowed and gleamed.

"Simon, I've had time to think this out. With the General's consent, I'll take charge."

"Right," General Morrow answered.

"General, you and Simon and the two girls start *down* the ditch. Latah can go with you, and you can have one of the rifles, though don't fire it except in the last extremity. Keep your heads down at all cost. We've got to try a feint."

"What about you and the natives?"

"Dasa and Puran and I are going up the ditch, with our friends the Jats. We'll show our heads from time to time, and the hunt ought to be hot. With any luck, we'll shake 'em off and circle back to you. Wait for us in the grass jungle where the ditch plays out. It's not as big as I hoped, but the best in reach."

By now the farmer was about fifty paces off, clamoring and gesticulating. Ronald waited until he drew within ten, then swung the rifle to cover him.

"Hear me, you barnshoot bastard," he began in fluent Urdu. "Tell your wife that if anyone asks which way we've gone to say we've gone up the ditch. The children, the same. Tell her your life depends on it, for it does. The last thing before we're caught, I'll shoot you in the back. Now speak out loud and plain."

The Jat obeyed orders implicitly.

"You and your boys will walk ahead of me, up the ditch. Now and then you'll show your heads as I tell you." Then, whipping to English, "You others had better start now. Our detail will wait till the enemy is in sight, then run for it."

"Don't wait too long, Major," General Morrow said.

"They're a sharp-eyed lot, and a native face shows dark a long way off."

"Yes, sir."

"Good luck, then."

Vivian, Mildred, General Morrow, Latah, and I walked quickly to the byre and dropped into the ditch. There was no enemy in sight as yet, so I did not go to the trouble of bowing my head, some inches above the General's, as we paced the hard-baked bottom. Nor need we worry about leaving tracks in the dust. There were scores of others running both ways where the Jat and his boys had used this path, seeking shade.

"Excuse me, Simon, but I thought Ronald told us to keep our heads down," Mildred said.

"Pardon me, I will."

Vivian, walking ahead of me, turned her head and grinned. "The King is dead, long live the King," she murmured.

There would be no more grinning by any of us for a long time. My cautious peep over the embankment revealed four horsemen and about fifteen foot soldiers, all armed with rifles, advancing up the road toward the house; another band of twenty hastened across the fields. With the latter was a white-clad figure, not as tall as the sepoys, whom I took for the Jat's missing son. If these continued their present course they would certainly intercept our path of flight.

They came on and became larger and more vivid in the strange olive-colored light. We stopped, half afraid that Ronald's plan had failed; then it was a thrilling thing to see them stop. One of them was pointing. All turned and stared. Then as their shouts rang faintly across the plain, we saw them break into a run almost straight away from us. The party on the road, never doubting that the chase was hot, raced to join them.

The figures became small and more and more hidden in dust. By now our ditch was becoming shallow, but there was an increasing heavy growth upon its banks until it flattened out in a marshy grass jungle of perhaps ten acres. That we could long evade determined hunters in such narrow cover was unthinkable. Moreover, it was in the nature of a cul-de-sac. Less than half a mile off we could see rougher ground with far-scattered bush stretching away at last to the dark blue smudge of distant forest, but the race would be too long to undertake in daylight, and between us and the first thicket was naked ground flat as a polo field.

215

"I wish to hell it would rain," I told the General. "We'd have a decent chance to slip through."

"Then I'll pray for rain," Mildred said, in what I thought a maudlin tone.

"I wish you would, Mildred," General Morrow answered, his voice low and resonant with emotion, his eyes glimmering.

I could not stay my eyes from sweeping to Vivian's. She replied to my glance with a vulgar gesture—putting one hand on her stomach and pretending to retch. Her eyes too were bright with emotion, although of a different order. I thought it reflected an elementary conflict, an ancient hate.

Although we could not make out the figures, undoubtedly the hunt was drawing closer. What we had at first thought might be far-distant thunder was soon revealed as far-scattered musket fire echoing and re-echoing over the plain, and curiously transformed by the heavy air.

I found myself speaking rather stiffly to General Morrow.

"You know, sir, if the mutineers get here in any numbers in anything like daylight, we'll have no chance to escape."

"I know it well, Simon. Of course Ronald won't come this way—much nearer, that is—with that pack on his heels. I think he's had to double back part of the distance, probably in another ditch. Whatever he's doing, it is the best he can do, with no thought of his own danger."

"You and the girls would be safer in the rough ground to the east. Why don't you try to get there, while I wait here for Ronald? The mutineers are a lot nearer, but I can't see any of them yet and I don't believe any of them would see you crossing the bare ground. You could stoop low——"

"What's the matter with your eyes, Simon?" Vivian asked. "Look in those sal trees along the road."

In the distance, small as king vultures and more ominous, perched the spies.

Suddenly we all knew that the game was touch-and-go. The shots were nearer and more frequent; I had a swift, sharp vision of three men, one white and two brown, running and dodging for their lives.

"God, I hope they make it," Vivian burst out in a violent undertone inaudible to anyone but me. "Anyone of the three is worth all of us three." She meant herself, Mildred, and me.

"I'd like to discuss that later," I answered, "but I don't think we'll have a chance. If they don't make it, we'll not.

And I don't think they will unless Mildred's prayer——"

"Don't be sacrilegious."

I saw that Vivian was wildly aroused, her eyes shining, her skin glowing, her breathing fast.

"Don't you be so prejudiced," I said. "I wish I knew what made you so—although I suspect you don't know yourself. I'd like to live long enough to find out."

"You're in good form, Simon."

"I'm trying to do what you told me, when scared to death. Either to be frivolous or highly contemplative. Remember that Mildred is one of the faithful. Unlike us black sheep, she prays in fair weather and foul. Of course we're permitted to pray too—it might indicate a change of heart—but usually it's because we're scared out of our wits and almost out of our self-respect. Actually, we don't do it often. We're afraid the Lord will laugh at us. He ought to. It's quite a joke, really——"

"Simon, you're hysterical."

"No, I'm trying to keep talking. So not to look——"

"At the clouds?"

"Yes."

"You're afraid if you look they'll—stop."

"Precisely."

"Simon, if you believe it was Mildred's prayer, they ought to stop."

"I don't believe it. What are they doing now?"

"They're churning—and lowering."

"Is the light going out?"

"It's getting awful dark."

"I don't hear any more shooting."

"No, they've stopped. They couldn't keep on making that little noise in the presence of the gods."

"There's not a sound."

"Yes, there is."

"I hear it now. A rustling, hissing sound. But it might be a dry wind——"

"Dry, my eye. It's the wettest wind you ever felt . . . Here it comes. Listen to it thrum! Simon, it's the Rains! The wonderful Rains!"

She did not know that in welcoming the Rains she tried to go to meet them. Rising on the balls of her naked feet, her radiant head high and thrown back, she did not know that her bosom rose and her breasts stood forth, pointing to the sky as might those of a nature goddess. The effect was

217

strangely heightened as the dams of the sky burst and the impounded floods roared down. The soiled silk became instantly clean, then transparent. The nipples raised and glowed as in an embrace of love.

If my soul was satisfied with the symbolism and the gods looking down were gratified by such beautiful response to their great stroke, all of us standing here sensed another climax that we could get our teeth in. The day's hunting was over. The rain was better cover than pitch dark. It hung a curtain in front of the eyes that thickened to impenetrability at a hundred paces, and no torch and not even the lightning could expose those in its care, and any sound they made was drowned out, and their very scent was washed into the ground. Except for the most evil fortune, we would live for another day. I nearly laughed aloud to think of Haran Lal trying to rally his men—standing out before them, brandishing a sword whose hard glimmer was liquidated by the rain, whose brave commands were muffled by its roarings until they seemed the poutings of a child, all his masterfulness washed away. Only deep in his waterproof chest did his zeal still burn. The mutineers could not feel it now. He had read too many books and had so forgotten that men cannot fight the gods. My evil mirth died as my eyes were drawn to Latah. She knew that men and women too could not fight the gods, and that knowledge brought a beauty to her face I had never seen before. It was greater than the beauty in Vivian's face and breast, and the beauty of the rain. She was small and brown, as are those who would escape the gods' notice. I went to her and put my arms around her and kissed her mouth. Her firm warm tongue glided about mine, as though to tell it something, if only that it need not speak. This too was a climax ushered in by the Rains, but I did not know its meaning.

We had not recovered from our first overpowering wonder, we were still looking and listening with the wide eyes and ears and the simple hearts of children, when a shadow in the rain solidified into Ronald's form. He was walking in long strides, with Puran and Dasa appearing to float behind him. We were standing just within the edge of the grass, gazing through the stalks. Vivian emerged so that Ronald could see her, and at sight of her he raised his arm in a joyous wave. I thought she expected him to kiss her. He did not, and I took malicious pleasure in her bland expression.

"All to the good, eh?" he cried boyishly. Then, sobering a

218

little, "General Morrow, I thought the ground looked rougher over to the eastward. Did you observe that?"

"It appeared gullied, and there was some thorn. It runs south toward what looked like a jungle-grown nullah."

"Then with your permission, we'll head that way."

"Right."

Ronald ordered Dasa to lead the way. As we came on the open ground it was no longer sun-baked and our bare feet sank toe-deep in thin, warm mud, and the warm rain seemed solid about us, as though we were wading on the bottom of a sky-deep river. The ground beyond was rougher than we thought, with scattered thickets. Almost at once we came upon a narrow watercourse, too small to be called a nullah even in high flood, bone-dry for months, but babbling with muddy water in the last few minutes. Undoubtedly it led to an ever-running stream that had watered the distant jungle.

"Follow this," Ronald instructed Dasa. Then to General Morrow, "Sir, I'd like to do a little scouting and will catch up with you within the hour."

"As you think best, but don't get lost in the rain."

Ronald looked for the drowned landscape. "Simon, your man Puran has a compass inside his head. I'll borrow him, if I may."

"Sir, I look to you for orders," I answered, turning the tables of only yesterday.

"You needn't much longer. I think we're fairly well out of the woods—but I want to make sure." Then, whipping to Urdu, "Come along, Puran."

The two vanished in the storm. We others walked a little way down the bank of the watercourse. Then Mildred called it to our minds that the rain would wash out our footprints as soon as we lifted our feet, so we white people stopped and put on our shoes. Dasa set an easy pace. The brook widened and deepened, the bush became heavier. Once I thought I heard a rifleshot somewhere behind us, but it could easily have been a dead tree falling as the dirt melted from its rotted roots.

In about an hour more, Dasa began to look for cavern-like holes in the bank, formed by the uprooting and fall of giant trees in great storms gone by. There we might huddle until the rain slackened, dripped on but not drenched. In spite of our late escape from a darker hole, we found it a dreary prospect. So the faces about me brightened at sight of Ronald waiting for us, a pleased grin on his face.

"Where's Puran?" I burst out when I had looked for him in vain.

"He's back in the bush, cutting dry wood for a fire," Ronald answered cheerfully.

"It will never burn in this weather!"

"We're not going to be out in it, old boy. On a short cut back, we found a path from a village over yonder, and by the dead flowers strewn along, he figured we were close to a shrine. We found it in jig time. It's not big enough to swing a cat, but it's dry. I'll show you."

He led us up an easy slope to a well-worn path. Our feet were magically lightened as we lifted them a hundred times more. Then we came on a dilapidated wooden temple whose gaping door revealed Siva the Destroyer, four-armed, with the skull-club and beggar's drum, carved in sandstone.

"Puran will have a fire going in a few minutes," Ronald explained boyishly. "It might be a bit smoky, but there'll be a good draft through the door and out that hole in the eaves. I think we can lie doggo until the rain slacks off—that ought to be no later than nine, if this is a typical monsoon downpour, and if we can make ten miles or even five before we hole up for the day, we'll score a big gain. I wouldn't be surprised but Dasa can contrive some sort of a torch before the time comes. As you see, cleanliness has nothing to do with godliness in the Hindu religion, but Latah can sweep this dirty floor with some wet branches."

Ronald glanced at me as he mentioned Latah, as though I owned her. I had had an impulse to correct his broad aspersions on Hindu cleanliness—in many respects we English were a dirty people compared to them—but decided against it now, lest too much be made of it. Anyway, I was fascinated by Ronald's charm of manner. At this moment he would arouse enthusiasm in any companion, and a young woman who had been through what Vivian had been through could hardly keep from loving him with great elated gusto, regardless of her other commitments. Vivian had put a mask of impassiveness on her face—I could not imagine why—but Mildred's eyes were shining in the gloom as might a young mother's over a triumph of her schoolboy son. A kind of juvenility is almost a standard ingredient of the best English officer class, again the cart before the horse for all I knew, and certainly its most delightful attribute; and I had never seen it more marked than in Ronald now. His tone was warm, jubilant, and just enough triumphant, his eyes were alive, and his face flushed. Yet this was the same man who had wanted Captain Maybank and Sergeant Gray to be buried in separate graves!

"We'd better try to dry our clothes," he went on. "You can be in a bout with fever before you know it. With the permission of due authority, I'm going down almost to my smalls, and I propose that the ladies be no more formal than at Brighton Beach."

"What precautions shall we take against surprise?" General Morrow asked.

"Well, sir, no Sivaists are coming here in this weather— that would be carrying bull worship a bit too far—and the mutineers have definitely retired. I suggest Dasa, Puran, Simon, and I take turns looking around in as few clothes to get wet as possible. That will be no hardship, and although I haven't the least uneasiness, it's good soldiering. Now we're going to have a better supper than you expect."

Meanwhile Puran had been laying a fire just back of the idol, putting a stub of candle under the damp wood in hunter style. I looked at his dark face and at the other dark faces and at the white faces and at the stern face of the god.

"Puran, will Siva be angry at the smoke and flame?" I asked when I had the chance.

"We will give him a smell of the young goat I stole before we eat her," was the grinning answer. Although he acknowledged all the gods, Puran yearned toward the big-breasted Yaksis of the Serpent Cult.

My next question was not in good-humored jest of the gods, but perhaps in fear of them. I did not ask it until it was my turn to survey our environs, as it happened in a weirdly silent intermission between cloudbursts. Puran wanted to come with me, whereby I decided to go with him when his turn came.

"You say you stole the young nanny," I began. "Did the sahib shoot her first?"

"No, I heard her bleat and found her tethered and forgotten in a thorn patch and mercifully cut her throat."

"I thought I heard a shot. Did the sahib shoot?"

"Yes."

"Did he kill?"

"Yes, he is a good shot."

"Was it the Jat who betrayed the bread and salt?"

I waited for Puran to say "Yes, sahib." Such an action

would somehow fit in with a new concept of Ronald lately shaping in my mind.

"No, sahib."

"Whom did he shoot? Speak plain."

"Sahib, he did not intend for me to know. He told me he wished to draw near our pursuers, and in that matter I served him well. Leading him back along the ditch, soon I heard an angry shouting. It was the voice of Haran Lal as he chided some twenty of his men, standing about like buffaloes in the rain. Then the sahib told me that we should both fan out to try to find the remainder of the band, and then meet at the junction of the two ditches. But I thought the sahib played me for a bumpkin. What was the good now of counting Haran Lal's scattered and impotent followers? And knowing that you and he desire the same memsahib and that under your smiles and good words you are deadly foes, I only pretended to obey him, and instead crept back to spy upon him."

"That was good. What did you see?"

"I saw him creep along the ditch, take careful aim, and fire. I was too far to make out his quarry, but the wailing and shouting told me who it was. Sahib, he had chosen the biggest head in the herd and laid him low."

"Haran Lal?"

"Yes, sahib."

"Are you sure it was not the raissaldar Hosain, who shamed his beloved?"

"It was Haran Lal. I heard his name cried a dozen times. Even now they carry him to the burning ghats of Mother River."

"Perhaps that was why he did it. To stop all danger of pursuit."

"In any case, it was well done. And this Blain Sahib is a sahib of parts, a man to reckon with, a foeman worthy of your steel. I think in the end that one of you will surely kill the other."

Chapter Twenty-nine

The rain on the temple roof while I slept dry beside a Hindu god wove into my dreams of danger and flight. The loud silence of its stopping waked me. The dying fire threw what

222

looked like a living flush on the face of the Sivan idol. Vivian's body was as relaxed as Latah's, both as a sleeping kitten's; they were in close proximity to each other and, although one was tall and the other small, closely allied in beauty. Even their faces had a common ingredient, and suddenly I thought it was imagination incarnate. Both imaginations were extra-busy just now, weaving dreams. Naturally they would be more visible than usual.

I thought Mildred was awake. I could not see her eyes or hear her breathe, but could not believe it possible for anyone to sleep in her present posture, flat on her back, her arms rigid at her side, her hands tight-closed, her legs flexed with her feet arched downward. Both brown men slept fully and deeply while they had a chance. General Morrow made movements indicative of dozing. Ronald was absent, evidently taking his turn at surveillance. That would put the hour close to eleven.

Ronald came in in a moment and crouched between General Morrow and me.

"Sir?"

"Yes."

"The stars are out, and I think we had better get going. Dasa saved fat from the goat and can rig some sort of fire pot. Better yet, if Puran has any more candles——" Ronald looked at me.

"I think Latah has some——"

"One of 'em burning in the cooking pot will save us many a misstep. There's a fair footpath down the nullah, but I don't know how long we can keep it."

General Morrow raised his voice. "Vivian, we'll be off now. Mildred, I wish you could sleep better, and I don't see how you can be so plucky on the road. Dasa——"

But Dasa, Puran, and Latah were already on their feet.

"Before we start, I've a suggestion," I said.

"Very well, Simon."

"I woke up with it in my head. When I first came out, I took an interest in Indian archaeology and remembered hearing of some ruins not very far from here. What attracted me about them, they were so little known. The only way to get to them is through a jungle-grown hill tract infested with Gonds and tigers, and no natives, including the Gonds, will come in a mile of 'em. There's been only two or three fragmentary reports from savants, although the Survey has a short sketch. Geographically they're classified as Nagara, and are in the style of the temples of Khajuraho." This last I said pedantically, for Vivian's attention.

"You say they're not far from here," Ronald remarked. "How far?"

"I was told to go to the town of Maihar and turn east."

"I dare say that would be in the Kaimur, north of the Son River," General Morrow said. "My guess would be three days' march for seasoned troops."

We took six marches, the first four by night and the last two in the long greenish dusk of jungle. We found our way by Puran's reconnaissance in the guise of a salt merchant, a trick he had once played on the road to Chittagong. The Hindus in the valleys and the Gonds in the forest knew of the ruins only as a place to avoid both in their walk and talk. When they must speak of them at all, they called them Murta Mahal—the Palace of the Dead.

We had found and followed the remains of a stone causeway until it crossed a jungle-grown ditch under a stone-and-earth embankment. The ditch was once a moat and the embankment was the foundation of a city wall. Since the wall itself had disappeared without trace, I supposed that it had been some sort of wooden palisade. The gate at the foot of the causeway stood in magnificent ruin. It appeared to be of creamy sandstone, very massive, of elaborate design. Its carvings of armed men, beasts, and gods were all but hidden under a dense growth of vines.

Within the gate ran row after row of empty cells that were once stone houses. They had been as full of people as the chambers in an empty hornet nest of grubs; now the thatch roofs had vanished, the wooden doors had rotted away, and the name of their great King was long forgotten. The cobblestones of the roads had been torn out and heaved up by a force greater than an earthquake—the silent, patient, almost irresistible thrust of growing things. Around the remains of circular wall, the stone flagging had been worn deeply and glass-smooth by naked feet. These and the broken masonry between the roots of a banyan tree indicated the ruins of a well.

The city had stood on the sides of one of the steep, isolated hills found throughout these highlands. The roads wound up to an inner wall enclosing three sides of a high shelf jutting out from the clifflike summit, enclosing in all an area of at least twenty acres. Within its several ornamental gates, wide and tall enough for the passage of elephants with towering howdahs, was a maze of palaces, towers, terraces, and courtyards, all with a wealth of decoration almost unimaginable outside the fabulous Indies. There could be no doubt that here lay the seat of mighty kings.

Because I had always been something of an outcaste, I had thought more upon the nature of man than those happy folk who accept one another and so take it for granted. In musing over the last king who had gloried here, and the swarms of people who fell on their faces at sight of him as though he were the viceroy of King Death—people greatly like the Calcutta swarm today except that they thought that this particular scene during a certain brief stretch of years was the very hub of the wheel of time and space—I dwelt concurrently on myself and my companions. We were beholding a wonderful thing. Each person's attitude toward it reflected his whole mind. It was as great an index to his inmost nature as his behavior in a crisis of life and death. It was not made plain in the face and words and actions of any of my companions; but I could make a few vague guesses.

The two most deeply moved of our party were the two most richly human—Latah and Vivian. They were the two most warm with the strange warmth of life, which might be a way of saying that they had the most active imaginations. Puran and Dasa stood close together, while their skins crept and became beaded with cold sweat. They had an understanding of the gods that we white men had lost—or never found—in the cold climes of the north. Perhaps they were more keenly aware of their own evil than we thickheaded barbarians late from the Groves of Woden, and they saw it reflected all about them here. General Morrow stood frowning and rubbing his chin. He did not approve of this sort of thing—well-ordered cities, with kings and revenues and armies and temples and trade, turned into silent ruins in the jungle. It indicated a lack of discipline. Someone had fallen down on the job . . .

Ronald refused to be impressed. He had a jaunty expression. He had seen the courts of living native kings, with all their pomp and peacockery, and this was all they amounted to at last. If there had been an English political officer in those days to tell his high muck-a-muck what to do, he'd have got along better . . . So I fancied the stirrings in Ronald's mind, but I might be very wrong. Instead of the most simple person here, he might be the most complex.

The face in which I could read nothing was the pretty

face of Mildred. It seemed likely that she was so preoccupied with herself that she felt nothing.

We walked on, getting a clearer concept of the ruins. The most beautiful of the buildings, set in a terrace of green-and-white tiles, was probably a queen's house. Its dome had fallen in, smashing down part of its walls: those that remained were a wonderwork in white marble, jasper, and agate. A fretwork summerhouse with trees bursting through its screens adjoined the main palace, which was a fortress of sandstone with towers and battlements tumbling in ruin. There were pillared balconies and what might have been temples and broken fountains once fed from sandstone reservoirs higher on the hill and a fishpool of red agate and white jade.

The shadow of the jungle-grown steep flinging out over the palace grounds felt cold, and the air about the ruins smelled of dank decay. Bats hung down like devilish inverted crosses from the lavishly worked cornice of a gloomy crypt; and beside a huge black stone of unrecognizable shape a mongoose whisked his tail and ran off. Presently we found the quarry that the little hunter was seeking. On top of the stone where once had risen some kind of monument, no doubt to some sort of god, lay a sleeping cobra.

What had become of the great kings, their dark-eyed beautiful queens, legions of eunuchs, court attendants, soldiers, courtiers, and mighty elephants arrayed for war? Some of their forms were carved on the long frieze of a stone balcony, along with the shapes of godlike beings that looked more Buddhist than Hindu. But the great god that had stood or danced, or squatted or slept above the black stone—I saw now that it was in the exact center of the enclosure, toward which all the avenues led, and was probably a meteorite weighing at least five tons—had vanished without trace.

The priests had taught that he was everlasting, and the people had made offerings and sacrifices to him, their eyes glowing or wet with tears. Instead he had been hardly more durable than themselves.

Ronald was the first to call attention to an arch-shaped shadow at the foot of the steep summit of the hill. As we came nearer we began to make out a row of pillars, half hidden in vines and undergrowth, that formed a kind of veranda to the nobly carved entrance of a cave. That would have been enough of a wonder without the cave itself being almost altogether the work of human hands. Perhaps there had been a narrow opening caused by water action, but the main of

226

its expanse had been hewn from the limestone as a dugout from a log. Each of its scores of ornate columns rested on the back of a crouching lion, and none had been erected and all had been cut out like roof supports in a coal mine. By the uncanny light trickling through rows of apertures above, we could see the domed ceiling with a pendant of a life-size winged lion suspended from its lace-like fretted work. The walls were adorned with lavish figure-sculpture carved in relief as are cameos.

"It's beautiful in a gaudy way, but what was it for?" Mildred asked.

"It's a rock temple. There are a good many in India, but this is one of the finest."

"I've heard of them," General Morrow said in a wonder-struck tone. "I was too busy to go and look at 'em. At least I thought I was."

"There will be priests' rooms overhead. They will be dry and the safest shelter we can find till we can get back to the English lines. The jungle will furnish plenty of meat, and Latah is good at finding wild fruit and edible plants. If need be, we could hide from a whole regiment of mutineers in the cells and passages of the ruins. We should maintain a watch, but I don't think we'll ever be disturbed. Unless all signs fail, this is forbidden ground to natives."

"To the natives of these parts, I don't doubt," General Morrow said. "But the mutineers won't know local superstitions or be much affected by them."

"What do you think about that, Puran?" I asked.

"Sahib, the mutineers who do not already know of this place will not hear of it. Those who do know will not speak of it."

"Haran Lal is a well-educated man. He may know of it already."

"Still I do not think he will come here." Puran's eyes grew very wide.

"I don't think so either," I said, without a glance at Ronald.

"Puran and Dasa and Latah came here," Vivian remarked in English, her eyes alight with excitement. "Of course that was a matter of loyalty—love, if you want to call it that—certainly that's the right word as far as Latah is concerned—but the mutineers may have motives just as strong. Hate, for instance. Desire for loot. Even, in some cases, loyalty to their leaders or to a cause."

"If you are speaking of mutinous sepoys, Vivian, I'll ask you not to apply the word loyalty to them in any sense," General Morrow said. "It happens to be a word of very deep meaning to me."

"I won't apply it to mutinous sepoys," Vivian answered gravely.

"Puran, did you come here in duty to me, your master?" I asked.

"Sahib, in the way of duty I could have come only to the outmost causeway. Not for love or hate or gold or for any god I know would I have come here, into the very heart of Murta Mahal. But when you bade me come, I came without great terror. Thereby you had taken upon your head all the evil that would otherwise fall on me."

"Dasa, is it the same with you?" General Morrow asked in Hindustani.

"Yes, sahib."

"What is that evil, Puran?"

"Wait, Simon," Vivian said. "I think we should learn all we can of the native attitude, so we can make a better guess of what will happen. Ask Latah."

My hill girl was looking at the sculpture, her face lighted with childlike wonder. When I called her name her luminous dark eyes met mine.

"Latah, when Puran told you of Murta Mahal, were you frightened?"

"No, sahib. I am not a Hindu or a Mohammedan and do not know their gods, whether good or evil. I trusted to my *nat* and to Sahib's gun."

"Is that satisfactory, Vivian?" I asked.

"Quite."

"Puran, it would be a great help to us if you told us the nature of the evil."

"How can I, sahib? It is not one of evil's manifestations but the thing itself. It has lingered here a thousand years, lying in wait for those who come here. It cannot touch Dasa or me because we came in obedience to our masters. Latah came by her own will, as she does all things, but it cannot touch her because she knows no evil. She knows of good *nats* and bad *nats,* but evil cannot come near her, for she has none in her heart. In that she is like a cheetal deer."

"Anyway, this looks a good place to lie doggo," Ronald broke in vigorously. "So let's cut the balderdash and, if the General's willing, pitch camp."

Mildred applauded him with a joyful clapping of her hands. Not quite able to lay the ghosts that seemed so barely out of sight and hearing, I rejoiced with the others at this respite from our long weary march and in what our reason told us was a reasonably safe retreat. The storm of mutiny sweeping the valley of the Ganges would not likely strike in this lost city of the dead. We believed we would live on.

Chapter Thirty

General Morrow and Dasa went into the jungle in search of a sambur deer or a nilgai antelope. It was true that the shot might be heard by a wandering Gond, but we agreed that the small brown men would not likely come into these environs. With one of Latah's candles lighting their way, Vivian and Ronald found a row of stone cells above the cavern, each with apertures in the face of the cliff, and above these the remains of earth-dug rooms walled with timbers. Above us the tree-green hill rose steeply for another four hundred yards, an eminence that would make a good lookout over many miles of jungle.

Vivian and Mildred chose to sleep in the same room. I took note of Vivian's agreement to this, since it would certainly interfere with her entertaining Ronald, which every other present factor in our situation would appear to serve. What was a first half-pretended surprise at her restraint, actually a self-protective cynicism against what I did not want to believe, became quite real as I looked down over the dead city, and I did not know why. Perhaps it was only a feeling of being out of the world and hence no longer subject to its decrees. The ruins were as much a testament to the inevitable cold and silence and negation of death as the lush greenery to the brief hungers of life. In such a scene, Vivian's native passion might become lasciviousness. The chained selves of all of us might break free and become our masters.

While I was investigating the water supply, Latah chose a room for me. It was one unoccupied by bats, and its niche could be used for a lookout. Here she put my belongings and the few articles Puran had obtained for me along the road, but nothing of hers. Following the narrow passage of a carved-out balcony, I saw her bundle lying in one of the small, dark inner cells. I searched for her and finally found her a short distance up the steep, washing her Gond raiment under one of the broken reservoirs overflowing with rain water. I sat down to watch her as in old days at the Tame Kuki village.

She wore only a long cloth tucked in at the waist. Her slender body with its proud breasts was never more lovely to my sight, and her face never more beautiful, although both were somewhat gaunt from the long march. As she pounded the clothes on a stone in the immemorial custom of washerwomen in the Orient, she sang me a washing song that was almost as old—of the beating of a faithless husband by his brawny wife, each blow punctuated, and the story told by witty verses and ribald refrain. Then she kissed me and crouched beside me.

"Do you see that I am thin?" she asked, stretching out her glossy arms.

"A little."

"I am no fatter than when you saw me the first time, when all we Old Kuki were half starved, before you killed Kharab-Bagh."

"I had thought to make you round-bellied long before this. But there is still time before the end of the Rains."

"No, sahib, the time has run out."

She spoke cheerfully with a little sideways cut of her head that always lent emphasis.

"That cannot be," I answered. "You promised to stay with me until the end of the Rains."

"The time has run out beforehand, like water from a broken jar. You are no longer an outlier, divorced from your tribe: when the guns began to shoot, you returned to your own. So it is not meet that I should any longer keep your house and share your bed. Both of us thereby lose face. In my own country, you may be my lover. In your country, you may be my master. But you can't be both, I being an Old Kuki and a daughter of a chief."

"In a little while we'll return to your country, the green hills of the Tripura."

"No, I'll go there alone. There I will make a house with a youth of my village. Such is the bidding of my *nat*, and behold, Shikra, how plain the writings of Kismet, and how fair and full our settlement with each other. Have you forgotten the day that you came to our village? It was the Day of the Tired Sun, when the shadow at noon is longest of all the year. I was thin from going hungry. That day you gave

230

me meat and jested with me and looked upon me with eyes of favor. Then in four days or such a matter, you slew Kharab-Bagh, and I went to your house and lay with you in love."

Her voice faltered as she said this last, and her eyes glowed.

"We lay together," I told her, "without debt."

"Now that is true. But all the Old Kuki owed you a great debt for the saving of their lives from Kharab-Bagh, and lo, the time came round for me, Latah, the chief's daughter, to pay it. This I did. Puran plotted to save you only from the death waiting you at Allahabad, but I prevailed upon him to save your companions also, even Ronald Sahib, who covets the memsahib with whom you yearn to make a house when I am gone."

"Ronald Sahib no longer covets her, to use the word rightly. She has already pledged her troth unto him and, I think, given him her flower."

"That I doubt."

"In any case, Latah, speak on."

"You saved many of my people, and to pay the debt, I saved many of yours. And now what is the season?"

"The beginning of the Rains."

"Aye, and today is the Day of the Strong Sun, rising early and setting late, when my shadow at noon is the shortest in all the year. So for three days I will gather good things to eat in the jungle, and show Puran what they are and where they may be found, and show him also a certain grass to make mats, and a kind of root to use for soap when the soap is gone, and other things known only to us jungle dwellers. On the fourth day I'll set forth down-river on the way to the far Tripura, and if you will have me bring word to the sahibs of your hiding place, that too I will do."

"No, I'd have you go straight to your village and remain there until the storm has passed."

"The danger of going to the sahibs, if any are yet alive, and giving them a message would not be great. And it is in my heart to do good to the old General Sahib and to his daughter of the fire-bright hair."

"To them more than to the others?"

"Yes, but I don't know why."

"Still, I'd have you tell no one where we are. In these days of unchained hates, I trust no one. Also, if English soldiers try to come here, some might lose their lives or

231

cause us to lose ours. Now that risk might be well run for a great prize, but in this case the prize would be the rescue of Morrow Sahib because he is a general. If in the soldiers' minds that is a great prize, it is not so in mine. I think that many younger officers may take his place in the councils and that the soldiers' time and sweat can be better spent."

While I said all this, greatly pleased with it, and in a somewhat dictatorial tone, an interesting expression was coming into Latah's face. It seemed at once tender and amused and a little forlorn. On my finishing my proclamation, she continued to gaze at me, as though she expected me to continue. Suddenly my face felt hot.

"Wah, but those are many reasons," she replied at last. "I doubt if I can remember them all. But, Shikra Sahib, is there not one more, the best of all? If you are the great sahib that I believe—justly chosen by Fate to slay Kharab-Bagh—I can tell you what it is."

"What is it, Latah?"

"You want the people to stay together—these and no more—until the business you have with them is done."

"Latah, we three sahibs are needed in the battle line. If I had any such business as you speak of, do you think I would let it interfere——?"

"Yes, Shikra Sahib, I think you would. In your heart you know that part of it, at least, is of great importance to the sahibs and to all men and to your gods—greater perhaps than any other in your reach."

"What is the business, Latah?"

"To find out who betrayed the fort at Diwanpani, and for what gain."

"Yes, because if the betrayer is alive or dead, I believe the evil that he wrought or was wrought upon him is with us still."

"If it was done in strength and not in weakness, it must be a very great evil."

I stared at her. "Latah, if it was done in strength, I think that Shaitan himself would not be equal to it, because he has never had the heart and brain of a man."

"Do you think that it can be brought into the light, where you can see and kill it?"

"I think that if we stay here until the moon waxes and wanes once more, I can see and kill it. We'll be prisoners of the jungle and the Rains, bound together night and day, conjured by the legions of the dead, and at some moment of dropped guard, it will show its face."

"When it shows its face, sahib, it may be only the face of a common man, its evil shared by all men."

"I don't know what you mean."

"A mistake-maker instead of an evildoer, who moved weakly instead of strongly. My *nat* thinks so but is not sure. But you, Shikra, must be sure. Until then, you cannot live with a whole heart." She drew a deep breath. "You can't make a house with Vivian Memsahib when I am gone."

As though to exorcise a bad *nat,* she sprang up, beat her clothes three times against the stone, rinsed them, and hung them up to dry.

"We'll speak no more of evil things," she told me with a broad, childish smile. "Nor of sad things."

"Not speaking of them doesn't change them. You have said you are going back to the hills of Tripura, breaking our bond."

"Not until the fourth day, Shikra Sahib. And although these hills of the Gonds are not quite as green as the hills of the Old Kuki, still they will do very well for a place of taking farewell."

"What of the cold cell in the stone where I am to sleep?"

"Sahib, I thought that now you have returned to your own people you would not want to share your house with a hill-woman——"

"I want you as long as you will stay with me."

"Then for three days and nights we will live again the old days and nights of Tripura. And although the nights will be short, our dreams flying faster than the wild pigeons, the days will be long and full of happenings to remember always. Did you not tell me that according to the 'Isai Book, all earth and heaven were made in twice three days?"

"So it is written."

"I believe it. I believe it could have been made in one day, if there had been need of haste. Look at the dead city. It may have taken a thousand years to build, and it has lain dead a thousand years, but a song written by the King's bard in three hours might live forever, and the cobbler's son and his bride might fly to Bihisht in the third part of an hour."

Latah's glowing eyes appeared to lift at the corners as they gazed into mine.

"Shikra Sahib, what would the Great King of Murta Mahal give for three days more of life?" she asked.

233

"All the jewels that lay forgotten in his treasure house."

"And where would he spend them, do you think?"

"I think with his most beloved, in the green hills."

Chapter Thirty-one

There was more danger in these hills than Latah and I had reckoned, but we had no intention of letting it mar our joy in being alive together while we had the chance.

Indeed we were given a little fright, of a spine-tingling rather than a blood-chilling sort, before dark of the first day. Dasa had brought in a young barasingha that General Morrow had shot, and after butchering it and cutting off steaks for our evening meal, he had hung it in a tree just outside the cave. As we sat on the "veranda" gazing out into the silvery dusk of the pelting rain, a great yellowish form sprang into our sight, reared up at the carcass, snatched it down with his jaws and forearms, and made off with it all in ten seconds of continuous violence.

A rifle had stood near Ronald, but he had had no time to snatch it up and level it. Perhaps we were better off on that account, not being at present prepared to settle a death feud with a wounded tiger. However, the fact that he had made so bold—creeping down the steep with no regard for smoke of our cooking fires—was a warning against blundering unarmed into his lairs.

A potentially serious threat appeared at rain-break the next day. Returning from a scouting trip, Ronald showed us a weak, ill-made arrow about three feet long, fletched with jungle-cock feathers and barbed with iron.

"I was making up the hill on the other side of the nullah for a good spy-out," he told us. "It was only moderately heavy cover, and I could have sworn nothing bigger than a fox could steal a march on me. Then I heard a *pinggh*, and this billy-do came buzzing out of the scrub."

Ronald was not quite as cool and collected as he liked to appear, I thought.

"It hit a bush about six feet from me," Ronald went on. "I whirled to shoot, but all I saw was a glimpse of brown in the thicket. The fellow instantly disappeared, and I had sense enough not to look for him. In fact I retrieved the arrow, made an about-face, and returned to camp. It's a good thing, too, that I didn't shoot him, for I soon perceived he hadn't tried to hit me. If he had, he would have."

"The shot was in the nature of warning?" General Morrow asked.

"I think so—not to go into the higher hills. That's the last retreat of the wild Gonds, and they don't like sahibs to come messing about. I don't think there was any animosity shown. It was just a pointed hint."

"But surely you're not going to take it," Vivian remarked, almost sneering. But it was no joy to me to see her with dagger drawn on Ronald: it was proof of a power over her that I had not been sure he wielded. "Surely a sahib mustn't yield an inch——"

"Don't talk rot, Vivian," Ronald answered, and turned to General Morrow. "Sir, it's my opinion we needn't have the least concern as far as our present plans are concerned. We'll have no need to go near their villages, and unless they're looking for trouble—which seems highly unlikely— they'll not come on this side of the nullah. We can hunt and the boys can gather produce all over this jungle. I intend to continue scouting, but I'll walk with care."

The iron-tipped stick that could be snapped in two by the fingers suggested a child's arrow more than a weapon of war—I thought it must be used only for small game. I too could not believe that Ronald had been attacked with deadly intent, although a Gond might have shot at him in sudden panic.

So while Puran, Latah, and I were weir-laying in the stream just after sunrise—the wattled enclosures should keep us in fish—we were more thoughtful of tigers, buffaloes, bisons, wild elephants, and snakes—especially cow elephants with young and a little dust-colored snake known as the krait—than of small, brown jungle men. My companions were happy in a way that grown-up white people have almost forgotten and recall in the eyes of a child. They gathered the branches; their clever hands plied fast; they made sober decisions how best to entrap the thin pike and fat perch; they waded neck-deep in the warm, muddy water. At high sun the job was done, at least two hours and perhaps four before the clouds would pack the sky and shatter down in rain.

Puran trotted off to join Dasa on a camp job. Latah and I went only fifty feet beyond the wall-like border of the vine-hung nullah jungle before we found a grassy glade where we could eat our lunch of cold venison and sun-warmed jungle fruit out of the reach of leeches, nettles, and other pests of the rank undergrowth, and in light good enough to satisfy my eyes. Standing off about two paces from her, I was delighting in her brownness as she sat cross-legged beside a shrub ablaze with shu'la blossoms. I would soon slip down her wet waistcloth for my greater pleasure. I rejoiced in our solitude, its security guaranteed, it seemed, by the great silence about us. My happy thoughts left no room for anxiety.

The silence was abruptly broken by a subdued sound. Later, when I tried to recapture it in memory, I thought that *pinggh*, as pronounced by Ronald, was good onomatopoeia. In spite of its softness, it was a strangely frightening sound, otherwise it would have been physically impossible for me to whirl in time to see any of its accompanying action. The sweep of my gaze intercepted the nearing flight of an arrow. I saw it the instant that the slight angle of its course made it visible—before then it had been a dot that became a dash—darkly stenciled against a sunlit opening in the greenery. Then it was about twelve feet from me, and instead of darting level, it climbed a little. Then or thereafter I perceived that it was going to pass at my eye level about six feet to one side of me and at least two feet over Latah's head.

Almost before the shaft had whistled harmlessly on, my brain had leaped eagerly and hopefully to Ronald's account of a deliberate miss. Before there was time to think, I knew enough to run—guided by those lightning-swift perceptions induced by danger . . . The bowman was already in flight. I heard the rattle and swish of thickets rise and recede. The tangle would hide him at ten yards. There he could stop, stand in ambush, and shoot again.

. I snatched up Latah with my right hand and my rifle with the left. Instead of a retreat such as Ronald reported beating, we ran our best. In twenty strides we were behind saplings and safe from attack.

Both my fright at the shot and the elation of our escape died away. In sudden rage I ached to send a bullet after the vanished archer—only the dictum to keep my gun loaded saved me from the folly. I was no longer at all certain of his peaceful motives. Latah and I had not been hill-climbing toward the villages of the little wild Gonds. I could not quite believe that this was a second warning . . .

"I'm going to retrieve that arrow," I told Latah.

Although more frightened than she wanted me to know —I saw it in her eyes—she gave me a quick nod. That would be unlike many memsahibs, but quite like her. Perhaps because she had always lived with danger, she had found out it could not be pandered to; it must be met in the teeth.

I advanced aggressively, my finger on the trigger, ready to shoot at the first stirring of a leaf. If the bowman had crept back and was waiting in ambush, he knew my intentions; and by absolute immobility—not the most stealthy drawing of his bow—he made sure that no leaf stirred. I had seen where the shaft struck, and finding it thrust into the moss of a rotted log, I backed away without lowering my guard. Together Latah and I withdrew another fifty yards into open forest. There I examined my find.

The arrow appeared identical with the one Ronald had shown us, except for one detail. The iron point was smeared with an amber-colored gum.

"What do you make of it, Latah?"

"It's a mixed trail, sahib," she told me, as when we had hunted sambur in the high Tripura.

"Did the Gond try to kill me?"

"No, sahib. No hillman worthy of the name would miss you by six inches at that range with a standing shot on a windless day, let alone by six feet."

I stopped and saw my breathing and the relaxation of my throat muscles.

"Latah, did he try to kill you?"

"No, sahib. That would make no sense. If he made war against all aliens, which of us two would he kill first? From where he stood, maybe he didn't see me."

She paused, her throat worked, and then said what her *nat* demanded. I did not know what a *nat* was in Latah's pantheon: to me it meant her soul. Her voice was low and her face was beautiful with a sadness I had rarely seen.

"What I have said pertains to the wild Gonds. They are hillmen and I am a hillwoman. If anyone sought my life with a poisoned arrow, it was the sahib."

We were in open forest now, and I could see in all directions far out of arrow range. I sat down and drew Latah beside me.

"What sahib?" I asked.

"Blain Sahib, whom you call Ronald. I know something that he did that he wants to keep hidden. I didn't think that he was sure I knew it, but surely he would suspect it. I did

237

not intend to tell anyone, for I believed and still believe he had made a mistake and is not guilty of great evil, but the time has come to lay the burden on your head, the head of another sahib. Now it has come to me, splitting apart my head with achings, that a sahib who aspires to be the greatest sahib in Hind might kill a hill girl, of no more worth in his mind than a barking deer, if thereby he could hide a mistake that would put him to great shame.

"What was the mistake, Latah?"

"Before I tell you, Shikra, hear my true word! The side of my head that says the archer was a Gond, trying to scare us so we would go away, speaks ten times stronger than the side of my head that says the archer was Blain Sahib, trying to kill me to stop my lips forever, and letting the blame fall upon the Gonds."

"Lay the trouble on my head."

"Sahib knows that I came too late to Diwanpani to warn the people of the great trouble. There were shoutings in the road that many sahibs, and soldiers true to their salt, had been killed by the mutineers, and the rest had fled to the fort and shut the great doors. As I came up behind the Mess Hall the killers were firing at the loopholes, as were some bad-zats who had stolen guns from the slain. Many more evil ones ran about shouting, but as yet none had entered the officers' houses along the field. Then I saw three men, two sahibs and one Indian, crouching by the garden hedge, but by now I was greatly frightened, and I came up to them unseen. One of the sahibs was Ronald Sahib. The other's face I didn't know, but Ronald Sahib called him Sergeant Gray. The Indian was a servant of the Mess—this I knew by his garments—and looking well upon his face, I remembered it when I saw it again on Mother River. His name was Haran Lal."

I did not have to take precautions against exciting Latah and getting her confused. She spoke quietly, and there was only a little tension in her voice. I was never more aware of the deep bond between us.

"As I came close, Ronald Sahib was writing a message on a paper," Latah went on. "This he folded and handed to Gray Sahib with an order spoken softly in a tone of command. In giving the order he spoke of 'Captain Maybank,' the name being one I had heard often among the Tame Kuki. No doubt the paper was to go to Maybank Sahib but Gray Sahib stared as though he did not believe his ears. Then Ronald Sahib told him something else, still in a low voice but with great force, and at the end of the saying were three words that I knew. Two of them I had heard from the Tame Kuki and one I had learned from you. The words were 'General Morrow's bungalow.' "

My imagination leaped, and I had a bird's-eye view of her, standing still, not needing to crouch, so small and brown she was, in the shrubbery of the Mess House garden, her frightened eyes missing nothing, her ears sharp, her mind storing every detail of the event. Yet I had to ask an urgent question.

"Those words could have meant very little to you at the time. When did you begin to think about them?"

"When Puran told me that the mutineers had found a passage from Morrow Sahib's bungalow into the fort."

"Haran Lal heard him, of course, and Ronald probably didn't know that he understood English." For I was ahead of her story and preparing for Haran Lal to follow Sergeant Gray . . .

"I do not know, Shikra, but when Haran Lal spoke to Ronald Sahib, his hands on his forehead, and his face shining with sweat, the sahib appeared to take pity on him, and Haran Lal and Gray Sahib went off together. The last I saw of them, they were creeping along the hedge toward the grass thicket. It would be their best way to go to Morrow Sahib's bungalow without being seen by the badzats."

I went over the story point by point, letting no heat come up from my heart into my brain.

"Well, then, Latah, the question of the betrayal of the fort has been answered."

"It may be so, sahib."

"In a desperate pass, with much that he had built in ruins, Ronald Sahib betrayed his soldierliness. The tunnel was to be the last resort for reinforcing the garrison or for its escape when all other hope was lost. The lives of all who had taken shelter there hung on the keeping of the secret. The sahib risked it in order to send a message to Maybank Sahib. It might have been an important message—a matter of great urgency to the defense. It might have been a message of great mercy, which no soldier must ever send at risk to his men and his cause—that Maybank Sahib's wife, Mildred Memsahib, had not been slain by the mutineers but was in hiding."

I stopped, because my brain was surging toward a distant gleam of light.

"If that was the message Ronald Sahib sent to Captain Maybank, its mercy was incidental to its great urgency," I went on. "Maybank Sahib was ill-fitted to be an officer. He lived and breathed for his wife Mildred, and he was also a coward. In his desperate terror for her, what would he do to try to save her? Would he send an armed force through the tunnel in search of her? Might he even surrender the fort on the mutineers' promise to save her life? It may be that Ronald Sahib knew he must relieve that terror, even at some risk to the garrison."

"What do I know of the way of sahibs, sahib?" Latah replied.

"Yet I will tell you my thoughts, to try to keep them straight. If Ronald Sahib was partly or even wholly justified in sending Gray Sahib through the tunnel to deliver the message, what excuse can he make before his gods and his chiefs for letting a native servant go with him? I tell you, there is none this side of the bar of heaven. It was true he had known Haran Lal for many years. Served by him in the Mess, relying on him as an excellent khansaman, he had come to trust him. Mark you, at this time he did not know that the mutiny was widespread, brought about by a great conspiracy—he thought that one company of sepoys had rotted and gone mad. Haran Lal begged to go with Sergeant Gray, for if the badzats caught him, they would kill him. Ronald Sahib took pity on his terror—and thereby brought about the slaughter of all the people in the fort."

"Is that why he showed no pity to Indra and Bahadur as they lay sleeping on the boat?"

"He gave other reasons, which Vivian Memsahib found good. There are many things to guess at, few that are sure. When Haran Lal had learned the way into the fort, he crept back and told the mutineers. Meanwhile Sergeant Gray had missed him—went down from the citadel to look for him—then in frantic haste ran through the tunnel trying to overtake him. When he reached the tunnel mouth, the mutineers were assembling for the butchery. He killed four before he fell, and then it was too late to warn Captain Maybank of the missing native—whereby the garrison would guard the passage and defend it for many hours. I've heard that Gray was of an excitable nature——"

I stopped, because I remembered who had said so. It was

Ronald. He had not openly charged Sergeant Gray with a fatal mistake—he had only admitted its possibility—and he had vigorously denied that Gray had deserted the gatrison. Even so, it was dishonorable conduct both for an officer and a gentleman. The first rule was stand the gaff . . .

Then the current of my thoughts checked and turned as I remembered a pertinent fact. Ronald had said this before we were taken prisoners. Perhaps no suspicion of Haran Lal's part in the betrayal had crossed his mind: if he had thought of him at all, it was as one of the dead in the slaughterhouse. The awful truth might not have burst upon him until he recognized Haran Lal in the gray dawn on the jeel.

"Latah, when Haran Lal and his followers came on their buffaloes to the island, Ronald alone wanted to fight them to the death."

"Puran told me so," Latah answered.

"Was it because he didn't care whether he lived or died, except to send Haran Lal on before?"

"It may be so, sahib."

"He asked permission to shoot at Haran Lal from a dead rest. I don't think he would have missed. That he was denied, but his chance came when Haran Lal hunted us in the rain. Ronald Sahib would not accept freedom at the price of leaving Haran Lal alive."

"Surely that is why he killed Haran Lal, rather than to shut his mouth. So it follows that he did not send a poisoned arrow to shut my mouth."

"Are you even sure that he knew you had seen him send the two men into the fort?" I asked.

"No, sahib, I'm not sure. When they had gone, I came up to speak to him, but he hardly glanced at me, so busy was his mind with his great concerns."

"He did not ask you how long you had been in the garden?"

"No, Shikra Sahib. Why should he, unless he had done deliberate evil? Only later he remembered seeing me there. I am ashamed that today I charged him with seeking my life even in one tenth of my head split off from the rest. I would not have thought of it, sahib, if he had not stolen away to kill Haran Lal. How could I know that he had gone to punish him for his treachery? We Old Kuki understand a man taking another's life for something that he greatly craves or to save himself a great harm, but we do not understand punishment. We are only jungle wallahs. We do not know what makes ourselves do wrong, let alone our brothers."

"Latah, every one of us is a mixture of good and evil. There is enough evil in many of us—perhaps most of us —to wish for the death of people whom we greatly fear. It is true that you are the last witness to Ronald Sahib's great mistake. He knows that if it is ever discovered he will be a marked man, and his hope of a great career will be blasted. Also, his izzat counts more with him than with any sahib I ever knew. Yet I swear that if he plotted against your life with a bow and quiver he had bought from a Gond met in the jungle, it is because shame and remorse and fear of what he had done have driven him mad."

"Sahib, I don't believe it."

"Nor do I, thank God! I think that the little wild Gonds spy on us from their secret places—one may be in a treetop watching us this moment—and they saw us cross the nullah to get vines for the fish weir. Likely that too is forbidden ground, and they gave us a stronger warning than the one given to Ronald Sahib. Is good so much more hard to believe than evil? In the last record, is it not more true?"

"Your eyes are shining, sahib——"

"With my joy in you as part of my joy in life. A great burden has been lifted from my mind. I'll do what I can to conceal Ronald's mistake."

"Won't you tell Vivian Memsahib when I am gone?"

"What good? She wouldn't cast him forth and make a house with me. He's my enemy, but I have done him and myself too a great wrong with my dark imaginings, and you have freed me from them as from my chains."

My pulse was throbbing in my fingers and my neck tingled and I was aglow the same as with the first insinuations of strong drink.

"It's as though I am well of a fever," I went on, my voice ringing strangely in my ears. "I'll put more trust in life— more faith in people. I'll get along better." And I started to say that I would charge no more windmills, then realized that Latah would not understand the allusion.

Suddenly brought back to her, I realized I had already said more than she understood. But what did I understand of her except her beauty?

"I have talked very fine, Old Kuki," I told her as a different kind of joy poured through me. "Let us hope it is not like the fox's talk when he could not reach the grapes in the old tale. And now let us find a small grassy place, screened from all eyes, and make better use of our mouths."

"And of our arms, sahib?" Latah asked, looking at me boldly.

"Assuredly of our arms."

"Of our whole bodies and the spirits that dwell in them?"

"We will merge them in a love that will never die."

"I'll be glad, Shikra. For this is the second day of the three allotted."

"We won't speak of that—yet."

"I did so with good intent. I don't want you to forget that tomorrow I start on the long journey to the Tripura, there to make a house with the boy of my choice. Thus there will be a blessing on all our joys. You will take more joy in your hill girl than ever before, not even your heart hanging back. I do not know why and I will not ask. I only know it is true."

Chapter Thirty-two

The passing and shallow interest I had once had in Indian archaeology had left me with a smattering of its lore. Thereby I had wondered how the beautiful queens had gone back and forth between their terrace house and the palace without being seen by greedy-eyed retainers, and had discussed the question with General Morrow. Since the grounds showed no trace of a hall, we had predicated an underground passage. After working on the fish weir, Puran had gone to help Dasa search for it.

Broken masonry among the roots of a great tree piercing the walls of the Queen's house had given them the clew. When Latah and I returned from the woods, they had dug through a mass of buried rubble to a black well that threw back their voices. By now the rain was lashing through the mango trees, but it was not this that delayed our exploration of the challenging void. Rather it was a temporary lack of adequate safeguards against miasma, mantraps such as jealous kings were not averse to setting in and about their harems, and the many snakes that love darkness.

I had suggested a bat for an air tester—they hung in thousands in some of the cells—but Ronald thought that such cave dwellers might thrive on poison air. So Puran rigged a box trap out of a giant gourd, and oblivious to the rain, he and Dasa set it to catch a wood mouse. Then they helped Latah make deer-fat candles, and you would never know by her shrill laughter setting off theirs that tomorrow was a day of parting with her lover. I sat alone at the cavern entrance while the rain fell in roaring sheets and then the night in blinding folds. My little wood fire caused strange flickerings among the carven kings, beasts, and gods, and a rigadoon of shadows. I wished I could recapture a little of my greathearted exultation of the afternoon. I hated to feel so empty . . .

All night I wandered in desolate deserts of dreams. When our whole party assembled at sunrise eager for the adventure, I alone viewed it with lackluster eyes. On the contrary, Ronald was boyishly excited in an indubitably charming way. He could not wait to look into Puran's trap, then came running back with the catch of not one wood mouse, but three. He took command of the enterprise by default, and gave orders in the blithe voice of a winning cricket captain. When he decided that the whole party would take the trip, I was sorry to throw cold water . . .

"Ronald, we haven't any safety lamps, and some of the gases accumulating in old wells are devilishly explosive. I think you had better appoint one sahib and one native."

His face fell. "It was your idea, so you are elected. Puran can go with you, but it's my turn next. If you're gone long we'll know you've found the King's treasure and are trying to ditch it."

I wormed down into the hole with a homemade candle lantern in one hand and a forked stick in the other, a live mouse in a perforated gourd hung around my neck, and my revolver handy in my belt. Puran carried a like lantern and the ax. There was a rustling sound ahead of us, and the rear three feet of a prettily marked snake disappeared in a crevice in the rock. Faster than a snail, but not as fast as a turtle, I worked around a heap of rubble and flung forward my light. I had the curious illusion of looking down a big, walled well —actually I was gazing into a horizontal passage dimly revealed in the yellowish light of my lantern, and running on into deeper and deeper dusk until it was lost in darkness. In this stretch, it was almost as good as new. Water seepage had worn pits in the side walls and undermined some of the flagstones of the floor; others showed no sign of their long neglect except a thin film of dust. I guessed that the rock-cut temple was part of this same limestone stratum, the bedrock

244

of the palace grounds.

My foot slipped on one of the dust-coated flagstones. I felt several of them, and all were worn smooth as glazed tile by small, naked feet and footless crawlers. But no basilisk eyes glared at my lantern, and the dull glimmer between two flagstones proved to be a two-tined ivory hairpin, its top bordered with dusty opals, turquoises, amethysts, and star sapphires. Had a lovely little queen dropped it on her last journey from the Queen's house to the palace on some day of doom? Was it an invading army that had emptied the city of human life, or was it plague?

Farther on, the passage appeared choked with rock. Puran, who was smaller than I, found a hole in the angle of the wall with the ceiling, and, enlarging it a little, let me through. We crawled down the debris into water that swiftly deepened until it was around our waists, but its chill was ameliorated by a warm, bright beam around a tree root that had burst a side wall, relieving the worst of our fears of poisonous air. The pool shoaled, and we climbed a flight of five steps that were once white marble. Light swift feet pattered ahead of us and were lost to hearing. We made our way around more debris, killed a cobra that would not give us the right of way, and found, hanging from a bronze chain, a lamp with a gold lid and an alabaster bowl.

Almost under this was a heap of rubble that I passed by without a second glance. "Wait, sahib," came Puran's low voice behind me. And when I turned back, "Where do you think it came from?"

I looked in vain for a break in the walls. "What do you think, Puran?"

"I think it was pushed in here from another passage in order to hide the entrance."

Puran held his candle flame at various points about the heap, and once it wavered a little as though from stirring air.

"We'll not speak of this to the others," I told Puran. "If Ronald Sahib wants you to take him through, try to divert his attention as you pass by. Later we will look into it in secret."

When we had climbed three more steps, the passage became sumptuous. The floor was a checkerboard of black-and-white tiles, and the walls were slabs of marble with multi-colored veins, cunningly fitted and matched. Many of these were cracked, but since there had never been any dust blown into this part of the corridor, they appeared newly washed. Soon our lantern-glimmer revealed a steep flight of steps. Above it was what appeared to be the stone wall of a small, square, low-ceilinged cell.

But the close-held lantern revealed that the slab of marble at the head of the stairs was larger than the rest and not as closely fitted. It gave a little to my first strong thrust: when I pressed close to its edge, it swung out with a slight, grating noise. The opening was gray from diffused light. I stepped through it into a dusky chamber with one ghostly-looking wall. This proved to be a marble screen of beautiful fretwork, faintly luminous from some aperture beyond. The stone door I had opened appeared to be a wall carving in high relief of a Yaksa with a raised arm, his outset wrist sash concealing bronze hinges. Obviously the stone had been hollowed out to save weight.

We found our way to the terrace, where all of our party except Latah waited with extreme curiosity and mild anxiety. We took them into the hall room and showed them the trick door; Ronald wanted to start back at once. Had I found any treasure? I told them about the alabaster lamp and showed them the jeweled hairpin. Vivian's and even Mildred's eyes looked rapacious as a hungry cat's.

"If nobody objects, I'm going to give it to a real heroine," I said.

"What right has anyone to object?" Vivian asked with a buttery tongue. "It's yours, isn't it? Finder's keepers——"

"Where is she?"

Only when the words were out of my mouth did I notice the expression on Mildred's face, and then its instantaneous and startling change. It had been a mixture of coyness, feigned modesty, saccharin, and greed. Pretty words of thanks, coupled with a declaration of her unworthiness of the prize, were ready on her lips: they would have made General Morrow swallow with emotion. Suddenly it gave way to pained astonishment if not self-righteous outrage.

"She's over there by the cave, drying meat," Vivian answered calmly, pointing to a brown figure by a smoky fire. "But let's hope she won't trade it for a monkey when she gets to a bazaar."

Without even looking at Vivian's bright eyes, I was sure that this was not for my benefit. If it were, it would not be at Latah's expense; whatever Vivian was, she was never cheap.

"How much do you think it's worth?" I asked.

"Two hundred rupees if an anna," Mildred broke in. "That's why I was startled at what you said. It's not my affair, of course, but I don't think it's a proper gift for a hill-woman. How can she realize its worth? If she doesn't throw it away for bazaar trash, someone will get it away from her by fair means or foul. Simon, I don't think you have the right to put her in danger——"

"Two hundred rupees is only twenty pounds," Vivian said thoughtfully. "It will bring fifty pounds in Calcutta and five times that much in London. As a museum piece it might bring a thousand pounds."

"Well, that would be only two hundred pounds apiece, divided up among us five," I remarked. "We'd have to give a share to the boys too. Under the circumstances, I dare say I'll give it to Latah as I intended. She can wear it in her hair at village feasts——"

"Oh, isn't she going to continue to live with you?" Vivian asked.

"Not for very much longer, I'm afraid." Suddenly the grim game was not worth the candle and I spoke solemn truth. "I'd like to give her something of real worth and beauty to remember me by."

By our baiting Mildred, Vivian and I had learned nothing we did not already know. She was shallow, greedy, vulgar, and inordinately vain. The fact remained that she thought herself deep, generous, genteel, and modest—and most people who saw her doll face and heard her chirp were in agreement with her. Again and again I played with the idea that she had betrayed the fort. I had rather reveled in it as the supreme irony—her misty-eyed sacrifice of all the inmates, including Phil, for a fake-noble cause—but I had known it was preposterous on the face of it. It fitted in with no fact of the tragedy. Even the gods of ancient India, some of which reflect men's darkest laughter, would not go that far. Still I had intended to find out her movements and whereabouts in those fateful few minutes before Ronald's bearer put her in General Morrow's charge, if only for their effect on others. Now that I had heard Latah's story, I had no excuse to do so, nor any desire. I wanted to forget.

I could not, for a long while yet.

"Latah, have you told anyone except me that you are leaving today?" I asked when I had gone to her smoky fire.

"No, sahib."

"Don't tell anyone. When your bundle is ready, put it in

247

the edge of the woods above the temple. After Puran has taken Ronald Sahib through the passage, I'll have him get it and take it to the shrine of Hanuman, near the path to the village where he bought tobacco for us, and to wait for us there. You and I will go forth as before. I will go with you that far, before I bid you farewell—give you a gift—and turn back."

"It is four koss [about eight miles], sahib."

"What is that to us, old hunter?"

"The direction is not toward the high hills of the wild Gonds, but toward Mother Gunga and the villages and farms. So I need no protector."

"I don't fear the Gonds. But I spoke of how a sahib's shame or remorse or fear or all three together might bring on a madness, hidden from those who know him best. I don't believe it, Latah, not in a tenth part of my head, but I want to go with you that far, and I will."

"My *nat* and I—we will sing many songs on any road that we must walk thereafter."

"At what hour shall we set out?"

"I will be ready an hour before noon. We can come to the shrine of the monkey god in an hour after noon if we make haste, or as much later as we dawdle on the way. Then we may take an hour or even two hours to make a good meal and to say farewell before the rain begins—if it keeps to the way it has set. And then I will walk in the rain to the village, and in its great fresh flood, every tear that I would shed will be washed away."

The time came, and as we made for our place of parting we were as happy together as in the hills of the Old Kuki. Indeed we saw the jungle in fuller light than ever before, with refreshened eyes; and its beautiful dwellers came forth from their coverts into our plain sight as though in some great portentous pageant put on by the old brown gods. All the beasts and birds were prodigiously alive. The snakes lay supine only to store their dynamics until the split second of their terrible application.

The vanity of the big, bright-colored birds took the form of strutting, flaunting their fine feathers, raucous cries, and impudent behavior; but the leopard, twice as beautiful, moved silently through the thickets, displaying modest manners and great civility to all until the dreadful instant that he sprang; and the devil knew him for ten times as proud as the noisy parvenus in the trees. His reddish-yellow hide was spotted with black, and truly he was the second most beautiful creature in all the jungles. But the most beautiful was the cheetal deer, her reddish-yellow pelt spotted with white, and she was his favorite prey.

"Need you have gone so soon?" I asked Latah when she spoke of the new-washed beauty of the forest.

"Yes, sahib. The air grows fresh and sweet, now we are away from the ruined city, but there it smells of death. I could not breathe it any longer. I too would die."

"I would have camped with you in the jungle if you had asked me to."

"No, sahib. It was required that you stay with your own people. Also, I am in great haste to see my father and my brothers and all the people of my village. I yearn to go into the fields with the other women and plant seed in the warm mud. I long to take my turn at the corn grinder, and to sing with the other maidens at the clothes-washing, and to sniff cheeks at the feasts. Truly, Shikra, there is not one little thing in my village for which I do not ache!"

"Have you decided what youth you will choose to make a house with you?"

"No, Shikra Sahib. But there will be plenty to choose from, and now that I've made house with a sahib and have seen the great world besides, I can pick the best. However, I shall be courted by several before I settle down. The beginning of the Rains is a good time for courting among the young people of the Old Kuki—our hearts leap up even as the grass, and our blood runs bubbling through our veins like new-fallen rain in a dry nullah."

"You will have much to fill your days and nights, saving you from sadness over our parting. But what will I have?"

"The whole world, sahib. A much greater world than I knew was under the sky. It is full of wonderful things to see, hear, touch, smell, and taste. You can win many prizes, and if you try hard and are lucky, win what you think is the best prize."

"In the first place, she is already lost——"

"No, sahib. She has not yet decided to make a house with Ronald Sahib. It is true that she has come to the very brink. Her bad temper lately is a sign of the struggle in her mind. So you must act quickly, sahib. She loves boldness—and you must woo her boldly. She is not one—how do you say it?— to bite off her own nose to spite her face. Now that she has found out she can't conquer you, the next best thing is to be conquered by you. And remember, sahib, she is very hot-blooded."

"How do you know?"

"We women know those things about one another, and we have talked together."

"You have!"

"She told me things, thinking I would tell them to you. They were to make you think that she had given her flower to Ronald Sahib and that she loved him more than you. But they were only to make you jealous of him, which I did not want. In the few days that remained before I went to my own people, I wanted all of you for my own."

"I wanted the same, Latah."

"So much we have had; more we cannot have. But you must not believe that I, coming between you and the memsahib for half a year, have caused you to lose each other. Instead, my coming has made it possible for you and her, lost in shadows of your own casting, to find each other again. I do not know why, unless I am like the woman in the 'Isai Book of whom you told me, a woman with tender eyes?"

"That woman was ill-favored, while you are very beautiful. Also, she was jealous of her sister. Latah, if Vivian Memsahib and I find each other again, would you be jealous?"

"Sahib, will you fast when I am gone? Will you not eat meat and drink of the spring? Now if you had had us both, dividing your favors between us, doubtless I would have been jealous. The women of the harems on the plains are said to feed each other poison. But look what I may tell my granddaughter when I am old! I was the first to make a house with Shikra Sahib! When it was the fate of both of us to go different ways, he made a house with the General's daughter, the most beautiful memsahib I have ever seen. Lo, what a beautiful maiden I must have been, to have had a lover who could so pick and choose!"

We talked of other things until we came to our rendezvous with Puran. When he had delivered Latah's bundle, he called my attention to a bank of dark clouds driving across the sky from the southwest. "I think the rain will not wait his usual time," he said.

I told him to stay within call, rain or shine. Yet it seemed that Latah and I must hurry our farewells to get them over with before the downpour. I had a sense of a mean and churlish Kismet. An inadequate ending would cast a shadow

250

backward, however faint, over the whole affair. I was already out of tune with Latah on account of my perturbation and her poise.

"Here is a farewell gift," I told her, putting in her hands the bejeweled ivory hairpin.

Her eyes and her mouth rounded and there was a kind of pallor in her face.

"Shikra!"

"It was worn by a queen long ago. I found it in the passage. You are to show it to no one until you are safe within your village, for when the war is over, it will bring a thousand rupees."

"Then you wish me to sell it to the Marwari?"

"If you like."

"Whoever heard of a hill girl, who will eat all manner of things forbidden to the Hindus, wearing a thousand rupees in her hair?"

"That's to be thought of."

"But whoever heard of such a girl wearing the love of a great sahib in her heart?"

"Did you know that, Latah?"

"That you are a great sahib, or that you love me?"

"Only that I love you. I would not like to have you doubt it."

"Do you think I ever did? Sahib, I knew both things. It was not only the killing of Kharab-Bagh that showed you a great sahib. If you had been a little sahib, you would have been busy proving that I loved you. Instead you were always proving that you loved me. No, you could not bear for me to doubt it. You did not give a small, cheap love. You gave a great, costly love. And that is why you can give me up when the time comes, and I can give you up. We have made each other wondrous gifts, and now we must go on our ways."

"What of the little gift?" I pointed to the jeweled pin that gleamed in her hair.

"I will put it in a box, and hide it in the ground, and get it out only on feast days. On those days my husband will walk proudly that he has won a woman beloved by a great sahib, and all the young men will envy him, and the old folk will tell again of how you came to the village, and slew Kharab-Bagh, and gave room on your couch to Latah. No, I will not sell it to the Marwari, unless the people are about to die from hunger. I will look upon the turquoise and remember our days under the sky. I will look at the opals and remember the dawn mists that we saw drawn across the hills by the rising sun. I will look at the sapphires with their bright points and remember our nights beneath the stars."

She stopped, because lightning hacked a great gash in the sky and an earsplitting clap of thunder roared from hill to hill. As we had talked, the scudding clouds had closed rank overhead and now churned and lowered.

"What will you have to remember this parting?" I asked.

"We haven't parted, Shikra, yet."

"In a few minutes the clouds will burst in rain."

"They are cracking even now. They are being shaken to pieces by the thunder."

The flash seemed far brighter than the other, because the day was so much darker. I waited until the mighty rumbling and roaring died away.

"Then we must make haste with our farewell, if we are to be on our way when the rain starts," I said, looking into her widening eyes.

"Is it so commanded by your gods? It is not so by my *nat*. No, they have joined hands to give us something whereby to remember our parting."

"What is the gift?"

"The rain! Here it comes, running. Listen to it roaring up the hill. Hear it singing in the trees. Oh, lift your face, Shikra. It is as warm as your lips on mine."

Our eyes spoke and our hands began to fly. The sky darkened, but the lightning turned every drop of rain into a miniature crystal lamp, and countless thousands of them shone on and about her, and at last I saw her beauty in its full. Not one of its aspects was veiled from me. It was the whole beauty of Woman, the same that Adam saw when he and his bride were driven from Eden amid the thunder of the skies. It was native to our rough earth. No other planet knew its like, I dreamed amid the luminance, and the great stars must bow. I saw it, and then I knew it by an ancient means and meaning. I was entwined in it and locked with it and became part of it. The might of the elements seemed only reflecting mine. The pouring rain became a symbol of a more procreant flood.

And the rain could never fall again, out of any sky we knew, without remembrance of our joining in farewell.

Chapter Thirty-three

Last year I had lost my fortune, thereby losing Vivian. Possibly the chance would come to recoup the first loss in Golconda, as my brother had cheerfully written, which would ease the shame and balm the defeat of the second. It would turn the tables in some way I could not quite rationalize.

The chance that a hidden corridor opening from the Queen's passage, evidence of which we had found, might lead to the treasure vault of the vanished kings was well within the possibilities of implausible India. So in due time, Puran and I went hunting ostensibly in the jungle, only to double back to the summerhouse. From there we made our way to the pile of rubble that Puran had thought concealed an opening in the passage wall.

The hole proved large enough to admit us on hands and knees. Beyond lay a man-dug tunnel, tall enough to pass a stooping man, noticeably no different from the main passage as far as it went. But after a hundred feet it interesected a long, low natural cave, caused by water action and common to limestone regions. Taking such bearings as we could, we deduced that it had once opened at the foot of the steep—a narrow cavern used as a crypt before the city grew to greatness and its kings to power. In the long centuries the dark den had been transformed into a fabulous temple glorifying the gods. One day its inter-opening channels had been summarily cut off by what appeared to be a landslip, so that now they stopped short in a maze of broken rock just below our entrance way.

Just above, the channel opened into a natural chamber with three other entrances. A massively but crudely carved god whom I took to be Indra stood guard over the largest, so for convenience we named this room the Hall of Indra. From this point Puran and I beat a careful retreat.

When we came again we had a line over six hundred feet long, no heavier than a cable length of cod line, and almost as strong, although it was made of elephant grass. Anchoring one end to the foot of the idol, we unreeled it slowly as we penetrated the passages, rewinding it as we emerged. Thus we spent three happy hours, our dim light searching hopefully the dwindling hallways. Obviously the whole cave was a small one compared to many in this part of India, honey-combing the part of the hill immediately above the temple, and our chance of finding treasure faded fast.

Then, as we were making up what we thought was the main channel, the walls crowding in and our rope running out, we made a startling discovery.

The narrow passage opened into a room almost as large as the four-mouthed Hall of Indra. As Puran held his lamp to the nearer wall of sparkling limestone, mine found a pale place in the farther blackness which disappeared like a spot before the eyes as I tried to outline it. Puran raised his lamp. A shape began to emerge, unrecognizable, wan, and weird. As he drew nearer, its shadow became monstrous. He stopped with a gasp.

Instead of wall sculpture, it was an idol of some sort, carved not from the native limestone, but of snowy alabaster. Indeed its whiteness amid the blackness in which it was hidden was suggestive of the horrid bleaching of fish and other cave dwellers shut away forever from the light of day.

By the same token, it would be blind. With a deep, chilling start I flung my light in search of its head. In the maze of shapes I made out a female figure, neither erect nor hori-zontal, and instead stretched at an angle over what might represent three branches of a tree. Her form was Yaksi-like in exaggerated breasts and hips, although her face was delicately moulded and expressed dreamy ecstasy, not unlike some of the Buddhist faces of Farther India. But my night-mare of a blind Goddess of the Dark did not come true. Her eyelids were merely closed to represent sleep or, more likely, heavenly bliss.

The light grew as Puran brought his torch close to mine. The whole statue began to have meaning. In all my journey-ings up and down India I had never seen its like. Suddenly I was quite sure that it had once crowned the huge meteorite we had seen in the center of the palace grounds and was no doubt the titulary diety, the holy of holies, of the royal city. Whether it had been banished from its place of honor or hidden here to await the passing of some awful storm, I would never know. I knew only that the storm had passed centuries gone, leaving a silence deep as death's, and a cobra lay sunning on the black stone from heaven.

Then my flesh crawled, because the chief figure in the sculpture was not a goddess but a gigantic snake.

What I had taken for tree branches represented his coils.

254

But even at the second of the discovery I did not mistake the monster for a python in the act of crushing its prey. This snake was very Shesha Naga, the manifestation of Indra. Instead of killing the earth-goddess, he held her in loving embrace.

The great trunk of the serpent coiled thrice around her to form both her couch and her shield, then towered so that his flat spade-shaped head hung over her as in protection. As the weak beams of my lamp found his eyes, they glared into mine.

"What are they, Puran?" I asked.

"I think they are rubies, blood-red and of first water."

"How large?"

"They are as large or larger than the one the Burmese trader offered you in old days."

"And in those days, if I had made such a find as this, I would have done the right thing. Mark you, Puran, this is a wonderful conception of the snake diety's union with the nature goddess, the basis of one of the oldest religions in the world. Truly it deserves a place in the great Wonder-House in London."

"What is the right thing, sahib?" Puran asked, staring into the red eyes.

"To protect it from vandals who would steal the rubies."

"Those days are no more, sahib, so what now?"

"Truly they are no more. And of late my fortunes that rose a little have again declined. I had long ago lost the beautiful memsahib, and now my hill girl has gone home. Also, our good hunting, to keep us at least wide awake, has played out. Instead of a great enemy, the winner of the memsahib is only a good officer whose one great mistake I can't play against him. The evil that we thought we smelled was only a spoiled durian fruit left in the road. My mouth is dusty and my heart is cold."

"Then for our souls' sake let us go into the light."

"Not yet."

I picked up a piece of limestone as big as my fist. The first sharp blow on the beautifully sculptured head broke it off in three pieces. One of the red eyes rolled on the floor; the other was easily worked out with my fingers.

I held the light close and then handed it to Puran.

"Is it worth half a lakh of rupees?" I asked, laughing.

"No, sahib. But its like may be bought in any bazaar for two annas."

"There has been no one ahead of us these thousand years, or the head would have been broken even as we broke it."

"I think that the temple priests saw to the matter when the god still stood in the palace square."

"Puran, again I have not done well. And it comes to me that my Fate has laughed at me once more."

Puran picked up the three fragments of the snakehead and laid them on the breast of the nature goddess.

"Sahib, if you wish me to mend the breach, I will. I can make plaster by burning and crushing a broken piece of marble and mixing the powder with water. At least it will hold the pieces together until skilled menders from the Wonder-House can fix them good as new. As for your kismet—I am not sure that it mocks you. I could more readily believe that it has tested your worthiness for great happenings to come."

"A test that I have failed?"

"No, sahib."

"It is fool's talk—but let us go into the light!"

We did so, and without admitting it to each other, we watched and waited with a sharp expectancy. No event moved that afternoon or all the next day: Puran's and my only occupation was to make a gourdful of cement and to hunt a lame tigress that had taken to hanging about the ruined city, so lean that we feared she might turn maneater. Finding out where she used, we planned to stalk her on the following day.

As we were starting out just before sunrise, I saw Dasa lurking in the thickets close to the Queen's house. He beckoned furtively.

"What is it, Dasa?" I asked as I looked into his ashen face.

"Sahib, in your bag you have a telescope with two eyes."

"Yes."

"Sahib knows the white rock near the top of the hill, close by the big tree where Bagh sharpened her claws?"

"Surely."

"Sahib, will you send Puran for the two-eyed glass and go forth with him as though to hunt below the ruins? Then while Puran goes on alone, I beg that you turn back in secret to the white rock, there to lie in ambush until the sun is about one hand high. Then if you will keep a close watch of the ring of thickets above the reservoir, you will have good hunting."

"The tigress would not come there in daylight——"

"I beg that you grant my plea, Protector of the Poor!"

Dasa slipped away. I began to follow his instructions, with the addition of telling Puran not to let any of the others see him get out my field glasses, ordinarily useless for hunting in thick country. When he had brought them to me, we paced downhill until well out of sight of the cave. Here we parted, Puran to remain out of sight in the jungle at least until noon, I circling back to the steep hill overhanging the temple. The sun was not quite an hour high as I made myself comfortable at the lookout, my back against the white rock, and my elbows braced against my knees. Thus I could hold the field glasses almost as steady as a rifle.

Actually I saw no need of a dead rest. The ring of thickets was about three hundred yards distant, and I could gaze through a rift in the trees down into its grassy center. A wild peacock could not run across unseen.

Presently I laid down the field glasses and picked up my rifle. There were footsteps in the scrub, swiftly nearing. Then my little alarm gave way to profound curiosity, because these were a woman's steps, light and quick rather than stealthy, and her business was with me. I saw a white garment in a rift in the bush, and then flame-colored hair.

"Simon?" Vivian called softly.

"Yes." As she came up to me, she took pains to remain screened from anyone who might be watching from below. I would be enlightened now, I thought. Instead——

"What's happened?" she asked.

"Nothing that I know of——"

"You sent for me, didn't you?"

I started to answer, then stopped to think.

"Did Dasa ask you to come here?" I asked.

"He said I was to sneak up here, without anybody seeing me, on a matter of extreme importance, and you would be waiting for me."

"I think the matter is of extreme importance, Vivian, but I don't know what it is."

"Why have you brought your field glasses?"

"To watch that patch of thicket above the reservoir. That's what I was told to do. You can see down into it——"

"That must be where Mildred goes. She walks off every morning—wants to be alone to think about Phil—but if Dasa thinks she needs spying on——"

Vivian sat down beside me. I did not look at her because she would be ashamed to have me see her white face.

257

"I believe she's coming now," I said.

As Mildred climbed the hill by the reservoir, her bright hair caught the eye. When I raised the glasses, she walked into the lens as Judy upon a puppet stage. But she was more doll-like than Judy, whose bad temper and tears and tragedy appeared to make her real. She walked slowly, her face a little lifted; when a vine got in her way she laid it gently aside with her right hand. If General Morrow caught a view of her, so pretty, going off alone to dream lost dreams of Phil, he would be touched.

"Has she got something under her arm?" Vivian asked.

"Yes."

"It's a mat. She lies on it and thinks about Phil and after a while she goes to sleep——"

Mildred passed through heavy growth that screened her from view of anyone below. At once she began to climb rapidly, thrusting away the greenery with vigorous movements. "Watch out, you'll tear your dress," I thought. In a few steps more she entered the ring of thickets where she thought she was shielded from all eyes. Instead she stood clear and sharp before me, it seemed in reach of my hand. Carefully she spread her mat. I thought she had chosen the softest grass. But she did not lie on it yet—instead she took her stand close to the edge of the thicket and peered through it.

"What is she doing now?" Vivian asked.

"Just looking."

"Looking, would you say, or watching?"

"It's a delicate distinction."

"Nothing about this is very delicate. I think I ought to be going—but what's the use?"

"None that I know of."

Mildred would make a good hunter, I thought. Except in war and the chase, I had never seen anyone stay so still. The two or three minutes of her watch drew very long. Sweat rolled off my cheeks, down my neck. Vivian sat with her hands limp in her lap. Then Mildred moved suddenly and quickly.

In an instant she was lying on her mat, her skirt pulled modestly down, her bright head on her arm, as though she had been there a good while.

"There's someone coming across the hillside," I remarked.

"Well, what did you expect?"

"Do you know who it is?"

258

"Who would it be? Phil's ghost?"

"I thought Ronald said he was going to——"

"He did. He said what he was going to do yesterday morning, too, and the day before. A very busy fellow, Ronald."

"Do you still want to stay? You've still time to leg it——"

"Give me those field glasses, Simon, and get out."

I shook my head.

"What are you trying to do, protect me?" Vivian demanded. "Who has the most right to see this show?" She had turned stark white.

"You have, but not by my help."

"Then I'm going."

"That's what I suggested. It's a good idea."

But she only turned her back on the scene. I thought that she was sickened at staying but was too proud to go. Mildred had stopped shaking her head and had her arms about Ronald's neck, and I could imagine her still protesting—almost pleading—asking him to help her resist . . .

"Maybe it's their first tryst," I said.

"Would Dasa know of it? If he did, would he peach on them until he knew the stuff? Even so, I wonder why he did. After all, it's the only thing remarkable about this affair——"

Her voice died away. I watched in silence.

"Let's both go," she said.

"Not yet."

"What difference does it make to you?"

"It may make quite a lot."

"Isn't your curiosity satisfied yet?"

"I'm not yet sure of the facts."

"Do you suppose she goes through the same show every time? Of course she does. Ronald wants it that way. It's like seducing a virgin."

"Or profaning an angel," I said.

I watched a moment more, then put the glasses in their case. At my nod, Vivian led the way down a deer path out of view of the scene below. I stopped her at the edge of an opening fifty yards farther on.

"We'd better wait here a few minutes to avoid any chance of being seen," I said.

"I wonder if it matters." But she stopped, her pale face turned away.

"While we're waiting, I want to ask a question. I hate to do it——"

"Go ahead and ask it."

"How long has this been going on?"

"What business is it of yours? But I'll tell you, to try to pretend I'm not ashamed. Months and months. Maybe years. I didn't know or even suspect it until now, but now I know it's true. That's why he banished her in Diwanpani—he knew it was too dangerous to his career—but he made up for lost time when he visited there. I remember——"

"Who else knew it besides Dasa?"

"I don't know of anyone. I doubt if Dasa found it out until lately. They've been terribly clever. And why did Dasa tell——?"

"I've got one more question before we can consider that. It's worse than the other. Did Phil know it?"

Vivian straightened her shoulders, looked me in the face, and shook her head.

"Are you sure, Vivian?"

"Simon, I'm sure. He couldn't have stood it. He would have killed Ronald——" Then her voice faltered and her eyes fell.

"You don't believe that."

"No, I don't. It isn't what he'd do. He would have told Dad—told everybody—got Ronald hauled up and broken—and then tried to get her back. But he didn't know it, Simon. I can swear to it——"

"You mean you could swear to it the last time you saw him."

"What?"

"You hadn't seen him for several days before the mutiny."

"No—I hadn't."

"You called them young lovers. Did they love each other enough to defy convention——"

"Don't make me laugh, Simon. My throat hurts——"

"Enough to defy the hangman?"

"That's an awful thing to say, Simon. And why take an awful risk for what you already have?"

"Ronald came out from Calcutta to meet you and your father. Do you know when he arrived at Diwanpani?"

"The day of the mutiny, I suppose——"

"Most men don't plan their trips to arrive in the morning. Especially if there's a rich dish——"

"I suppose he got in the night before."

"What happened then? People in desperate lust—I didn't say love—forget to be clever. They weren't even very clever today. If they made a mistake—if Phil happened to return unexpectedly from some duty—then the ill wind of the mutiny blew somebody good, after all."

"Oh, damn you, Simon. Damn you to hell!"

"Why, I thought that after the performance——"

"You thought you'd take one final satisfaction. It wasn't enough to win hands down all along the line. You lived with a native girl—and she proved the best and most beautiful of us all. You proved yourself a better man than Ronald. Today you saw me shamed as few women have ever been. Still you're not content. You want to see me give way to hatred and revenge—it would do your eyes good. You want me to believe that the man I took in place of you is a—— I can't even say it. You do hate me, don't you? You swore you'd get back at me when I threw you over—and you have. Still you won't forgo——"

Suddenly she stopped. Her pupils spread until they filled the irises. Deliberately she left me waiting while she quieted her breathing and steadied her voice.

"I underestimated you, Simon," she said quietly.

"In what way?"

"I didn't give you your full due. Now I can answer the question I asked a while ago. The question was, 'Why did Dasa tell on Ronald and Mildred?' The answer is, he didn't."

"What do you mean?"

"And that gives the answer to another question—one of yours. You asked who knew about the affair. I know of only one person."

"Who?"

"You. It was you who found it out—you're very clever at finding out people's weaknesses. Dasa didn't tell you to come here. You told Dasa to send me here. A final victory for you, a last shame for me."

She struck me in the face as hard as she could, but could not turn in time to hide her tears.

Chapter Thirty-four

I needed to think hard without interruption. Meanwhile it was important to stay out of sight of both Ronald and Mildred, who had seen me leave for the lower jungles with Puran. If they had cause to wonder what I was up to in and about camp, they would become very conscious of what they had been up to. I had better not show myself until I could appear

261

to be returning from the hunt, some time after twelve o'clock. Although it was hard to believe, the hour was barely nine.

The future held only one sure thing. As soon as possible, I would try to find out the exact contents of an order Ronald had received a few days before the mutiny, a copy of which was probably preserved at General Headquarters in Calcutta or Barrackpore, and which the author would no doubt remember if still alive. This was the order instructing Ronald to proceed to Diwanpani, there to become General Morrow's aide in taking immediate action against threatened treason. Ronald had let fall that he had received such an order when we had met in the grass.

If it named Haran Lal as the ringleader of the traitors—he could have been under investigation by a native member of the Survey—then I was in the midst of prodigious evil.

There was no alternative but my own death to making a full report of the case to the first responsible officer I could find. It could not wait, it must be done at the first possible moment. The fact remained that many hours must pass before Puran and I could set forth on the long, cold trail. Our vanishing in the jungle must be carefully planned. That meant that I would have time for two things I wanted to do, neither of them necessary to the cause, but both deep urgings of my nature. I could afford to indulge myself, I thought. I had not many affairs left.

One was to have Vivian acquit me of her charge. Dasa's declaration could work that. The other was a matter of izzat and perhaps honor with myself—to make minor atonement to some old gods for an act of vandalism against a great scientific curiosity and, I thought, work of art. It was only to cement back the pieces I had broken off so they would not be lost.

By attending to this at once I could kill two birds and perhaps three with one stone. It was a good way to keep out of Ronald's and Mildred's sight, and the cool, quiet chamber of Yaksi-Naga should be a good place to think.

By a long sneak around the hill and into the native city, I came through a break in the royal wall by the Queen's house. Screened by the ruins, I picked up the gourdful of plaster that Puran and I had cached near by, as well as a new candle lamp we had hidden for emergencies. My revolver was already on my hip and a stout stick armed me against snakes. Diving into the passage, I made for the four-mouthed Hall

262

of Indra. From here our grass rope led straight to the chamber of Yaksi-Naga.

Looking at Naga's broken head, I was glad I had come. When I had finished with it he would still be blind, I thought —he had no need for eyes down here in the dark—but the seat of his wisdom, so famed in folklore, would appear intact. Meanwhile my own head would be well served by the exacting task. Instead of aching with burdensome thought, it could take pleasure in communion with my hands. Anyway, what good was thought in confronting Evil? It was not amenable to logic, no more than is Good. It could hardly be hypostatized except in poetic reverie. The only thing to do with Evil was to try to kill it.

I poured the crushed clinker from the gourd on a dry stone. Puran and I had intended to bring water from above, but there was seepage here and there throughout the cavern, and with patience I collected half a gill from a trickle out of the opposite wall of the room. Pushing aside a little of the powder—quite like a journeyman plasterer, I thought—I mixed it with water to make a thick paste. Working quickly, I cemented together the three shards and put them aside to dry. By the time I was ready to affix the piece in place, my plaster was too hard to spread. I pushed aside another portion of the powder and went after more water. This time I did not bring my candle lantern nearer to the spring, intending to get the little I needed in the fitful gloom.

While holding my gourd to the trickle, I received a crushing blow. It struck almost in the middle of my back, knocking me down, filling my whole being with climactic pain, sickening my brain, causing geometric forms of light to flash before my eyes, and finally, an almost instantaneous reaction, shocking me into a sink of consciousness of only dull terror and torment.

Through this heavy pall my first returning impulse toward survival worked its blind and tortured way. It reached my brain as an instinct to fight back to awareness, without yet knowing its own need. My most inward, naked, intrinsic self made a nightmare journey before it could again realize its own being. With it, there dawned from the darkness the two corollaries of self-realization, the sense of time and space.

All this was probably a matter of a few seconds. I could not yet move a finger, but I knew that I had been struck down by a living enemy, and that he stood above me now. In a second or two more I identified him as Ronald. He

263

was busy at something, and I divined rather than perceived that he was searching my pockets and pouch. I became aware that he had found the glass eye of the idol, looked at it, and thrown it away in disgust. My sick vertigo became less and my bursting eyeballs admitted light in normal patterns.

Ronald picked up a piece of limestone—no doubt the missile that had felled me—and held it in his hand ready to hurl again if my returning consciousness put him in any danger. The first resurgence of cunning in my brain made me abstain from any attempt to stir. Satisfied, he removed the revolver from my belt to his own and took from his pocket a three-foot strap of raw deer hide. Drawing my arms behind me, he tied my wrists together. With another strap he lashed my ankles. By now I was sufficiently awake to be mystified by the act, since his ultimate intention was so plain. On no account could he let me live.

I caught my first glimpse into his mind when he slid his arm under my back, heaved me up, and carried rather than dragged me within a few feet of the idol. This was the beginning of the setting of a stage. During the process he had made sure I would not rouse up and fight. Some further preparations were required for the signs to tell a story of my death by accident or at least of his own innocence of murder.

Suddenly I was no longer his completely helpless victim. Although my body was still inert, my mind was rallying with great force. It did not seem possible that I could deal him a surprise blow with my feet. Although I was lying on my back, the terrific exertion was utterly beyond me at present and for many minutes to come, and probably he was too cautious to come in range. It seemed that my only hope lay in delaying the *coup de grâce* until the situation had time to change. As far as I dared count, that was not even possible within the next two hours. Puran would remain in the jungle at noon or after noon, as I had told him. But when he missed me, this would be the first place that he would look for me.

Two hours! And a lethal blow can be aimed and dealt in two seconds.

My brain was in desperate search of some way to gain time when Ronald spoke.

"I say, Simon, you're not as comatose as you're making out."

I made no answer.

The toe of his boot rammed hard against my side, the

264

shock carrying through to the pulpy flesh and battered bone of my injured back. I did not scream, but I could not stop a deep gasp of pain.

"I thought that would fetch a grunt out of you," Ronald said in an exultant tone. "And a few bruises more or less won't cut any ice in the end. Fact, there'll be what's called corroborative evidence of a terrible accident."

The words were clear in my ears, their meaning sharp in my brain, but they told me nothing I could make use of. On the contrary, I took note of Ronald's accents and tone. They were more vulgar than any I had ever heard him use and could be expected to accompany low language. They were too deep-seated ever to expel completely; they had remained dormant in his throat even though his intelligence plus dogged practice had made his use of tolerable English a second nature. It was instantly plain that he was of humble and probably low birth and had hidden the fact with amazing success behind a pukka-sahib veneer.

The demon that dwells in the bottle has been known to expose a pretender. In this case it was exultation over a fallen enemy that would soon be out of his way.

"What accident?" I asked hoarsely, as though struggling to understand him.

"I haven't quite decided. Any man fool enough to come alone into a hole like this is likely to have accidents—our friends would tell you so. Suppose, Simon, you were bending over, looking at the lower part of this heathen what-is-it, and a rain of stones came down from above. One hit you in the middle of your back and another on the back of your head—the last one with fatal consequences. All I'd have to do is collect a couple of armfuls and strew 'em around——"

"You'd be caught and hanged," I broke in with only a little show of weakness.

"You've about come round, I notice. Well, just lie quiet and we can talk this over like two sensible men. What's wrong with my idea?"

"Do you think I'm going to tell you? But I can promise you the police would see through it in two minutes. They're not as dull-witted as you would like to believe." I had paused between sentences to save a morsel of strength, a modicum of time.

"The police are rather busy right now," Ronald said, grinning boyishly in the candlelight. To my growing amazement, he showed not the least haste.

"General Morrow would see through it. Anyway, he'd make a full report to the police."

"All I'd have to do is move you where there's water seepage from the roof and a good many stones already on the floor. I'd have plenty of time for it, if I wanted to go to the trouble. You see, Simon, old boy, there's not the slightest danger of us being interrupted."

"What do you mean?" And I could not hide the terror welling up into my voice as I waited for him to tell me he had killed Puran.

He did not. Instead he laughed, then suddenly grew tense.

"You love the black bastards, don't you?"

"I don't know what you mean."

"At least for one little minute you were more worried about Puran's life than your own. Don't think I failed to notice it. I can read people like you like a book. All the real toffs loved 'em—and that's the one consolation I get for their house falling down about their ears. No, I haven't played any tricks on Puran. But I heard him shoot not twenty minutes ago at least four miles upwind in the scrub jungle. If he missed he'll keep on hunting—that's the shikari for you. If he hit he'll stop to butcher or skin. That means two hours clear—and I need only five minutes. But I'll take twenty—just to be sociable with an old chum."

What he need not tell me was that these twenty minutes were perhaps the most thrilling in his life. They were in wild celebration of what he believed was his great victory over circumstance and its proof of his glorious future. I saw it in his face and heard it in his voice. For no slight danger would he cut them short.

"I tell you, you'll be caught and hanged," I warned him in low tones that rang against the stone. No longer was my goal only to gain time. I was clutching at every straw of hope. "You've already made a dozen mistakes——"

"For instance, leaving tracks in that long dusty stretch? I saw your tracks there, with Puran's, when I came through following your string last night. All I did was take off my shoes. When the pallbearers have come and gone, no one will ever question but that they're Puran's or Dasa's. I've got my shoes on now, you notice, but there's a shorter route you don't know about, hard stone all the way. In fact it's only a skip and jump from here."

"But it's not worth the risk," I cried, playing another all but hopeless chance. "Those rubies are likely flawed. Even if you're in desperate need of money—and you must be, to kill for it——"

"Oh, chuck it, Simon," he broke in. "I'm not such a fool as that!"

"I don't understand you."

"Latah told you I sent Haran Lal with Gray into the passage. I knew she'd seen me, but I thought she'd make nothing of it, and by the time you saw her again she would have forgotten it. That's why her showing up on the boat gave me such a start. I failed in my first attempt to shut her up; and after she told you—I knew she'd done it by the way you acted—then the gain of trying again was not worth the risk. You wouldn't tell Vivian or the General until you'd made your case—you were too much the gentleman—and you wouldn't live that long. Latah would go back to her hills and stay out of trouble. Moreover, I think you've guessed the whys and wherefores. If you haven't, I want to tell you now it was not just a stupid mistake on my part. I'd come up too far from where I began—at too great effort—to lose it all through one weakling officer who took a grudge against me. Can you fancy me worrying about a parcel of half-castes and natives who got in the line of fire? I was sorry about Gray and his wife, but there's a thousand like them in England to one like me. Do you understand that?"

"I hope there are a million to one," I said.

"Many a true word spoken in jest, so they say. Well, I've talked enough. I'm going to tip over the thingumajig so it will smash your noddle. Puran won't come here to wonder how it happened or what became of the jewels. I'm going to meet him on his way in from hunting and scare him clean into the Sundarbans, and don't think I won't. He's a good, loyal man, but he can't draw pay from a corpse, and there's no other prize but death."

I did not answer because I could not trust my voice. While Ronald was speaking I had seen the end of the grass rope twitch like a dying snake.

Chapter Thirty-five

Perhaps a live snake had run across it.

"You know, Ronald," I said slowly and, it seemed, with the calm of resignation to my doom, "I've never met you before."

"Explain that a little better." His tone told me he was flattered.

"I mean the real you. The man behind that amazing façade. What is your real name?"

"Barney Blount. The broken-down minister who adopted me—his wife thought I had pretty hair—was named Blain. And I'll be General Blain before I'm through."

Ronald Blain—Barney Blount—leaned against the idol, testing its weight. Using a stone as a fulcrum and my stick as a lever, he could not quite raise its edge off the floor. Then he tested the knots of my rope.

"You won't have to wear those things very long," he told me with a grin. "There's a stout piece of tree root in my private entrance not fifty steps from here, and as soon as I fetch it, I'll set you free. You'll be surprised how free you are, my boy. Free from trouble—free from pain——"

Chanting now, he picked up the candle, and its flame grew smaller and the light it threw became more narrow and pale as he advanced up the passage. I watched it being blotted out by Ronald's body. His shape became indistinguishable from his black shadow cast backward on the floor. Then the blackness that had already rolled over me ran and caught and blotted out his last fading aspect.

All that while there was someone coming toward me down the corridor. I had heard the twitching of the grass rope like a snake's rustle on dry stone and at last a swift, stealthy footfall. But now the candle lamp was coming back. I saw it as a bright disk in jerky movement amid a growing space of slowly fading blackness. The footfall hastened and the grass rope rustled on the stone floor with a hushed violence, but the far-thrown beam of the little candle would get here first. Unless the newcomer had a knife ready, unless he wore dark clothes, unless he could feel me over and find my ropes and cut them all with super-human efficiency, he would be shot down.

I knew this by instantaneous calculation. In a second or two more he too grasped the fact and the patter of feet stilled and the rope lay still. I believed with all my heart that he was almost to the entrance of the chamber. My heart ached for me to speak to him, but my mind would not assent. My lowest voice might echo from wall to wall to Ronald's ears.

Ronald came with a short pole-like piece of tree root on his left shoulder, steadied by his left hand. In his right hand he held the candle lantern high. The metal bracing of the revolver butt thrusting up from his belt glimmered in the light. He loomed taller and more tall until he towered above me.

"I was starting to tell you——" he began.

"If you drop that lamp, I'll fire!"

Strained to the breaking point with terror, the voice jumped out of the dark entrance of the room. It was a woman's voice that was not Mildred's, so it had to be Vivian's; and in spite of its distortion, both Ronald and I recognized it without process of thought. He did not drop the lamp or move at all. He stood at bay, not yet striking back, too startled to do anything but obey the frantic voice; but he remained more dangerous than a tiger.

Out of the blackness of the entrance first emerged the highlights cast by the lamp on the smooth steel of a leveled rifle. Vivian's bright hair and vague shape were close behind; and then her skin showed white, her face drawn, her drenched garments clinging and streaked and daubed with dirt. She stepped about six feet from the entrance, five paces from Ronald. I thought her eyes were shifting a little in their sockets as she tried to take in the details of the scene and thus know what to do.

I spoke in low tones, calmly as I could.

"Keep your eyes on Ronald," I told her.

"All right," she answered, to let me know she heard and understood.

"Don't take your eyes off him for a single instant. Keep your finger tight on the trigger and fire at his first move. You're an old hunter. Don't jerk your aim if he drops the lamp or snatches for his revolver—just pull that trigger. Don't wait till you see what his movement is. At the first twitch, fire."

"All right, Simon," she said again.

"Now I'll tell you what's wrong with this situation. You can't hold that aim for more than a few minutes. You'll

269

begin to tremble and he'll drop the lamp and try to leap free of your aim at the same time. He's a brave man with nothing to lose, everything to gain. There's only one way to circumvent him. That's to kill him now."

"I can't kill him in cold blood."

For the first time Ronald spoke.

"I don't think you can kill me in hot blood either, Vivian."

"I will! If you make a move——"

"Don't talk to him, Vivian," I broke in. "Listen. He betrayed the fort in order to kill Phil. The Grays and the half-castes and their children and a little girl who hid under the table and the sepoys who stood fast, all had to be killed with him. I wish you had been there to see, and smelled the blood and heard the flies buzzing. He went back and killed Haran Lal to shut him up and tried to kill Latah. He did all that to prevent the ruin of his career. Vivian, will you put a stop to it right now?"

"I tell you I can't kill him in cold blood——"

Ronald laughed. "You see it's no go, Simon," he told me in jubilant tones. "Now you'll find that hot blood won't work any better. Vivian, the reason I didn't take any of the hints you gave me was because I could get Mildred."

Vivian did not answer.

"You heard me, didn't you? Mildred's a real lady, in some ways like an angel in human form, yet she yielded to me. She didn't surrender her modesty, mind you—I've never even seen her breasts. She cried every time. She wanted to resist but she couldn't. Do you think I'd want you when I could have her?"

"Don't answer him, Vivian," I broke in.

"I proposed to you so I could be old Sorrow Morrow's son-in-law, but I never intended to do more than go through the motions. She's the pukka memsahib, and compared to her you're a born whore. Besides that, when you get hot you smell like hell."

The leveled piece began to have a barely perceptble tremor.

"Do you know why he's saying that, Vivian?" I asked.

"I tell you it's not all true——"

"He doesn't know what a lady is, of course, but he's studied people like you. He can't understand, but he knows what civilized people will do. The more he enrages you, the less you're likely to shoot him. You might shoot him in self-defense, but he's making you afraid you'll commit murder. He's

270

setting in motion a whole train of reflexes against pulling that trigger. Keep your finger on it a minute more!"

"I will, Simon."

"I love you, Vivian."

"I've always loved you, Simon."

"When he dies, everything he's said dies too. The same with everything he's done. There's only one way to conquer evil, and that's to kill it."

"Simon, I can't——"

"Watch him!"

"I'm watching the barnshoot——"

"Good for you. I saw his hand quiver—he almost dropped that lamp. Hold hard for ten seconds more."

"She's not going to do anything, Simon," came Ronald's easy voice. "Wait and see."

"Where are you leveled?"

"In the center of his breast, but I can't——"

Now she's found out she can't conquer you, the next best thing is to be conquered by you. Latah was speaking of Vivian on the day of our parting. I heard her plain.

"Vivian, I am going to give you a command."

"You can give all the commands you please, but she won't obey——"

"Take steady aim."

"I've got it."

"FIRE!"

The yellow flame of the candle lamp had not even flickered when the red blaze from the rifle barrel wiped it out. The brief violent glare revealed all the moving things in the room as stopped dead-still as the stone, and thus their images were fixed on our eyeballs, and so they would remain forever in our memories. Vivian was caught with her shoulder twisted back from the recoil. Ronald's head had bowed so that his position gave the effect of deep thought, and his knees were slightly bent, but although his hands had opened, the lamp still touched his fingers and the log on his shoulder had not begun to tip. The snow-white idol was half bathed in red light and threw a vast, grotesque shadow on the sparkling limestone.

Then the waiting darkness leaped, engulfing all. The roar of the gun rebounded from wall to wall with such blasts as might deafen and cast down an eagle flying through a thunderstorm. They grew less and the echoes died away. If the strange lovers carved in alabaster knew time and event, per-

271

haps they thought that this was the setting in of another silent night to last a thousand years.

But Vivian groped her way to me through the absolute black and, reaching in my shirt pocket, found my box of lucifers. She scratched one and it ignited with a crackling sound. We looked upon death, and then our eyes were drawn to a carving in alabaster that in the brief, flickering light seemed alive. It was of a nature goddess in the progenerate embrace of the serpent. Then we looked quickly into each other's widened eyes because we had been given one brief glimpse of its awful meaning.

The match went out. Vivian lit another and brought it to the fallen lamp. The wick was slow to catch, then the uncertain flicker became a steady flame.

I had never seen a more lovely thing, nor one more true.